D0392785

Hillsboro Public Library
Hillsboro, OR
A member of Washington County
COOPERATIVE LIBRARY SERVICES

PRAISE FOR THE BLOOD OF EARTH TRILOGY

Breath of Earth

"The book as a whole strikes a nervy balance between easy-going charm and suspense. . . . As brisk as Cato's plot is, it's also straightforwardly simple. But she embroiders it richly with gorgeous period setpieces, imaginative speculation and the charismatic Ingrid herself, a hero-coming-into-her-own full of gumption and dimension. . . . Cato's exhaustive research of the time and place gives the book texture and grit, and she hasn't whitewashed what was a very problematic chapter of America's history."

—NPR

"Readers in search of steampunk and alt-history can find them here charged with magic. . . . A strong cast and an unconventional approach to alternate history and magic . . . [in] this extraordinary world."

—*Locus*

"The acclaimed Cato creates an alternate early 20th-century San Francisco of stunning detail. Drawing on the power struggles of the refugees and women's work, this vivid reality will keep readers intrigued to the very end."

—*Library Journal* (starred review)

"Cato . . . begins a new steampunk fantasy series with supernatural creatures, action-packed adventure, mystery, humor, a touch of romance, and more to come."

—*Booklist* (starred review)

"With an interesting mix of steampunk, alternate history and urban fantasy, this mystery and slow-building romance—first in Cato's new series—is excitingly different. Her marvelous star is multifaceted and her costars are colorful. Her fantastical fiction is unique."

—RT Book Reviews

Call of Fire

"A powerful, fast-paced, entertaining enigma, a fantastic melding of alternate history and urban fantasy with a definite taste of steampunk thrown in. Memorable costars, a protagonist with real star power, picturesque scenes and her use of mythical Asian creatures, plus flowing dialogue, make it a real page-turner."

—RT Book Reviews

"Cato's sequel to *Breath of Earth* takes readers further into an alternate turn-of-the-20th-century America, wrapping a dark time in U.S. history in a bright fantasy veneer. The incorporation of sympathetic characters results in a gritty, imaginative, and unforgettable read."

—*Library Journal* (starred review)

"Cato brings increased nuance and skilled characterization to her second Blood of Earth historical fantasy. . . . [She] ably juggles historical fact and fantastical elements to create an alternate 1900s America as finely adorned with Asiatic touches."

—*Publishers Weekly* (starred review)

"An entertaining installment in a series that tackles an ambitious reimagining of history."

—*Kirkus Reviews*

"It's been a long while since I've looked forward to a book as much as this one and I'm happy to say that it delivers."

—Nameless Zine

ROAR
OF SKY

ALSO BY BETH CATO

THE BLOOD OF EARTH TRILOGY

Breath of Earth
Call of Fire
Roar of Sky

THE CLOCKWORK DAGGER SERIES

The Clockwork Dagger
The Deepest Poison: A Short Story
The Clockwork Crown
Wings of Sorrow and Bone: A Novella
The Final Flight: A Short Story
Deep Roots

ROAR
OF SKY

BETH CATO

HARPER Voyager
An Imprint of HarperCollins Publishers

This is a work of fiction. Names, characters, places, and incidents are products of the author's imagination or are used fictitiously and are not to be construed as real. Any resemblance to actual events, locales, organizations, or persons, living or dead, is entirely coincidental.

ROAR OF SKY. Copyright © 2018 by Beth Cato. All rights reserved. Printed in the United States of America. No part of this book may be used or reproduced in any manner whatsoever without written permission except in the case of brief quotations embodied in critical articles and reviews. For information, address HarperCollins Publishers, 195 Broadway, New York, NY 10007.

HarperCollins books may be purchased for educational, business, or sales promotional use. For information, please email the Special Markets Department at SPsales@harpercollins.com.

Harper Voyager and design are trademarks of HarperCollins Publishers LLC.

FIRST EDITION

Map and interior book designed by Paula Russell Szafranski
Map image © THEPALMER/Getty Images.Istock

Library of Congress Cataloging-in-Publication Data has been applied for.

ISBN 978-0-06-269225-2   33614080791675

18 19 20 21 22 LSC 10 9 8 7 6 5 4 3 2 1

For my mom, who always promised me Hawaii

but gave me Morro Bay

We infinitely desire peace, and the surest way of obtaining it is to show that we are not afraid of war.

—President Theodore Roosevelt, 1903

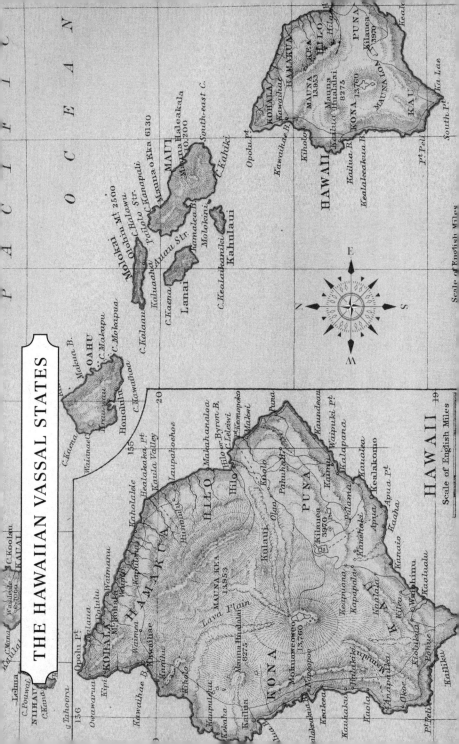

THE HAWAIIAN VASSAL STATES

PACIFIC OCEAN

OAHU

MOLOKAI

MAUI

LANAI

KAHULAUI

HAWAII

Scale of English Miles

ROAR
OF SKY

CHAPTER I

FRIDAY, MAY 4, 1906

☼

"Hide me! Now, now, now!" Ingrid whispered, her gaze on the man across the street.

She scarcely had the chance to ready herself for the jolt as Cy rolled her wheelchair off the cement walkway and onto the hard mud of a small park. The seat bucked as the wheels thudded over dozens of small roots that spiraled out from the trunk of the wide banyan tree. Once she was hidden, he lifted the chair briefly to turn it around. The metal frame squawked in protest. She slowly leaned forward to peer across the macadamized street.

Ingrid understood quite well that her visit to the Hawaiian Vassal States included the risk of potential capture and abuse by Unified Pacific soldiers, an immediate death in the event of an earthquake, or that her now near-constant pain might actually trigger a seismic event, possibly resulting in volcanic eruptions and tsunamis.

And so, of course, she had encouraged Cy to escort her to one of the most dangerous places for her to visit in Honolulu: the local geomancers' auxiliary.

The Hawaiian Isles Auxiliary looked far different from the other auxiliaries she had known. With its white paint and three tiers of ornately styled porches, the building resembled a magnificently frosted square cake. Everything about it stood as testament to the wealth created by a consistent harvest of earth energy.

The consequences of that constant flow had almost given her away just now.

"There," she said in a breath. A short man in a suit sat on a landing along the exterior stairs leading down from the second floor. A young man squatted beside him and fastened lengths of metal to his legs.

Ingrid ducked behind the tree again as the seated man glanced up. Her heart threatened to gallop away in terror.

"Who is that?" Cy asked.

"Warden Hatsumi. He can see auras."

As a child, Ingrid had been trained to recognize him by his photograph in case he ever made a surprise visit to San Francisco. She didn't dare linger around a man who could possibly observe her ability to hold energy—a skill no woman was supposed to possess.

"What?" The word sounded strangled. "You didn't mention there was anyone here who—"

"He often travels around the islands doing contract work for the Unified Pacific, but I had hoped he might have been sent to the mainland or even Vesuvius. This is a hard place for a geomancer to live. Hear that sound?"

Cy casually leaned on the tree to gaze at the street. "Leg extenders? I've only seen the like in book diagrams." The metallic ping of springs announced Warden Hatsumi's every footstep.

"We kept a pair at the Cordilleran Auxiliary as part of the boys' training. I used to wear them for play, too. They are damnably difficult to walk in, worse than high-heeled shoes, and for me that's saying something." She struggled to reach into the pocket where she had kept her empty kermanite. Her fingertips met the small crystals, and immediately the energy she held was pulled away. "He can never walk on the ground here or even linger on the first floor of a house."

"Ingrid, how much power were you holding?" Cy said this in a way that implied she might be in big trouble. In the past, his patronizing attitude would have irked her, but she knew he was right to be wary of her in this regard.

"Barely anything, in truth. Scarcely enough to cause a rise in body temperature, but enough to tint me in blue. The energy here . . ." She frowned, struggling for the words. "I have never felt such a *potential* flow of power, though there's no miasma over the ground."

"Are geomancers constraining the outflow?" He kept his voice low, his gaze across the street, where Hatsumi departed with springing steps.

"No. The temperamental geology requires that geomancers avoid most direct contact with the ground and take special care during seisms." She grimaced, realizing that she was quoting a textbook. "When energy emerges here, it lashes out as fast as a whip and as heavy as a boulder."

She peered around the tree again. Warden Hatsumi had

3

bounded to the end of the block. The shiny orichalcum extensions to his legs bowed at an angle, like the hind legs of horses, granting him leaping strides and several feet of additional height. An extra-long walking stick helped him maintain balance. The young man scurried in his wake, a briefcase in hand.

"Let's cross the street. This time of the afternoon, we should catch Mrs. Kealoha preparing for supper," said Ingrid.

But Cy didn't move to position himself behind the chair. "Is there anyone else here who sees auras?"

"No. I say that with certainty. It's a rare skill."

"You didn't think that man would be here either. Good grief, Ingrid. I don't like this. Every time we visit an auxiliary, something awful happens."

"You met me at an auxiliary, remember?" she murmured in a teasing tone, her head tilted to one side.

Cy couldn't help but smile at that. "And meeting you's been one of the great blessings of my life. Hardly your fault that you've been dogged by chaos and misery ever since."

"Some of that woe *is* my fault," she said softly, looking down at her lap. Her left calf tingled.

Loud footsteps announced other passersby. Two young men strode into view. They were attired as many local dandies had been around downtown, wearing white linen suits and broad-brimmed straw hats. They caught a glimpse of Ingrid sitting there and simultaneously burst out laughing.

"Is it the time of afternoon to take your pet *kanaka* out for an airing?" one asked, gesturing to Cy and laughing again as he strolled along.

Cy remained still and quiet as the men continued on their way. "I don't know what that word means, but I gather that I should take offense."

"I recall Mr. Kealoha saying *kanaka* is actually the Hawaiian word for 'people.' Not a bad word among Hawaiians, but when used by others—yes, it's meant to be derogatory."

Her explanation sounded clinical to her own ears, and she realized she hadn't even been offended at the slight. She felt a kind of detached fascination, really. With her deep brown skin, she was accustomed to being sneered at for being Mexican, Indian, Filipino, even in the relatively tolerant San Francisco. The people who mocked her likely didn't care about her actual ethnicity; they simply needed to look down on her for being some sort of dark-skinned *other*.

If anything, this was the first time an epithet had carried a degree of accuracy, by recognizing that she was part Hawaiian. She almost smiled at that.

"I see." Cy was tense, his fingers clenched in a way that made her afraid he might actually pursue the two men.

"Cy . . ." She gently touched his hand, smoothing the tension out of his fists. "I've been called far worse." She shrugged.

His anger faded to sadness. "You're a lady and should be treated as such." His fingertips stroked her cheek as he moved to the back of the chair.

Ingrid's lips quirked in a small smile. Cy had such a big heart. Maybe someday the world would follow his example.

Then again, maybe someday mermaids would swim in the sky and politicians wouldn't lie either.

The chair shifted as he placed his hands on the bars, but

he still didn't push forward. "You're certain about this visit, Ingrid? We're taking a terrible risk by crossing the street."

"I know," she said softly. "But we need information, and I have faith that Mrs. K can help us."

She wondered if he'd resume the arguments they'd already repeated a dozen times over the past day, but instead, the chair rolled forward. She grunted as the wheels rocked over the banyan roots and walkway.

"It's a wonder there aren't soldiers here to guard the place, considering what's happened at other auxiliaries of late," he murmured.

"I suppose the way they see it, if everyone here died, it wouldn't be a public safety catastrophe like in San Francisco or Seattle," Ingrid said, tone bitter. "This auxiliary functions more for military support—to keep airships and naval ships moving around the islands and across the ocean."

"A layperson likely wouldn't know that."

"True." She leaned forward as he heaved the chair up onto the sidewalk before the auxiliary. The wicker seat back creaked. "But the heavy military presence around the islands also helps to discourage attacks. Japanese law holds here, not American. Guilt is presumed and trials are fast. I imagine the system is all the more ruthless with martial law in effect. The security measures at the dock seemed effective at keeping out personal weapons."

He grunted. "It bothers me to walk around without so much as a Tesla rod."

Any guns, rods, or knives with blades longer than four inches had to be left aboard vessels or checked into lockers at the gates into the docks. Though Ambassador Roosevelt's people had informed Cy of a particular dock to utilize and a certain superintendent to request for ease of entry, that access hadn't precluded them from the weapons restriction.

Ingrid craned back her head to take in the looming presence of the building as she rolled through the gate. She pointed to the right. "I know the kitchen is in an outbuilding. Let's follow our noses."

The smell of roasting chicken lured them around the building and through a lush fruit and vegetable garden growing a bounty that Ingrid couldn't fully identify. Flower-laden bushes lined the back wall. An entire garden bed overflowed with a rainbow array of squashes. A nearby rosemary bush stood taller than her chair and radiated a powerful scent that complemented the cooking chicken in a delicious way. She was surprised to see bananas growing in a massive upside-down cluster from a tree with leaves broad enough to function as umbrellas. Another tree held a heavy burden of deep green alligator pears, most of them larger than her fist. She wouldn't want to linger beneath that tree on a windy day.

A tin-roofed cook house stood on stilts set about five feet high. White-painted plank walls looked austere against the surrounding greenery and blooms. The windows that wrapped around the building were covered by tight netting, not glass. A solitary figure bustled around inside and glanced up at the noise of wheels on pavement.

Ingrid could sense Cy's tension. "She'll keep our visit in confidence," she murmured over her shoulder. "I've known her for over ten years through correspondence and telephone."

"There's likely a reward for your capture," he returned. "Matters of trust aren't what they once were."

"Mrs. K holds no magic of her own, but she effectively runs this auxiliary and she knows these islands. She's better than a library. It's worth the risk."

The screen door squawked open, ending their conversation. Except for new strands of silver hair, Mrs. Kealoha looked as she did in the photograph that her husband had kept on his desk. She wore a loose, waistless dress in the Mother Hubbard style, as many women had throughout downtown. Flour powdered the chest and belly of her blue attire.

"The auxiliary's shut for the day. You need to come back tomorrow if you are looking to buy kermanite." Mrs. Kealoha squinted as she looked down at Ingrid. Her face paled as recognition crossed her features. "You—you're—" Her hand went to her mouth. "Hurry, get her inside the kitchen," she hissed, holding the door wide. "I intercepted the missive, but there are bound to be more. If one of the men looks out a window, they'll see you on the path. *Wikiwiki!*"

Cy rolled Ingrid to the base of the stairs. She pushed herself up, giving the six steps ahead a gimlet eye.

"Do you want me to—" he started to say.

"No, let me. We'll stand out even more if you pick me up," Ingrid said. He had all but carried her down the long staircase of their docking mast. This was the first chance that she had to try stairs for herself. "I'll be fast."

She eased both feet onto the ground and stood, bending forward as if bowing. As she levered herself upright, she felt terrible tightness in both legs, though it was far worse on her left. The magnitude of magic she had wielded in Seattle had caused infinitesimal damage to the nerve endings in her extremities; both Pasteurian and Reiki doctors had speculated that the harm was permanent and recommended a life of convalescence.

To hell with that notion.

Ingrid had spent much of the *Palmetto Bug*'s weeklong trek across the Pacific doing laps up and down the airship's corridor, at first managing only a pathetic shuffle, but eventually learning to lift her knees higher to avoid dragging her toes all the time. Blum's tainted healing of her had undoubtedly aided her recovery beyond the physicians' expectations, but Ingrid wasn't sure how much more improvement she could expect.

That made it especially vital for her to somehow make it to her grandmother; and if anyone knew how she and Cy could endure that dangerous trek, it'd be Mrs. K.

But first: surmount these damned stairs.

Ingrid clutched the low railing as she lifted up her right knee in an exaggerated motion. Her boot-encased foot landed on the step, the partially numb sole prickling as if she stood on pins and needles. She cringed as she brought her weaker leg up to the same step. Cy hovered right behind her. She sensed his impatience, his desperate need to help, and wanted to swat him away, though she knew that was foolish. She needed him there more than she needed her stubborn pride.

"Are you hurting much?" he asked, low enough that Mrs. K couldn't hear.

It was impossible to look him in the eye and lie. "Enough to aggravate locals, if they could be aggravated."

His tight-lipped concern showed that he knew exactly which locals she referred to: nearby geomantic fantastics, creatures who empathetically shared in her pain, to disastrous results. That was the other reason he had insisted on acquiring a wheelchair for their errands in Honolulu. To act as a minor buffer between her and the earth.

"If my presence was going to rile anything, I think we would know by now with the energy flow here as present as it is," she mumbled, panting slightly as she made it up the final step.

"Oh, Ingrid. In God's name, what happened?" Mrs. K stared at her with wide, moist eyes, both hands to her flushed cheeks. Ingrid accepted her help to make it to a rattan chair beside a battered wood table.

Cy latched the screen door behind him, his bowler hat held to his chest. "Ma'am, excuse my familiarity, but it's best if I simply introduce myself to you as Cy. Is this a good place for a private conversation?"

"This is my kingdom. None of the men dares to come here or into the gardens, or they'll meet my rolling pin." With pressed lips, she motioned to a wall that held numerous kitchen implements.

"You said there was a missive?" Ingrid asked, consumed with dread. She took off the simple straw hat she'd bought on her way through town.

"Yes. A telegram from the Unified Pacific, asking the auxiliary to be on alert for Ingrid Carmichael, 'a dark-skinned woman who might be traveling in the company of a tall, white man known to use aliases.' I'd show you, but I burned the letter straightaway."

Mrs. K appraised Cy with an uplifted eyebrow, and Ingrid didn't mind giving him a once-over herself. He towered near six and a half feet, his body slim and face bookishly handsome with a pair of pince-nez perched on his nose. He'd made an effort to alter his appearance by growing a mustache and beard, both of which had developed a surprisingly red tint. Over the past few weeks, his brown hair had grown long enough for him to style it in a samurai-like topknot positioned to accommodate his hat.

"Ma'am, was this note specific for the Hawaiian auxiliary?" asked Cy.

"I don't believe so, sir."

It made sense for Blum to put auxiliaries on alert for Ingrid; she would eventually need more kermanite to help her cope with energy flow. A number of wardens and adepts worldwide would know her by sight, too; San Francisco's auxiliary had been one of the largest in the country, and had trained and hosted many geomancers.

"See, Cy? I told you it was fine to visit the auxiliary. Now we only need to worry about the thousands of military personnel here perhaps being put on notice, too," Ingrid said with a flippant wave. Cy's expression did not reflect amusement. He stood at the corner near the door, positioned to monitor the screens that faced the house and the main path through the garden.

"What kind of *pilikia* you gotten yourself into, Ingrid?" Mrs. K asked, her eyes filling with tears again.

Ingrid didn't know the word *pilikia,* but the meaning seemed clear enough.

"Everything started with the explosion at the Cordilleran. That day, your husband . . ." Ingrid struggled to find words. Warden Kealoha had been one of her mentor Mr. Sakaguchi's dearest friends, and she had come to love him, too. "I think I poured him five cups of coffee during the meeting that morning. I'd made his favorite shortbread cookies, too. He had a handful for his breakfast. I had to tell him he had crumbs on his suit jacket."

Mrs. K's face crumpled, the sheen of tears in her eyes. "Good. I'm glad you were looking after him. I've made your mother's shortbread recipe for the men here as well, but I never had the chance to make it for my husband." She paused a moment to control a sob. "I have missed him so much."

Ingrid had to look away in an effort to check her own emotions. Mr. Kealoha hadn't been approved for a visit to the Vassal States in over five years. He had reached the high status of warden due to his geomantic prowess, but as a native Hawaiian, he was looked down upon, judged to be primitive and untrustworthy. He had not been allowed to travel beyond San Francisco without proper paperwork and an approved adept as escort. The kermanite that he filled was even priced lower than that of more esteemed white and Japanese wardens.

Meanwhile, Mrs. Kealoha had been refused annual passes to visit the mainland to see her husband, even as she continued to manage household functions for the Hawaiian Auxiliary.

"I talked to Mr. Sakaguchi right after the Cordilleran explosion, when he called regarding the urgent need for geomancers in San Francisco," Mrs. K said, her voice hoarse. "I was so relieved that you two had survived. What a miracle that was. Then the earthquake occurred days later, and since then the news from the city has been confusing at best."

"It's been confusing for us, too." Ingrid took a deep breath. Cy wouldn't approve of her next words, so she avoided looking at him. "I . . . I have something to confess. I'm a geomancer." She felt strange saying the words aloud. "A powerful one. That's how we survived the explosion. I used my power to shield myself and Mr. Sakaguchi." She paused, briefly overcome by despair at the thought that she might have saved Mr. Kealoha, too, if he had been close by. "After that . . . I tried to hide what I could do, but the Unified Pacific became suspicious of us." She thought of the horrid, arrogant Captain Sutcliff with a shudder. "And then an ambassador became involved, and—"

"Roosevelt?" Mrs. K cut in sharply.

"No." Not at that point, and she would not implicate him in this telling. Nor would she speak Ambassador Blum's name aloud and risk attracting her attention from afar. Ingrid had recently learned a great deal about the magical potency of names.

Her hand formed a fist on her thigh right above where she'd burned the kanji character for "earth" into her own flesh. Ingrid had almost died from the effort of infusing that magical ward against Blum; the life force she'd expended in that act was likely what had damaged her legs.

However, the ward *should* prevent Blum from tracking Ingrid. Should it fail, the distance between Hawaii and the continent would strain even Blum's mighty powers. And surely Blum was bound to stay in America right now, with her Gaia Project ready to go public.

Ingrid continued, "Amid all of this, I discovered my father wasn't dead. He lived in hiding until late last year. He somehow ended up in the custody of Thuggees—"

"The Indian rebels are involved in this?" Disbelief rang in Mrs. K's voice.

"Yes, ma'am. The papers blamed the Chinese from the start, and that's exactly what the Thuggees wanted everyone to believe," said Cy. "I assume you knew Warden Thornton at the Cordilleran?"

"Thornton? Of course. He even came through Honolulu a time or two. You're telling me that pompous windbag was a *Thuggee*?" She barked out a small laugh. "The dime novels certainly don't depict *that* right."

No, the cheap paperbacks preferred to romanticize an insulting cliché—dark-skinned pagans with swooning white women in the backdrop.

"The Thuggees had stolen an unusually large piece of kermanite," Cy continued. "They needed energy to fill it."

"Therefore they needed the guardian geomancers gone, leaving San Francisco vulnerable to an earthquake." Mrs. K accepted the logic behind her husband's death with a stoic expression. "There were stories about your father, Ingrid. He was . . . said to be profoundly gifted. I take it the Thuggees knew this and used him to channel energy?"

"Yes. He died soon after the quake." Putting it so simply felt like a lie. "The Unified Pacific now knows that I'm a . . . profoundly gifted geomancer, too. They want to use me in their war against China. I want no role in that. I fled. They've chased me."

Mrs. K would assume that the Unified Pacific wanted Ingrid for her ability to channel energy, which was fine with Ingrid. There was truth in it. But most of all, they wanted to use her as they had Papa: as a weapon to level whole cities.

"You, a geomancer." Mrs. K studied her. "It's never set right with me that only men are supposed to have that skill, that training. But I wouldn't have wished that burden on you, Ingrid. Women like us, women who *think* . . . we're seen more as tools than people." She shook her head, her gaze resting on Ingrid's legs. "You haven't mentioned the whereabouts of Lee and Warden Sakaguchi amid all this."

"They are both missing right now," Cy said in his gentle way. Again, a statement so simple and misleading it felt like a lie. The last time Ingrid had seen Lee, he had been on the verge of death, evacuating Seattle via submarines with other Chinese refugees—and a captive Mr. Sakaguchi.

"I'm sorry, *keiki*." Mrs. Kealoha stooped to hug Ingrid in her chair. "We are steeped in grief right now." Ingrid braced her head against Mrs. K's soft shoulder. "Now. You took the risk of telling me all of this for a reason. How can I help you?"

"The best place for me to hide is where no geomancer is expected to be, on the Big Island." She paused, taking in Mrs. K's aghast expression. "While we're there, though, I want to do something more. You know my father's origins have always been a mystery to me and everyone who knew him. I think . . . I have reason to believe that his mother might've been Pele."

At that, Mrs. K physically recoiled, her face darkening like a storm cloud. "Ingrid. You're in the islands now, not reading some geomancy textbook. You call her *Madam* Pele."

"I—I'm sorry. I meant no disrespect, to Madam Pele or to you. I'm ignorant." She ducked her head in chagrin. "That's why I came to you for advice, Mrs. K, because when we go to Hawaii Island, I—"

"Oh no. Oh no. Only Hatsumi is foolish enough to go there and he's paid well for it, and *no one* goes near Kilauea. The energy always flows there. Leg extensions aren't enough of a buffer. Geomancers in hovering airships can absorb power. And you think you can waltz in there for an audience with Madam Pele?" Mrs. K rolled her eyes and looked toward heaven. "I won't help you commit suicide. I won't."

"That sounds like a familiar argument," murmured Cy.

Ingrid shot him a glare. "I'm aware of the danger, Mrs. K. I've been . . . injured through the use of my power. That's why I'm in a wheelchair."

"You were in San Francisco, when the earthquake . . . ?"

"Yes." Ingrid let that answer suffice.

Mrs. K shook her head, her lips slightly parted in awe. "Surely some grace was upon you, for you to survive that cataclysm. You can't test that kind of blessing by trying to confront Madam Pele. The books in there"—she dismissively waved toward the main building—"like to classify her as a

Hidden One, but she's not one to hide. She *is* lava, whether it's boiling red or cooled black. She *is* sulfurous air. She changes forms the way normal people change clothes."

The way she said it made Ingrid think of Ambassador Blum and her many skins. She shivered.

"Most of our old gods are fluid in form," Mrs. K said as she absently tapped the cross at her chest. "The Japanese here have come to regard her as one of their kami, those nature spirits they like to see in every stream or significant rock. My people, most of us are Christian these days, but we still regard her with respect. We must. Parts of her past bodies are still strewn across the islands as rocks and other landforms."

Mrs. K clicked her tongue against her teeth as she looked to the counter, where partially cut biscuit dough waited. "I don't know if you're aware of this, but years ago, Mr. Saka-guchi had me research to see if there was evidence of your father coming from here. I found no proof. But I told him, Abram Carmichael *looked* like one of us. So do you." She cast a fond smile at Ingrid. "You wouldn't be the only family of Madam Pele either. The districts near Kilauea look to her as a goddess *and* as an ancestor."

Ingrid leaned forward in her chair. "Are there women there who—"

Mrs. K held out a hand as she shook her head. "If men or women there are geomancers, they keep it secret. As well they should." Grief rippled across her face again. "People like *us* aren't supposed to be blessed in such a way." Her voice shook with barely repressed rage.

"Well, my secret is out," Ingrid said quietly. "Ambassadors know. Common soldiers know. I only hope I can avoid the UP's intentions."

"You have to hope. You can't lose that." Mrs. K moved to the counter and began to press her biscuit cutter into the dough with savage speed. "I need to get these in. The bells will toll for *pau hana* soon."

"Pau hana," Ingrid repeated. "You never used Hawaiian words like that on the telephone."

"Of course not. The telephone is for business. An operator or official is likely listening in." With practiced hands, Mrs. K re-formed the remaining dough and stamped out more biscuits. "My husband told you that speaking or writing in Hawaiian is illegal?"

Ingrid nodded, somewhat bewildered at the change of topic, but sensing Mrs. K's need to vent.

Mrs. K moved the loaded baking sheet near the stove with the chicken. "Here in Hawaii, you'll hear *haoles,* that means 'foreigners,' white or Japanese, using select Hawaiian words— like *pau hana*. That means the end of the workday, a chance to relax. A very Hawaiian thing. *Pilikia* is popular, too. *Haoles* think it's a fun word to say, so we are graciously allowed to still use it."

"Mr. Sakaguchi used to say that language can be used like shackles," Ingrid murmured.

"Yes. We use the words we're permitted to use. We take the jobs we're supposed to take. We try to stay alive." Mrs. K stared down at her flour-whitened hands. "You're going to go to Kilauea no matter what I say, aren't you?"

"We've come this far," said Ingrid.

Resignation weighed on Mrs. K's face. "You know about the declaration of martial law?"

"Yes, ma'am," said Cy. "Something to do with strikers on sugarcane plantations?"

"Yes, and there are even more plantations on Hawaii Island, especially around Kona and Hilo, so you can expect more soldiers, more scrutiny. The landowners brought in a lot of Filipinos and Koreans to work the land in recent years, thinking these people beaten by Japan and the UP would be easy to control. That they'd be *grateful* to work under contracts that essentially made them slaves. Well, the workers found out that newly arrived Portuguese make a third more than they do, and they get family housing and more . . ." She shook her head. "I'm sorry. I'm rambling. But all this means that you need proper papers and a solid reason to travel inter-island. Especially you, Ingrid." Her look was severe. "You're most likely to find Madam Pele at her home of Halema'uma'u, and that chair of yours won't make the journey."

"Cy has almost completed walking aids for me. I'll get where I need to go." Ingrid rubbed her left calf in an attempt to ease a cramp, and pushed away worries at how a prolonged hike might affect her. Cy's rig for her shoes had to work. It had to.

"I had a thought," Cy said in his mild way, "that it might help our mission if we posed as a married couple. I've heard that such relationships are allowed here."

For once, Ingrid was speechless. She gaped at Cy, trying to gauge if his suggestion was purely intended to be an act on their parts or perhaps something more.

Mrs. K regarded him with wariness. "Mixed relationships aren't *uncommon,* but that doesn't mean they're accepted or welcome. You'll hear *haoles* and Hawaiians alike talk up racial purity. The children that result from such unions can be treated with special cruelty, but I don't need to explain *that* to Ingrid." Ingrid acknowledged this with a wry smile. "But you are going to attract attention. Saying you're married would make your proximity more proper."

"We've survived a lot over these past few weeks, including the earthquake," Ingrid said, feeling the need to provide some context for their relationship. "We've become close." She managed to get this out without blushing, though Cy's cheeks flushed slightly.

"Close." Mrs. K's eyebrows rose. "Well. When you both book your passenger craft—"

"Beg your pardon, ma'am, but we have our own airship," said Cy.

She perked up. "That changes everything! Do you have room for freight?"

"Our ship's Sprite class, so it depends on the freight. What have you in mind, ma'am?"

"I was thinking that a feigned honeymoon trip *might* be adequate to allow you to book a ticket, but it depends on the ticket agent and the inspector at the dock. Any man could judge your marriage as illegitimate and prevent you from taking the trip. But if you have your own airship . . . well, that presents a different option."

Mrs. K motioned Cy to the chair beside Ingrid. "Take a seat, young sir. I'm going to get these biscuits in the oven and make a telephone call or two. I think I can get your airship all of the right paperwork to travel interisland, and earn you extra yen for your pocket, too." She paused and looked over the two of them, her gaze finally lingering on Ingrid as if to memorize her face forevermore. Once again, Ingrid saw the sheen of tears in her eyes. "Oh, Ingrid. I want to help you. I *will* help you. But God forgive me, I hope I'm not helping you along to your death."

CHAPTER 2

Cy wheeled Ingrid away from the auxiliary an hour later. "How does it feel to be a married man?" she airily asked as she held out her left hand, now adorned with a simple gold band. Mrs. K had insisted that she take the ring—a family piece that she had never been able to wear—saying that the gift was surely meant to be since it fit Ingrid perfectly.

Cy came around to stand in front of her, his handsome face troubled. "I . . . well . . . I thought to ask you about that before we disembarked, but Fenris was everywhere at once, and I never had the chance. I hope you're not offended that I introduced it as a—"

"Offended?" Ingrid laughed, a deep belly laugh, one that caused Cy to grin in relief. "Oh, Cy. I certainly planned to spend my remaining time with you, one way or another. So this is perfect. And brilliant."

He crouched down beside her. His heart shone in his

eyes, and he glanced around before leaning forward to press a quick kiss to her lips. "I'd be honored to be your husband, in all truth, Ingrid." He looked at his empty hand on the armrest. "I'd like to find a ring of my own."

Ingrid leaned back, her face warm from his words and his touch. "I'm glad to hear it," she said matter-of-factly. In truth, the idea of Cy wearing a ring that matched hers caused an almost frighteningly intense feeling of joy to well up inside her. "Now, as much as I'd like to draw out this moment, you had better move my wheelchair or we'll be run down." A veritable parade of well-dressed white women with parasols was approaching. Cy hurried to take the handles again in time to roll the chair onto the grass. He greeted the women politely, but received no acknowledgment for his efforts.

"If I were to take offense to anything, it'd be these narrow sidewalks and uppity people," Ingrid muttered, bracing herself for the lurch up to the sidewalk again and a subsequent rough patch of root-uplifted cement. Her teeth jarred together.

"I'm chagrined to say I never noticed how cities are so poorly accommodated to wheelchairs," said Cy.

"I hope I won't have to use one again, though this one has served its purpose well enough. Please thank the officers at the dock for the loan." She gave the wooden armrest a grateful pat.

Down along Nuuanu Avenue, the business district overflowed with an evening crush of people, autocars, rickshaws, and bicycles, with sporadic horses and wagons in the mix. Bells tolled from some unseen church.

"Every place must be closing up soon," she said. "They take their *pau hana* quite seriously here. I'm glad we bought our supplies earlier."

Cy chuckled. "The one thing I can say is that our previous experiences have trained me to buy whatever we need right prompt when we land. Now let's just pray that Fenris didn't decide to refit the *Bug* while we were out this afternoon."

Mrs. Kealoha's contact needed their shipment on its way first thing the next morning and was paying well for their speediness. They couldn't let such an opportunity pass by. In truth, Ingrid was relieved that they were leaving Oahu so quickly. Beautiful as downtown Honolulu was—and as nice as it was to be off the airship after a week aloft—soldiers and sailors swarmed the streets like ants on spilled ice cream.

"We will still need to buy those gifts Mrs. K recommended for my grandmother." Ingrid chose her words carefully, mindful of the crowds.

"That shouldn't be too difficult. There was a shop by the dock that ought to be open late. They're bound to sell cigarettes and maybe salt pork, too." He thoughtfully hummed. "I daresay, it's been some years since I bought tobacco. Fenris used to smoke."

"Really?" Ingrid tried to imagine Fenris smoking while at work on machinery, as many engineers did, and she couldn't quite picture it.

"Yes. From about age eight," he said, "and all through our academy years." He bent close to Ingrid's ear to murmur, "He did it to give himself a deeper, raspier voice. Once he had that, he quit. Without a quiver or craving after." Cy straightened again in time to angle the chair around a light pole. A woman squatted at its base, weaving unidentifiable blooms into a delicate *lei*.

Flowers abounded here in a way Ingrid had never known, their scent penetrating the sharp stench of autocar exhaust. Walls contained waterfall cascades of blossoms in almost unreal shades of purple, red, and pink, while nearby trees and bushes swayed beneath their fragrant burdens. Non-flowering vibrant greenery sprouted on lawns and small parks even in the thick of downtown.

The natural beauty stood as an odd contrast to the heavy presence of the military and the patriotic signs and swags that lined the street declaring EMPEROR BANZAI, NAVY BANZAI, and ARMY BANZAI in both kanji and English.

The predominant language spoken around them was English, and many of the people here looked white as well; the Japanese government ruled the land on paper, but America's agreement for use of Pearl Harbor predated Japanese dominion.

As a lanky white man in working-class clothes, Cy would have blended in fairly well had he been traveling by himself, though he was more youthful than many men around. Most men his age and younger had been conscripted.

"Something's going on up ahead," Cy muttered as their progress slowed.

Ingrid's low vantage point only afforded her a view of suited backsides and hats and the brick buildings across the way.

Autocar horns honked and voices rose, many in complaint, as brass instruments struck up a festive tune nearby.

"What can you see?" Ingrid asked.

"Nothing yet," said Cy.

"You're not missing anything," said the white man beside them. "It's a damned parade again. They're doing it every night. Support for the war effort. Ooh-rah." He spoke, deadpan. "As if anyone feels otherwise. All it does is clog the street."

The parade consisted of a caravan of flatbed trucks garishly adorned in banners for the United States, Japan, and the combined flags of both as the Unified Pacific. The first truck held the band—a dozen men in suits, with a drummer a half beat ahead of the rest. Two more trucks rumbled by hosting children who tossed wrapped candies into the crowd. A few boys darted from the sidewalk to scoop up loot, and were nearly squashed flat.

The next truck hosted three Chinese men hanging in effigy.

Ingrid sharply inhaled, the sound of her reaction lost amid the cheers that erupted around her.

The leaf-stuffed cloth bodies bobbed and swayed. They wore yellow brassards on their upper arms that bore the characters for "Shina," as all Chinese were required to wear in public. This attention to detail was repeated in the paper identification booklets that jutted from their shirt pockets.

The third figure looked smaller, younger than the other two, its face slender and black hair shaggy.

It looked like Lee.

She swallowed down her nausea, but she couldn't seem to avert her eyes, even as the truck drove on and vanished behind a line of men that jumped and hollered.

"Ingrid. Ingrid?" Cy's hand was heavy on her shoulder. That's when she realized she was leaning forward in a way that threatened to tip the wicker chair. She sat back as the crowd roared again. The next truck held attractive women, both white and Japanese, who smiled and waved to their captive audience. The music of the first truck faded and people around them began to move again.

"The last truck makes the damned wait worthwhile, eh?" said the man, giving Cy a nudge as he shuffled on. Cy didn't bother to respond.

Other people shoved by, the resumption of traffic creating a deafening cacophony. It took a minute or two for the congestion to ease up enough for the wheelchair to roll onward.

Ingrid stared down at her lap and tried to create a blank canvas in her mind, but she had never had a knack for Zen meditation. She ached to know where Lee was, how he was doing. She twiddled the unfamiliar ring on her finger, trying to think of something to say to break through the gloom that had descended on the two of them.

"You know, we need a different name for our new lives together," she finally said, twisting to look back at him. Her heart wrenched at the dispirited expression on his face.

"Do you have any preferences?" he asked, his tone a bit gruff.

She thought for a moment. "I don't mind the name Harvey. I once had a cat by that name."

Cy snorted out a laugh. "Fenris would be greatly amused by that, with the grief he gives me about attracting cats."

"It's a nice, nondescript name. Not royal or pompous,"

she teased, alluding to his true identity as a member of the Augustus family.

"That name'll do just fine, Mrs. Harvey," he murmured as he stroked her shoulder. The contact tantalized her. She wanted to feel more of him, to take comfort in his warm and strong body. That's what she wanted most of all right now: a hug, improper and scandalous though it might be. And later, perhaps, much more than that.

She and Cy had experienced one glorious, intimate night together before all hell had broken loose in Seattle, and she yearned for the opportunity to be with him again. She knew he would be hesitant, though. Not for lack of desire on his part, but for fear that he'd hurt her somehow. He couldn't seem to accept that she was going to endure some level of pain no matter what she did these days.

Sitting included. She shifted in her seat with a grimace.

"I spy a bakery sign up ahead," he said. She had to take his word on that; all she saw were heads and backsides. "I bought some kashi-pan this morning, but Mrs. Kealoha's descriptions of the Big Island's wilderness make me want to buy more rolls, as a precaution."

"Good idea. I don't believe there is such a thing as too many pastries," she replied lightly.

By some miracle, an OPEN sign in English and Japanese still draped crookedly against the door glass, and an employee still lounged behind the counter. But before she could express her relief, another issue immediately became apparent.

"Blast it all." Cy heaved the wheelchair up the slight lift to the door entrance, but no matter how he angled the chair, it refused to fit. Pedestrians cursed them in multiple languages as they blocked the walkway.

"Mr. Harvey, you may as well stop trying. You can't squeeze a kraken through a keyhole. Roll me down there." She motioned past the building, where tree branches draped low enough to threaten passing hats. Once they were in the shade, she twisted to look up at him. "Now go inside and buy whatever stock they have."

"Mrs. Harvey." The name rang as strange on his tongue, but the warning in his tone came across clearly. They could both see a cluster of soldiers across the street harassing a man of dark coloration beside a parked rickshaw.

"I trust you'll be fast. Come now, we're lucky this place is still open at all, and that could change any minute. The more pastries we have for the sylphs, the less likely we'll have a mutiny."

"That sounds like the setup of a horrific dime novel. Trapped aboard an airship with ravenous fae," he said in a grim tone. He adjusted the angle of the wheels and rolled her back into a paved recess off the sidewalk. A shoulder-high stone wall stood behind her. "Don't go anywhere without me," he said, and dashed away.

Ingrid curled her fists toward her belly, keenly aware of her vulnerability. In the past, she would have been confident in her ability to wield energy to shove away attackers or raise a shield in her defense. Now she was afraid to expend anything at all lest she draw on her own life force again and worsen the damage to her nerves.

A group of older Japanese businessmen walked by, arguing the merits of mail-order brides. The music of the brass band carried from somewhere distant, and she grimaced at the thought of that horrid parade passing by again. She understood the reason for the crowd's enthusiasm, though. People wanted the war to be done, for their men to stop dying, for the survivors to come home. They wanted *peace*. The most straightforward way to achieve that was to obliterate the Chinese people so that Japan could continue to settle the Asian mainland.

Ingrid wanted peace, too, but on far different terms.

"I heard there's an ambassador coming through," a white-haired man said.

Ingrid's head jerked up, her breath frozen in her throat.

"Coming through, or staying a time?" asked another fellow. "Are they going to do something about these damned strikes? I have three freighters here and no molasses barrels to load. Why, it don't even smell right down at the docks right now . . ."

She was tempted to roll after them to ask if they knew which ambassador, but she also knew men of that ilk would probably be stupefied that she was conversant in international politics at all.

Her breaths came fast. What if Blum could still track her despite the ward and the distance they'd come? If so, Ingrid was doomed. The sylphs couldn't hide her for an extended time, not for all the kashi-pan in the world. Cy and Fenris would surely die in an effort to save her. Lee and the rest of his people would be slaughtered.

And Blum would visit Ingrid in her imprisonment and persist in her delusion that they were the best of friends, all while torturing her to the brink of death time and again.

She breathed deeper, not to calm herself, but to see if she could detect that nightmarish, musky odor that denoted Blum's presence.

The only smells she could identify were autocar exhaust and frying fish.

Maybe this visiting ambassador was Roosevelt. His people had surely told him of the *Palmetto Bug*'s destination. He might have pursued her for some reason.

Or it could be any of the other ten ambassadors, several of whom were Japanese and certain to stop here during their flights across the Pacific.

The cool logic of those odds eased her back from outright hysteria, but her heart still raced, her body slicked with sweat despite the cool evening shade.

The heavy clop of boots caused her to jump in her seat. She looked up to find Cy, his fists burdened by two laden paper bags. His relieved grin faded as he took in her mood.

"What happened?" he quietly asked as he checked the area around them. His hand lowered toward his waist, as if to grab his Tesla rod or pistol, and in their absence he clutched the bags tighter.

"Some men mentioned that an ambassador was visiting Honolulu. They didn't say a name, but . . ."

Cy went a little bit pale, but his voice was even when he spoke. "Maybe we can find out more, and if it is her, we'll know to be ready." He passed the two bags to her. She set them on her lap and resisted the urge to laugh maniacally. They had no weapons at hand, but by God, they had pastries!

"'Be ready.' What does that even mean, Cy? We can't shoot her. She's almost invincible between that ring and her own inherent powers. She killed three men to keep me alive, and she wasn't even in direct contact with any of us." Her breaths came faster again.

Cy knelt to face her. "Ingrid. Sweetheart. Keep your voice down. We're in public. If it is Bl—the fox—we won't go down without a fight."

"A fight. We know what the outcome of that will be." Despair threatened to drown her.

His eyes searched hers, and she read in them his desperate need to kiss her and hold her close. Instead, he rested a hand on her shoulder. "Wait until we have more information before you decide all is lost," he said, straightening as he took the handles of her chair.

"Very well. I'll schedule my existential despair to resume in a short while."

"That's the spirit," he said.

"I love you, Cy," she whispered over her shoulder.

"And I love you," he whispered back.

She feigned nonchalance as they reentered the crowd. "What did you buy?" She rattled one of the sacks.

"A bit of everything. An-pan, melon-pan, croissants, cream puffs, palmiers. I bought out the place. The shopkeep turned the sign to 'Closed' as I left."

Ingrid laughed a little at that. "Well, our small friends will experience European pastries for the first time. If they won't eat them, I happily will." She resisted the urge to dig into a bag at that very moment. Her hunger had been relentless as her body recovered.

"Can you believe it!" A man stood with a group at a street corner, a newspaper held up in both hands. "Look at the size of that thing! We're living in an incredible age."

"What size of kermanite is needed to power a craft like that?" asked one of his companions.

Cy brought the wheelchair to a stop just behind the group. For a moment, he was very still, reminding Ingrid of a cat ready to pounce. "Pardon me, gentlemen," he said in his graceful way, "I couldn't help but overhear. Are you referring to something in the evening paper?"

The papers he had bought that morning had repeated the mainland headlines of the previous week: the prospect of gold continued to lure men north to Baranov, where clashes with Russians were imminent. Across the United States, the Chinese were being imprisoned "for their own good"; an editorial viciously examined if the Chinese could exist in civilized societies at all—the answer, of course, being no. The fires in San Francisco had stopped, and survivors were still scattered in camps across the Bay Area. There had been no mention of the fate of Cy's missing father.

"Why, yes, this is the very latest news!" The man with the paper turned to assess Cy, and seeing a neatly attired white man like himself, he grinned and spread the sheets wide again. "Look at this on page two!" Much to Ingrid's frustration, she couldn't see anything.

"Wonder what the damn invention cost?" muttered another man, shaking his head as he walked away.

"'The debut of the Unified Pacific vessel *Excalibur*,'" Cy read aloud. "'A craft that is in truth more city than ship, an offensive vessel capable of dropping payloads to level cities while safely transporting as many as ten thousand soldiers along with supplies to keep them aloft without resupply for months.'" He settled back on his heels. No one but Ingrid would have been able to tell that the news had shaken him like a titan.

"And that picture . . . !" This time when the man flared out the paper, Ingrid caught a glimpse of the full page.

The black-and-white print fuzzed out fine details, but the photograph was still extraordinary. *Excalibur* resembled a castle hovering high in the sky. The high sheen of the hull indicated it was some kind of metal, most likely orichalcum, which was incredibly light and nigh bulletproof.

This was the culmination of the Gaia Project, Ambassador Blum's top secret endeavor to subjugate the Chinese. This vessel may have been made in America for the cause of the Unified Pacific, but the ultimate purpose was for the glory of Japan, firmly establishing it as the supreme power in Asia. A war machine of this might would certainly intimidate Britannia as it struggled to maintain control of India, and likewise challenge the Russian Empire, which had been engaged in border scuffles with Japan in recent months.

It might very well intimidate America, too. Theodore Roosevelt had expressed fears that the union of the United States and Japan was bound to fracture, with Japan positioned to dominate its former ally.

"I bet my bookie is running odds on how fast that *Excalibur* is versus a Behemoth-class airship. If he's not, he needs to start a pool going!" A man cackled. "I just got paid, and now I know where that money's going."

"If that monstrosity's going to China, my God, it'll have to fly to Honolulu en route! I need to tell my boss. If we hooked that supply contract . . ." The fellow rushed away.

"Much obliged to you for sharing such extraordinary news." At that, Cy tipped his hat. The street traffic stopped, and he wheeled Ingrid across the way, dodging oncoming folks by juking left and right. He harshly brought the chair's wheels up over the next curb. Ingrid caught herself on the armrests.

Along the next block, there were too many people close by for them to speak with any sort of privacy. Cy's continued silence draped over her, thick and heavy. She wished that she could see his face or offer some comfort as he rolled her along as fast as the scant walkway space allowed. An industrial area lay ahead. Just beyond, airships hovered like oval clouds attached to tall steel mooring masts. The ocean was hidden from view.

She looked left, and all she could see were more buildings and a plume of smoke. When she had first seen the smoke, she had been afraid that the Chinatown here had been set afire, forgetting that it had been razed years ago after the Chinese experienced an outbreak of bubonic plague. Cy had identified it earlier as a garbage fire that constantly burned in a swampy area.

Finally, the crowd thinned enough around them that she chanced a whisper. "Cy, please tell me what's on your mind."

"Excalibur." The word rasped out. "Of course she named it *Excalibur.*"

Maggie. Cy's twin sister, by his account the most brilliant engineer he'd ever known. Newspapers had announced that she'd died in a tragic laboratory fire, but in truth she'd faked her own death in order to escape an oppressive life as an administrator in their father's company. It was her engineering genius that had made Ambassador Blum's Gaia Project a reality.

Ingrid thought back to the day she met Cy. "You mentioned once that *Connecticut Yankee* was a favorite childhood book for the two of you."

"Yes," he said shortly. "She maintained a fascination with Arthurian tales ever since." He drew silent again.

"We're a week's flight away from the States. How long would it take *Excalibur* to get here? Should we wait in the islands?" She wished she had the words to cut through Cy's jumble of emotions about his sister, but she didn't. In truth, she didn't know how she felt about Maggie herself.

He pulled her chair to one side. She twisted around to look at him. His head was bowed, his eyes narrowed.

"The article mentioned *Excalibur*'s route will take it across the southern states and territories to where it'll pick up its full crew in Los Angeles. By the time we get back to the mainland, more information will be available. Photographs. Film reels. Articles. We need to know what Maggie's made."

"Just the greatest war machine the world has ever known, backed by the might of one of the greatest militaries of all time, all of it orchestrated by a power-mad kitsune at least four hundred years of age," Ingrid said, tone light.

"Is that all?" Cy's chuckle sounded strained. "Well, I do have some true good news. That newspaper also mentioned the ambassador making a stop in town. It's Morimoto."

She released a long breath. Ambassador Morimoto was one of the most public Japanese representatives.

"That *is* good news," she said.

The airships loomed larger, the noise of engines creating a consistent background drone. Men in military and company uniforms huddled in small and large groups and blocked the way ahead. Cy rolled her off the sidewalk and around stalled autocars in wait of passage through the gate.

Ingrid clutched the chair arms. "I see Fenris out here."

Fenris Braun leaned against a building, his hands thrust into his pockets. He was of average height and reed slim, his skin a socially acceptable shade of tan, though he rarely endured the sun. Stains mottled both his khaki trousers and untucked denim shirt.

"Didn't expect to see you out here." Anxiety edged Cy's voice.

"Circumstances required that I take a walk. I decided to wait here afterward. This is a good place to see who comes and goes." Beneath a brown bowler hat set at a cocky angle, his gaze tracked the other men around the outer gate.

"What circumstances?" asked Ingrid.

"A man was watching the *Palmetto Bug*. He was about as subtle as a dragon with heartburn. I decided to make his acquaintance. He then decided to take a nap. And a swim. Unfortunately for him, he did both at the same time."

"Are you saying you . . . ? *How?*" She dared not say more with other people so close by.

Fenris's glance was cold enough to make her erupt in goose bumps. "I'm saying yes, I did. As for how . . . well, I can still possess weapons *within* the dock, can't I? My efforts were proved worthwhile, in any case. I found this." He tugged a folded sheet from his pocket and passed it to her. "The man was clearly incompetent. I expected Bl—the fox to hire better lackeys. At least his ineptitude was to our advantage."

She unfolded the single sheet as Cy leaned over her shoulder. A list in light pencil included numbers, names, and airship classes. The *Palmetto Bug* was about two-thirds of the way down the page, its line marked by a drawn star in darker lead.

"He was watching for us," Cy said softly. "Did he—"

"He had no chance to report to anyone, no. I observed him the whole time. And before you begin griping at me, yes, I took care of him with proper efficiency." Fenris continued to assess everyone who walked by.

Had Fenris had much experience with this sort of thing? From what Ingrid knew of him, it didn't seem likely. And yet . . .

She opened her mouth to ask, but no sound emerged. Suddenly she wasn't sure she wanted to know the answer.

"Let's hope your work remains efficient through the night," Cy murmured, passing the notepaper back to him. "We're taking on freight in the morning and heading off for Hawaii Island. I assume the ship is still flyable, even with your recent distractions?"

"The *Bug* will be ready." Fenris waved a hand in dismissal, then tilted his head, a thoughtful look on his face. "Truth be told, I was almost hoping someone would try to break on board because I rigged a new alarm that will shock—"

"Fenris." Cy said a great deal in that one word.

Fenris sighed. "I *suppose* we shouldn't leave too many bodies in our wake."

CHAPTER 3

SATURDAY, MAY 5, 1906

"The sylphs are *molting*." Fenris made the statement with all the drama and dread of announcing that the *Palmetto Bug* was plummeting to its doom. He cast a glance at Ingrid over his shoulder.

"And good afternoon to you as well," she said, rubbing her eyes as she yawned. She dropped her body into one of the wooden seats that flanked the door just within the control cabin. Her muscles felt stiff, but at least her clothes were unrestrictive today. She wore cotton drawers for their day flight to Hawaii Island. The male underclothes fit her loosely and featured larger buttons than their feminine counterparts; her legs had absorbed the worst of the nerve damage, but her finger coordination wasn't what it once was, so small buttons were troublesome.

Certainly, wearing such attire would have been scandalous to much of society, but she was comfortable, fully covered, and her company didn't mind, and she didn't particularly give a damn about society at large.

"I don't see any kind of molting here," she said, examining the doorway. The sylphs hovered near the ceiling, their presence like a buzzing bonfire to Ingrid's senses. Their scent flared like lavender as they greeted her as a bobbing gray mass. There had to be about a thousand sylphs, each resembling a gray-winged moth with a humanoid body. Ingrid had rescued them from becoming oil-fried enchanted appetizers for wealthy diners overseas.

"The gray fluff is in their rack. I cleaned it up as best I could, as very unpleasant things would happen if that mess entered the ventilation system. At least they aren't shedding near the control cabin." He shot a glare over his shoulder. "They have taken to their training quite well."

"Fenris, they're fairies, not poodles!"

"I don't discriminate. In fact, people need those same kind of boundaries. Have you ever been around small children?" He shuddered head to toe as if he were speaking of spiders. "If you do see any fluff on the floor, let me know immediately. We need to clean it up before . . ." He uplifted a fist and flared out his fingers to illustrate a small, dramatic explosion.

"Wonderful. Because there weren't enough ways this mission might kill us. Now we have to worry about fairy dander." She leaned forward on her knees and studied the dials and meters and toggles. "I often wonder what all this means."

"I'm not the one to come to with your life dilemmas."

"You know what I'm talking about. How the two of you

pilot the *Bug*. I can't comprehend what any of this means, yet . . ."

"Are you expressing an interest in learning to fly?" Fenris looked at her sidelong, an eyebrow raised.

Was she? Ingrid couldn't say she had ever daydreamed about flying an airship on her own, but she *did* detest her ignorance about operations aboard the *Bug*. And with her legs as they were, the idea of new independence in movement held special appeal.

"I think I'd like to understand more of how things work," she said. Fenris accepted this with a grunt.

Ingrid gazed out the glass. Patches of green and red land peeped from beneath a blanket of gray. "Where are we? Is the Big Island beneath those clouds?"

"No. That's Maui."

She slipped into the vacant copilot's seat to better see. "Oh! That's Haleakala! It's huge!" Maui's massive volcano poked from among the clouds. "I'm glad I woke up when I did. I was afraid I'd slept too long and missed the sights."

"Well, you shouldn't have exhausted yourself helping us this morning."

Before dawn, they had loaded their freight: twenty small pots of vanilla orchids. The little plants had surprised Ingrid; she hadn't even known vanilla beans grew from a kind of orchid.

Fenris and Cy had done the hard work of ferrying plants by the armful up the mooring mast and into the *Bug*; Ingrid had merely lashed the pots in place along the corridor. Not something that would have tired her out before.

"I had to help load," Ingrid said. "I can't abide laziness. It's not as if I drew on my magical power."

"Magical power, physical power. Those two overlap quite a bit in regard to your body."

"That's why I'm certain my grandmother will be able to help in some way."

"Delusion is wonderful while it lasts," said Fenris.

Ingrid recalled Blum's parting words for her in Seattle. *Hope is a form of gangrene.* Her hands formed fists atop her thighs. "You really don't think I'll get better."

Beneath his goggles, his thin lips pursed together. "Define '*better*.' Will you be able to move like you once did? To jump, climb, run? That might be asking for a miracle."

"Madam Pele *is* a goddess."

"She doesn't go around healing erstwhile relatives who knock at the door of her volcano, does she?" He arched an eyebrow. "No. Of course not. She's too busy burning down villages with lava."

Ingrid conceded that point with a frown. "Actually, I'm most concerned that she won't show herself to us at all. As a shapeshifter, she could be *anything,* anywhere. If she wants to hide from me, she will."

"Shapeshifting. Such an interesting skill." Wistfulness flickered over Fenris's face, and he shook his head as if to shed the unfinished thought. "Ah, well. To bluntly change the subject, I spy something of great interest to you." He pointed ahead. Ingrid sucked in a sharp breath.

Mauna Loa. She could recite its data from oft-overheard lessons at the Cordilleran Auxiliary. The volcano scraped the heavens at fourteen thousand feet, about the same height as Mount Rainier back in Washington, but Mauna Loa existed on an entirely different scale. Geologists speculated it was the largest mountain in the world in terms of mass. Whereas many mountain peaks formed a rough triangle, Mauna Loa formed one that was squat and wide, like a sumo wrestler in position to start a bout. Even though it was early May, a dusting of snow was still visible at the peak.

"I've never seen a mountain that big in all my life," said Fenris. "And that's a volcano? Christ."

"Yes, and there are actually several other volcanoes around it. That peak to the left is Mauna Kea. It's actually the same height as Mauna Loa, but the mass is considerably different." She stared in awe. Mauna Kea appeared puny in comparison. "Straight ahead, I think, is Kohala, and then Hualalai is over on the right somewhere beneath those clouds. That one last erupted about a hundred years ago."

She suspected she was pronouncing the latter name wrong, as she had read it more often than she heard it. That bothered her. This place was part of her identity, and she wanted to grant it proper respect.

"The lava rocks all those volcanoes left behind will create a rough flight for us soon." At Ingrid's puzzled look, Fenris continued: "Black lava rocks absorb and radiate heat. By early afternoon, that can cause thunderstorms to develop. Like *that*." He motioned to the clouds ahead and below them.

As if to illustrate, the craft made a small lurch. "I hope Cy can sleep through it."

"Eh. We've had to bunk in cheap flats beside railroad

tracks more than once. The man has evolved, per Darwin's theory, to sleep whenever and however he can. The little tub of beeswax he bought back in Honolulu won't hurt either. You know, maybe if you plug your ears, you'll sleep better."

She shrugged. Her sleep issues had little to do with noise and a lot to do with leg cramps. "I'm going to stretch my legs and check on the plants."

"Be extra careful walking through this turbulence." As if to illustrate, the *Bug* hit another rough patch. It bobbed up and down as if on a stormy ocean current.

"Be extra careful yourself. An airship crash would bring unnecessary excitement to our day." Ingrid had to pivot her hips around to lead with her right leg in order to step out from between the pilots' chairs.

The sylphs dipped and swarmed around her as she entered the hallway. They had been ecstatic when the orchids had arrived that morning, buzzing like a hundred cats purring at once. They must have been starved for greenery, Ingrid decided. They hadn't expressed any desire to leave the ship in Honolulu, instead lurking in their rack. When she had checked on them, they conveyed that the bustle and scents of the dock were reminiscent of the Seattle port where she had rescued them from death.

"I'm glad to see you, too," she said. She extended her arms to either side, catching herself on the walls as the airship jostled. The fairies followed her.

Ropes secured the orchid pots to built-in holes and fasteners. She frowned as she tentatively lowered herself to the tatami mat. The slender vines and broad leaves looked noticeably larger than before. She studied the next plant, and the one behind her. They *all* looked larger. One plant had even developed buds, and none of them had been budding when she tied them down.

"Is this your doing?" she murmured to the sylphs. She didn't reach into her power to formally ask the question. That had been less necessary recently, as the sylphs had begun to understand more verbal communication from all three humans aboard the *Bug*.

The sylphs responded with a high-pitched clicking sound.

"Don't make them grow too big, not this time. The man buying these plants *wants* them small."

The happy buzz took on a querulous tone. Ingrid sighed. Even if she delved into her power to clarify what she meant, she wasn't sure how she'd go about it. Instead, she switched to a word they knew quite well. "Pastry?"

At that, the sylphs reached a euphoric decibel that Fenris could probably hear in the cockpit. Ingrid opened the pantry, which currently had an entire shelf devoted to kashi-pan wrapped in newsprint bundles. She grabbed two packets and, with a high-stepped gait to prevent her feet from dragging, walked to where the four beds flanked the corridor.

Sitting down, she tore a pastry in half and extended a piece to the sylphs. They dive-bombed it, the weight of the yeast bread dissipating in a matter of seconds. Not a single crumb remained on her palm.

She usually didn't rely on equal distribution when she fed the sylphs these days. Their relationship had become more casual. The fairies had accepted the *Bug* as their new nest, and Ingrid, Cy, and Fenris were part of the deal.

Examining the remaining bread in her other hand, she concluded that the middle of this particular bun contained some sort of yellow marmalade. Ingrid suspected it was lemon, but biting into it, discovered a much tarter flavor than she expected. Still delicious, though, despite numerous little seeds. It must be some local fruit.

She ate the rest of the soft bread roll, then reached for the second. This one was an-pan. The red bean paste inside was the slightest bit chunky, just the way she liked it.

Across from her, Cy occupied the bunk that she often used. Blackout curtains obscured him from view, but she could hear the soft noises he made as he slept.

Good. He wasn't awake to stop her. Fortified by bread, she climbed the ladder to the rack directly above.

She proceeded slowly, her feet dragging against each rung. About halfway up, the muscles in her left leg spasmed with an electric-shock jolt from her toes to her buttocks. Her calf went painfully rigid. She kicked it out in an effort to loosen the tension. Her right foot lost its grip. She gasped as her body dropped—then immediately stopped.

The prickling sensation of the sylphs' touch brought a different kind of pain, but one that was preferable to smacking her head and back on the floor below. She gritted her teeth as she clenched the topmost rung with her sweaty hands and dragged herself upward, the sylphs providing an extra boost.

At last, she made it onto the bunk. Sweat drenched her body. She sat and rubbed the troublesome calf muscle.

The sylphs fluttered into the large, bowl-like nest they'd made for themselves in the blankets. Their buzzing was subdued out of courtesy for Cy.

She had climbed this ladder in mere seconds several times before. Now the effort reminded her of trudging up Telegraph Hill in San Francisco with a laden pack.

In the far corner behind the sylphs' nest, the Green Dragon Crescent Blade of the Chinese god Guan Yu lay hidden in its bag beneath folds of blankets. The holy presence of the pole-arm's blade radiated heat that was distinct from that of the sylphs. The fairies had gladly accepted Ingrid's request that they guard the weapon from any strangers who might come aboard the *Bug,* and they had otherwise shown no reaction to it.

Lee's carving of the *qilin* stared at her from the back wall. The image of the chimerical combination of dragon, goat, and unicorn was undeniably crude but still recognizable.

The kirin and *qilin* were regarded as among the most powerful beings in the Japanese and Chinese pantheons, so rare and obscure that they were considered extinct or mythological. They were creatures of peace, and also ones of divine portent, said to visit people destined to be sages or powerful rulers.

Previously, the *qilin* had shown up of its own volition and counseled Ingrid to save Lee's life for the sake of the world—as if she had needed additional motivation to save the boy she loved as her brother. It had also told her that it could perceive the world through reproductions of its image, but it hadn't returned since then. And she was damned sick of waiting for the next visit.

She stretched out her fingertips to touch the triangle-shaped divots of splintered wood, relying on the tactile sensation to help her reach out to the celestial being.

"*Qilin.*" Ingrid placed as much emphasis on the name as she could without utilizing her power. "Thank you for watching over us. I am keeping the *guandao* close by your image here. I hope I can return it to Lee, or give it to someone else whom you deem worthy enough to wield it." She knew she didn't qualify, and in truth, she was still embarrassed that she had tried. She wasn't Chinese, and it was arrogant of her to presume she could handle the holy weapon.

It was unquestionably arrogant of her to invoke the *qilin* like this, too, but she was desperate.

"I need your help, *qilin.*" She kept her tone humble. "If Lee is alive, you are certain to be watching over him." She struggled with her emotions, thinking of how she and Lee had clung to each other in the weeks after Mama had died. "I ache to watch over him myself, to talk to him, but I have no means to do so."

She went quiet for a moment. There was still no sense of the *qilin*'s holy presence, no tintinnabulation of bells or whiffs of wonderful smells from the past that made her feel at peace.

"I would be humbled and honored, *qilin,* if you could act as a medium between us. I know this is a bold request on my part. I'm grateful to you for even listening to me." She shook her head, chagrined. "Even saying that is a presumption on my part. I'm sorry."

She waited and waited. Minutes passed. Five, ten.

Nothing.

She conceded defeat. Despair weighed on her as she eased herself down the ladder. The sylphs, unbidden, rose from the nest to hover behind her. She reached the tatami mat and released a sigh of relief. At least she hadn't broken her neck by falling off the ladder.

She couldn't dwell on her failure to connect with the *qilin*. She needed a pleasant distraction.

The metal rings of the curtain squawked as she pushed them to either side. Cy slept flat on his back, his head tilted back and his mouth agape. Wavy tendrils of hair framed his face. His legs bent to one side so that he could fit in the confines of the rack.

Ingrid ducked her head into the space, close to his chest. Her hairpins tapped the base of the bunk above. Cy's eyes flew open, and she almost laughed at his startled expression. Grinning back, he pried the beeswax lumps from his ears.

"Hello!" she said.

"Hello to you as well. Can you set this in the nook? And pass me my glasses?"

She let her hand drift down to rest on his chest after handing him his glasses. His white shirt had been pulled askew as he slept, stretching to show more skin at his collar.

His elbow thudded on the wall as he placed his glasses on his nose. "Fenris hasn't made some dire statement about the fate of the *Bug*, has he?"

"Not in the past few minutes." She paused for dramatic effect. "I want you."

His brown eyes blinked rapidly behind his lenses. "Oh. What? But you. Your body. I wouldn't want to—your legs— and Fenris is just up the hall—and the racks, we'd never—"

"I'm not suggesting we take immediate action on the matter, but I thought it best to warn you of my intentions."

He arched an eyebrow. "I see."

"Do you?" She kissed him, the pressure of her lips and the touch of her tongue evoking a ragged groan from his throat.

"But your—" he started to say against her lips.

Ingrid pulled back. "If you say the word 'legs' again, I might be tempted to bite you." She sighed, her levity fading. "Cy. I'm aware that I have new limitations, but I am willing to adapt. If one technique doesn't work, we'll try another. That's the scientific way, isn't it?"

His lips quirked together. "You're asking me to experiment with you?"

"Good God. Yes. That's it exactly." She kissed him again.

The airship rumbled and bounced. Ingrid's head smacked the ceiling, and would have smacked a second time but for Cy's hand acting as a buffer at the last second.

"Are you all right?" he asked.

She withdrew from his bunk to sit on her backside in the hallway, rubbing her head. "I'm fine. Just a bump." She braced both hands against the floor as the *Bug* jostled more.

"Expect turbulence! We're flying over those lava fields and some storm clouds!" called Fenris.

"I had best lend some aid." Cy helped her upright. They stood together, bodies a breath apart. Despite his statement, he seemed reluctant to move. The ship jolted again, pushing them together. His arms wrapped around her waist as she rested her head on his chest. She let her eyes drift shut, his heartbeat her lullaby.

"I so enjoy the freedom to do this." His words were hot and muffled against the top of her head.

Anger and frustration caused her throat to tighten. She wanted to show affection to Cy no matter where they were. She wanted the freedom to walk along with him, hand in hand. For him to plant even a chaste kiss on her cheek in public without it being a scandal. For them to legally marry, and for that document to be irrefutable here and across the United States.

He stroked her back, and her body melted against his. Some of her frustration faded, but only some. She had a hunch her rage at the societal injustice would never fully go away.

"I suppose the *Bug* is like our own independent country," she said. "Laws and propriety be damned." She tugged on the hip of her pajama trousers for emphasis.

"Almighty preserve us. Don't tell Fenris about this simile of yours, or he'll endeavor to make it a reality."

Ingrid giggled. "A crown would suit him quite nicely, I think."

"He's never fancied hats, really, but I think he'd feel differently about a crown." Cy held her close, their bodies fitting together just so. The ship rocked again, and she would have stumbled off balance except for his secure grip.

"Cy! Are you awake? Come here! Ingrid, you too! The coast is blackened wasteland for miles and miles! It's fantastic!"

Ingrid wistfully sighed. "We'd better both share in this glorious vision of a wasteland." She gazed up at him. "Please give some thought to ways we can experiment, Cy. I assure you, I'll be doing the same."

His eyes gleamed with mischief. "I might need to chart out some possibilities."

"Be sure to share them with me later," she whispered. She pressed her ring-adorned hand against his chest and gave him a final, lingering kiss that made her feel warm from head to toe.

She moved toward the control cabin and attempted a sultry walk, even as she continually balanced herself on either side of the hallway as the craft lurched. A glance back confirmed that Cy's gaze followed her all the way. By the look on his face, he wasn't simply thinking of catching her if she fell.

"Cy!" Fenris's voice hit an unusually high pitch. All of the gaiety in the cabin evaporated in an instant. "Get up here, now!" The airship wobbled again.

Cy flew down the hallway. Ingrid pressed herself against the wall as he rushed past. "What happened?" he asked briskly.

"We're losing pressure." She saw Fenris gesture to dials on his right. "Take the chair." With that, he ran past her, to the engine room.

Ingrid remained frozen for a moment. Fenris's face had blanched, becoming almost ghostly; she had seen him like that only one other time—when he'd been stabbed. She edged into the doorway, desperate to help, but also smart enough to stay out of the way.

The window showed the ship at about the same elevation

as before. Ocean sprawled to the right, the view below of broad swaths of black lava rock divided by brief bands of verdant jungle. There were no landing masts. No towns.

Ingrid reached into her pocket. Kermanite crystals dissolved at her touch. Power whirled into her bloodstream, heady and delicious and wonderful. Oh, she missed this feeling, but damn it, she couldn't let herself become intoxicated by the sensation.

"Pipe leak!" Fenris shouted.

"Can you shut it off?" Cy yelled back.

"Working on it!"

Cy and Fenris were at opposite ends of the *Bug*. If the ship went down, Ingrid wouldn't be able to shield everyone. She could have screamed in frustration. She glanced at the control cabin, her heart in her throat, then hurried to the center of the crisis.

Fenris wore elbow-length thick gloves as he gripped a valve and grunted as he slowly turned it. A low whistling sound brought her gaze up about a foot above them, where a small white plume emerged from a T-shaped joint of pipework.

"Do you want me to seal it?" she asked.

Fenris didn't look up. He worked the valve with all of his slight weight. "Hell yes."

Ingrid didn't need a reminder to be delicate. Demolishing the pipe would blast fatal steam over both her and Fenris, and even if she managed to shield them in time, the internal engine might very well fail completely and send down the ship.

She braced her legs wide for steadiness and drew on her magic. The concentration of heat in her right hand felt as if she'd immersed it in a pot of simmering water. She leaned toward the pipe above her, about a foot down from the leak. Uncomfortable warmth wavered against her fingertips. Magic shielded her skin like a glove as she gripped the metal.

Ingrid closed her eyes to block out the rest of the world. Fast-moving condensation thrummed within the pipe. Pressure was building. More and more steam rushed this way. The weakness at the joint was expanding, millimeter by millimeter.

She willed magic to flow from her fingertips and outward along the pipe to find the leak. The incredible power of the steam fought against her as she sealed the minute crack. So much deadly might, packed into one small conduit—a metaphor for her own life, really. She gritted her teeth and held the plug in place.

"Keep doing whatever you're doing!" Fenris said, gasping. "I almost have the access closed!"

"Will the engine continue to run? Will we stay aloft?" Her voice sounded distant to her ears.

"I already opened a secondary valve to divert some of the flow. Once this is shut off, yes, the *Bug* will get us to port."

Ingrid sensed the moment that Fenris succeeded. The thrum within the pipe abruptly slowed and stopped. She opened her eyes but maintained her grip. "I won't let go until you give me the okay."

"Stay exactly as you are for now." Fenris hesitated. "Or is this power use . . . ?"

"I could stay here for a while. I'm not fighting the flow of steam now, so sealing the pipe isn't taking much from me."

"Good." Fenris released a relieved huff. Sweat glistened on his skin. "A few minutes is all I need." He began to check other pipes and valves.

"We're holding steady," Cy shouted. "Everyone well back there?"

"Yes! Fenris stopped the leak," she called.

"Meanwhile, you're holding a pipe that should be burning your fingers off," Fenris said, his voice low. "But I don't suppose that kind of feat is noteworthy these days."

"We can give him the full account once he sees that I'm walking as well as before. No point in vexing him unnecessarily."

"A wise course of action." He nodded. "Okay. Gradually release your seal on the pipe."

She did so. A tiny wheeze of steam escaped from the joint, but no more. She sagged against the doorway as she checked her hand. The skin was unblemished.

"Crisis averted." Fenris worked off the large gloves. "Can't say that I'm surprised something like that happened, though. We've put a lot of pressure on the *Bug* in the past few weeks." He gave the wall a fond pat.

Fenris was being unusually gracious in his statement. "I'm sorry," she hoarsely whispered.

He glanced back, blinking in surprise. "What? Oh." He took in her emotional state. "No need to feel guilty about it. Sure, we flew around because of you, but just think. If you hadn't met Cy, the two of us probably would have died in the quake or conflagration in San Francisco." He shrugged. "Here we are. We're not dead yet."

She stared after Fenris as he walked to the control cabin, the long gloves flapping in his grip. He was right. They weren't dead. Yet.

CHAPTER 4

The *Palmetto Bug* docked after dusk. Ingrid lurked in a pilot's chair, restless as the men conducted necessary business
on the mooring mast. Male voices carried up through the
open hatch, but she couldn't discern any words. She tugged
at the side of the nearest woven privacy screen that blocked
a cabin window and peered outside.

The dock consisted of about a dozen mooring masts
sized to accommodate small passenger vessels like Sprites
or Portermans. She could only spy four masts from here, and
judging by the presence of people, two of the other docked
ships appeared to be new arrivals as well.

She had fully expected the ground to be misted in blue
because of the active volcanic vents close by, but there was no
visible outflow of power at all. She wasn't sure if she should
take that as a positive sign or not.

It's not as though she had reason to relax, though. Soldiers were everywhere, their navy uniforms almost black beneath the blue-hued glow of the mast lights. Mrs. K hadn't exaggerated about the military presence on the island. They hadn't even docked near a major port like Kona or Hilo either. This was out in the wilderness. But then, that made this an even better place for the strikers to try to sneak through weapons and supplies.

Ingrid walked to the open hatch, still surprised at the ease of the movement. Cy had finished assembling a mobility aid he'd worked on for days, something he'd once seen used by a professor at his academy years ago. Her new and rigid boots featured a thick band of elastic that attached at the toe of each boot and stretched to the top eyelets of each shaft, creating a forty-five-degree angle of taut elastic. The movement of her thighs therefore helped to pull up her toes with each step.

The rig wasn't a permanent aid by any means. Cy had elaborated on the many ways it could fail. And, of course, it did nothing to prevent her calf muscles from misfiring, as they were wont to do. But the device was certainly better than nothing.

The men continued to talk down below. What if their paperwork was inadequate? What if they had to go elsewhere—or couldn't dock on the island at all?

Metal vibrated within the pantry. She slid open the door. "Shush. You have to be quiet and still."

The digestive biscuit tin, salvaged from Mr. Thornton's airship, rattled and danced at the back of the cabinet. The sylphs had been ushered into most every enclosed food box in

59

the pantry. The ship now hosted sylph-biscuits, sylph–saltine crackers, and sylph–coffee beans, among other products; ironic, really, since the sylphs themselves were regarded as a gourmet delight. The actual food had been wrapped and stacked, as neatly as possible, in the drawers below.

Cy hadn't trusted the sylphs to remain hidden and silent as strangers meddled with *their* orchid plants, and Ingrid had to agree. Even her imagining such a thing had sent the fairies into a buzzing fury.

"Wait a short while longer. There. Stay quiet like that." She straightened the misbehaving tin and wedged it behind the chunk of cheese kept on board in case of a gremlin swarm. She shut the door.

Heavy footsteps shuddered up the mast below. She glanced down and caught a glimpse of moving figures through the steel mesh deck. Fear and relief simultaneously flowed through her. Cy had said the physical inspection of the ship should be the last stage of this rigmarole.

She hurried over to berthing, where she had dumped the clean, spare bedding and mussed it up. She sat and had just picked up a sheet when a stranger's head emerged through the hatch. Her heartbeat galloped. The two men were white, their hat brims pulled low, their scowls blatant.

"You take the control cabin. I'll go this way." The man came all the way inside, followed by a companion, and walked toward her. "You. You're Mrs. Harvey."

Ingrid glanced up, not meeting his eye, and bowed her head again. "Yes, sir," she murmured, the very image of domesticity with laundry on her lap.

He grunted. His pen scratched at his clipboard. "How many plants aboard? Do you know how to count?"

Her work at the auxiliary had trained her well for these kinds of encounters. She swallowed down her impotent rage. "I believe there are . . . twenty?"

He grunted in reply. The other man thudded around in the control cabin. Ingrid knew Fenris must be a seething bundle of nerves as he awaited permission to come on board his ship again.

Ingrid slowly, carefully folded the bedding as the men continued to poke and prod at the ship. The inspector closest to her made a circuit of the engine room, going so far as to open some tanks and shine a flashlight into the far recesses of the chamber. The man in the control room worked his way down the hall. As he opened the pantry, Ingrid risked tapping her magic to call out to the sylphs in her mind.

"Stay still. Quiet. Invisible. Predator is close." The few seconds of speech weren't enough to drain her, thank goodness.

A subdued confirmation came from the sylphs. The man reached into the cabinet and rustled around, but apparently the kind of contraband they were searching for wasn't expected to masquerade in digestive biscuit tins.

"Get up, woman," snapped the other soldier. Ingrid stood. He panned his light over the dark space in the bunk behind her, then stepped up the ladder to check the bunk above. He lifted the mattress, swiped an arm beneath, then let it fall into place again. He then did the same to the beds across the way. Cy had anticipated all of this. The top bunk was neatly made, every shred of fairy molt discarded.

The Green Dragon Crescent Blade was hanging on the wall in the engine room alongside other tools.

The inspector landed hard on the floor, then whisked past Ingrid to begin a thorough inspection of the plants. The other man was doing the same. With the laundry folded, Ingrid could only sit again, hands demurely folded in her lap, as the soldiers finished their duty. They exited the vessel without another word to her.

She had scarcely released a heavy sigh of relief when rapid, light footsteps on the stairs announced Fenris's return. "What'd they meddle with?" He looked up and down the hall, his slender face a mix of rage and terror, and scurried past Ingrid to the engine room.

"The man opened some lids—" she started to say.

"Damn it, I should probably change out all the water, clean the tanks. As if I didn't have enough to do, patching that pipe—"

Fenris's frenzy distracted her. She didn't hear Cy until he was right beside her.

"My apologies for the wait. That process was more grueling than anticipated." He squatted beside her, elbows propped on his knees. "Thank the Almighty that Mrs. Kealoha arranged for us to deliver freight here, or we'd be revving our engines about now."

"But I've always heard tourists were commonplace here . . ."

"The incoming flights all seem to host whites and Japanese folks of undeniable wealth. There's a Porterman yacht one mast over. The thing is girded in *steel*. The weight must make 'em fly like a pegasus with colic." He shook his head in disgust, then lowered his voice. "As new as the *Bug* is, it's designed to be more functional than pretty. We don't look like we belong. Apparently, the riffraff usually comes in by naval ships."

"I'm guessing that these critical comments about the *Bug* weren't said in front of Fenris, or he'd surely be under arrest about now."

"No, I encountered the arrogant attitude straightaway when I disembarked. Fortunately, our customer here is an important local businessman." He frowned. "The inspectors didn't harass you, did they?"

Fenris pushed past Cy, muttering beneath his breath. If Fenris could work magic, he'd surely be evoking some sort of vengeful dark wizardry about now.

"The plants received far more scrutiny than I did." The soldiers had probably regarded them as more valuable.

She thought she had masked her annoyance, but Cy leaned over and placed a kiss on her cheek, his whiskers grazing her skin as he stood. "It's better for you to be invisible to them."

Ingrid knew he was right. "I'll start unfastening the plants so you can carry them down."

He shot her a grateful grin that made a warm, fuzzy feeling arise in her chest. His brown eyes were shining with affection. "Good. Soon as we get this done, we'll see about getting to that crater. Apparently, a nighttime tour leaves in a short while. Here's a-hoping it's not booked up."

"I had hoped this would be a place we could hide in plain sight for a while," she said, expression wistful.

"I know. Me too. I didn't expect *this* many soldiers myself, even with our warning. We need to push on soon as the *Bug* can fly."

That's all the encouragement Ingrid needed to hustle along. The vanilla orchids had sprouted three inches in their day aboard and many had started to bud. She wondered why she'd never heard of sylphs being utilized to help farmers—it seemed like such a natural use of their abilities—but the fairies were probably worth far more as niche cuisine. She shook her head in disgust.

Cy returned with several crates and hauled the plants down the mast. Ingrid turned her attention to the food pantry and the captive sylphs. Their buzzing was quieter than usual, their demeanor wary. After she let them out, they fluttered throughout the cabin to verify the plants were indeed gone. She wondered if they were sad, but instead, the sylphs began to fly in their usual happy loops around her.

Images and feelings flashed in her mind. The sylphs regarded the *Bug* as their home. It had been threatened, but all was well now. Their shelter, good people, and baked goods remained.

Ingrid laughed. The sylphs' emotions reflected her own, right down to the inclusion of pastries.

With the engines off and the hatch open, a chill began to penetrate the ship, reminding her that they were moored at about four thousand feet elevation along the southern flank of a fourteen-thousand-foot volcano.

"Do you need any help in the engine room?" she called to Fenris.

"No." His tone brooked no argument.

Ingrid took the opportunity to retreat into the lavatory to dress for a chilly hike. She had just emerged when Cy returned.

"The delivery's done, and I've already spent almost every penny we just earned. An autocar will be at the gate in a few minutes to take us to the rim." He assessed her apparel and nodded. To Ingrid's relief, he looked excited about their excursion, not consumed with worry for her. "Fenris, how're things here? Any gifts left behind by those inspectors?"

"Do you think they left whirly-flies?" asked Ingrid, alarmed. Her slicker jostled, causing the empty kermanite in her pocket to jingle.

"That's not the kind of gift I meant. Whirly-flies are an expensive resource. They wouldn't be left on just any airship that docked. I wonder more about planted contraband left to get us in trouble at the next dock. I already had to pass along some extra yen in my handshakes."

Fenris leaned back to glare up the hallway at them. "They made a mess of things, but I haven't found anything insidious. I'll have the *Bug* ready to fly in a few hours, but we *cannot* head to the mainland straightaway. I must do more thorough maintenance before we dare another week in the air."

Ingrid felt another small rush of guilt twist through her as several horrible what-ifs flashed through her mind.

"We'll be out past midnight, Fenris. Take a nap, if you can," said Cy. Fenris snorted at the suggestion.

"That late?" she asked. "Is the whole trek on foot?"

"Shouldn't you know more about this?" Fenris asked her as he joined them in the corridor.

"Everything I know about Kilauea is from dry text written by mundanes. Remember, no geomancer dares to set foot here, quite literally." She didn't elaborate further; they had argued over the risks time and again. She maintained the vain hope that maybe, just maybe, her grandmother wouldn't want to kill her, and might restrain the energy flow for a while.

If not, well . . . Ingrid might fall over dead as soon as she stepped off the mast. At least it'd be instantaneous.

Cy looked grim. "Only the last part of the trip is on foot. I told the tour agent that my wife"—Fenris made an amused choking sound—"had a leg injury that made prolonged walks difficult. He said, and for the sake of my physical well-being I'll quote, 'many weak-willed women and elderly take our tours.'"

"Weak-willed . . . !"

"I had to stop myself from laughing when he said it." Cy's broad grin softened her indignation. "The descent into the Kilauea crater is done on horseback," he continued. "I was cautioned that you'll be required to ride astride, as they use Mexican saddles."

"Is this when I'm supposed to faint at the indecency of the suggestion?" she said wryly.

"Have you ridden?" Cy asked.

"Yes, but not since Mama's passing." And not for months before that. They had stopped riding after Mama had discovered she was pregnant. "I'm a fair rider. Get me into the saddle, and I will manage from there."

Cy nodded as he turned to Fenris. "If there is any sign of volcanic activity—an earthquake, a plume—don't wait for us. Take the *Bug* and go. Same if you see soldiers flood the dock. Go."

"I get it. The moon rises, I go. A cat meows, I go. But where am I going, exactly? Or am I to assume you're dead and we won't be meeting again until the afterworld?"

"Preferably not," said Ingrid. From a drawer, she pulled out gloves Lee had packed for her in San Francisco.

"I think the nearest public mooring masts are in Hilo to the northeast," said Cy. He fumbled in the lower cabinet to pull out a readied travel pack, only to find that it had been left open by the inspectors. He quickly checked the contents then belted it shut again. "We can plan on meeting there, worst comes to worst."

"Unless my presence triggers a major volcanic event, in which case Hilo could be at risk from lava as well as from a tsunami," she added as she wiggled on the gloves.

"I suppose I shouldn't look into properties in Hilo, then. Now go. Shoo. I have work to do. Ingrid, don't die." Fenris's scowl added weight to his words. "Don't be out all night either. I *won't* be happy if I have to come looking for you two."

INGRID DIDN'T DROP DEAD UPON MAKING CONTACT WITH THE ground. That pleased her.

Beneath her feet, the earth thrummed as if she sat up front at the Damcyan Theater as a full orchestra played. She looked to the tour company's horses as a kind of barometer, and was relieved to note that they didn't act skittish like horses did in San Francisco before the quake.

Cy, on the other hand, was appalled to realize his elastic rig for Ingrid's boots prevented her feet from slipping into the stirrups.

"I think that's just as well," she murmured as everyone mounted up. "I can't angle my toes up, anyway. My foot would have slipped forward in a dangerous way. I'll be better off without using stirrups."

Worry shone in his eyes. "We could ask for some rope . . ."

"Mr. Harvey." The false name had a nice ring to it in an icy tone. "You're a horseman. You know how dangerous that would be if the horse tripped or rolled. Help me mount up." She motioned to the tall stump that was serving as a stool. "I'll be fine."

Cy snapped his mouth shut and did as she asked, but she could tell he was still worried.

Once she was in the saddle, Cy modestly situated her skirt then gave her a little nod, clearly more at ease. Ingrid's mother had always told her she had a natural seat, and apparently Ingrid hadn't lost that knack amid her spasticity issues.

About a dozen people were in their group along with two native Hawaiian guides, one to lead and one to play caboose. Ingrid studied the horses. They looked older and well used, but in good care, her own bony mare included.

The trail took them away from Volcano House, a renowned inn, and through thick woods. A waxing gibbous moon played shy behind a tattered sheet of clouds, granting them little illumination through the canopy. A few flashlight beams flickered to reveal brief glimpses of thick vegetation.

Birds were quiet, a fact that emphasized the murmur of voices and the jingle of tack and the plod of hoofbeats.

Far ahead, the leader waved to direct everyone right. The lead horses emerged from the trees, the rest following. Ingrid brought her horse to a stop and stared downward, breathless in awe and terror.

The Kilauea caldera stretched miles in circumference, the edges fringed by the dark silhouettes of trees. Off to the right, a long stretch of the steep cliff released billows of steam, but as if by gravity, her gaze was pulled into the abyss below. It was impossible to judge the drop in the scant light, but it had to be several hundred feet. The land below consisted of absolute blackness. Perhaps a mile in the distance, color returned in a splashing cauldron of red, orange, and yellow.

"That down there is the lava lake of Halema'uma'u," said their guide, his pronunciation of the place like lilting poetry. "That's the home of the goddess Pele. That is our goal." He reined his horse to the right. The rest of the pack followed. Ingrid couldn't help but continue to look left, utterly dazzled, until the trail began to slope and trees obscured the view.

To Ingrid's surprise, she couldn't smell any sulfur despite the vents in the cliff nearby. The thickening forest around them dominated her olfactory senses with moisture, fresh greenery, and pleasant rot. The horses huffed as the incline grew steeper and the lead horses rounded a switchback.

She leaned back in the saddle for balance, grateful to be on a well-trained trail mount that knew her job without need for guidance on Ingrid's part. Her hands dropped to where she could grab the pommel, if necessary. Her lower legs actually felt strangely relaxed as they draped down.

"How are you, my dear?" asked Cy.

"Quite well, really." Her double layers of tights couldn't prevent cold from creeping up her skirt, though. She shivered. With one hand, she unfolded and angled her cloth headband to partially cover her ears.

They continued to zigzag their way down the cliff. The steep embankments along the well-worn holloway were alive with moss and ferns. The chill made her fingers curl and lock in their grip on the reins, the pressure of the wedding band unfamiliar and uncomfortable within her glove. As time went on, the cold brought stiffness to her leg muscles again, escalating to an edge of numbness and pain.

An animal rustled in the brush, and she caught the brief sight of some large birds dashing away—chickens, perhaps, or pheasants. She rested a fist on the pommel, ready for the horse to react, but the mare only flicked an ear, unperturbed.

The foliage began to thin. The bleak blackness of the crater was like gazing into a sky without stars, the infernal lake a red sliver in the distance.

The path abruptly leveled out. There were no more trees. Hooves clopped on the dry lava bed and sent up small sparks.

"Everyone dismount! We leave horses here," called the guide. Groans abounded as people heaved themselves from their saddles. Cy surrendered his horse and led Ingrid's mount to a tall rock where he helped her to the ground.

Her feet touched down, her soles zinging with pain as if

she were walking barefoot on the nearby *a'a* rocks. She drew in a hiss of breath.

"I'll fetch your umbrella from the packhorse." He headed toward a corral made of stacked lava rocks and planks.

"Well, Madam Pele," she whispered. "If you can hear me right now, please know that I truly hope that my pain doesn't irritate you as it does other Hidden Ones. No one should have to feel like this."

Cy returned with the tall umbrella he'd purchased for her in Honolulu. It made for an excellent societally appropriate walking stick. She was grateful to lean on the crook handle as Cy shared his water canteen with her. Then they joined the tour group, situating themselves near the back, and began to move. Walking hurt, but not as much as standing still. The umbrella's metal ferrule made a small, hollow *clink* every time it struck the *pahoehoe* lava that formed the ground. The black surface was smooth and uneven, set in ridges and waves.

Ingrid glanced back. The cliff blocked over half the sky; the steam vents along the edge sent small plumes heavenward. Looking forward, a much larger plume of gray and a gleaming line of red marked their destination. Flashlight beams angled this way and that. Sporadic knee-high stacks of chunky *a'a* rocks marked their path. Her modified boots helped her lift her feet, but the dark, uneven ground made it difficult for her to judge her steps. She relied on the umbrella to prevent her from kissing the lava. Cy hovered close as a shadow but gave her space to walk on her own. The night's chill soon faded, replaced by the heat of exertion.

"Hey, you brave to do this, walking like that," said the rear guide, trotting alongside her. He gestured with his own walking stick. "I use this, and I still fall sometimes."

Ingrid gritted her teeth. She knew her limp was visible, but she didn't appreciate the reminder.

"She's recovering from an accident," said Cy.

"Oh yeah? Well, we almost to the lake. It'll be worth the effort, savvy?" The line ahead slowed for some indiscernible reason.

Cy motioned to a scraggly bush growing nearby. "I'm surprised to see plants growing in such a desolate place."

"These bushes here are *ohelo*." The guide's light tone turned serious. "I think you missed Harry's talk since you came in the last autocar, so I tell you now. See, these sacred berries are always offered to Madam Pele first, *then* visitors here can try them. Otherwise, she gets mad. People joke, say they want to see her mad, because they hope to see active lava. But no, they really *don't* want to see when she gets angry."

"I assure you, we have no desire to see Madam Pele angry," said Ingrid. The guide nodded, somewhat placated, and moved onward.

As they continued to shuffle forward, Ingrid could finally see the reason for their delay: a bridge across a chasm. Flashlights aimed downward gave no true indication of its depth. She eased her way across and was stunned to realize she could still sense the earth's energy, even with empty space beneath her.

As they neared Pele's home, the earth felt like a living, breathing, aching being. It wasn't moving, but it *yearned* to.

The lava lake wasn't in view as they walked through a shallow valley, but she felt its pulsations, like how a person could sense the sea through the heaving deck of a ship.

"Are you pulling in energy?" Cy murmured.

"Not much. I am starting to feel feverishly hot, though."

"So am I," he said, unfastening his leather coat. Sweat sheened his face.

With the help of Cy and the umbrella, she trudged up a rocky slope. Tephra shifted underfoot. Cy caught her as she began to slip. As she stood upright, her left calf muscle seized. She bit back a yelp at the sudden agony.

A woman dropped onto a rock nearby, nursing a banged knee with both hands, and all the others had slowed their pace, struggling not to fall on the steep terrain. Ingrid took the opportunity to pause and work her fingers into the back of her boot. The knotted muscle hurt to touch, but she rubbed it nevertheless.

"Do you need to sit?" Cy asked. He propped his bowler hat up higher on his head.

"No. Let's get over the rise."

The heat increased as they climbed. The entire tour group was panting and gasping for breath. Some removed their jackets and shawls. The ground crunched underfoot, revealing a crusty layer of sulfur atop the black lava.

The leaders reached the top. Gasps and squeals carried down the slope. Ingrid pushed her reluctant legs to move faster, and with Cy at her side, she reached the crest.

Before them lay a living vision of hell. Ingrid had never seen anything so beautiful in all her life.

CHAPTER 5

The lava lake looked to be half a mile in length and glowed in lurid red, gold, and yellow. Black islands crested along on molten waves. The fiery surf emitted an angry roar, punctuated by rattles and bangs like gunfire or cannons. One of the men nearby dropped to the ground as if he'd been shot. Other people hunkered over him, but his companion shook his head and waved them back. "He's not hurt. He was in the war." A simple statement that said so much.

Cy flinched at the rattles and pops, but stood like a statue. Most of the others did the same, even the tour guides, who had surely visited this place times beyond measure.

Ingrid had never known such a sense of reverence. She took in the sight of the earth's raw majesty, the contrast of liquid creation against the broad span of twinkling stars on high. Most of the clouds had cleared, though volcanic gases fuzzed the view of the far edges of the lake.

A sharp, human whistle split the air. The tour guide waved both arms to catch their attention. "Wander around. Walk closer to the lava, but always watch your feet. If your shoes are smoking, get out of there! We do have extra shoes if people need them, but remember, the walk back will feel especially long in shoes that don't fit, right?" A few people laughed as they moved down the embankment toward the lake. After a minute, Ingrid and Cy were left alone on the crest.

"If hell looks like this, I want to go there," she said. "This is my idea of heaven."

Cy cocked his head to one side. "Back in Seattle, you *did* express an interest in possessing a lake of fire of your own, so I can't say I'm surprised by your reaction."

"I was jesting back then. I didn't know . . . I *couldn't* know. I read Twain's personal account of this place years ago, and I dismissed much of it as hyperbole."

"Can any words do this place justice?"

Ingrid didn't need to answer that. Cy wrapped an arm around her back, his hand a perfect fit above the curve of her hip. Exhausted and emotional as she was, the sheer comfort of his presence and touch in this exquisite place almost made her weep. They worked their way down the incline. People had been rendered into silhouettes against the bright lake.

The oppressive heat increased, as did the sulfurous and almost industrial stench. A coughing man hurried past them, clearly retreating from the fumes. Ingrid felt a harsh tickle in her throat.

Just ahead, the two tour guides tossed small branches into the lava and backed away. Ingrid experienced a surge of envy and a yearning to understand this place as deeply as they did. Even though she now knew she was of Hawaiian blood, she also knew she could never *be* Hawaiian. That thought left her feeling bereft.

Where *did* she belong now? The San Francisco she knew and loved was lost to the earthquake and conflagration. Her definition of home had shifted to an airship and the people she loved, but when all was said and done, she wanted permanent roots. She wanted to be like the hardscrabble bushes of Kilauea and find a place to grow and bloom, even if it was amid desolation.

Ingrid and Cy stopped walking about thirty feet from the lava. Lines of red, like veins, illuminated cracks along the lakeshore. Two women squatted near one of these fissures and held pieces of paper close to the ground. Ingrid realized they were searing the edges of postcards; cards like that had been mailed to the Cordilleran Auxiliary over the years.

Not far away, a group of men had skewered sausages on sticks and dangled the meat over the lava. They roared with laughter as one man lost his sausage to a molten sputter.

"They are cooking *frankfurters*?" Ingrid became angrier with every word. "Don't they feel the holiness of this place? Would they cook sausages in the middle of a church? The lava itself is Madam Pele's body!"

Cy swung his pack off and rummaged inside. "Pardon me for playing the devil's advocate, but by that logic, we've tread across her body for some distance."

"We walked with a light tread and treated the area with respect as we passed through." She shook her head in disgust as a few other men tossed coins into the lava to see how fast they melted.

A chorus of cries caused Ingrid's gaze to focus far out in the lake. Lava spouted in a brief, violent fountain that sent glowing tephra high in the air. Some men scampered back from the edge as the hot rocks arced their way.

"Here's the meat," Cy said. "I found the cigarette papers, but the tobacco's slipped further down in the bag."

"The pork will be enough of an offering to start, I think." She braced her legs, the umbrella leaning on her torso as she unwrapped the large green *ti* leaves that had been knotted to hold the salted meat.

Cy cleared his throat and gazed past her. She turned to see the guide from the back of the group.

"Hey!" His smile revealed gaps between his teeth. "You could get closer if you want. Lava not sputtering too bad over here."

"Beg your pardon, but I don't believe I caught your name?" Cy asked as he extended his hand.

The tour guide gripped him with both hands and they vigorously shook in greeting. "Call me Sam. Hey, that pork there? You leaving that for Madam Pele?" He regarded Ingrid with more scrutiny.

She glanced at Cy, debating how best to answer. "My father was from the islands. I never knew him. I'm trying to connect with my past. Silly, I know . . ." She tried to sound flippant, though she meant every word.

"Nah, nah. We see lot of that. Maybe Madam Pele will like." He nodded toward the lake, where a veritable geyser of lava had erupted out in the middle. "It been quiet here recently. Tonight, well, something different."

"I'm glad," she said with a renewed sense of excitement and relief.

Sam tipped his hat to them both and continued on his way. Ingrid set the meat on a tablelike rock a few steps away and laughed.

"What?" asked Cy.

"Madam Pele's favorite things include some of my own, like pork and strawberries. Mama couldn't stand either. I wonder if Papa favored them, too." There was so much she wished she knew about Papa. He hadn't been a good man—he had done terrible things—but she knew she'd probably always feel wistful about his absence in her life.

"Should we maybe throw the pork into the lava like they did those branches?" Cy asked.

"Goodness. As if I know!" She glanced at the burbling lava and frowned. "Since I hope for her to show up as a human, let's leave her offering in a palatable form. I should try to formally evoke her, too."

"Should I grant you some privacy?"

"No. Please, stay with me." She gripped his hand. His fingers were sweat-slick against her leather glove. She bowed her head.

"Madam Pele. My name is Ingrid Carmichael. I know there is power in names, and I give you my name because it's my understanding that you've given me a great deal already." She paused, chagrined at her clumsy words. "My father went by the name Abram Carmichael. Like him, I channel the earth's power in a way that sets us apart from other geomancers. I've come here, knowing the dangers of this place, because I seek answers about my body and my blood. I'd be honored if you would speak to me."

After the words emerged, she realized they sounded much like her appeal to the *qilin*. She could only hope for much different results.

She raised her head to search the lava, seeking another fountain, or a human figure emerging from the molten pool. Something. Anything. "I am leaving this pork as an offering for you. I hope it meets your liking. Thank you."

They remained quiet for a few minutes. Cy's thumb stroked the back of her glove. "It's a precious thing, to hold your hand in public like this."

"Public being a remote two-thousand-degree-Fahrenheit lava lake."

"We'll enjoy whatever romantic moments we can find." He nodded toward the lava. "Do you see any blue miasma?"

"No. Those fumes, though . . ." The lava lapped at the thin gray haze. The fog itself seemed to stretch downward at a multitude of points, as if with arms, fingers skimming the red flow and flicking away spatter. Ingrid shuddered as she recalled a geomancy textbook that described ghost-gods residing in Halema'uma'u with Pele, though she couldn't recall all of the details. "I don't know. I may be seeing things out of desperation." If there were any other minor fantastics nearby, she couldn't sense them within the heady geomantic energy.

"Or maybe you're weary enough to hallucinate after the

exertion of that hike. Let's retreat a ways and you can rest before the long trip back."

"Cy, if I sit, it'll be awfully hard to rise again." Though sitting sounded nice, especially if she had time to slip off her left boot.

"Do you realize the longer you stand, the more you're bent over that cane umbrella? You'd end up on the ground soon anyway." He gave her hand a gentle squeeze and guided her farther away, where rocks stood at about chair height.

With her legs angled away from the group, she removed her boot. Pain dappled her vision for a moment.

"We need to come up with something better," Cy muttered. Sorrow glistened in his eyes. "It breaks my heart to see you hurting like this. Where's the pain the worst?"

"The arch of my foot, which is different than usual. The top of the boot is so tight it's almost like a corset, and that's helping the muscles there."

"We could try wrapping your foot with bandages back on the ship." He gnawed on his lip.

"That might work as a temporary solution."

"Temporary. Yes." Frustration twisted his face. "We'll figure this out, Ingrid. I promise."

"I know you will." She tilted forward to stroke his jaw. He leaned into her touch. "I wouldn't have made it this far without you. Quite literally."

"I'm here with you, every step of the way. Never forget that."

She nodded, wordless with emotion, conscious again of the strange presence of the ring on her finger and all the wonderful things that meant.

Shoes crunched on rocks as people came closer, and she sighed as Cy drew back. She leaned down to tug the boot back on. Once that was done, Cy pulled a simple supper from his pack: rolls, a jar of honey, and dried meat. The food settled some of her shakiness from the hike, but her anxiety escalated as the minutes passed with no sign of Pele.

"I'm holding some power now," she murmured. "Should I try to reach out to her?"

"Is it wise, to directly call on a deity in such a way?"

She thought of the *qilin* with a jab of guilt. "I don't know. I suppose it depends on the being involved. I'm feeling desperate, though."

Terror flashed across his face. "You're not thinking to harm yourself, are you?"

"No! That'd be akin to stabbing a dragon with a dinner fork. I want to *evoke* her, not provoke her." Besides, if Ingrid's pain could irritate Pele into showing herself, Pele would have appeared by now.

"Thank goodness for that."

The tour leader blew his whistle. "We going to start back in ten minutes. Last chance to do whatever you want to do!"

"We risked so much in coming here," Ingrid whispered. "It can't all be for nothing, it just can't."

"Ingrid." He leaned close to whisper her true name. "This wasn't for nothing. The flight served a good purpose. Remember, T.R. advised us to travel far in case the fox could still track you. Hawaii worked out well for that. Plus, you had the chance to meet Mrs. K at long last—"

She pressed her lips to hold back petulant words. She

had known her hopes for a miracle cure were silly and ill-placed, but . . .

Hope is a form of gangrene. She shivered at the memory of Blum's words.

"Maybe we can lurk on the island for a while," Ingrid croaked out. "She's most likely to be around the lava lake, but she could show up anywhere."

"For your sake, we can't stay," Cy said gently. "Think of all the soldiers. We already know someone in Honolulu was on the lookout for the *Bug*. That could happen here, too. We can't forget about *Excalibur* either, and that we need to find Sakaguchi-sama and Lee."

The thought of *Excalibur* only deepened her despair. How was she going to help stop the citadel when she could scarcely walk on her own?

"Inu, dog, inu, dog!" The little boy in the tour group bounded past them excitedly, vivacious as a pixie despite the late hour.

"Come back, Thomas!" His nanny panted heavily as she pursued him across the uneven ground.

"I have him, ma'am." Cy snared the boy with an arm and gave him a spin for good measure. The child squealed, and Cy grinned. The whole scene made Ingrid's heart ache. She really didn't need to think about Blum's revelation about why she couldn't have children, not when she was already feeling as low as a grub.

Thomas pointed over Cy's shoulder. "Dog! Inu!"

"Smart boy, speaking both English and Japanese so well when so young," Cy said, setting him down.

"It's the best time to learn, his teachers say." The nanny cast Cy a grateful smile. The boy continued to point at the lake. "Come, Thomas, leave it be. We need to walk back to the horses."

"Nooooo!" he wailed, stomping on the hard lava as she dragged him away.

"How's a dog surviving out here?" Cy asked. Like the boy, he pointed out toward the lake. A small white dog was picking its way along the edge of the lava. That close to Halema'uma'u, the poor animal should have been yelping as its paws burned.

"I'll be damned. There *is* a dog." One of the other men joined them, a few others following close behind. "Where did it come from?"

"Hey!" Another man jostled Sam the guide. "Don't you people eat dogs? That one's a mite skinny, though."

Ingrid noted the tightness and twitch in the guide's smile at the man's ignorant words. "This dog's been seen many times here. No one would eat him. He belongs to Madam Pele."

The dog bounded away from the lake and toward them. Sheer power billowed over Ingrid like a fifty-mile-per-hour gale. She reeled in place, and would have fallen if not for Cy's hand on her shoulder. She couldn't manage words. She could only stare.

Cy brushed her side with his elbow, concern in his eyes. "Dear?"

The dog paused to eat the pork offering left on the rock a short distance away. One of the men laughed. "Well, now we know how the mongrel stays alive out here, thieving from that goddess of yours. Reminds me of when I was a hungry lad, slipping Communion wafers from the bowl during Sunday service."

"We're going!" the tour leader called down from the crest. The other men turned away, leaving only Sam beside Ingrid and Cy.

The dog scarfed down the meat in mere seconds—too fast even for a starving animal. It trotted toward Ingrid, tail wagging. Power buffeted her, leaving her nauseous and terrified.

"That's no dog," she whispered.

CHAPTER 6

Ingrid could picture this dingy white dog in any San Francisco alley, rummaging in trash. The breed was indiscernible—maybe a terrier or a bichon cross, perhaps with a poodle. Tight, curly fur covered its body, with the hair slightly longer along the muzzle and around its tufted ears.

She had encountered diverse and powerful creatures of sea, air, heaven, and earth over the past month. Each had been distinct in its ambient power. This animal's presence radiated heat and smelled of hot rocks.

That thought jolted her. Ambassador Blum once mentioned that Ingrid stank of hot rocks, like her father.

This dog wasn't simply property of Pele. It *was* Pele, in some aspect.

Ingrid felt the profound need to humble herself as she had before the celestial glory of the *qilin*, but there were still other people nearby. Pele herself was acting with subterfuge in her appearance, so Ingrid could only hope that the goddess wouldn't take offense if she likewise played nonchalant.

"Hello," she softly said as the dog trotted within five feet of her. Ingrid could scarcely breathe; she felt as though she'd stuck her head into an industrial kiln, though the power didn't physically pain her like the mental and physical touch of the thunderbird and selkies. The dog radiated the magic of earth and fire, after all, the same elements that Ingrid evoked. The dog just embodied *so much*.

"What can I do?" Cy asked, a hand close to his Tesla rod.

"Don't hurt that dog," said Sam, his tone sober.

"I assure you, we'll do nothing to hurt her," she said.

Sam stepped closer. The man could have passed for her brother. "You recognize *her*."

What was she supposed to say to that, to this stranger who could harm her, turn her in to the UP, do any number of terrible things? Cy sidled closer and pulled out his rod, but subtly so, angling it where only she and Sam could see.

The dog sat and panted, pink tongue dangling. Ingrid had the impression she was amused.

"Yes." Ingrid decided to keep it simple.

Sam cocked his head and waved them all forward. "Come on. It's a long trek back to the horses." He walked away.

Ingrid stared after him. "That's it?"

"This is Madam Pele's business. Not mine." He vigorously shook his head as he kept on walking.

"Huh." Ingrid looked between Cy and the dog. "That went differently than I expected."

Cy sheathed his rod again. "Indeed. Still wouldn't trust

him, though. If he gossips, we're in a heap of trouble. We can't dally here, that's for certain."

"Madam Pele? Are we supposed to follow you?" Ingrid asked. The dog remained sitting. "Or are you coming with us?" The dog stood and barked.

"Are you getting any words or images along with that?" Cy asked, keeping his eyes respectfully averted from the animal.

"No. The dog speaks like a dog."

Cy shook his head, wonder etched on his face. "Walks with you always end up interesting, Ingrid. Shall we?"

He helped her trudge up the crest. The dog followed close behind.

She felt Cy stiffen, and followed his gaze to the two tour guides, who were speaking together apart from the group. As if in response, the guides looked their way, expressions unreadable in the dark. They then split up to conduct their duties.

The group started out across the ebony wasteland, the cliff oppressive in the distance. Ingrid and Cy dragged toward the back, with Sam and a few older gentlemen lurking farther behind.

Ingrid checked to see if the dog reacted to their concern about the guides. The white mutt simply plodded along, paws unharmed, as if out on a normal, midnight stroll across a desolate caldera. "If both the guides respect the dog's presence, I can't imagine they'll be a problem," she whispered.

"Perhaps." Cy looked thoughtful. "But being followed by a white dog makes us memorable to our other tour companions. They're bound to tell tales about this adventure."

The oppressive heat of Halema'uma'u faded, but the night's full chill did not return. To Ingrid, the dog was like an ambulatory furnace. She became more accustomed to breathing in the dog's presence, which was good, as the hike soon had her panting and sweating. She would be due some extra pain tomorrow, of that she had no doubt.

The corral was in sight when the elastic support band on her right boot snapped.

She staggered forward a step, catching herself on the umbrella handle.

"Good grief. We almost made it." Cy stared at his handiwork in dismay. With a quick swipe of his pocketknife, he removed the flaccid band. He wrapped an arm around her waist to help her forward. "The heat back there must have weakened it."

"My skirt's been catching on the bands, too."

He sighed. "I knew it'd be a temporary aid, but I hoped it wouldn't be *that* temporary." He didn't ask how she was feeling. Her limp had grown more pronounced, requiring her to roll her hip forward to prevent her feet from dragging.

The white dog trotted ahead of them and barked, looking between them and the horses ahead.

"I'm moving as fast as I can," Ingrid snapped, belatedly remembering that she probably shouldn't show irritation to a goddess of volcanoes, especially when standing *in* a volcano.

"Sorry. I hope we can rest on the airship for a while. I . . ."

She gawked as the dog went into a sudden frenzy at her words. "You seem excited at the mention of the airship. Do you want us to fly somewhere?"

The dog spun in a happy circle, as if she could go airborne on her own. Which she likely could, though not in this form.

"I'm not quite certain how Fenris will react to our new passenger," Cy said dryly.

"It may come as a surprise to you that the *Palmetto Bug* is not Noah's ark." Fenris greeted them from the engine room. Goggles were propped on his forehead, a wrench in his hands.

The white dog had followed them aboard and sat in the hallway before the cockpit, gazing around with blatant curiosity. Ingrid could sense the sylphs up in their bunk. They offered her a subdued greeting but otherwise remained still, perhaps even invisible. She understood their caution in the presence of a deity and had no intention of drawing them out.

"Obviously, this can't be Noah's ark. We haven't gathered creatures by twos." Cy shrugged off his coat.

"We *cannot* have a dog on this ship." Fenris squeezed past Cy to stand by Ingrid, staring across the open hatch at the offensive beast. "Look at it! It's filthy, and even worse, it's *furry*. There's no way to effectively barricade it from the engine room, and if that fluff gums up the machinery—"

"You haven't even complained about excrement and urine yet," said Ingrid. She sat on her rack, boots off. The soles of her feet tingled as if feasted upon by a thousand ants. Her calves didn't feel much better.

"Oh, yes. *Let's* complain about the excrement and urine. We can't set the *Bug* down just anywhere for the mutt to take a walk. Oh! Oh! Look!"

The dog lifted a hind leg, back end aimed toward the cockpit. Her gaze focused on Fenris.

"Now you're just doing that for spite," scolded Ingrid, then pressed a hand to her face, appalled at her lack of tact yet again. She was too tired to deal with recalcitrant deities. "Sorry, Madam. With you in that form, it's easy to forget who you truly are."

"Madam?" echoed Fenris.

"Fenris, do you think we'd bring just any wandering dog along for the ride?" Cy asked.

He mulled this for a moment. "No. You'd do that with a cat."

The dog remained in pose, waiting for further reaction from Fenris.

"Madam, please don't vex him," Ingrid said. "He loves this place like you love your island."

The dog sat with a slight grunt.

"So. That's not a real dog," said Fenris.

"It's an aspect of Madam Pele," said Ingrid.

"The goddess. Your grandmother."

"Yes."

"Huh. Interesting." Fenris frowned.

The dog entered the control cabin and sat beside the main pilot's chair, her gaze on the controls.

"I take that as our cue to fly. Fenris, is the ship ready?" Ingrid asked.

"Ready for a short flight, yes."

"I'll see about getting us cleared for departure." Cy bowed to the dog and hurried down the stairs.

"Does this"—Fenris waved at the dog—"have anything to do with that dog sorcery you used in Seattle?"

"No. That enchantment didn't even last the night. This dog form of hers is apparently well-known to the locals."

Fenris snorted and moved down the hallway. Ingrid gripped the bed rail to push herself up, and failed. Rage flared through her and she barely held back a scream of frustration. Her legs were as useless as that broken elastic band. She was twenty-five years old. Twenty-five! Her body wasn't supposed to be like this. She should feel tired, yes, but not . . . broken.

That very word popped her bubble of self-pity. She refused to be broken, damn it.

She used her hands to set her feet in a different position, and tried again. This time, she made it upright, though walking felt as if she were moving through setting concrete. She gritted her teeth together. She didn't have to go far. Almost there.

At the hatch, she stopped, overwhelmed by the urge to sob and laugh at the same time. The hatch was open. She couldn't control her feet well enough to angle around it. She sagged against the wall, her breaths fast and heavy. Here she was, the granddaughter of a goddess of volcanoes, and she couldn't step around a two-by-two-foot square hole.

Searing heat warned her of the dog's approach. Ingrid's rage was suddenly replaced by shame. She didn't want anyone to see her like this, and certainly not this dog.

The mutt emitted a soft, concerned whine and pressed against her legs. Ingrid bit back a yelp, but to her surprise, the contact didn't induce more pain. In fact, her legs hurt just as much as before, but they felt more . . . solid. Pele had somehow empowered her in a way that kept her from collapsing.

"Thank you for the help," Ingrid said, gratitude bringing tears to her eyes.

Together they maneuvered around the opening to the control cabin, where Fenris was muttering to himself and oblivious to all else. Ingrid lowered herself into her usual seat by the door.

"I'm glad you brought up dog sorcery, Fenris. Maybe I should try that again," she said. The dog looked up at her with a face of disgust. "Or not."

"What?" asked Fenris, his focus on his dials.

"Never mind. I'm talking to the dog," said Ingrid, smiling at the white mutt at her feet. "As you don't want me to utilize sorcery, I assume you have something else in mind?"

The dog stared at the rudder wheel, tail wagging.

CHAPTER 7

SUNDAY, MAY 6, 1906

Fenris and the dog worked out a communication system that involved canine nods, head shakes, and pointed noses. Fenris handled the situation with aplomb, his usual caustic wit subdued. Ingrid lingered in the cockpit long enough to make certain that they were getting along like butter on toast, and then retreated to her rack. She had scarcely rattled the curtain shut when she felt Cy's hand grip her shoulder.

"Ingrid. We've arrived."

"Already? Arrived where?" She lay flat on her back, legs straight and tingling. In an instant, she took in the presence of the sylphs, still dormant in their high bunk, and the dog at the far end of the airship. She also sensed . . . *more.*

"Are we over that lava lake? How long was I asleep?" The *Bug* bobbed against a high wind. That she slept through that said a great deal about her exhaustion.

"You've slept over an hour. We're out in the godforsaken nowhere on the southwestern side of the island."

She rolled onto her side with a groan. Her lower body felt like one big bruise. "Has Fenris continued to handle things well with a dog as his copilot?" Ingrid helped her legs to swing out into the hall. Her purple dress was wrinkled and smudged, smeared green where plants had whipped her along the crater trail.

"They've become a good team. I may be out of a job. Here." He helped her up with an arm around her waist. She leaned into him, enjoying his touch.

Loud shudders rattled through the belly of the *Bug*. Cy stiffened, his gaze jerking toward the control cabin. "Fenris?" he called. "Are we—"

"We're docking." Fenris's tone was stoic and even.

"Who can possibly dock us?" Cy almost dragged Ingrid as he hurried down the hall. She didn't mind, weary as her legs were. "We're at a mooring mast all by its lonesome in the middle of lava fields," he said to her as they entered the control cabin.

"The mast isn't quite so lonesome now," said Fenris. "A woman spontaneously appeared and waved us in." Out the window, the ebony bowl of sky sparkled with a full array of stars. Lights beneath the *Bug* revealed the ropy, braided gleam of an old *pahoehoe* flow below them.

As he spoke, someone rhythmically knocked at the hatch of the ship. The dog hopped to the floor and padded that way. Ingrid shared a wide-eyed looked with Cy and Fenris. "When I woke, I thought we were over the lava lake. That's the intensity of energy I feel below us. Madam Pele must be out there."

"How many pieces is she in?" Fenris muttered.

"As many as she wants. She's a goddess," Ingrid said, her voice tight. Her grandmother, a goddess. Ingrid had wanted this meeting, and now that she was on the verge of having it, she felt more like crawling into her cot and pulling her blankets over her head. Why was she here? What did she really hope to gain from this family reunion?

At the hatch, the dog barked, encouraging her to come. "Are you going to help me down the steps?" she asked. A tail wagged in response.

"Pardon." Cy slipped past her to unlatch the hatch. He glanced up at Ingrid. Love, pride, and fear shone in his eyes. He had vowed to be with her every step of the way, but they both knew there were some steps she had to take on her own.

He believed in her. She wanted to live up to that belief.

She gave him a nod, and the door dropped down, the stairs springing into place.

Intense heat boiled and coiled around her as if he'd opened Nebuchadnezzar's oven. She gasped, a hand to the wall. The dog sidled against her, the warmth of that body minor compared to what awaited below.

"Let's go." The words trembled, her voice raspy. She gripped the hatch edge as she eased her stocking feet onto the short staircase. A fierce wind slapped her in the face. Her hair, falling loose from its pins and headband, tangled and lashed her cheeks. She would have fallen for sure without the helpful aura of the dog. Even so, God helps those who help themselves, and she was glad to reach the deck and use the rusted railing to propel herself along.

With each step, a sinking feeling increased in Ingrid's gut. She knew the old stories about Pele. This was a being more persnickety and violent than even Ambassador Blum. Ingrid might very well die in these next few minutes, depending on how Pele took her request. She might very well deserve it—who was she, to pester a deity? But most of all, she shouldn't have brought Cy and Fenris into this danger. The *Bug* could be immolated with a glance.

Madam Pele stood on a deck one flight down, her forearms on the rail. She wore a red Mother Hubbard dress like that of many women in Honolulu. The wind caused the skirt to billow, revealing bare feet, broad like Ingrid's own.

Ingrid, scared as she was, experienced a strange spike of envy. Pele would never be forced to wear shoes—men's wide shoes, at that—while in public, and deny to the world her natural ability as a geomancer.

The goddess turned to confront her directly. She was an old woman, her silver hair loose and waist long. It flowed in the wind like a banner and did not tangle. Her skin was dark, her cheekbones high, jaw slightly rounded. Her eyes gleamed, black and shiny as the *pahoehoe* below.

The dog trotted forward and vanished within the voluminous skirt, their essences merging in a single blink.

"Madam Pele." Ingrid was relieved that she remembered to say "madam" at the last second. She managed a small curtsy, the grace of her grandmother's presence still lending her legs some much-needed strength.

"Granddaughter. Ingrid."

The power embedded in the invocation reverberated

through her skull like a thunderclap. "What should I call you, Madam Pele?"

"Some call me *tutu,* but you're accustomed to *haole* ways. You may call me Grandmother."

Pele was certainly unlike any grandmother Ingrid had ever encountered. She was ancient, yes, but strong. Her gown, waistless though it was, couldn't hide the generous curves of her figure beneath the pleated, billowing fabric. Barefoot, bright-eyed, haughty, she defied every expectation of a woman of the Western world.

In that moment, Ingrid knew she adored her. She wanted to *be* her. She cast her eyes down again, not wanting to cause offense. "Grandmother, I . . ."

"Here, use my stick."

A wavy stick was thrust into her line of vision. She gripped the glossy dark wood, her hand immediately finding a perfect grip. Then she realized what she held. "This stick. Is it—"

"No. It's not my *Pā'oa.* I do not hand *that* stick to just anyone." Her laugh was as deep and rich as the earth itself.

Ingrid nodded, feeling rather weak with relief that she hadn't been handed the legendary magical stick used to dig volcanoes.

"We will walk to the bottom of the mast together to talk. But first, Cy?"

Pele's casual use of Cy's name caused Ingrid to jolt in surprise.

"Madam?" His voice echoed down, dimmed by the whistle of wind across the top of the mast.

"You brought tobacco to offer me at Halema'uma'u. I'll take it now."

Of all the things Ingrid had been expecting, that wasn't it.

"Yes, ma'am," Cy said at once.

Pele continued to stare upward in expectation, so Ingrid remained quiet in wait, wondering if the white dog's keen nose had detected the tobacco. A minute later, Cy scrambled down the stairs. He was hatless, his eyes downcast as he stepped beside Ingrid. "Ma'am." He bowed and held out the pouch and sheaf of papers.

Pele sniffed at the pouch without opening it. "Bull Durham? Good. You may go back aboard. I will not kill your beloved. She's done enough damage to herself already." Her tone was both chastising and kind.

Cy nodded as he took in the goddess's words. "More than enough, yes, ma'am." He faced Ingrid, his eyes full of love and concern. His lips parted as if to speak, but then he gave his head a small shake and leaned forward. His kiss grazed her cheek, his whiskers soft on her skin. Her hand found his. Their fingers clenched, briefly anchoring each other. She remained reinforced by his love and strength even as his feet banged up the creaky stairs again.

"Come." Pele gestured for Ingrid to follow her.

INGRID AND PELE SAT AGAINST THE STEEL FEET OF THE TOWER. The goddess's fiery presence kept Ingrid warm despite the brutal wind. It was a wonder Pele didn't melt through the metal structure, but Ingrid supposed that was all a matter of focus, just as when she wielded her own power.

The underlighting of the *Palmetto Bug* cast an eerie spotlight as the airship bobbed and rotated in place at the top of the mast. The flow of lava had cleaved to preserve the structure, creating an island amid desolation. Whatever civilization had once existed here was buried beneath feet of volcanic flow.

As Ingrid tried to find a somewhat comfortable position for her legs, Pele rolled a cigarette with deft, slender fingers. Neither the papers nor a shred of tobacco dared to blow away, though she did pluck a few small twigs from the tobacco tin.

"You're not what I expected, Grandmother."

Pele lit the cigarette with a tap of her finger. "No. I *am* what you expected. I could appear before you as a young woman, but it might be uncomfortable to call me 'Grandmother' then, yes?" Pele took a long drag of the cigarette. The smoke undulated into the figure of a woman dancing the hula that dissipated with a pivot of hips. "I could speak Hawaiian, or Japanese, Chinese, Tagalog, or any of the other languages I've picked up in recent years. For you, though, I will speak your bland tongue so that I may be clearly understood."

"Could you have spoken as a dog?"

"No. When I'm a dog, I am a dog. Pork tastes so much better to that tongue. Ah, the smells." Her grin was wide as she seethed smoke from both nostrils like a dragon. "Tobacco, however, is much more enjoyable in human forms."

Ingrid thought of how Ambassador Blum employed different bodies for different purposes. She had utilized the form of an older Japanese woman who had apparently been a master of Reiki, and though she could tap into that healing power in her other bodies, it was strongest while she was in the originating skin.

Pele's use of shapeshifting seemed decidedly more pleasant.

Pele gave Ingrid a thoughtful look. "So, you inherited some of my affinity for the earth. You can use *mana*. Talk story."

The prompt baffled Ingrid for a moment until she remembered "talk story" was a common Hawaiian phrase. And so she began to talk, beginning with childhood, with Mama, Mr. Sakaguchi, and her long-lost geomancer father. Pele rolled a second cigarette as Ingrid told of what happened in San Francisco, and Portland, and Seattle. She fought tears as she explained Blum's designs, of what that meant to Lee, to China, and inevitably, to America.

"Show me the burn on your thigh," Pele said, and snorted at Ingrid's scandalized expression. "Such a prudish regard for bared skin. Come now. The men on board can't see you."

Ingrid stood, leaning on a steel beam, and worked down the doubled layers of stockings. The hosiery hobbled her around the knees. She lifted her skirt to show the kanji of "tsuchi" to her grandmother.

Pele leaned close, squinting, then nodded approval. "Yes. This is what damaged you so. You poured your own *mana* into creating this ward, and it works. That old kitsune would have found you by now otherwise."

Ingrid hadn't encountered the word *"mana"* before this conversation, but the meaning was evident from the context. She lowered her skirt again. Then she reached for her courage and asked the question that had been burning on her tongue. "What can I do to fully regain my strength?"

"Nothing."

The blunt word struck Ingrid like a blow. "Nothing?"

The word echoed in her mind. *Nothing*. Her body would never recover. The pain would stay as constant as her shadow, the level of agony varying hour to hour. She'd never again sleep through the night uninterrupted by excruciating calf cramps and burning tingles in her toes. And how would she get around if she couldn't walk? She thought of her experience on the airship just now, how she tried—and failed—to walk ten feet without aid. She remembered how she used to walk all over San Francisco, up and down those steep hills. How she'd haul heavy laundry baskets along the servants' stairs at the auxiliary. How she had exulted in the full potential of her body during that one blessed night in Seattle with Cy. How afterward, with their legs intertwined, she'd tickled his calf with her toes until he chuckled and squirmed.

Pele gripped Ingrid by the shoulder to anchor her upright. In her eyes, Ingrid saw compassion and sorrow.

"Your body will never be as it was, but that *does not mean that you are not strong.*" The raspy words embodied centuries of experience, but Ingrid still wanted to find a way to argue otherwise. Pele smiled and shook her head as she released her hold on Ingrid's shoulder. "Remember what I said about using the physical form that is best for your needs? *This* is your best form now. Even if the fox cut off your leg, the ward would hold. It's part of your breath and flesh."

"But I . . ."

"We destroy." Pele crushed the stub of her cigarette against a steel flange. "That's what our blood is known for. I traveled across the Pacific. I visited each island in turn. I dug in my *Pā'oa,* and I stayed here. But our kind of destruction is not wanton. When you walked across Kilauea, you saw the bushes, yes?" Ingrid nodded. "Plants begin to grow soon after the lava cools. In a few more decades, centuries, the forest will return. Along the shore, I create land where there was nothing. Out there." She pointed down the slope. "I cultivate an island that won't emerge for centuries yet."

She finished wrapping a new cigarette and lit it with a spark sent from her lips. "Of course, you're human. You don't think on the scale of centuries. You're impatient after mere minutes of listening to me speak." She grinned, taking a puff. "You said yourself that the energy flow in San Francisco almost killed you, yet you placed yourself in similar circumstances in Seattle. This was your choice. Yes, yes." Pele sliced her hand through the air, a warning gesture. "Blame the fox as the instigator, but *you* made your own choices. You live with the results."

Every word seemed to weigh on Ingrid like a ton of rocks. She took several long, deep breaths. She had done this damage to herself. She had known that all along, but now it felt real. Now she knew there would be no true recovery. And as much as she wanted to cry and scream and beg and rage, she knew it was pointless.

"Our fight against the ambassador is far from over. I need to be able to do more," Ingrid said. But as the words hung between them, she immediately wished she could take them back. They seemed petty—and none of this was Pele's fault or burden.

Pele exhaled smoke, an eyebrow arched. "Do you? You're not stupid, most of the time. You'll figure out a way." Her tone was matter-of-fact.

"Grandmother, you speak in riddles like the *qilin*."

"No, I don't." Her voice grew harsh. "I'm saying words you don't want to hear. That does *not* mean I am speaking in riddles. Listen. Listen well." The terrible heat swelled, causing Ingrid to gasp in shock as Pele leaned toward her. "You came to me saying that you want information. In truth, you want a miracle. You're not the first person, nor will you be the last. Your father came here with high expectations, too."

"My father?" Ingrid's mind raced over what she knew. Papa had lived under a false identity for twenty years, but he had finally been captured by the Unified Pacific in January—in the Hawaiian Vassal States.

"He'd had something of an awakening, it seems. After years of idleness, he decided to return to the land of his childhood. But what he saw didn't match his idyllic memories. He was horrified at how foreigners outnumbered his people, at how they are bound into callous labor on sugar and fruit plantations or in other servile roles. He said we could fight back. We could free them. He said all this, but I had not revealed myself to him. I merely listened. Therefore, he shot himself in the foot to try to provoke me to appear." Pele's eyes were glimmering midnights. Her breath reeked of sulfur. "That wasn't wise of him."

"No. No it was not." Ingrid felt the need to say something agreeable, reminded yet again that she was in the presence of a goddess.

Pele considered Ingrid for a moment. "You mentioned that the fox treats humans as game pieces." She spoke in a low voice. "After centuries, after one realizes that immortality means endless boredom, it's easy to use tedium as an excuse to toy with people. Treat them as objects of amusement. I don't. I see the suffering around me. It has always existed. The Menehune warred among themselves, then the Tahitians came, and the Hawaiian people grew and changed. They knew my ways, and I knew theirs.

"Our blood is the blood of the earth, Ingrid." Pele stood, and a stick appeared in her hands. It didn't look that different from the one that Ingrid had propped beside her, but this new stick crackled with holy energy, not unlike the Green Dragon Crescent Blade. "I'm ancient, but the earth is older yet."

Pele tapped the bare ground between the mast's base and the dry lava flow. Ingrid felt the shudder through her bones.

"I was drawn to Hawaii because of this well of magma that reaches deep into the core of our planet. I can direct this energy, but I don't create it."

"Auxiliary textbooks often say that geomancers are conduits between the earth and kermanite," Ingrid murmured.

Pele nodded. "Conduits. Yes. Each of us with limitations. I can direct lava at my whim, but not even I can completely prevent the earth here from shaking. It *needs* to move and grow. Nor can I change how an earthquake flows, rippling outward and into the ocean. Nor can my brothers and sisters in dominion over water contain a mighty wave that grows as it stretches across half the world."

"A tsunami," Ingrid said to herself.

"Abram was foolhardy. The way he injured himself would have provoked a baser being—like that double-headed snake you mentioned—to shift and destroy the land above. By trying to provoke *me* in that way, he could have killed many of the people he professed hope to save. And yet he continued to rail against me. He thought he could convince me to go to Japan, to awaken Fuji." Pele barked out a laugh.

Ingrid felt sick at the thought. "I hadn't even considered that I could choose to attack in such a way."

"Does that appeal to you?" asked Pele, her smile amused.

"No! It's horrible!"

"You've seen the destruction caused by your father in San Francisco. Imagine, then, what I could do, if I *chose* to do so." She gestured around her. "I don't want to wander anymore. I don't want to meddle in human affairs. Not much, anyway. I want to stay here, in my beautiful home. I want to guide the lava's flow and build this land, then seed it with new plants, new life. Maybe, in time, I'll move to my new island that still grows below the waves. But even by my perception of time, that's a long way off."

Ingrid remained quiet for a moment. "Tacoma mentioned that I should find my own mountain. I see the appeal in that. A month ago, I never would have considered living anywhere but San Francisco. Now I'm not sure where to find a permanent home."

"You'll find a place that offers the peace and balance that you seek. I wish that Abram might have had the presence of mind to do that." Grief weighed on Pele's beautiful face, her eyes downcast. She mourned her son. The depth of Pele's sadness surprised Ingrid—and made her feel ashamed. She knew from the old stories that gods like Pele loved and hated and acted all too human, but even so, she had expected more . . . divinity than humanity. Perhaps that expectation arose from Ingrid's own selfish desire to be healed.

"Abram stayed for days to persist in his argument. His injured foot became infected, and he was very ill as he left Kilauea. He blamed me for that, too, of course. As if I owed him miracles." Pele shook her head and sighed, then tilted an ear toward the ground. "We cannot talk much longer. The earth needs to move soon. You'll be safest at a high elevation through the night."

Ingrid had come a long way for such a short conversation, but there was no arguing with the needs of the earth. "You're right. I came here with hopes for a miracle. I wasn't any better than my father, really." Shame weighed on her. "I thought . . . I thought the extent of my problems called for the aid of a goddess. I was wrong." She blinked back tears. "What I needed most of all was a grandmother."

"Ah, Ingrid." Her gaze was fond as she motioned for Ingrid to stand. She did, relying on her new walking stick, and quickly found herself enfolded by two powerful arms. Ingrid stiffened, overwhelmed by the need to flee the intense heat. Pele's tendrils of hair felt like flickering sparks against her face, while the goddess's stick crackled as it almost pressed against Ingrid's back.

Despite Grandmother's incredible presence, after a few moments, the heat became oddly soothing since it wasn't accompanied by pain. Her hand rubbed a comforting circle over

Ingrid's back. The gesture was not reminiscent of Mama—
she had never been much for physical affection—but felt all
the more profound for that very reason. This was a kind of
tenderness Ingrid had never known from the women in her
life.

"I've been so scared." The confession blurted out. "About
my legs, about the fox, about Lee, and Mr. Sakaguchi—"

"And your Fenris and Cy, too, yes. You've gone through a
lot, Ingrid. You should be scared. It's smart to be scared. Fear
will keep you alive, eh?"

Ingrid half laughed, half sobbed. "That is a very grand-
motherly thing to say."

"Well, you are not my first grandchild. I have *some* experience in these things."

Wind whistled through the steel tower above. "Do you
ever feel lonely out here?" Ingrid asked, then immediately
regretted her nosiness. To her relief, the arms around her
didn't relinquish their loving hold.

"I might lack human company, but I am never alone. I can
speak with birds, bushes, bugs, the earth itself." Grandmother
hesitated, seeming to realize she had missed the heart of
Ingrid's question. "But sometimes, yes, I know loneliness."

Ingrid nodded against her grandmother's shoulder, taking comfort in her profound humanity, even amid the searing
heat. "I've only known you for a few minutes, but I hope I can
see you again. You're family. I . . . I need my family."

Grandmother pulled back to look Ingrid in the eye. "I do
not know if we'll see each other again either. I look downward
more than I look outward. But know this, Granddaughter."

The wind paused, adding gravitas to her words. "You are mine, and you are loved."

She stepped back, leaving Ingrid to stand on her own. *"Aloha, a hui hou."* She uplifted a hand in good-bye.

Ingrid didn't understand all of the words, but the tenderness in the farewell required no translation.

CHAPTER 8

Ingrid could not sleep. Her brain repeated her conversation with Madam Pele in an endless loop.

Stories about Pele fixated on her chaotic nature, that she was an impulsive and violent woman. In reality, though, Pele had not tried to manipulate Ingrid—a stark contrast to Blum, the *qilin,* and even humans like Mr. Sakaguchi and Mr. Roosevelt. Pele had left Ingrid empowered by her words, not by lava or some show of godly power.

Ingrid laughed quietly to herself. All the male storytellers over the years had every right to foment fear of Pele. She was a woman who would never submit. She would spit lava at the concept of fate.

And Ingrid adored her. She wanted to be her, in so many ways. Mama would have loved her, too.

She smiled up at the ceiling. She had a grandmother. A grandmother who loved and accepted her.

Her leg muscles twitched as if zapped by electricity. Her good mood sobered in an instant. She rolled to her side and scooted to the edge of her cot. The worst of the pain subsided with the change of position, dwindling to a burning sensation in her toes. She stared down at her legs.

They would never truly heal. She'd never again be able to take walking or climbing or other basic ambulatory functions for granted.

For years, Ingrid had ached for respect as a geomancer, as a woman, as a human being, only to have that repeatedly denied. And now, injured as she was, some people treated her as even *less*. That struck at her own deepest fears: that she was a burden. That in their current circumstances, her inability to act or to help or to simply walk could prove fatal to those she loved.

But what was it Grandmother had said? *Your body will never be as it was, but that does not mean that you are not strong.*

She stood with a muffled groan and glanced down the hall to where Cy piloted the *Bug*. The window still showed darkness. Fenris lay in the rack behind and above her. He was a twitchy sleeper, constantly shifting and muttering, busy even as he dreamed.

She stepped forward and gripped the rungs of the ladder across the way. The sylphs responded to her proximity, stirring for the first time since Pele-as-a-dog came aboard. They fluttered down in a gray cascade.

help? pastry? The sylphs flashed her an image of when they caught her when she last climbed the ladder.

"Yes, but stay quiet," she whispered, a finger to her lips.

The sylphs lowered their susurrus.

Ingrid climbed slowly, steadily, the sylphs at her back as a precaution. By the time she sat at the top, both legs quivered and twitched. The sylphs returned to their nest and watched her in a fluttery mass.

She leaned toward the back wall to touch the carving of the *qilin*.

She didn't plead with words this time. Instead, she opened herself as if in Zen meditation. She focused on her breaths, in and out, and tried to dwell in mu. Nothingness. Receptive to whatever news came her way.

A minute passed. Two. Terrible thoughts barged into her attempt at mindlessness. Was Lee dead? Was that why the *qilin* couldn't act as a bridge? She forced away the dark possibilities by imagining Mr. Sakaguchi's peaceful expression as he sat at their old household shrine. She tried to channel that solace herself.

If not for the pervasive pain in her legs, she might have fallen asleep at last. Instead, she stared at the carving, her attempt at nothingness filled by melancholy.

"I just want to know if he's alive. Can I learn that much?" she whispered.

She heard nothing but the roar of the engines, smelled nothing but the indescribable odor of sylph dander and the sour funk of bodies and bedding after a prolonged time aloft.

Her thoughts flicked this way and that as she descended the ladder. Was it worthwhile at all to continue her attempts to initiate communication? Or was she merely irritating the being?

Was she acting like Papa?

Her feet slipped. Her hands alone couldn't support her weight. The sylphs caught her almost immediately, their close contact like being pricked by a hundred pins at once.

The fairies released their hold as soon as her soles met the floor. She crumpled forward, rendered limp in agony. The pain from their contact dissipated within seconds, but she still found herself unwilling to move.

"That wasn't particularly fun," she whispered.

"Falling from heights and hurting yourself isn't recommended, even when we're aloft." Fenris's voice was soft and raspy from the other high bunk. "Nor will it ever be fun."

"Noted," she said.

"*Are* you actually injured? Because if Cy finds out how it happened, you know he'll gripe like a molting harpy."

Ingrid couldn't help a quiet laugh at that as she sat up. Fenris peered down through a gap in the curtains. "How long have you been awake?"

"Long enough to observe you climbing your own private eight-foot-high Matterhorn, conversing with the *qilin,* and engaging in a catch-me game with the sylphs that could have easily left you with a broken spine or skull. Was it worth the effort?"

"No. The conversation was one-sided. I keep trying to connect with Lee, but . . ."

"You tried this before?"

"I first reached out to the *qilin* on our way to Kilauea, for all the good it did." She couldn't keep despair from her voice.

"You've climbed that ladder twice, then?" He scowled at her nod. "Damn. Why can't that heavenly being just show up in the hallway like it did before? For that matter, why are you climbing the ladder at all? You didn't even know that carving was there the last time the *qilin* showed up."

"I've always been rotten at meditation. When I'm touching the carving, connecting with something Lee made, it makes it easier to focus." She shrugged. Her excuse sounded silly when said aloud.

"Like using rosary beads, huh? Well, unless you truly want to risk life and limb on the ladder again, I *could* actually remove that portion of wall so you could keep it in the safety of your rack."

"You could?"

"Sure. I'd need to wait until we were docked so I could patch that section immediately. If the sylphs worked their way into the walls . . ." He violently shuddered.

"Even if I'd thought of removing that bit of wall, I wouldn't have dared to suggest that kind of desecration to you."

"Good." He haughtily gazed down. "You shouldn't be thinking of ways to maul my ship."

"I'll leave all the mauling to you."

"It's only mauling when someone else does it. *I* know what I'm doing. Now, why don't you utilize that auxiliary secretary training of yours and start coffee on the burner? Two hours of sleep is enough for me." He pushed the curtains back the rest of the way.

"I can start some of that god-awful brew for you, but *only* because I like you. And the sylphs seem to like you, too." The fairies' low, polite buzz rose to a motorlike roar as they swirled around Fenris in greeting. "They don't greet Cy like that. I suppose there's a reason we're working through pastries at such a fast rate?"

Fenris's expression was of mock offense as he hopped down the ladder to the floor. "They were starved and poisoned when you first staggered in with them. I think they are finally looking healthy. That's nothing to complain about."

She stifled a yawn. "You're right."

"Try to sleep. Use some of the beeswax stashed in the nook and you might sleep through our docking. And, Ingrid?"

"Yes?"

Fenris gave her a cool glare. "If you feel the urge to go up that ladder again, give me a nudge. Don't rely on the sylphs alone."

"I won't. Thank you," she said softly.

"Someone has to do the thinking around here," he said. "I can make my own coffee, too. You rest."

INGRID AWOKE TO THE SCREECH OF HER CURTAIN BEING YANKED back. Her eyes opened wide to be blinded by a brilliant white light.

"Leave her be!" Cy snapped.

"Back off!" growled a husky voice. The beam shifted away, and through bright spots she recognized the navy cloth and gleaming buttons of an Army & Airship Corps uniform. "Get up, woman."

What was happening? Did these men know who she was? Her heart felt as if it would pound out of her chest. She used the railing to pull herself out. Cy stood behind the soldier, his expression one of barely checked rage. Two more soldiers stood behind him. Fenris's voice, at a strangely high pitch, carried from the control cabin.

The bearded soldier scowled and motioned her to stand.

"I have an injury, I can't move quickly." Her voice shook.

"Just move." The soldier stepped to one side. She stood, feeling defiant and vulnerable all at once, standing before armed men while she wore men's loose undergarments. Thank the Almighty she still wore a brassiere.

The man assessed her with a sneer. "An 'injury,' eh?" He glanced back at Cy. "You shouldn't use her so hard." Without waiting for a reaction from Cy, he flipped up her mattress. "No guns here!" he called to his companions.

"Nothing here!" called a deep voice from up the hall.

The sylphs. She sensed them in the bunk above, rendered still by the invasion of strangers. She mentally screamed confirmation of the threat as one of the soldiers behind Cy bounded up the rungs. The mattress thudded as he shifted it. He was on the floor a second later.

"Nothing up there," he said. Ingrid breathed out a tiny sigh of relief.

"Give me your paperwork," the bearded soldier said to Cy, walking back to the hatch without giving Ingrid a second look. "If you're planning to put her to work as a seamstress, you need another sheet. And hell, why couldn't you have brought a pretty blonde? Got enough of *them* around here." He gestured a thumb her way.

A seamstress. Ingrid knew that vernacular from San Francisco. They assumed she was a prostitute.

Cy went deadly still, and Ingrid was terrified of what he might say or do. "She's not a woman of that sort, sir," he said, voice quiet and even.

"Sure." The soldier signed a sheet and shoved it back at Cy's chest. "If you're caught, it's not my jurisdiction. Take this to the depot."

The soldiers exited. Ingrid gasped, a fist to her heart. She sank to the jutted edge of her rack, her legs rendered boneless. Down the way, Cy leaned against the pantry, his body rigid, one fist straight at his side. His body heaved as he took in massive breaths.

"Don't you dare punch my cabinets," said Fenris, sliding around Cy.

"I could have pounded that bastard's head in," Cy said between gasps. He sounded more scared than angry.

"But you didn't, which is good, because otherwise we'd likely be dead, too." Fenris continued toward Ingrid, his eyebrows drawn tight in concern. "You're all right?"

"Rattled, but unharmed. What was all that about?"

"That was our welcome to Hilo."

AS THE BASTION OF CIVILIZATION ON THE EASTERN SIDE OF THE island-state, Hilo bustled with activity like a riled wasps' nest. Unfortunately for the *Palmetto Bug,* much of the fuss was orchestrated by soldiers in Unified Pacific blue.

"It's all about the sugarcane plantation strikes," said Cy. He rubbed his beard and paced in the doorway. "Word among other pilots is that it's just as bad in Kona and Waimea. Riots are busting out on plantations across the islands. Any Chinese person is being interrogated as a potential gunrunner—"

"Of course they are," muttered Ingrid. "The fox would have them blamed for the setting sun, if she could."

She sat in the cabin. The shades were partially down, granting her a vantage point on the chaos down below while still shielding her from view. Twenty minutes had passed, and she couldn't quite stop trembling from her rude awakening.

So many soldiers were here. All it took was one person to recognize either her or the *Bug*.

"Our personal firearms and Tesla rods are registered and must remain on board or in lockers at the depot, like in Honolulu," Cy continued. He seemed to take comfort in the recitation of information.

"Should we fly back there to restock?" Ingrid asked.

"Oahu is probably just as bad," Cy said. "Besides, we already know people there are on the lookout for our ship."

Fenris stood by his chair. His slender fingers twitched on the seat back as he glared toward the figures below. "We're not going to Honolulu. I need to work on the *Bug*. I won't risk another flight."

The finality of that statement left them all quiet for a minute.

Cy stared out the window. "Strange, to see a port this busy on a Sunday. It reminds me of Seattle amid that awful Baranov rush." He shuddered. "Only good thing about this hubbub is that many businesses will be open to accommodate the influx of soldiers."

Ingrid knew Cy and Fenris would busy themselves in a

myriad of tasks in the next while. She had to do her part, too. "Cy, can you bring me any recent newspapers? I'll scan for more news on *Excalibur* or anything else of relevance."

He nodded. "I'll hit the shops lickety-split and start placing orders. I can bring you some papers." He started to move past her, and hesitated. "About those soldiers, what they said . . ."

"Cy. I've heard that kind of nonsense since I was old enough to wear a brassiere. Since Mama died, I've also dealt with insinuations that there must be something crude between myself and Mr. Sakaguchi, because *surely* he would have no other use for a woman of my complexion." She said this flatly, and she could see the revulsion in his eyes—not for her, but for people who were vile enough to believe such things.

"I hate that you have to endure such abuses."

"I hate people in general sometimes." She shrugged.

"I think that's why we get along so well," added Fenris. "We have banded together in a sort of antisocial club."

Ingrid laughed and shook her head. "Confronting horrid people like that gives more merit to my grandmother's suggestion that I find a remote, safe place, away from civilization, someplace where I can be myself. I think, so long as I have books and pleasant company and access to good chocolate, I could get by."

Cy's expression softened. "Maybe that can be arranged." His arms curled around her shoulders, bringing her head against his ribs. Ingrid melted against him, even as he leaned on her. His fingers trembled as they stroked her hair. She wrapped an arm around him, a hand on his hip.

Out of the corner of her eye, she noted Fenris politely turn his attention elsewhere, a tablet and pencil in hand.

"Just so you know," Cy murmured, "I can make bookshelves."

"Are you trying to seduce me, Cy?" She kept her voice as low as possible.

His hand paused on the back of her head. "Is that all I need to do? Build bookshelves? How many hundred do you need?"

She looked up at him, smiling. "I'll let you know once we're settled in someplace and start compiling a library."

His eyebrows furrowed, pained. "I want that time to come. More than anything."

Ingrid thought back on what Pele said about choices. From Hilo, the *Bug* could fly anywhere in the world. They could find a cozy, isolated spot. Cy and Fenris could have their machine shop. She'd have a library—and what else?

Guilt. Tremendous guilt. The knowledge that she'd abandoned Lee and Mr. Sakaguchi, allowed Blum to render the world to scorched earth. Blum, who would most likely never leave her in peace, even if she did run and hide.

She pressed harder against Cy, and he responded by strengthening his embrace. He didn't ask what she was thinking. He didn't need to. She clenched her eyes shut and forced her focus onto him, his touch, his heat, his smell. Her terror—her guilt at even considering a coward's route— gradually subsided.

After several minutes, Cy relinquished his hold and crouched to look her in the eye. "We'll survive this. You'll get your bookshelves. I promise."

"I'll hold you to that," she said with a wobbly smile, forcing hope into the words.

Cy responded with a kiss. Tender, soft, a stroke of lips, a rush of hot breath. A kiss of promise. "I'll be back soon." He headed toward the stairs.

Ingrid knew she should go back and get dressed, but she wasn't quite ready to walk around just yet. Her legs didn't feel awful right now, but they sure didn't feel *good* either. She needed to get accustomed to this, her new normal.

My body will never be as it once was, but that doesn't mean it's not strong. She had a hunch she'd be invoking Pele's words often in the coming days and years.

She looked out the window again. Through a bobbing sea of airships, Hilo proper and its bay were visible to the north. The town existed at the base of a slope that led to verdant green hills and continued upward to the magnificent, massive peak of Mauna Kea.

Her gaze dragged down to the dock again to try to find Cy in the vicinity of the gate. "Pardon, Fenris, what are those machines over there?"

"What machines? Where?" Fenris, frowning and distracted, leaned toward the glass. She pointed to the gate in question. Only a mast and a cluster of buildings stood in the way.

The orichalcum contraptions looked like nothing she'd seen before. Two legs, about as high as a man and twice as thick, bent back like the hind legs of a cat. Above the legs was a bowl-like indentation and some sort of metal cage. There were six of these devices lined up in a tidy row, and apparently Ingrid wasn't the only one marveling at the sight. Quite a crowd had gathered, soldiers and civilians both. She imagined Cy was somewhere in the melee.

"Huh. I read about those in a mechanical journal some months ago. Some new creation by Augustinian, an automaton unit controlled by one or two pilots sitting in the top. It's like a more mobile Durendal. The legs can run fast as a horse and jump over canals. Eventually, they are supposed to have arms with guns controlled by the pilots." He shook his head. "Damn, but those machines do look shiny and new. They must plan to try these out on the strikers."

Try them out. That painted a terrible picture in red. "Augustinian. Did Cy's sister work on these?"

"Anything brilliant that developed there over the past ten years, you can bet money that Maggie had some role."

What would go through Cy's mind as he passed by those automatons? Would he return, mired in grief again at the reminder of his twin sister's choices?

"I don't want to be around when the UP decides to test the firepower of those machines." Ingrid stood.

Fenris stilled, his face thoughtful. "You know, normally I'd *like* to witness such a demonstration, but in consideration of our recent encounters with the UP, I must agree with you this once. Let's get the hell out of here as soon as possible."

CY RETURNED, BRIEFLY, WITH ASSORTED GOODS, THEN HEADED out again. With Fenris immersed in maintenance, Ingrid sat on her rack and read through the stack of newspapers he had brought.

A short while later, Cy marched back on board and bustled about the ship putting parcels away. She watched him, biding her time to speak, as he was clearly lost in thought. He finally stopped near berthing and leaned on the wall, saying nothing. She took that as her cue.

"The only news of interest I've found is a growing anti-Russian sentiment because of the attack on the Seattle Auxiliary. There's even an editorial from Portland that calls for the UP to send more troops to Manchukuo to reinforce Japan's claims there. Otherwise, the mainland news remains the same. The same photograph of *Excalibur* is repeated five times over."

He stared to one side, frowning, but otherwise showed no reaction.

"Cy? What are you pondering?"

"Your legs." His fingers tapped on the wall.

"My legs?" she said, surprised. She had fully expected him to mention Maggie and those automatons.

"We've been thinking about this all wrong. The human body's a machine. We need to reinforce the natural movement of your lower legs. The rigs on your shoes don't do enough." He motioned to storage nearby, where he'd replaced the elastic attached on her boots. "When I saw those Bayards out there, how their legs can flex and move, all I could think is that I could replicate that on a smaller scale." He spoke faster as he continued, his eyes gleaming.

"Bayards? That's the name for those contraptions?" At

his nod, she grinned. "They're named for Paladin Renaud's magical horse in the old French stories, right? The steed that could expand to fit more riders."

"Why am I not surprised you're well versed in horse mythology?" His smile was fond. "The brace should fit within your boot. Therefore, it must be light and thin."

"Five-plate orichalcum or less." Fenris's voice echoed from the engine room. He sounded as though he were speaking into an open duct. "But unless we've suddenly inherited a mine up in Baranov, we have no means to afford that."

"Five-plate?" she repeated.

"Orichalcum is one of the hardest materials on earth, and damnably difficult to refine," said Cy. "A forge requires substantial enchantments on its tools to work ori down to thirty-plate, which is the thickness of the *Bug*'s hull. That's expensive enough. We scraped and saved for years to put our ship together. Single-plate is the stuff worn by the mikado. It's lighter and thinner than most cloth, and still nigh impenetrable to bullets."

She sighed. Roosevelt had said he'd provide them funds, within reason. She suspected this expense would be too extravagant to qualify. Still, for a moment there, she had been caught up in Cy's excitement.

He crouched beside her. His giddiness had not diminished. "We should only need strategically placed plates from the arches of your feet up along your calves. We're not encasing your entire body—"

"Not that it's a terrible idea. You do have a propensity for getting shot and otherwise injuring yourself in disastrous ways." Metal clanged, and Fenris emerged from the engine room, his slender arms folded over his chest. Goggles granted him buglike eyes.

"May I study your legs?" asked Cy. "I need to envision the plate placement."

Ingrid arched an eyebrow. "Yes?"

Fenris cackled. "Congratulations, Ingrid. You now get to see Cy in the thick of creative mania. These moods strike about as often as Saint Nicholas makes a circuit around the world. When he came up with the Durendal design, he didn't sleep for three days straight."

Cy didn't even seem to hear. He lifted her skirt to knee level, his manner entirely clinical. He tapped along the length of her right calf to just above the knee, muttering beneath his breath. Ingrid watched with a sort of detached fascination.

"Cy. Cy!" Fenris kicked him in the shoe. Cy blinked rapidly and gawked upward. "Listen to me. I have a hell of a lot of work to keep me busy through the night. You people need sleep." He said this with an expression of disgust. "Ingrid, you take Cy. Find a hotel nearby that doesn't look too flea-infested. Get him some paper and space to work. Use a tablecloth and some paint, if you need to. Just give him means to exorcise his creative demons."

That somehow penetrated the fog of Cy's thoughts. "But you need help with the *Bug,* and more supplies'll be delivered this afternoon—"

"You will be utterly useless as help right now. Trust me, I speak from experience. Put the receipts in the pantry and I'll verify we get what we ordered."

"The soldiers—" Cy started to speak.

"Are here. If they want to capture us . . . well, here we are, too. Stuck. The *Palmetto Bug* is grounded for the time being." Fenris held out his arms, hands brushing either side of the hall. "We can't stroll out of here right now. I imagine the roads out of town abound in checkpoints where soldiers are inclined toward suspicion and violence. If we're separated in town . . . well, at least we're more inconvenient to catch."

"Thank you, as always, Fenris, for grounding us in the unpleasantness of reality," said Ingrid.

"Mmm-hmm." Cy frowned as he stared at her feet.

Fenris shook his head in exasperation. "Watch out for him in the streets. He's likely to walk into traffic while muttering to himself." He laughed, a rare, light sound. "Thank God I get to foist the parenting duties on someone else for once."

INGRID HAD COME TO KNOW CY INTIMATELY IN THE WEEKS OF their acquaintance. She'd seen him terrified witless when he walked with her along the bottom of San Francisco Bay, and overwhelmed with grief after finding out dire news of his parents, and enraptured with her body as they explored each other during their peaceful interlude in Seattle.

Now she observed him the way a cryptozoologist might analyze some rare fantastic encountered in the wild for the first time in a generation.

"You're rather like those rainbow-maned flying unicorns that are rumored to exist on banks of cumulus clouds high above the Pacific Ocean." Ingrid pressed her chin to her forearms as she leaned forward on Cy's makeshift work-station.

They had traversed several blocks to find a hotel that did not feature women of a certain occupation at the front door ready to greet passersby, and the quarters they'd found consisted of no more than a bed squeezed into the same space as a screened-off lavatory. There was no table to be found, and Cy *needed* a table. Fortunately, the mattress sat upon a large wooden box. The mattress now occupied the floor, its edges curled up against the wall and the bed frame, while Cy used his new table to ink out schematics on brown paper bought from the butcher next door.

"That so?" Cy muttered, lost in his work.

"Yes. You have a lovely, shiny white coat, though I doubt it's ever been touched with a curry comb. Your colorful mane flows when you walk. Your hooves are shiny gold."

"I think we might need to use tin for the prototype. It's light enough . . ." He tapped the blunt end of the pen against his lips.

Cy had drawn designs and figures on a full dozen sheets of paper, scowling and muttering and conversing with himself all the while. Ingrid had always had a gift for mathematics—one of the many reasons she'd been an effective secretary for Mr. Sakaguchi—but Cy spoke an advanced language of numbers that could have been some fae tongue, as far as she knew.

However, he'd also been at this nine hours straight, with one prolonged break in the middle to check on Fenris and acquire victuals for their evening meals. Cy had gobbled up the contents of his bento box without noticing what he was eating.

Fact was, for the man's health, he needed to turn off his brain for a while and sleep. That wasn't going to happen without her intervention.

Her words had been incapable of distracting him. She had a hunch there was another way that might prove more successful.

She scooted herself across the limp curve of the mattress to peer through the thin curtains to the street below. All was quiet. Curfew in Hilo had come down as swift and sharp as a guillotine. As sunset neared, yells and whistles had echoed through the streets. Soon afterward, a Bayard had marched through town. Ingrid felt its approach through shuddering steps that caused the ceiling lamp to chime and sway in their second-story room. Somehow, the heavy, resonant steps made its approach even more terrifying than that of the loud, rumbling treads of a Durendal tank. The Bayard passed by along a nearby block, unseen and nightmarish. She imagined being a sugarcane striker, protest sign in hand, feeling those things approach from the distance. She wondered how many men and women would hold the line against such machines.

Hours had passed since then. Cy stifled a yawn as he continued to work, his back bowed in a way that'd surely make him ache tomorrow.

Ingrid hiked up her skirt and worked her stockings down. She considered a balled-up stocking, wondering if throwing it at Cy might gain his attention. She unfastened her obi-style belt, then the large buttons down her chest.

"Ingrid? What're you doing?"

She was down to her chemise and panties by that point.

She looked at Cy. "I'm removing my clothing, of course."

"Why're you doing that?" His gaze still looked bleary, as if he'd just awakened.

"Did you know it's approaching midnight?"

"It is?" His brow furrowed. "I recollect curfew falling, and the Bayard walking by, but I didn't think that was so long ago."

She sighed. "You need to sleep soon, Cy. You can't afford a second night with more coffee in your veins than blood. We can't all function like Fenris." She motioned toward the makeshift table. "Have you reached a good stopping point?"

"I'd rather not stop at all," he said with a rueful smile. "But sleep sounds like a wise course of action . . . and the sight of you brings other scientific endeavors to mind." He cleared his throat.

"You haven't forgotten our discussion on the *Bug* the other day, then."

He had a roguish twinkle in his eye as he stood. "I've given it a great deal of careful thought, actually. You were right to chastise me for regarding you as fragile. I know better."

"Yes, you do." She couldn't help but stare, breathless and eager as he slipped his suspenders off his shoulders and reached for the buttons at his collar. "I'd volunteer to help unbutton, but I'm not sure if my fingers would cooperate." Her voice sounded husky to her own ears.

"I wouldn't mind if you relaxed for a time." His shirt dropped to the floor. "I'd like a chance to do more of the seducing this time around. It's only fair, seeing as you did much of the initial work in Seattle. And I have some things in mind I'd like to try," he said airily.

Her body surged with pleasant warmth. Good God, but she wanted this. She wanted him. "It sounds like you do indeed have some plans."

"Mind you, none of these plans have been committed to paper yet. I'd rather engage in some tests first to see what works. To see what you like."

"I want everything to be to your liking, too."

"Oh, Ingrid. I wouldn't worry about that." The look in his eyes made her heart pound fast and hopeful.

She opened her arms wide to accept Cy. His arms wrapped around her, his kiss on her lips searing and hungry as they fell back on the mattress together. They paused, breaths rasping, as they stared into each other's eyes.

"I will gladly do my part for the sake of science," she murmured, and snared his lips in another kiss.

CHAPTER 9

MONDAY, MAY 7, 1906

Though her legs were stiff, Ingrid had a new spring in her step as she walked with Cy toward the dock. He carried a burdened pack, rolled schematics sticking out the top like a bouquet. A giddy smile lit his face. He kept casting Ingrid fond looks, which she couldn't help but reciprocate. They both sobered, however, as they came within a block of their destination.

"Good grief. Did a Behemoth class land during the night?" she muttered, self-consciously trying to avoid eye contact with swarms of soldiers in blue.

"Probably. Look at the skies, too."

A torrential downpour had fallen during the night, but the morning was crisp and clear. The sky, however, was dotted with airships of various sizes that idled over the island. Her gaze shifted to the masts ahead. "Every mooring mast is full. What's going on?"

"Nothing good." He tugged his hat brim lower. "I had really hoped for a few days here to do thorough maintenance. Reckon we'll need to vamoose as soon as we can, and pray to stay aloft until we see California's shore."

"As if the prayers will stop then. I'm glad you didn't tell me the risks of flight before we initially flew to Hawaii. Or maybe you did. I was so medicated at the start, I can't recall."

"Would warning you have helped?"

"Certainly. It's almost nice to distract myself with a worry that doesn't involve war and the deaths of millions."

"I suppose it's good to diversify, have some worries that are personal, others that encompass the fate of the world."

"You know I love you, right?"

The corners of his eyes creased as he smiled down at her. "I do. I hope you know with a certainty that I feel the same."

"I don't doubt that one bit, I—" A blue flash radiated from the ground. With one hand on her stick, she gripped Cy, squeezing his elbow in warning.

Ingrid pulled in a lash of heat that lasted all of two seconds. Cozy tingles swirled up her legs and eddied through her arms, causing her skin to break out in goose bumps.

"Mrs. Harvey?" Cy asked, alarm in his eyes.

"Did you feel that?" she murmured. He shook his head.

"How bad?" He kept his voice low.

"I'm fine. No. Don't argue. I've coped with such events hundreds of times, and here, Grandmother is keeping things well in hand." She did not feel comfortable saying more. People pressed too close to them at the bottleneck of the gate. Cy glanced at her, tight-lipped, and she was grateful that his words were held in check.

The jostling crowd made it impossible to see the ground underfoot, and she tripped twice before they were through the gate, though Cy and her walking stick managed to keep her upright.

"I need to get our debarkation paperwork," Cy said, motioning toward a two-story stilt building. "That'll speed up the process." He warily eyed their surroundings, tension evident in his posture. He wasn't alone in that either. The mood of the place had gotten uglier since their visit the previous afternoon. At least the *Palmetto Bug* was visible on its mast a short distance away.

Ingrid glared up at the building with narrowed eyes. "I used to think of spiders as my greatest nemeses. Now they've been replaced by stairs and ladders."

"Let's hope that you never encounter a spider on a ladder or staircase, then. You can wait here. This should take just a minute. No point in tiring you out when we need to climb the mooring mast next."

"I'm amenable to that plan," she said, waving him along. He bounded up the steps.

She wistfully stared after him. She *could* use her held power to give her stride a boost up the stairs, but she knew better. Nor did she want to pour the energy into the empty kermanite tucked in her pocket. That could wait until they were safely aloft.

She stood to one side of the stairs and looked toward

the dock. There had to be some thirty masts, all occupied by various Sprite-, Pegasus-, and Porterman-class vessels. On the neighboring acreage, taller masts held three docked Behemoths bearing Unified Pacific colors. Their gray-and-parchment-toned envelopes almost entirely blocked the view of the massive volcano on the horizon.

Boots struck a discordant rhythm. Ingrid turned toward the noise, and before she knew what was happening, she found herself surrounded by soldiers. She bit back the urge to scream as several pairs of white-gloved hands grabbed her arms. Someone tried to pull away the stick, and she jerked it closer with a gasp.

"Are you Ingrid Carmichael?" A mustached man barked the words in her face.

She froze, her heart pounding against her rib cage. Where was Cy? Was he captured, too? She looked around and up the stairs. Cy looked down from the porch, utterly still. No soldiers were near him. A rush of relief rolled through her and she quickly pulled her gaze away. She couldn't implicate him, too.

"Answer him, woman!" A man jostled her arm.

"What are you doing? Let me go!" she snapped. Her power flared against her skin. She could knock these men down like ninepins, but even boosted by geomancy, she couldn't make the run to the *Bug* with so many other soldiers around.

"She doesn't need to confess her name."

She looked up. Cy was gone, replaced by a Japanese man. Ingrid went very still. *Warden Hatsumi*. He could see the miasma in her body.

"Bring her up to my office," barked Hatsumi. His war-denship seemed to have afforded him considerable power here.

A soldier tried to pry away her stick again. She gripped it tight. "No! I need it."

To her surprise, he let go.

The other men yanked her up the stairs. Her feet tripped on almost every step, and if not for the pressure on her arms, she would have fallen. They released their hold at the top. Another soldier gestured her inside.

"Walk," he growled.

She clutched the staff with both hands. The soldiers eyed the stick and her with suspicion, but they didn't make an-other move to steal it.

Good. Let them underestimate her, judge her to be a crip-pled, weak woman. Hatsumi might know her identity, but he didn't know what she was truly capable of.

Hope and rage burned through her in equal measure, hot as the energy she held.

The hallway contained a nook with brackets designed to hold Hatsumi's leg extenders; she imagined that he rarely left the building here. The soldiers pushed her up a long, nar-row staircase, to a breezeway open to sunlight and air at both ends. Hatsumi awaited her there, scowling. She couldn't sense the earth's energy on this floor. The building's stilts must have been reinforced with metal, which would conduct little supernatural energy.

A desk, filing cabinet, and several wooden chairs granted the stark white space no personality; not so much as a picture adorned the wall. A large window showed the wavered edge of the overhanging metal roof of the building next door.

A young man sat at the desk doing paperwork. He jumped to his feet, his gaze only for Hatsumi. He was the same man who had accompanied the warden in Honolulu.

"Ducey," snapped Hatsumi. "You have the wanted-person bulletin from yesterday." It was not a question.

"Hai." He hurried to the cabinet and opened up a file. Ingrid remained standing. The tread of heavy footsteps carried from elsewhere in the building. "Here, sir." He passed a sheet to Hatsumi.

Warden Hatsumi read and began to chuckle. "Oh, you are a valuable find." He waved the paper in Ingrid's face, too fast for her to see anything but a gray photograph. "Where's the man you were traveling with? Is he here?"

"I don't even know who *you* are, or why I'm here." She tried to keep her voice nonchalant, but she didn't have Lee's talent for these kinds of games.

"Ducey. Go telegram that I found the woman. I'm going to speak privately with her for now." He shoved the sheet at his assistant. The younger man bowed, and taking the paper, he exited the room. The door shut behind him.

Hatsumi circled her, his arms folded. "A woman geomancer. I feel like I have found a Hidden One." Ingrid bit her lower lip to hold back her retort. "You worked at the Cordilleran Auxiliary. I never met you there." His fingers stroked his wispy beard. Knobby rings flashed from each of his fingers. Three of the facets held filled kermanite, while the fourth ring had an empty stone. He carried no energy within his body.

"I don't believe you have introduced yourself," she said coolly.

"I'm Earth Warden Hatsumi. And you're Ingrid Carmichael, Sakaguchi's pet. I suppose he must have known what you are. I have so many questions."

Which Ingrid had no desire to answer. She needed to escape. She drew on the power in her veins, just a touch, well aware that Hatsumi could see any major fluctuations. She cast out her awareness. About a quarter mile away, she found the sylphs. They stirred at the brush of her power.

"Resist Fenris's training. Show him that he needs to make the airship buzz," she told them, imagining the roar of the revving engine. *"Then cast yourselves invisible, and fly to me."* She pictured the building and the view from the office window.

A wave of happy emotion flowed over her as the sylphs began to move. *earn pastry! yes!*

"My instruments downstairs observed the tremblor that just occurred. It was a mere burp of energy. Not worth the effort of slipping off my shoes for a rare moment on the ground here. But you, stupid girl, were on the ground, as if without a care. You must not have been here long or you'd already be dead," he mused. She gripped her staff as if to strangle it. "All those years at the Cordilleran, and you obviously learned nothing. Typical."

"Typical for a woman, or someone of my color?"

"Either. Both." He made a flippant motion with his hand.

"You do remind me of your father. He is also a deviant geomancer with incredible ability but no sense."

His use of the present tense provoked her to speak. "What do you know about my father?"

"I know he's a fool. All those years he hid from the UP, but he couldn't hide from *me*." Hatsumi puffed up with pride. "Last winter, I had a strange call from a doctor here in Hilo. He had a man with a terrible foot infection who was delirious with a fever that couldn't be broken. Some earthquakes had occurred recently, and the doctor suspected that his patient might be near death from energy sickness as well as infection. Imagine my surprise when I arrived and recognized the patient as one of my long-dead colleagues."

Ingrid's breaths came rapid. *This man*. He was the one who had turned Papa over to the UP. They initialized the Gaia Project. All those deaths in Peking. The scourging of San Francisco. It all led back to this pompous mugwump.

"He was too sensitive to the natural energy flow," Hatsumi continued, oblivious to her reaction. "A problem with lesser peoples. I saw the same in Chinese geomancers years ago. They are physically and mentally too fragile to handle the gift bestowed on them. And for a woman to pull in the earth's power?" He shook his head, tsking. "Look at you, unable to even walk upstairs on your own. Such degeneracy can't continue. It sullies reputable geomancers."

Ingrid couldn't hold back anymore. She burst out in laughter. Hatsumi stared at her, baffled.

"Really? You're trying to use my existence as some argument for racial supremacy, even as the Unified Pacific offers that ridiculously high reward for my capture? *Your* value to them is certainly clear, Warden Hatsumi. You're assigned to a place where any significant energy release will boil your innards in your skin in under a minute. You're disposable." His face flushed deep red while his jaw soundlessly opened and closed like a fish. "By all means, continue to gloat. I could use the laugh right now."

"Uppity bitch!" The words were hoarse with rage.

"You're threatened by me." She stared him down. "Just as you were threatened by my father's very existence. Our sensitivity can be a weakness in some ways, true, but it also makes us your superiors. And you can't *stand* that."

Hatsumi lunged forward as if to slap her. She stepped back, swinging her staff. He dodged and moved forward again, this time gripping Pele's stick. Just as she had hoped he would. He reared back, ready for her to try to pull the stick away. Instead, she adjusted her grip and laid her fingers over his knuckles. His eyes widened in surprise at the intimate contact.

That's when she pulled the power from the charged kermanite in his rings. The crystals dissolved to powder, the vacant facets hard against her fingers. Energy hot as blood slipped through her skin and twined up her arms and into the well of her chest.

Hatsumi stared in slack-jawed awe. He could *see* what she felt as she drew in magic. He was the only person who ever had.

Rage consumed her senses. She shoved him away.

Things tended to break when Ingrid was angry and held

power, but rarely had she been *this* angry, *this* frustrated, *this* disgusted at the world entire, and all of it centered on this one horrible man.

He flew backward. A blue fireball surged into his body, searing a hole that briefly showed the white wall beyond. His body flopped to the wooden floor some ten feet away and slid to rest by the wall, a broken doll. The heaviness of his impact shuddered through her feet.

Hatsumi was dead. She had blasted a baseball-sized tunnel straight through his chest. Left a smear of blood and charred tissue across the entire room.

Ingrid stared at her hands in disbelief. *Mana* trailed from her fingertips in blue wisps.

"I killed him?" she whispered aloud. She breathed in the horrid malodor of cooked meat, and turned aside to retch.

She had killed him. She had. She was a murderer. She hadn't just killed him, she had scorched a hole through him. She hadn't even known her power could do *that*. She shuddered and fought against being ill again.

As she wiped her mouth on her sleeve, the door flew open. The assistant, Ducey, stood there. He looked from Ingrid to Hatsumi and back, his face pale with horror. She waited for him to yell, to draw a gun, something.

"The soldiers heard, too. They're coming up from the first floor." He kept his voice low.

"You're not— I don't understand. What are you doing?" She remained immobile, awaiting judgment.

"Did he hurt, at the end?" Ducey's voice was husky, his words rapid.

"What did he do to you?" she whispered, shaken anew at the cruel gleam in the man's eyes.

"Things that don't leave bruises. You need to go."

She did. She could hear boots thundering up the stairwell. "Are there any other stairs down—"

"No, I'm sorry, and the window is a sheer drop—"

She was already moving that way. She lashed out the staff, shattering the glass, then swept the wood along the sill to knock out the jagged edges along the frame. Using the staff for leverage, she vaulted out the open window. The arc of her fall brought her near the neighboring building. Heat leached away as she adjusted her angle and slowed her descent. She impacted on the ground with a puff of dust and god-awful jolts of pain up both legs. She panted for breath, her heartbeat at a gallop. Shouts rang out from above.

A buzzing swarm whirled around her. As the sylphs' glamour covered her, Ingrid drew on her remaining energy to shield her skin against the fae magic.

"Thank you," she whispered. "I really should not make a habit of self-defenestration from the upper floors of buildings."

She started walking. Her left calf screamed in agony, the muscle locked from the impact with the ground, but this was no time to idle and work out the tension. She had to get off the dirt around the buildings and onto the pavement, where she would leave no tracks. Whistles pierced the air all around her. More soldiers came running. Several almost ran into her, but the fairy glamour diverted them at the last second.

She made it onto the pulverized lava rock pavement beneath

the masts. Airship envelopes blotted out sunlight like low, oppressive clouds.

The *Bug* wasn't far. She could see it. She could get there. She tried to avoid relying on her staff too much, lest the tapping give her away.

we are hiding your sound. we will get you to nest. safe there. She sensed the sylphs' anxiety for her. They were picking up on her pain and terror.

Soldiers ran all around her. They'd likely shut down the dock soon and search all of the vessels. Someone had surely seen her go to and from the *Bug* the previous day. Even if the soldiers couldn't find her, they'd nab Cy and Fenris.

"Not letting that happen," she whispered between gritted teeth. She pushed herself into a faster limp, her staff's thuds striking a heavy, steady beat.

She rounded a mast where workers had stopped to stare toward the entrance and wonder aloud at the fuss. The *Bug*'s mast was just ahead. Up top, the airship's engine was on. Several dockworkers were at the top, ready to disengage. Cy stood there, too.

Between them: some fifty steep stairs.

She switched her staff to her left hand and gripped the rail with the right. Relying on her upper-body strength, she climbed, left leg dragging. She focused on one step at a time. Upward. Forward. Keeping a rhythm.

Halfway up the mast, her foot dragged over a metal stair. She fell forward, catching herself on her knees and hands. Her face hovered just above the next steps up. She pivoted on her hip to glance down. The left elastic band had been sliced through.

Her legs quivered as she pulled herself up. Unbidden, a few sylphs diverted their paths to help her stay upright. The others maintained the glamour over her.

"Thank you," she gasped, envisioning bonus pastries for them all.

The wind picked up as she neared the top, bringing with it the clamor from far below. It sounded as though the whole damn A&A was mobilizing.

God—would the murder of Hatsumi be blamed on her, or would it be shifted to the strikers? Or the Chinese? Had she just provided an excuse for all-out war against civilians?

Ingrid was indeed too much like her grandmother and her father. Everywhere she went, she left death, fire, and destruction in her wake.

She swallowed down her soft sobs as she reached the top deck. The stub-wing engines roared. The two dock boys conversed, their gazes on the entrance. Cy stared that way, but also had an eye on the stairs.

She stood as close to him as she dared while still enabling the sylphs to encircle her. "I'm here," she whispered, the words shaking as if she spoke through an earthquake. She sensed the sylphs allowing her sound to escape their geas.

The change in his expression was instantaneous. "That's it, boys. I don't like the sound of that fuss down there. I guess I'll need to give up on that last delivery."

Ingrid hobbled up the final few stairs into the *Bug*. Once she was inside, her knees dropped to the tatami, the staff falling from her hand. She willed the sylphs to disengage. Their heat dispersed, and Ingrid released the shielding on her skin. Sweat and tears poured down her cheeks.

"Fenris!" Her voice sounded ragged and ancient.

"Ingrid!" He scrambled toward her from the cockpit. "Do you need kermanite or—"

"No! I'm fine." Fine, as in not near death. "Are we ready to take off?"

Fenris retreated to his chair again. "Yes! We just need Cy—"

Cy's heavy feet clanged on the stairs. He leaped into the airship, yanking up the hatch. She recognized the sound of the stairs jostling and falling flat as he latched the door into the floor. An instant later, he was on his knees next to Ingrid. He wrapped his arms around her with a soft, agonized moan. She buried her head against his shoulder.

The floor wobbled and surged beneath them, the engines whining high. The *Bug* was aloft.

"Oh, Ingrid. Oh, Ingrid." Cy rocked them back and forth. "What happened out there? How did you get away?" He reared back to look her in the face, brushing a tendril of black hair from her sticky skin. "You're not feverish or cold?"

"No. I kept my energy in balance. Aren't you proud?" Her giggle was high and hysterical.

"Is she okay?" Fenris yelled.

"Mostly." He assessed her and grimaced when he saw her boot. "Damn, the elastic broke again? I'm sorry—"

"Don't be. It only broke near the end. I wouldn't have gotten far at all without the lift those rigs offered."

"What happened in the depot?" Cy asked.

"Warden Hatsumi isn't going to be spending the money he's due for capturing me." Her tone was light, but she pressed a fist to her stomach, sickened anew at the thought of what she'd done.

143

"I thought I recognized him from Honolulu. Did he try to harm you?"

"Yes. And I killed him."

His arms tightened around her. "Ingrid. You did what you had to do to survive." His voice was soft. He understood.

She nodded as she pressed her head against his chest, trying to force away the memories that threatened to overwhelm her again. His hand stroked the back of her head, her neck, easing the tension there. She closed her eyes, taking in the deep comfort of his touch. His heartbeat galloped against her ear.

"Can you please come up here and involve me in the conversation so I know what the hell is going on?" Fenris yelled.

Ingrid laughed a little shakily. Then she let Cy help her to her feet, leaning heavily on her staff. "Are we flying for California?"

"Yes." His grin was tight. "Situation's not ideal, but what has been, these past few weeks?"

Fenris was flipping switches as they entered the cockpit, his gaze flicking between the ocean view ahead and the panel dials. "Cy, I need you to take a seat. Ingrid, buckle up." As if to punctuate his point, turbulence shook the craft.

She wedged the staff between her knees as she fastened the harness with shaking fingers.

Cy slid into his place while checking the panel and mirrors. "We have company."

"Pegasus gunship. It was aloft over Hilo. It's been signaling for us to return to the dock," said Fenris.

The view ahead revealed a horizon in a gradient of blue and white from the ocean to the broad expanse of sky. "What've you said to them?" she asked.

"This might impress you, Ingrid. The system of coded light-blinks that airships use to communicate underway has developed some succinct ways to advise a pilot to do the anatomically impossible." Fenris turned the rudder wheel.

"I'd like to learn that language," she said, using her hands to adjust her legs to better brace herself.

"The gunship's reply is equally succinct," said Cy.

"Bullets need little translation," said Fenris.

"I don't suppose our envelope is enchanted against bullets?" She grunted as the airship heaved hard to starboard. "I don't recall if that came up the *last time* we were shot at."

"I regret to inform you that I didn't choose that upgrade option. Most enchanters of that ilk are in federal employ, anyway, and the black market is booked up months in advance."

"Sometimes it's worthwhile to wait in a queue, Fenris." The *Bug* bucked to and fro, Ingrid's stomach left behind with each lurch. Even the sylphs, retreated to their nest, sent her a flash of dismay.

"Well, we're not idling in a queue today!" Fenris cackled, and reached above the curved glass, to where a playing card–sized picture bowed out from between two dials. "Saint Pollendina is looking out for us!" A cloud bank swallowed them, gray mist whizzing past the glass.

"Saint Pollendina?" Ingrid repeated with a gasp as her stomach jumped.

"Patron saint of airship pilots and mechanics," said Cy

with a small shrug. "But entirely a joke, as the famed mechanic in question was an atheist. Still, it's tradition for pilots to hail him in certain situations."

"Hallelujah!" said Fenris, with another laugh. They breached, and before them lay a prairie of cumulus clouds stretching out to the curve of the globe. He hummed a victorious-sounding song.

Ingrid leaned forward, looking between Cy and Fenris. "What happened? Where's the gunship?"

"Left in our dust, to misuse a metaphor." Fenris rotated in the seat enough to give Ingrid a smug look. "Pegasus gunships *look* sleek, but their gunnery and large portions of the ship aren't made of orichalcum. That heaviness, plus a large crew, means they're like inflated sloths."

"Not that we'll be arrogant about this pursuit." Cy glanced back at Ingrid as she stood. "I need to stay up here for a while to monitor our flank. Can you manage on your own?"

"I'll be fine. I need to massage my leg, wash up, and feed the sylphs." She pressed a hand to her cheek, finding it stiff with dried tears, sweat, and dust.

"We had to throw some freight onto the beds. If you need to nap, just shuffle things over," said Cy.

"I just might do that." A nap sounded heavenly.

She'd made it to the doorway when Cy spoke again. "I'll let you know if I see any rainbow-maned horses gallivanting about."

She turned, gasping. "You *were* listening!"

"Maybe." He glanced over his shoulder, mischief in his eyes, then returned his attention to the mirrors.

Ingrid staggered down the hallway. In a week, they'd be back in California, where, just maybe, they'd find Lee and Mr. Sakaguchi. Blum would expect them to land somewhere along the West Coast, too, but they had dodged her thus far.

Not even the thought of Blum caused Ingrid's determination to fade. There'd be troubles aplenty ahead, no doubt, but today she'd killed a man in order to remain alive and free. She would never again take such things for granted.

CHAPTER 10

MONDAY, MAY 14, 1906

Ingrid had expected her return to her home state to be cathartic, that she would step onto the earth and feel a renewed connection to a place she loved and missed desperately. However, after hours of being docked in Southern California, she had yet to step onto actual dirt or to see anything beyond mooring masts, a cluster of buildings, and slightly rolling grasslands.

She all but pounced on Cy upon his return to the *Bug*. He smiled and waved her back, his expression tense. "I apologize that it took me so long to get the lay of the land. We haven't been to Los Angeles in a few years. I know you're as restless as a selkie with a rediscovered pelt." He softened the words with a kiss on her cheek. "The good news is that there aren't any wanted posters for you posted at the depot here. Not yet, anyway." Ingrid slumped in relief. "Fenris! We'll be moved to our private hangar momentarily."

"Finally!" Fenris groused. "I need to tear into that stub wing again and—"

"License numbers first," said Cy.

Fenris's face twisted in disgust as he scurried past Ingrid down the hall. "My poor ship, not even airborne a month, and already living under a false identity."

"That's what happens when you associate with the wrong sorts of people," said Ingrid, earning a soft snort of amusement from him.

Cy set a stack of newspapers beside her. "I didn't even get a chance to skim beyond the front covers, but it looks like *Excalibur* has come to dominate the news."

Indeed, the vessel was shown in a picture on the topmost paper. "I'll take a look," she said, feeling the need to reassure him. His smile was tight as he turned to exit the ship. Fenris followed.

Ingrid opened up the top paper, dated three days before. She had started on the next paper when the airship began to move. It was an odd sensation with the engines off and no one else aboard. She yearned to peer out the window to witness the ground crew pulling on the lines and guiding the ship into the private hangar, but she remained sitting in her bunk with her legs set indecently wide for balance.

By the time Cy and Fenris came aboard again, she'd gone through the papers and was more than ready to head to the ground.

A simple one-flight staircase had been locked into place against the open hatch door. She slowly descended in her elastic-rigged boots, staff in hand. The small hangar was sized for a Sprite-class ship, and stank of dust, oil, and the lingering mustiness of machinery.

"How's the earth feel?" Cy asked as he hopped down the stairs.

"Normal. Los Angeles has fault lines aplenty, but there are a few geomancers stationed here to harvest from the flow."

"Any of them see auras?" Cy asked sharply.

"No. That's a rare skill. Rarer now," she added softly, thinking of Hatsumi.

"Good." His brusqueness shocked her. "A person should feel regret over ending a life, but don't waste any more time feeling guilty over Hatsumi's death. He would've sentenced you to a life of torture that'd have caused countless more deaths, had he been able to go through with his plan."

She bowed her head. He'd said as much to her several times since they'd left Hilo. Whenever she'd drawn quiet and stared into the distance, he'd read her thoughts, sure as any book. "I skimmed through the newspapers."

Cy walked to the side of the hangar where supplies had already been delivered in wait of this second docking. "Tell me all as I ferry these to the stairs."

"Foremost, I didn't find any word of your father, Cy. I'm sorry. Mentions of San Francisco were confined to local fundraisers for money or goods to send to refugees."

Cy paused, a hand on more boxes. "I think I've come to accept that he's dead." His voice sounded oddly empty. "That part of downtown was obliterated by the earthquake and then consumed by the fire. I saw it from the air. I saw it from the ground. I know what happened to the people there." He shrugged, a helpless gesture. Tears stung Ingrid's eyes. "If anything, we can hope that Captain Sutcliff was caught up in it, too." He shook his head, a hand to his forehead. "No. I shouldn't say that, not even about him. God help me."

"The other headlines didn't bring any surprises," she continued, worried that Cy would fall into a dark mood if she didn't distract him. "Baranov figures prominently in articles and in ads for transports or supplies. There've been more Thuggee attacks in India, and subsequent British retaliations. Atlanta's been hit by a bad influenza that has caused a quarantine and shut down a lot of manufacturing there. Then, of course, there's talk of the Chinese."

"I can imagine how that reads," he said over his armful of supplies.

"Yes." Ingrid thought of how Mr. Sakaguchi had recently railed against people who debated the citizenship rights of the Chinese. Now editorials questioned their very humanity—questioned if they had a right to exist in America or anywhere at all. She couldn't grasp that way of thinking. How could someone look at Lee and deny that he was a living, breathing human being? But then, Ingrid knew some people regarded her in the same light. As *other*. As *less*. People like Warden Hatsumi. Her stomach twisted.

"Ingrid." The sharpness of her name dragged her back to the present. "Did you see anything about yourself in the paper?"

"No. I even looked through the Deserters sections. As for *Excalibur*, an advertisement for a theater in downtown caught my eye. It's showing a newsreel of the latest footage of *Excalibur* every Monday and Friday. You said the nearby tracks take us straight into the downtown station, right?"

He paused, thoughtful. "Yes. The Pacific Electric line goes right to Main Street Station." Their moorage at Dominguez Field was not along the coast like the major stops for freight and passengers. The way Cy described it, the clientele here wasn't *exactly* dealing with black-market goods, but most folks passing through minded their own business. That was both a blessing and a curse, as it meant Blum's agents might keep an eye on such a place, too. Fortunately, there were probably a hundred other docks like this in Southern California alone.

"Seeing some footage of *Excalibur* in action would be mighty helpful," he muttered. "Better than a mere article. I need to shop in downtown, anyway. We need to reach out to Roosevelt's contact here."

Fact was, they needed money. Their trip to Hawaii had cost far more than anticipated, and the private hangar was another major expense. Cy's plans for her braces would send them into debt, even without the use of orichalcum.

"I still think we should sell some kermanite. With the supply at the Cordilleran gone and the geomancers in two West Coast auxiliaries exterminated, we'd make a fair mint." She almost managed to speak of the incidents in a blasé, businesslike tone.

"That's a last resort. Your health comes first, and we need kermanite handy."

"One more thing. A paper made mention of strange submarines being spotted off the coast of Southern California.

An official from the UP said the fishermen had probably spotted whales."

"I can imagine what the fishermen would have to say about that." Cy pursed his lips in thought. "Before Lee parted ways with us at the rink in Seattle, I talked with him about what might possibly happen if Uncle Moon didn't let him leave, where the Chinese might go from there. Los Angeles was one of the most likely destinations. With that in mind, I asked him to memorize a mailbox number I maintain in the city. That way, no matter where he ended up, he might be able to send a note our way."

"Why didn't you tell me this before?" Her voice rose in both aggravation and excitement.

He gave her a pointed look. "Because I didn't want to get up your hopes without need. Because the last time we saw Lee, he was a breath away from death. And even if he recovered, he'd likely be kept under close watch."

The possibility of a message from Lee made her want to run as fast as she could for the rail depot. "We'll be checking this box when we go out, then?"

His lips quirked at her intentional use of "we." "I reckoned we would, yes. You'll need to do your utmost to remain nonchalant, whatever we find."

"I understand," she said softly, even as her thoughts turned to fervent prayers to God, the *qilin,* to any kind entity who might pay heed to her desperation.

"Fenris! Will you be okay if we make a run into town?" Cy called.

After a few dense thuds, Fenris bounded down the hatch

steps to stand at the top of the stairs, the airship hovering above his head. "I'll be fine without the two of you underfoot, yes. If our current pattern holds, we'll need to skedaddle from Los Angeles as if a swarm of wyverns is on our tail. I want to have the ship ready to fly by nightfall."

"Let's hope we break that pattern at last," said Cy, grimacing.

"I'm not about to rely on some airy concept of *hope*." He started back up the stairs. His head was inside the *Bug*, causing his voice to echo strangely. "When you're out, make sure you get more pastries. See if you can bring back some tamales, too." He headed on up.

"What's a tamale?" Ingrid asked.

Cy grinned. "I reckon you'll find out today."

INGRID HAD OFTEN HEARD LOS ANGELES DESCRIBED IN GLOWING terms—glorious sunny days, mild winters, fresh citrus, etc. Instead, as she ventured out with Cy, she encountered a cool, drizzly May day. The weather suited her quite nicely, as it reminded her of home. The rain also gave her an excuse to wear her slicker and keep the hood up, which made her feel safer, more anonymous.

No conductors hassled Ingrid as she boarded the bright red Pacific Electric railcar. She found it surprisingly clean. Many of the occupants were women in work attire, some with children in tow.

Cy wore rugged yet clean work clothes beneath his leather coat, his battered bowler hat on his lap. "It's not that long of a ride," he murmured, "though it looks like we're in the middle of nowhere."

The train began to move with a harsh squeal. The view through the windows showed that the Dominguez dock was set up on a mesa. Rolling grasslands spread out all around, demarcated by a gridlike pattern of dirt roads, groves of eucalyptus and citrus, and scattered bungalow roofs.

Cy leaned toward the window, his gaze on the sky. "I heard news in Dominguez that pilots have sighted peculiar glints, like heat mirages, way up high. Some say it's a type of dragon that's cloaked itself, or some kind of Hidden One."

Ingrid frowned at him. "These sightings are brand-new?" She used to make a hobby of studying fantastics, and this didn't sound familiar to her.

"Yes. At least a dozen cases in the past week, all along the California coast. I even saw a bulletin for someone gathering a hunting party."

"Good God," she muttered. "They don't even know what kind of fantastic it is, but they want to kill it and tack it on a wall. That figures." She shifted in her seat. She didn't want to spy some mysterious creature in the sky; she'd had enough bizarre sightings recently to last her a lifetime. Besides, she'd be much better served by keeping a wary eye on her fellow passengers.

"I'm scared, Ingrid." The words were barely decipherable. Surprised, she turned to look at him. "Being here on the mainland, feeling vulnerable every moment of the day. Wanting these braces to work and offer you the mobility you need. The quest to come."

"I'm scared, too," she murmured. "I like how you call it a quest, though. That makes me think of paladins and wizards and dangerous journeys to the moon."

That brought a smile to his face. "I reckon we have enough troubles on earth. Let's leave the moon out of it."

She couldn't hold his hand, much as she wanted to, but took comfort in how their hips touched in the seat. Amazing, really, how good it felt to be in the mere proximity of someone who loved you.

It didn't take long for them to enter the thick of the city. She craned her head to take in the view of the famed Main Street Station. The building was Los Angeles's first skyscraper and the largest building in the city—indeed, the largest building west of Chicago, if Behemoth-sized airship hangars were left out of the reckoning. Ingrid and Cy exited the railcar and passed through a marble-tiled hallway to emerge in a waiting room with soaring, painted ceilings and gilded ornamentation. A wall featured a stunningly realistic depiction of an ancient Roman imperial airship over golden hills that could either be in Italy or California. Voices echoed and rumbled together in the grand space. Cy's discreet tug on her sleeve reminded her not to stand around like a slack-jawed yokel. She scurried to keep up.

Halfway through the chamber, she felt the tickle of nearby magic at the same time as she began to hear whispers.

Just above her: *ingrid carmichael her magic tastes like hot rocks*

Across the room, barely audible: *she's not here*

To her left: *ingrid carmichael her magic tastes like hot rocks*

On her right: *she's not here*

The words surrounded her on all sides, identical in voice, some close, some soft and distant. The signature musk of Blum's power was unmistakable.

"Mr. Harvey," she said.

Cy glanced back, a hand resting near his Tesla rod. "Yes, Mrs. Harvey?"

"I do like that name. You should call me by it all the time."

He nodded, taking her hint. "I will as long as you desire."

"Watch what you say. As you know, I have many desires." Her attempt at levity rang flat even for her, scared as she was.

Whatever sought her in the station was broadcasting *how* it was supposed to find her, essentially reading its orders from Blum out loud. Blum had no idea just how sensitive Ingrid was to fantastics and magic. That advantage just might save her yet again.

She casually glanced around. The voices were stationary. From what she could ascertain, two originated from nearby pillars, while three more were near major doors into the building. The ploy made sense. Why send agents to search hundreds of individual docks across California when traps could be laid at major metropolitan junctions like Main Street Station?

Ingrid had no desire to spring the trap, but she did need to take a closer look.

She altered her trajectory to pass by one of the pillars. "Mr. Harvey, if you don't mind, glance along that column to see if anything looks peculiar about ten feet up, the side facing the window."

She didn't stare upward, but continued to mosey along. She carried no power at the moment. The beings shouldn't be able to sniff her out. She hoped.

Her fierce heartbeat drummed behind the repetition of her name and her magical signature. She passed by the column. Nothing in the chant changed. Cy craned his head up and all around, doing a fine job of playing a tenderfoot in the big city.

"I caught a gander of a small fox figurine, painted white to blend in with the column itself," he murmured, his voice dim against the loudness of so many people.

In Japan, foxes—living or as statues—were said to be messengers to the kami Inari, worshipped in both Buddhist and Shinto faiths. It made sense for Blum to somehow enchant fox idols to be messengers for her as well. *What other traps has she laid?* Ingrid thought, sick with dread. She had been lucky this time. Next time . . .

The echoes decreased when they stepped outside, but the overall noise did not. The city pulsed around them. Electric streetcars clanged and rattled from nearby tracks, horseshoes clip-clopped on the asphalt pavement, autocars whirred and sputtered, and newsboys hollered.

She welcomed the metropolitan cacophony. It was familiar.

They passed a corner that hosted a cluster of singing Salvation Army soldiers in their usual attire. Cy lingered long enough to toss some coins in a cymbal that was being passed around to collect donations.

"Is it safe to talk here?" Cy asked as they crossed the street. A hymn in fine harmony rang out behind them.

"Yes. We are out of the range of those . . . things, in any case." She explained their placement throughout the room. He listened, brow furrowed.

"She knows you well, to assume you'd carry yourself prepared for any situation."

Ingrid rather liked that as a publicly acceptable way to reference her magic. "One of the soldiers' reports from Hilo must have mentioned how Hatsumi recognized me. She can't deploy sensitive geomancers to stand guard at major transportation centers, so those figurines are her substitute."

She dreaded to think of what would have happened if they had recognized her. Would they have sounded an alarm? Attacked her?

"Similar traps may be set at larger docks and train depots across the west. They might even show up in Dominguez."

"I'll remain vigilant," she said softly. "We'll need to catch the electric rail line elsewhere, if we can."

Ingrid looked around, taking in the sights and the people around her. The sense of space was different here than in San Francisco, where the density of humanity and the steepness of the hills made everything feel tight. Los Angeles was a fairly flat city that had only begun to grow in the past twenty years, and it showed. Like Honolulu, it had a sparkling newness to it, even with the grime of exhaust and the stench of factory fumes. While Main Street Station's Huntington Building was the largest structure around in height and width, other towers rose high above a maze of flat and angled rooftops, church spires, brick chimneys, telegraph poles, and palm trees. The Japanese architectural influence was surprisingly minimal.

They walked onward. Cy paused at an autocar mechanic's shop tucked along an alley, where he spent a few pennies for a new map of Los Angeles. Deep black lines showed city streets, with the electric rail lines in blue and red. She was relieved to find there were several good alternate stops to get them back to Dominguez.

With a few glances at the map, they walked around the block to a post office. Ingrid's anxiety from the rail station had just begun to subside, and now she felt jittery anew.

Cy had written a letter to Roosevelt's contact in the city. He dropped that in the mailbox at the doorway as he entered; Ingrid followed him inside. The rented box was located far at the back. He worked a code to unlock it and withdrew a small pile of letters.

"We're not going through it here," he murmured with a wary glance around. The hallway of mailboxes dead-ended to their right. Ingrid nodded, and clenched her fists to resist the urge to impatiently grab the stack from him.

They found a spot just outside and tucked in the shadows beside an alley that stank of sweet rot. Cy angled the envelopes so they could both see. He flipped past an advertisement, a catalog, another flyer, and finally to a letter in an envelope so small it almost slipped from his grip. He caught it just in time.

"That's his handwriting." Ingrid's throat was tight with emotion. The address was written in a hand that was somewhat unsteady, not unlike her own handwriting these days, but still distinctively Lee's.

Cy slit it open with his pocketknife. A slip of paper the size of a baseball card was inside. The chicken-scratch writing in soft pencil read:

In city. Mount Whitney Building on Tringa. Guard dogs. Basement cabinet 36C. For Cy and Fenris.

"That's it?" she asked, and Cy flipped it over to reveal part of a typed business invoice. She blinked fast to hold back tears. Lee was alive, alive, alive! She could only hope that Mr. Sakaguchi was still with him. She gave Cy's hand a discreet squeeze, unable to release her emotions in any other way, even sheltered as they were in the alley.

"That's it. And it's plenty." Cy tucked the letter into his shirt pocket, his grin exuberant. For all his caution about acting nonchalant, he couldn't hold back his own relief. "I'll need to burn that later."

"Lee *is* in the city. Or was. Where's that address?"

"There's no date on the note and the postmark was smeared, so there's no telling when he sent that along. He might be long gone." Cy kept a wary eye on their surroundings. "We'll check the map later, and maybe we can find the actual building tonight."

"By saying 'we,' you had better be including me. I'm the one who can directly converse with the sylphs, and yes, I'm quite aware of how dangerous the trip will be, especially if Lee's friends are around." She chose her words carefully.

BETH CATO

"I'm not much inclined to trussing you up in the hangar, and that's what I think it'd take to leave you behind," he murmured, a twinkle to his eye. "But I should add, we don't know the circumstances behind this note."

"Meaning?"

Cy sobered. "It could be a trap." He gestured to the street and they began to walk.

Horrible as the idea was, it had merit. Uncle Moon knew Ingrid was a woman of unusual magical skill. He'd be fine with exploiting her—and Lee—if they could help his people survive. Lee wouldn't want to set a trap for them, but he might not have had much choice. He relied on Uncle Moon's *lingqi* to recover right now, and Mr. Sakaguchi's well-being could be used to control him, too.

They continued down the next block before Cy spoke up again. "I hope we hear from T.R.'s folks in the next few days. I'm antsy about lingering here too long. In the meantime, I might look for some odd jobs around the dock as I work on your braces."

"If there's a kitchen nearby, I could work, too. I can do *something*."

The look that Cy gave her almost broke her heart. "Even if you could stand for a duration without your leg seizing," he said quietly, "you're a kind and true woman. Can you befriend new folks and lie about who you are, where you're from?"

She tightened her grip on the staff. She still wore the wedding band on her left hand. Marriage between them wouldn't be possible in California, but the sentiment of the ring was true nevertheless. "I don't know how you endured this kind of life for years."

"Pretty simple, really. We tried to keep to ourselves, and when we did form attachments to places and people, we knew it was time to move on."

"You moved an awful lot."

"Yes."

"I suppose it's a good thing I threw in my lot with you two. Otherwise, you might have borrowed those Twain books and run."

"You should know by now that I'd *never* abscond with someone's books. I'd be sure to return them, even if by mail." They shared a fond smile, then at the same time noticed a bakery across the street.

"I've never tried Mexican pastries," she murmured as they crossed over.

"I believe they'll meet your approval, and that of our other companions."

The shop had little stock left, but they bought a full bag that mostly consisted of shell-shaped cookie-topped buns called *conchas* that Cy swore were similar to Japanese melon-pan. That was enough to entice Ingrid.

That important errand done, they rounded the block to their next destination. They found the nickel cinema tucked between a cigar shop and a pharmacy. Cy paid the fee, and they passed through a short hallway to the theater. Half the seats were already full. Folding metal chairs formed crooked rows, the chair legs squeaking and scraping the floor as people sat. Most occupants were working-class men, but there were also scads of young boys in knickerbockers and caps—undoubtedly in attendance because of the advertised footage of *Excalibur.*

Cy found them two seats at the end of a back row. More people filed in. The room stank of sweat and rank bodies and cigarettes and cloying perfume.

After a few minutes, a hatted man sat at the piano at the front of the room. Ingrid waited to see if anyone else would emerge.

"They don't use benshi here?" she murmured, referring to the performers who often read the title cards during motion pictures in San Francisco.

"I reckon not. There's not as much Japanese influence around here."

He had a point. The use of benshi stemmed from traditional Japanese theater like Noh. Ingrid had grown up listening to benshi and had assumed most American screenings used the technique nowadays.

The crowd rumbled and hushed as the lights blinked out and the pianist began to play. Projector images flickered to life on the slightly askew screen.

A jaunty tune accompanied images of flowers and a verse on the virtues of spring, followed by baseball news from around the country. Team names evoked cheers and groans. The grainy footage made it difficult to tell one man from another. The fog of tobacco smoke didn't help either.

The seat ahead of Ingrid barely contained a boy of about seven. His legs swung nonstop, the chair wobbling with each sway. She found herself looking at him more than at the screen.

He was at the age when a slim percentage of the population manifested geomancy or other magical aptitudes. But he was likely normal. He'd grow up here, a bright future ahead . . . maybe. Or in another ten years, he could be sent off to war like so many other young men were these days. To die or be maimed or to simply vanish in some bombardment of hell-fire.

That was one kind of grief she'd be spared, she supposed. She couldn't have children; she could never contribute to the war in *that* way.

Her infertility had never bothered her until Blum informed her that the alteration was surgical, not natural. Now she thought of it at random times, haunted by a future that could never exist.

If they found Mr. Sakaguchi tonight, what would happen? The Chinese likely would be more reluctant to part ways with him now that he'd agreed to fill kermanite for their cause. If she got to talk to him, what would she say? That she loved him, certainly. But how would she broach the subject of her . . . sterilization? She already knew how he'd justify it—her monthly pains would have aggravated Hidden Ones, and the agony of childbirth would have likely had catastrophic consequences, even with other geomancers nearby to absorb the energy released by the earth's agitation.

That didn't lessen her anger, her grief, that he and Mama had taken something precious from her . . . and from Cy, too. Really, that bothered her most of all. Cy had already lost so much. She would have loved to have been able to provide him with something more.

Cy nudged her with an elbow. She pulled her gaze up to the screen as the pianist began to play a martial tune. The framed white text of the intertitle read:

BEHOLD! AMERICA'S *EXCALIBUR*!

The boys in the row ahead whispered and wiggled.

The words were replaced by a moving picture of a massive crowd adorned in hats, with many of the people waving Unified Pacific flags. The view panned up to show an island floating in the sky. No, not a mere island—a castle, a Mont Saint-Michel with a thick keep and multitude of towers. The sheen of its orichalcum hull boldly stood out against the pale sky. It looked like an impossibility, a whimsical toy created on some studio lot in New Jersey and somehow spliced onto the film.

A woman in the cinema emitted a loud gasp.

MADE IN ATLANTA BY AMERICAN LABOR, A SECRET EFFORT YEARS IN THE MAKING! FACTORIES WORKING ON PIECES, NEVER KNOWING HOW THEY WOULD FIT TOGETHER—UNTIL NOW!

"It *is* impressive how it was kept secret," Cy whispered. "Though I wonder at the true conditions of that 'American labor.' So many Chinese have been sent to Georgia in recent years, under the auspices of labor contracts . . ."

"You think it was more akin to prison labor?" she whispered, aghast.

"I suspect so. Many companies have inhumanely treated their workers as they compete with Augustinian. How would they treat those they don't regard as truly human? Numbers of Chinese have simply vanished. The dead keep their secrets very well." His face looked gray in the light reflected from the screen.

THE WAR MACHINE TO CONQUER CHINA, TO QUELL THE AMBI-
TIONS OF CZARS, KINGS, AND QUEENS! BEHOLD THE WHITE CLOUD
FLEET.

The footage changed. *Excalibur* looked different, its shiny
orichalcum now painted white. Against the daytime sky, it
scarcely showed up on film, but it still looked like a toy. There
was no sense of its size or scale.

"See the faint white spots around the citadel?" Cy whispered. "Pegasus gunships, I reckon. All in that special paint
to make them less visible." He shook his head. "Early on in
the war, the UP painted airship bellies black so that they
didn't reflect spotlights at night and attract gunfire. The
Chinese can't counterattack in any such way now."

Below *Excalibur* lay a grassy plain not unlike the area just
south of Los Angeles proper. A cow grazed, oblivious to the
hulking technological wonder above.

Black blurs dropped from beneath *Excalibur*, followed by
an unfurling, expanding cloud. The cow lifted its head and
began a clumsy, panicked run almost directly at the camera.

The boys in the crowd howled in delight.

Ingrid felt herself slip into a memory. Hoofbeats thundered through pavement. The cows set free by the earthquake stampeded through downtown San Francisco, their
eyes wild. A man was caught among the churning bodies, his
body tossed upward and then vanishing in the crush.

Cy gripped her hand, hard. "Stay with me, here and now,"
he whispered. Only then did she realize how she had started
gasping for breath. Sweat soaked her dress. His hand was
likewise slick. Their eyes met. She saw that he was warring

with his own memory of that awful day. She managed a small nod, and he released his grip.

EXCALIBUR CAN DROP A PAYLOAD DIRECTLY BELOW, BUT IT CAN ALSO MOOR AIRSHIPS AT MASTS AT VARIOUS LEVELS! BEHEMOTH CLASS, PEGASUS, SPRITE: THERE ARE MASTS FOR THEM ALL!

The view showed a close-up of *Excalibur;* judging by the shaky footage, it was shot from another airship on approach. Dark windows freckled the pale citadel. A dozen towers encircled the central keep. Their curvature reminded Ingrid of the sleek, undulating surface of Durendals. Cy leaned forward on his thighs, his gaze narrowing.

THE MOORAGES ARE PROTECTED BY GUNMEN WHO CAN STRIKE TARGETS OVER A HALF MILE AWAY.

The airship docked, and the footage skipped ahead to show a line of men with billowing coats, hands on their hats to keep them from blowing away. Their movements jerked in an unnaturally fast way, as if they were marionettes bleached in shades of gray. They walked along a parapet, past massive guns and soldiers at parade rest. The camera skipped again to a closer shot of a soldier swiveling around a deck-mounted gun with a tapered barrel. The view shifted inside a spacious cargo bay. Several Durendals sat in a row.

EXCALIBUR CAN CARRY A HUNDRED TANKS AND AUTOCARS, UP TO TEN THOUSAND SOLDIERS, AND ENOUGH SUPPLIES TO SUSTAIN THEM FOR MONTHS! THERE ARE EVEN GARDENS ABOARD, FED BY RAINWATER CONTAINMENT.

The screen showed a broad greenhouse unlike any Ingrid had seen before. The camera moved to show the massive space—the length of an airship hangar, perhaps—but with a ten-foot ceiling. Low tables of plants stretched out in a multitude of long rows, followed by more rows of floor-to-ceiling pillars with tiers of vegetation growing along the lengths of the columns.

The view switched to a map, a dashed line showing a route from Atlanta across the southern states.

EXCALIBUR IS IN TEXAS TODAY. SOON ENOUGH IT WILL BE IN CALIFORNIA, WHERE OUR BOYS AWAIT A RIDE OVERSEAS!

What looked to be thousands of troops stood in perfect formation in a field. At some signal, they all began waving, some even jumping up in the air. A band marched along, its members' jerky movements discordant with the tune played by the theater piano.

WATCH OUT, CHINAMEN! AMERICAN-MADE JUSTICE IS ON THE WAY.

A cluster of cherubic children waved fistfuls of flags, American and Japanese colors together.

A man at the front stood up as he applauded, blocking the screen; more applause scattered the room. The piano music abruptly stopped. The screen flickered and went blank. Ingrid felt flattened against her chair, unwilling to move even though the hard metal seat made her backside ache.

Somehow she, Cy, and Fenris had to stop *that*. The craft already being dubbed the technological innovation of the twentieth century. How could they infiltrate it? Stop it with minimal deaths and damage to those below? The task seemed impossible, and Ingrid had become something of an authority in confronting and surviving the impossible.

The next reel began with sober, soft piano keys.

SAN FRANCISCO. WE REMEMBER. WE MOURN.

A wagon rolled down a wide street flanked with piles of rubble that almost blocked the thoroughfare. It passed by a decapitated statue with upraised arms—but only one arm was intact, pointing toward heaven as if in admonishment.

Ingrid knew that statue. This was along Market Street. The wagon followed the streetcar tracks. There should be a Bank of Italy across the way. The French bakery the next corner down had the best croissants. And there was a barbershop with a swirling pole, and a restaurant that often blared a Marconi so loud it could be heard from a block distant.

Gone. All gone.

She stood, Cy following her a second later. He led the way out through the minuscule lobby. The afternoon light blinded her as she stepped onto the sidewalk. She took in a deep breath, gladly taking in the foulness of autocar exhaust and a whiff of manure in a gutter nearby. Those scents were better than falling into memories of the distinct malodor of collapsed buildings with the fog of pulverized bricks still in the air and shattered wood and the dankness of leaking pipes, and smoke, smoke so pungent she'd never fully wash it away.

"I'm better now," she said, and wondered if she was lying to herself.

He was quiet for a long moment, considering her. Rain dribbled down, and Ingrid pulled up her hood. Cy tucked the pastry bag beneath his coat.

"If the rain's coming in again, we should head on back.

You up to eating? We can grab tamales from a yatai on the way."

"You never did explain what a tamale was," Ingrid said, relieved to change the subject. "Is it some kind of bird?"

He chuckled, and kept chuckling as they began to walk. "Good God. I needed that."

"I'm glad my ignorance serves a purpose." Her own laugh was shaky. "To see *Excalibur*, then to see Market Street, like that . . ."

"We're here. We're together. Alive and free," he said softly. "And tonight you'll dine on tamales. Pork, if we can find it. And pie, too. The carts often sell pie. You'll see yatai everywhere in downtown once evening starts, and they stay out until after midnight. Some of the stands are little more than wheelbarrows loaded with hot stones and food parcels, but what they serve up is practically divine, and for mere pennies."

"That sounds perfect," she said, and stayed quiet as Cy babbled on, working out his own anxiety through talk of ground corn and husk-wrapped deliciousness and the food cart where he found the most amazing slice of pecan pie one time.

Her thoughts drifted back to the cinema and the juxtaposition of *Excalibur* and San Francisco. If the citadel completed its journey, it'd leave cities razed in just the same way. All at the behest of Ambassador Blum.

And Blum would use Ingrid for the same purpose, if she caught her. With *Excalibur* and Ingrid in her arsenal, the Unified Pacific would rule the world.

Ingrid could not let that happen. God willing, they'd find a way to do the impossible and stop that machine. Stop Cy's sister. Ingrid would continue her fight to stay free, to fight for peace.

But for now: tamales, and perhaps some pie.

CHAPTER 11

The address supplied by Lee was in a newer business district, one with fresh paint and mud-packed streets. A lack of streetlights left Ingrid feeling conspicuous as they walked along. The sylphs followed at a distance of twenty feet. They weren't drawing on their inherent magic but were almost invisible just the same, gray smudges that most anyone could dismiss on this night without stars.

"This is it," Cy muttered. The block-shaped structure featured black lettering that read MOUNT WHITNEY BUILDING. "You two wait here for a few as I take a gander round back." He left them at the opening of an alley across the street. His leather coat gleamed briefly in the darkness, then he was gone.

"Lovely night for breaking and entering," murmured Fenris. He kept his hands tucked into a corduroy overshirt that looked two sizes too big, more suited for a husky farmer. However, it did an adequate job of hiding the Tesla rod sheathed at his hip.

"I suppose it's good weather for all varieties of chicanery." The sylphs roosted on the roof above. In the distance, dogs barked. Ingrid gnawed on her lip for a moment then faced Fenris. "You reviewed Cy's latest plans for my braces earlier, but you didn't say much. What do you really think? Can you two create a workable prototype in time?"

"*Excalibur* is like a ticking doomsday clock, isn't it?" Fenris fidgeted, frowning. "So many things look plausible on paper, but reality is considerably more complicated. These braces need to effectively support you *and* be comfortable enough to wear." He paused, and they both listened as more dogs struck up a fuss. "The latter is the tricky part, the one that will take more time to get right. I agree that orichalcum is the best metal, though. Not for the bulletproofing—though that's a nice perk—but because it's strong and light."

"This kind of project isn't quite the same as your incredibly fast airship assembly work, I suppose."

"That's proven technology. I based the *Bug* on existing machinery and innovated from there. When it comes to you, Ingrid, nothing is proven."

She softly snorted in reply. There was no point arguing with that statement.

Footsteps pattered in the puddles. Cy emerged from the shadows. "There's no outward sign of folks around. Back lot is empty." He motioned them forward.

They fell into an agreed-upon order, with Cy in the lead, followed by Ingrid and Fenris. The sylphs trailed them. Cy walked up to the building and around a shed to a side door. The neighboring business cast a deep shadow over them.

Cy pulled out his Tesla rod and gave it a twist. Thin blue light shone from the crystal tip. Ingrid dryly swallowed and fought against the memory of how that very rod had burned her skin to form the ward against Blum. There'd been no pain, but the stench of her searing flesh, the very act of harming herself in such a way . . . She shuddered, turning her attention back to the door.

"Maybe it's wired on the inside," Fenris muttered. "Window might be alarmed, too."

"Or it might not be." Cy held up a hand for silence. A soft canine whine carried through the door, followed by the sound of claws scratching on wood.

"They're not barking!" Ingrid said, grinning.

Cy managed a tense smile. "Did you notice, we didn't have a single dog bark at us as we walked together? As soon as I walked around the block by myself, though, I was getting barked at from almost every other yard."

She pressed a hand to her chest where she had painted the kanji of inu to utilize dog sorcery again. This time she didn't inlay an enchantment to ward against kitsune, but instead reinforced that she and those with her were friends to dogs.

"You think the dogs are the first line of defense, then?" she asked.

"I surely hope so. I'm reluctant to use the radio flash, in any case. If the Chinese *are* protecting something here, I want their security to continue to work against other burglars."

"My turn to work, then?" At Cy's nod, Fenris pulled out a lockpicking set. Using the thin light of the Tesla rod, he twiddled with the doorknob.

"I'd like to hear more stories about your decade on the run from the UP sometime," Ingrid murmured. "You both certainly acquired an interesting variety of skills for mild-mannered machinists."

"You may not like those stories," Cy said.

"Oh, come now. Ingrid would surely approve of your Robin Hood–like antics, Cy." The door emitted a small click and Fenris's face lit up with a grin.

The conversation was forgotten as Cy reached for the doorknob. He gave them grim nods and slowly opened the door outward. Ingrid scarcely breathed. Through the gap, three Dobermans bounced in eagerness to greet them.

"Down, down," Ingrid hissed, gesturing. The dogs sat, tails still wiggling.

"Was that the magic, or do they know English commands?" Cy asked, opening the door wider to inspect the room ahead.

"By command. That drew nothing from my fever." She had absorbed energy from a few small pieces of kermanite to wield the dog sorcery and converse with the sylphs, and carried more with her as a precaution. Blum's trap at the station had left her leery of holding too much power.

She beckoned the sylphs forward. They balked. "The sylphs don't want to follow us. They don't like dogs or enclosed spaces. They'll wait here."

Fenris closed the door, inspecting it as he did so. "Just

a lock here. The windows on either side, though, do have alarms."

The room appeared to be an average office space, with several desks, shelves, and stacked boxes. Ingrid scrutinized the dogs and tried extending her awareness over them, as she did with the sylphs. To her delight, it worked. Images and emotions flashed through her mind.

"The dogs are well fed and cared for, just lonely during the night. There's no one else here."

She blinked back tears of disappointment. Where were Lee and Mr. Sakaguchi?

Cy, however, sagged with relief. "Good. We don't have to fuss about direct confrontations."

"No, just traps that may electrocute or poison us," said Fenris. "That's all."

"The dogs don't expect people until sunrise." She scratched a Doberman's head, her hand well licked in turn. She was glad for her staff, as the dogs' enthusiasm might otherwise have toppled her. "Even if my sorcery wears away, I think the dogs have accepted us. We shouldn't have any problems with them as we exit."

"One less worry, then. Let's find our way to the basement."

They found the access tucked at the back of a storage room. Furniture had been stacked in front of the door, hiding it. Cy and Fenris shifted the items over just far enough to allow them passage.

"I have a hunch that the folks who work here during the day haven't a clue what their basement is being used for," said Cy.

Fenris crouched to pick the lock.

As the door swung open, the dogs backed away, whining. "That's not a good sign, is it?"

Cy looked to Ingrid. "What do they know that we don't?"

She frowned. "Something smells bad to them. Can you smell anything?"

They murmured in the negative. Ingrid's unease increased tenfold.

The stairs griped underfoot, every sound as loud as a scream. The Tesla rod provided their only light, its blue glow spectral. The steps were shallow, forcing Ingrid to slowly ease down sideways while relying on her staff for support, as there were no rails.

They reached a corner landing. The light revealed a short flight downward, and a large empty space beyond. A presence prickled at her, as if she'd fallen into blackberry vines.

"There's a fantastic out there," she whispered. "Something . . . powerful. It's completely still, about fifteen feet dead ahead of us. It's . . . angry. Focusing on us."

Cy did not move. Behind her, Fenris shifted to pull out his own Tesla rod.

"It's not moving. I don't think it *can* move." She frowned, closing her eyes and focusing. Whatever this was, it didn't draw on elemental magic like selkies or thunderbirds. Instead, it exuded a strange combination of heat from magic, but coldness within its physical being. "I'm reminded of the two-headed snake—it's cold like that—but this doesn't have that kind of ancient presence or great size."

"Something serpentine, but young, angry, and unmoving?" Cy asked.

"This sounds like a dangerous sort of children's guessing game," said Fenris.

"Shush." Remembering the sorcery in place on her body, Ingrid *listened,* as a dog listens. "Hissing. I hear lots of soft hissing. Not at floor level. About head height, I'd say."

"God Almighty." Cy breathed out the words. "Do they have a gorgon's head playing guard?"

Ingrid's gaze dropped to the floor. "A gorgon? Like *Medusa?*"

"One of her line. She was the only mortal gorgon of the three in Greek mythology. I've heard of gorgon heads being used to guard valuables in Europe, but how did the Chinese get hold of one?"

"The Chinese are scattered all over the world," said Fenris. "Why not pick up a gorgon's head as a souvenir of your travels? It's more useful than an engraved spoon."

Ingrid extended a greeting via magic. Her reply: a lash of fiery rage. She tried again. The very essence of the creature tried to snap at her as if with a hundred fanged mouths.

"There's no heartbeat. No ability to speak. No *desire* to speak." A chill went through her. "How horrible, to be used in such a way."

"That's how fantastics are treated, Ingrid," Cy said softly. "You know that."

She did. And she hated it. "I suppose we need to follow the example of Perseus. There was a mirror in the facilities upstairs. We can use that to get close enough to cover the head."

"Question," said Fenris, holding up a hand. "Are we certain what's down here is worth the risk of perhaps turning into a statue?"

Ingrid wanted to laugh at that—the idea that they were standing in a stairwell seriously debating whether or not to risk getting transformed into stone.

"Lee wouldn't have wanted you to endanger yourself." Cy's gaze on Ingrid was sober and eerie in the scant light.

"Whatever is down here must be important for us to find. Lee couldn't have been aware of the trap they were setting."

"Ingrid. You know Lee may not have had much choice in laying the bait."

"That may be true, but I don't think that's what happened here. Uncle Moon wouldn't want me turned into a statue. He'd want me alive so I could help his cause. And he'd want you alive, Cy, in order to control me."

Cy conceded the point with a grim nod.

"As far as I'm concerned, the presence of the gorgon is further proof that there's something important here, and I intend to find it." She glanced toward the darkness. Now that she knew what to listen for, she could hear the headful of hissing snakes. "I can take care of the gorgon. Even if I'm blindfolded, I can sense exactly where it is and what it's doing. I can uncover it again when we leave so that it can still do its job."

Cy looked aghast. She glared at Fenris. "Come now, where's your rebuttal?"

He shrugged. "You've made up your mind. Just know that I'm not hauling around a statue of you in the *Bug*. You'd go well over our weight allowance."

"I can't jest about this," said Cy tightly.

"Then don't," she said, giving his arm a soft stroke as she

started up the stairs again. "Fenris, will you give me a hand with supplies?"

Not far from the door, they found a length of gray-stained rag to cover her eyes, and a gunnysack that didn't allow light to shine through.

"Be careful," Cy said as he knotted the blindfold at the back of her head.

"I will be. Stone skin wouldn't suit me one bit." As she spoke, she wondered what happened if a person was bitten by the snakes of a gorgon. She couldn't recall that being addressed in the old tales, and she certainly wasn't going to broach the question to Cy.

"Can you see this?" he asked.

"I can't see anything except the color black." She touched the blindfold to verify it was secure.

"Good. I just waved the lit rod in front of your face. Here's the sack." His voice was thick.

She extended her staff to Cy, and he exchanged it for the gunnysack. She folded back the bag's lip to create a ready opening.

"Cy?" She found his chest with her outstretched fingers, and leaned forward. His beard scraped her face, and then their lips met. His kiss seared her senses, his hand on her waist needy, desperate, but his fear did nothing to change her mind. She took the final step to the floor and turned toward the hissing, magically radiant presence ahead.

She took small, mincing steps. She was conscious of how her muscles moved through her calf and foot, how the elastic band helped lift up her toes with each stride. The hissing grew louder. Ingrid felt the intense focus of the gorgon, how it craved for her to come closer, closer.

Something crunched underfoot. She stopped.

"What was that?" called Cy.

"I have no idea." She took another step, kicking some sort of small object. It skittered away. She continued forward, finding more and more objects underfoot that were akin to small, brittle rocks. Finally, she stood within arm's reach of the gorgon.

The unseen, writhing, hissing presence unnerved her more than the massive two-headed snake in Olema. That snake, she could communicate with. This . . . well, maybe once upon a time it could speak on a human level, but now its only language was fury. She felt the power of those human-like eyes that could turn her to stone. To her senses, they glowed like lit coals.

She held her arms wide as she brought the bag down. The gorgon's annoyance flared, the snake hair flailing against its cover. She found the hard corner of a wooden crate, then another, and continued pulling the sack down. The gorgon's head had been set up as if on a pedestal. She unrolled the sack until it dangled down a good foot below the base of the decapitated head.

"I think it's covered," she said. Now came the most terrifying part of all.

They had to turn on the lights.

CHAPTER 12

"I'm going to flare the Tesla rod," Cy said. Ingrid remained still, her breath fast, her world still rendered black by the blindfold. "You did it, Ingrid. I can see the snakes rustling against the cloth. God Almighty." She heard his deep sigh of relief. "Fenris, let's check for nonmagical traps before we head to the light box."

Fingers shaking, she pried off her blindfold. In the thin light, the burlap cloth rippled as dozens of little snakes tried to pierce the thick weave. Footsteps caused her to turn. Fenris passed her Pele's staff. He held a second gunnysack ready in his other hand.

"Better to be redundant as a precaution," he said, and covered the head a second time. Then he scurried to join Cy.

Ingrid leaned on her stick, still not quite ready to move. Getting that close to a gorgon was probably not among the most intelligent things she had ever done, but she had faith it was worth the risk.

Cy and Fenris spent several minutes examining the room before daring to turn on the overhead lights. Ingrid blinked rapidly, momentarily blinded.

When her vision cleared, she saw the basement had no windows. The solitary room was the size of the building above, the space filled with barrels, crates, heaping piles of books, small bags, large vases, discarded clothing, and all matter of detritus.

These were the artifacts of people's lives and livelihoods, abandoned.

"Look at all of this." Fenris peered inside a burlap bag, then through the slats of a crate. "There's anything and everything in here. Dinnerware. Silks. Sacks of rice."

Ingrid looked around in despair. Were the owners of these belongings still alive? So many Chinese were being attacked or imprisoned. She glanced down and gasped, a hand flying to her mouth.

"Good God. It was mice. I was stepping on *mice*." The little creatures had been rendered into statues. Her footsteps had scattered some pieces across the floor, and she saw an intact mouse a few feet away. It sat up on its haunches, gaze toward the gorgon. The figure could have passed for an intricate garden ornament. "I hope these creatures didn't feel pain."

"Turning into a statue would be a quick process, I'd think." Cy motioned to the far side of the room. "I found that drawer, 36C, and it's in quite a peculiar space."

"I found something you should see, too." Fenris waved at them from the middle of the room. He had an open box in front of him, his expression strangely excited. "Look!"

he said as they approached. In both hands, he held plates of orichalcum, each about the size of a dime novel. He held them spanned out like handfuls of playing cards.

Cy plucked one away, holding it to the light to inspect the edges. "This looks like ten-plate. That's a small fortune in your hands."

"Yes, it is. Quite fortuitous." Fenris's expression was pointed.

Cy shook his head. "These belong to refugees. Raiding from them is unconscionable."

"Even if this happens to be exactly what we need to help Ingrid do her part to help them? To help their prophesied leader?"

Cy backed away. "We can't. It's wrong. We must only look where Lee told us to. You shouldn't be rummaging around at all."

"What do you say, Ingrid?" Fenris extended a handful of orichalcum to her.

She couldn't help but grip a piece of ori. If she dropped the thin plate, she could imagine it drifting like a feather. "I . . . I don't know. Cy's right. The thought of stealing from them is horrible." She bit her lip as she stared at the metal. These could change everything for her. "At the same time, we know the fox is hunting for me . . ."

"Fenris." Cy's tone was sharp. "That crate's not why we're here, and we can't deliberate morality until dawn."

Ingrid reluctantly handed the ori back to Fenris. She hobbled around towers of boxes to the back corner of the basement, where she found a sectioned-off area with tables, drawers, microscopes, and glass tubes in shapes and sizes that she couldn't even name.

"This looks like the room the Chinese were destroying in Seattle as the UP moved in," she said.

"The similarity struck me as well," said Cy.

"It's also like the one we saw in San Francisco." Fenris joined them, his hands stuffed in the deep pockets of his overshirt.

"I don't recall that being mentioned," Cy said, a question in the statement.

Ingrid was stunned to realize they hadn't brought it up before. "I think that detail fell by the wayside, with Fenris being injured so soon afterward. In Chinatown, deep in a guarded building, there was a room like this around the corner from where Mr. Sakaguchi was held to convalesce. We stopped inside and Lee . . . Lee asked to inject me with a syringe. He didn't specify what the contents were."

"You'll find this interesting, then." Cy slid open a drawer labeled 36C along with other characters in Chinese. Inside were clear liquid-filled glasses nestled against plush blue fabric.

"'For Cy and Fenris,' Lee said in his message." She looked up, eyes wide. "He intends for you to be injected as well."

Cy nodded, mouth set in a grim line. "With what? That's the dilemma. There's nothing here in English to identify what's what. There are plenty of empty drawers, though, and a bin of empty syringes."

She touched her arm where the needle had pierced her almost exactly a month ago. "Lee asked me if I trusted him with my life. I said I did, of course."

"Lee didn't offer me the same treatment at the time. Not that I would have accepted." Fenris shook his head. "I suppose I should be flattered to possess an invitation now, though I should state that it's against my beliefs to place any liquids other than coffee inside my body."

Cy's gaze sharpened. "He said this would save your life, Ingrid?"

"Yes, something along those lines," she said. Fenris nodded.

"Lee'd want you kept safe no matter what." Cy tapped a fingernail on a glass barrel in the drawer. "The Chinese surely have some counterattack or defensive strategy in the works."

"Like a poison attack?" asked Ingrid.

"You can't inoculate against poison. Work up a resistance, maybe, but that tends to be a gradual and fraught process." He grimaced. "If you had any symptoms of illness in the days that followed your injection, they may have blended with your energy sickness or been remedied by the fox's dark Reiki. I suppose there's only one way to be certain of what this does." He worked off his coat with a rustle of leather and began to roll up his shirtsleeve.

It was more worrisome to see Cy in this position than to endure the mysterious treatment herself. "You wondered if Lee had mailed that note under duress. Now you're willing to take his word on faith?"

"Ingrid, I question everything. It's my nature. I wonder at the spin of our planet, at the rise and fall of the sun each day. I question why and how you can love a lout like me, a man with the graves of thousands on my conscience." He shrugged, but his quick confession struck Ingrid like a dart. "One thing is a certainty. I don't doubt Lee's devotion to you. If this is the same substance—"

"—which we have no way of knowing," cut in Fenris.

"True." Cy held the syringe to his arm. "I'll take it on faith." Ingrid had to look away to avoid the sight of the needle entering his flesh.

"Oh, hell. If I turn keel-up, I'll haunt you," Fenris said, pointing at Ingrid. His overshirt was baggy enough that he simply rolled up the sleeve. Cy applied a light touch to hold Fenris's arm still as he injected him using a fresh syringe.

"The night's halfway done. Let's rig up their security again and head out. No need to linger," Cy said when he had finished.

Fenris kept pace with Ingrid as they crossed the room. "What if we take the gorgon's head with us? It might stop Bl—the fox."

Cy turned from where he stood near the light box. "Can't risk anyone else who may be around her at the time, us included. Besides, the ambassadorial ring makes her almost impervious to harm."

Fenris sighed. "I suppose we must leave it, then, though I've known some wretched examples of humanity who would be greatly improved by becoming statuary."

Cy secured the blindfold over Ingrid's eyes and shut off the lights. She again walked toward the angry essence of the decapitated head. It wasn't nearly as nerve-racking this time, though the crunches beneath her boots made her cringe with every step.

She lifted up the layers of gunnysack one by one. The snakes hissed their rage. As Ingrid retreated a step, she reached into her power to send the gorgon a deep apology for its plight and her inability to provide further help, to which she received no comprehensible reply.

She faced the staircase as Cy untied the blindfold for her. Fenris held Cy's rod for him, the tip at a minimal glow, and passed it back to him. "You're well? No bites?" Cy asked, his worried gaze examining her. At her nod, he started up the staircase. "Be ready for any threats in the building or on the street." Fenris kept pace with Ingrid as they ascended the bend in the stairs.

Ingrid frowned and slowed. She heard a soft, subtle clinking sound with each step. Could it be another trap?

Cy stopped short a few stairs up. "What's that sound?"

"Maybe some stones are stuck to my boots?" Ingrid wondered aloud.

"I don't hear anything," said Fenris.

"No. I know that noise," Cy said, holding out the rod to illuminate Fenris.

He rolled his eyes. "Congratulations. You found me out. My pockets are filled with orichalcum."

Cy rubbed his face with his free hand. "How much?"

"As much as would fit." Fenris held his head at a defiant tilt. "It should be more than enough for the braces. Enough to do a few versions, if need be. What, should we have Ingrid drop a bag over the gorgon again so that we can repack the ori in its box, nice and neat?"

"Good grief, Fenris." Cy groaned.

Ingrid opened her mouth to speak but Fenris spoke first. "Yes, good grief. We *need* this orichalcum. And I will gladly apologize to the rightful owners for my thievery, *if* they aren't already dead." He advanced another step, bringing him closer to Cy.

Cy's defiance crumbled as he looked away, his face tight with grief. "You're right. I hate it, but you're right. I deliberated taking it myself, but I hadn't the nerve."

"Thankfully, not all of us ride such a noble high horse," said Fenris.

"Since I have absolutely no desire to go near that head again, let's consider the matter resolved," said Ingrid, though guilt still weighed in her gut like a stone. "The fact is, we needed ori. Now we have it. That is that."

Cy nodded, relaxing more in the face of Ingrid's resolve.

Minutes later, they were outside. The sylphs fluttered down to fly a few quick happy loops around Ingrid. She shook her head, smiling, and made a note to take the sylphs on more outings that didn't involve perilous situations.

Stars shone through the tattered sheet of gray clouds. They walked in silence for a while, each lost in thought. Distant autocars rumbled, as did a railcar along unseen tracks. Somewhere close by, a cat yowled, seconds later followed by a man yelling for it to shut up.

"We still need more money," Cy finally said. "We need to make prototype braces and the orichalcum still needs to be processed."

"The urgent work on the *Bug* is about done," said Fenris. "I can start on the braces tomorrow. Damn, but I wish we had our old shop in San Francisco and all that beautiful equipment." His face went wistful.

"If *Excalibur* continues along at its present rate, it'll take how long to reach Southern California? A week?" she asked.

Cy nodded. "Thereabouts. Then it'll idle for a time to load people 'n goods for the trip overseas."

"We keep talking about stopping the flying citadel," Ingrid said softly, "but what does that mean at this point?"

"I've been pondering that a lot," Cy said at last. "We need to disable it. We need to disable the Unified Pacific. We need Maggie."

"Are you suggesting that we kidnap your sister?" she asked.

"*Excalibur* is her project," muttered Fenris. "She's probably on board to make sure this initial flight goes well."

"Yes. The fox would make sure Maggie had a berth. The UP might try to fight against having a woman on board, but . . . well." She shrugged. Blum was tough to beat. "How can we get to your sister? Do we wait until the craft comes to Los Angeles?"

"Maybe, though that means contending with thousands more people aboard or in its vicinity." Cy frowned. "She's not one to gambol around town. She can stay in her laboratory forever, so long as she has decent food and facilities. You saw how I was when I started designing your braces. She's like that most all the time."

That was a frightening thought.

"Good ol' T.R. could get us aboard, maybe," said Fenris.

"God willing, we'll get word from his contact here, and

then we can bring up other subjects, if we dare," said Cy, weariness seeping into his voice.

"What about—" Ingrid tripped. She caught herself on her staff. Cy helped her straighten. It was only when she looked down that she realized the elastic rig on her right foot dangled loose. The fastener at the toe of her shoe had ripped free. "Damn it."

"This clearly isn't going to work." Cy shook his head in disgust. "We've got to get those braces made. Are you well, Ingrid?"

"I'm fine. We're almost to the rail stop." She tucked the elastic into the top of her boot and focused as she walked forward, her toes still dragging at times.

How were Cy and Fenris going to make effective braces in a matter of days? What if Roosevelt's people offered no reply, leaving them bereft of funds to process the ori? What if— heaven help them—Cy and Fenris somehow reacted to their injections? What else could go wrong?

Ingrid stared at the sky with the sudden need to wish on a star, but full cloud cover had returned. There was not a sparkle to be found.

CHAPTER 13

FRIDAY, MAY 18, 1906

"This whole situation stinks like a steaming pile of wyvern dung." Fenris scowled, his fingers tapping on the rudder wheel of the *Palmetto Bug*. "I think the trap could only be more obvious if it featured a large, neon-lit sign saying 'trap' in flashing letters, perhaps with a marching band present to make everything more festive."

"Roosevelt's contacts haven't failed us yet." Ingrid sat in her customary seat at the back of the control cabin.

Her skirt was indecently hitched above her knees as she tugged at her stockings. Thin tin plates were fastened together by modified garters within the shaft of her left boot. Cy had dubbed it her alpha brace, and she was already eager to move on to a beta brace.

"There's always a first time," said Fenris. He kept his gaze focused forward.

Ingrid hated that she made Fenris uncomfortable, but by

God, she *itched* inside her boots as her stocking kept bunching up. She felt as twitchy as a toddler ordered to sit still in layers of Easter lace.

"If this contact wanted to spring a trap on us, they could readily do so in Los Angeles," said Cy. "They could guess our general vicinity."

"Instead, we're told to go to *Bakersfield* to get our allowance." Fenris spoke the place-name as if it were an inner ring of hell.

Ingrid let her skirt fall into place again and focused on the view. Sporadic dark green oak trees freckled the gently rounded golden hills. "Tell me, what's so wrong with Bakersfield? It's something of a boomtown, isn't it?"

"Oil has brought in a lot of people, true. Bakersfield's not unlike the Los Angeles area. A lot of real estate, a lot of promise with oil and agriculture, but also a lot of nothing," said Cy.

"Which makes it perfect for a trap," said Fenris. "We're being told to go to a specific dock, to a specific farmhouse nearby. We could vanish as if we're covered by the sylphs. Poof."

"If Roosevelt's contacts are compromised, we're in a heap of trouble anyway," Cy said softly.

"Never mind if Roosevelt himself changes his mind." If Roosevelt knew that Mr. Sakaguchi had agreed to help the Chinese fill kermanite, if he knew that Ingrid plotted against *Excalibur* for the sake of the Chinese . . .

Not that Roosevelt wanted Ingrid in the custody of Ambassador Blum, though. No. He would likely have her killed instead. Regretfully. With mercy. That thought didn't bother

Ingrid as much as it should. But then, she had asked Cy to kill her back in Seattle, when Blum had them snared; he hadn't been able to pull the trigger.

"We'll play this smart," Cy said, a statement that made Fenris snort out a laugh. "Fenris, you'll stay with the *Bug* and be ready to lift off. The two of us will head to the farmhouse, with the sylphs as company. Ingrid'll send the critters back to let you know if you should power down and join us, or be ready for us to come a-running."

"Hopefully, the sylphs won't try to actually pilot the *Bug* like they did in Hilo," Fenris groused.

"I'll go check the engine status." Cy stood and edged past Ingrid. "If all goes well, we'll be back in Dominguez tonight, and with money to get that orichalcum cut to measure this next week."

She and Fenris sat in silence for a few minutes. Beyond the hills, she spied the flat horizon of the southern San Joaquin Valley. Bakersfield wasn't far now.

"'If all goes well,' he says. How often do things 'go well' for us?" Fenris asked.

Ingrid slipped her fingers into her pocket and dissolved a thumbnail-sized chunk of kermanite between her fingertips. Energy flowed through her in a delicious swirl, the amount low enough that Cy shouldn't be able to detect a fever if he touched her skin.

"Not often," she said, her fists clenched on her lap.

MULTITUDES OF OIL DERRICKS ADORNED THE FIELDS AND HILLS, and at a distance, their structure and height were similar to those of mooring masts. It took a while for them to find their necessary dock, and then the *Palmetto Bug* had to wait at a hover for a man to hurry in from the nearby fields. "Hurry" was a relative term, as he moved slow as molasses. When he was close Ingrid realized he was sluggish because he wore a prosthetic leg—a poorly done one, by its lack of flexibility and his heavy limp. Her impatience was replaced by a flare of shame at her unkind thoughts.

The man started to moor them, and was quickly joined by a younger fellow who looked to be a son. Soon enough, the hatch dropped, and Cy engaged in his usual pleasant banter as he disembarked.

Fenris and Ingrid stared out the glass. "See? Bakersfield. Isn't it exciting?"

"Actually, that's my very concern—that this *will* be exciting." She stood. For all the brace's irritations, it did support her leg. It also made her feel as if her calf was a sausage crammed into a small casing.

"Ingrid." The sober way Fenris said her name made her turn. "Here." He held out a gun to her.

"I— Where did you get that?"

"Remember our drunken guests aboard ship a while back?"

She recalled all too well the men who had commandeered the *Palmetto Bug* while Lee and Fenris hid in a water tank in the engine room. The thieves soon discovered the supply of fine whiskey aboard and drank themselves into a stupor, allowing Lee and Fenris to regain control of the ship. Apparently, this had also granted Fenris the opportunity to acquire a weapon.

Ingrid arched an eyebrow. "Shouldn't Cy have claimed this on the paperwork when we landed in Hawaii? I saw his sheet, and he only mentioned his pistol and the rods."

Nor had this gun been found when the ship had repeatedly been inspected. Well, well. Fenris had built hidey-holes into the *Bug* that even Cy was unaware of.

He shrugged away her question. "The gun is already loaded. Perhaps a mundane weapon will suffice in an emergency."

His tone was flippant, but his gaze held particular gravity. She nodded as she shifted all of her kermanite to her left dress pocket, leaving the right pocket for the gun. She'd need to check the gun's chambers when she had a moment alone.

Fenris had given her a pistol in case she needed to kill herself.

This was a gesture of love from him, really. "Thank you," she said, voice thick. "I hope I don't have to use it."

"Ingrid?" Cy poked his head through the hatch. "You ready?"

"Yes." She extended her awareness to the sylphs. They zoomed down from the bunk.

go? go? They swirled around her, a gray tornado.

"What has you so excited?" she muttered.

"They're Sierran sylphs, right?" Cy threw some canteens and food into his pack.

"Yes?"

"If they're from the southern Sierras, we're not too far from their old home. Maybe that's why they're stirred up."

"Oh." As soon as he said that, she felt silly for not realizing their proximity to the mountains—and then she began to worry. The sylphs had saved their lives more than once, and the invisibility they offered might be essential in their plans to confront Maggie.

She should ask the sylphs if they wanted to leave, for the business transaction to be declared done. It was the right thing to do. Instead, she motioned them to follow and tried to ignore a pang of guilt.

By the time she reached the bottom of the mast, her stocking and brace were a bunched-up mess again, but there was nothing to be done for it. The farmers lurked about fifty feet away, watching them.

"The brace is being a bother, isn't it?" Cy asked. "I'm sorry."

She looked at him in exasperation as they walked on. "Cy. You're inventing this device under tremendous pressure. I'm grateful to be able to walk around at all. I'm thinking I should try several different stockings to find a type that works best. Or perhaps the braces could be lined by cotton, and I wear no stockings at all. I assume you wouldn't mind if we experiment a bit?"

"Mind? I will never complain of your apparel—or lack thereof—beneath your skirts."

"My, my. You're being more blunt about such subjects now," she teased.

As she expected, he blushed at her words. "You have obviously corrupted my innocence."

"Obviously." She paused. "I hope I get the chance to corrupt you more soon."

"As do I." His glance at her was shy yet warm with affection.

Light as their banter was, Ingrid could not forget where they were or the potential dangers they faced. The dock was small, consisting of a mere three masts accompanied by a shed and an outhouse. A lone, shaggy tree could supply shade for a solitary person, if the tree was feeling generous. A dirt road led east, toward the golden humps of hills. Derricks stood everywhere like a strange industrial forest.

"There's nowhere for people to hide close by," she said. It was a beautiful late spring day, the sun a tick away from its zenith. Sparse, feathery clouds contrasted with a deep blue sky dappled with distant fast-moving airships.

"That we can see. Be alert with all your senses."

That took her aback. "You act as though we'll be ambushed by ninja garbed in sylph-wing gi."

"The fox has those resources."

"You're right. She does." She motioned Cy to stop, and on a whim, extended her awareness. The wide countryside let her magic flow unimpeded by the clutter of humanity. She sensed no fantastic presences in the immediate vicinity, so she let her magic drift higher, like dandelion puffs cast to the wind.

ingrid carmichael her magic tastes like hot rocks
she's not here

Fear drenched her with icy cold. "No. No. Those things—they can't be here!"

"What do you—"

She focused to find the voice. The entity floated on high.

199

Blum's tainted magic drenched the being with the stench of wild animal musk melded with the underlying sweetness of rotting garbage.

And as she noticed the thing, it noticed her.

The muttering being began a slow, deliberate turn in her direction.

ingrid carmichael her magic tastes like hot rocks

she's . . . here?

if ingrid carmichael is found she must be coiled up and flown straight to the mistress

ingrid carmichael her magic tastes like hot rocks . . .

"God help me, I'm luring it in." Coiled up? What did that even mean? Panic scattered her thoughts, and then she felt the strength of Cy's broad hand on her arm. She wasn't alone. She had slipped past Blum's traps before. She could do it again.

"Kermanite. I need empty kermanite." She opened her eyes wide and shoved a hand into her left pocket. The mingled stones would have flummoxed her in the past when she relied on vision alone to tell them apart. Now she could feel the ambient heat in the filled kermanite and mentally sorted them to one side.

"Is it a fox figurine, like in the train station?"

"I don't know what it looks like, only that's it's airborne and it's coming straight at me from that way."

She gazed upward, motioning her staff in that direction as she drew the vacant crystals to her open palm. For a few seconds, she spied nothing but blue sky, and then she saw an odd ripple. It moved like a broad, iridescent ribbon, sinuous and long.

"What is *that*?" asked Cy, his voice thick.

"Damned if I let it get close enough to make an acquaintance." She pushed power into the kermanite. Heat drained from her body and filled about a quarter of the rocks.

The creature drifted closer, Blum's magic looming like a toxic cloud. The sylphs hunkered low and rendered themselves invisible.

hide you? they asked.

She should have thought of the sylphs seconds before, when she still had power. Now, to rely on them to hide, she would need to draw in energy again—or try to endure the pain of the sylphs' touch—or spend her own *mana* to shield her skin.

"Should you push out more power?" Cy asked.

"I have nothing more to vent!" The thought of Blum, of capture, of being coiled up and flown somewhere by that *thing,* had her near hysterical. What more could she do?

"Can it be scenting your magic on the kermanite?"

"No! I don't think so! If it did, it should go straight to the *Bug* because of the engine crystal there." At that, Cy paled. "Or also any of hundreds of other places that host crystals that I filled."

ingrid carmichael her magic tastes like hot rocks
she's not here

The being resumed its original mantra as it slowly but surely turned away, arcing back to its original elevation. The foulness dissipated. Ingrid remained, quaking in place.

That had been close. So terrifyingly close.

"It's going?" Cy asked.

"Yes." She croaked out the word.

"Now's a good time to ask again, what was *that*? It didn't have wings like a dragon."

"I can't match it with any fantastics I've ever heard of. Maybe it's a construct?"

Cy adjusted the brim of his hat as he continued to gaze upward. "Good God. This is what other pilots have been spying up and down the state. How could she make something like *that*?"

"She could take her pick of cultures that practice magic that'll create semi-alive . . . things that do a person's bidding. We'd have to get unpleasantly close to identify any glyphs or words of life. The fox must have this thing, or more than one, flying all over the state in search of me." She felt ill at the very thought. "It wanted . . . to coil itself around me and fly me wherever she is."

Cy released a heavy breath. "The way it's flying, I reckon it's trying to catch you in the *Bug* while you're carrying energy. If that creature met us dead-on, flying as fast as that, we might have had no warning at all."

"Yes." What would it have done to the airship? How many times had that entity or its brethren flown over Dominguez Field, with her none the wiser?

Ingrid started walking again. She had to move before she cowered and sobbed.

"Today was the first time I've carried power since we ventured to the gorgon's basement, but I think . . . I think we're okay. It can't sniff me out now." She had to believe that, even as she remained wary for the creature's return.

Cy looked at her and then the sky. "Well, can't say I'm

eager to fly out of here right away, knowing that thing's up there somewhere. Better to walk and see what awaits us at the farmhouse."

They plodded past a homestead, and after about a quarter mile, they spied their goal. Tall palm trees flanked a long drive to a small home painted in robin's-egg blue. A matching tower stood behind it, the surrounding lot filled with gnarled trees with wide-spreading branches.

"Lots of space here for a ground-lander airship," Cy muttered. He glanced upward at regular intervals.

"Does the UP even use ground landers?" She lightly tapped the gun in her pocket; the weapon would be useless against a military airship, but its presence made her feel slightly less helpless all the same.

"They are a more recent civilian fad, but the UP might utilize them in flat areas like this. Ground landers' cushions are unreliable, but they can land where a traditional ship cannot. Here. Don't walk directly down the lane. We're too exposed to the house there."

He walked to one side of the drive, beneath the palms. Dried fronds crunched and rustled underfoot, the ground beneath as hard as concrete. Ingrid was glad to have her staff in hand for balance.

As they neared the house, they entered the welcome shade of a grove of walnut trees. Birdsong belted out from the branches above. The sylphs' susurrus grew louder.

"They should watch their noise," Cy murmured. "Most people would assume them to be bees, but some might recognize what they are."

Ingrid nodded and motioned for the sylphs to quiet

down. They acquiesced, somewhat abashed at their own carelessness.

Cy didn't walk toward the front door, instead circling the small home. A window was open, the sounds of clinking dishes carrying outdoors. Out back, a small plot of furrowed ground was dark with recent watering but showed no signs of plant growth. The wooden tower had an unlocked door; peering inside, they found that it housed a metal water tower. Cy continued around, headed toward the barn. The sylphs continued to follow in a sort of aerial dance from tree to tree. Other than birds, Ingrid heard and saw no other animals. If the property contained an autocar, it was either in the barn or elsewhere.

"Do you want me to see if the sylphs can scout out the house or barn?" she whispered.

"That level of communication would require you to utilize magic, right?" At her nod, he shook his head. "The sylphs would recognize some threats, not all. I'd rather trust my own eyes for our reconnaissance."

Ingrid couldn't argue with that. She tread as softly as possible as they rounded the back of the tall barn. White paint bubbled and peeled from the walls, reminding her of sunburned skin. Metallic taps and thuds carried from inside—the sounds of a workshop.

Cy stopped to peek through the gaps in the planks. "Wall's blocked, can't see a thing." They continued to the front, where half the barn door stood open.

An autocar faced them, its engine compartment exposed and its contents disassembled across an oil-blotched white sheet on the barn floor. A thickset man had his elbows braced on the front of the car.

Cy angled his body to shelter Ingrid behind him. She glanced at her own flank. No one else approached them. The sylphs clustered along an eave just above them.

Cy tapped on the barn door with the copper length of his Tesla rod. The dense sound rang out. "Pardon, but I was provided this address to meet someone here."

The man jerked up from the cavity of the car. He wore grubby dungarees and a plaid shirt like any workingman, and his face— Dear God!

"Barty?" cried George Augustus, opening wide his arms as he rushed to embrace his son.

Chapter 14

"Father? You're alive?" The words croaked out. The sight of his father had rendered him completely immobile.

Cy had seen beings extraordinary and ancient over the past month, but now, when he found the person he most wanted to see, he couldn't believe his own eyes. Ingrid wanted to yell at him, shove him forward, make him move, make him accept this wonderful reality, but she couldn't. He needed time to absorb the fact that his father wasn't dead. That his hopes hadn't been in vain.

George Augustus circled the dismantled equipment on the barn floor and barreled into his son. Cy kept his arms out for a moment, like tentative wings, before lowering them into a hug. The two gripped each other as if trying to keep hold during a tornado, their arms wrapped tight.

"My God! My boy, my boy! Theodore said you were alive, but to see you with my own eyes . . . !" Mr. Augustus pulled back to gaze at him.

"You have a beard?" Cy asked, with a sound halfway between a sob and a laugh.

"So do you!" Mr. Augustus embraced his son again. "What a glorious surprise this is. And you, miss! It brightens my heart to see you." He offered Ingrid a dignified bow, leaving her abashed.

"I'm relieved to see you, too, Mr. Augustus. We saw notice of your death in a newspaper." She curtsied with one hand on the staff. A tear slid down her cheek. This was indeed a glorious surprise orchestrated by Mr. Roosevelt. She had a hunch it was more for the elder Mr. Augustus's benefit than for Cy's—Roosevelt had not masked his disgust at Cy's status as a deserter of the A&A. To him, military service was akin to godliness.

Mr. Augustus pulled a red handkerchief from his pocket and mopped his cheeks. He had a long, angular face like his son, with blue eyes almost buried in padded layers of wrinkles. "I plan to remain dead in the public eye for the rest of my life, Lord willing."

Ingrid heard the scuff of shoes behind her. Her legs braced wide, she spun around, staff held outward. A dozen feet away, she recognized Reddy, Mr. Augustus's manservant. He wielded a shovel, blade up.

He recognized her at the same instant and lowered the tool. "Miss Car—?"

"Don't say my name here," she interrupted hurriedly. "I'll explain more later." She cast a worried glance to the heavens. She surmised that Blum's scouts were attracted to her magic more than to her name, but she wasn't going to gamble on her guess.

"I see." Questions sparked in his eyes. "Did you bring along our boy again?"

"Of course I did," she said, smiling as she stepped back from the doorway to let Cy past. His embrace with Reddy was almost as emotional as his reunion with his father.

"You both made it out of San Francisco." Cy stood with a hand on Reddy's back.

"We did, by the grace of God and Captain Sutcliff," said Mr. Augustus.

"Captain Sutcliff?" she asked sharply.

"Yes. I understand he was of your acquaintance as well." Mr. Augustus walked with a distinct limp in his step. As he passed by, a strange chill draped over Ingrid for a matter of seconds. She stifled a gasp. What was *that?*

She looked sidelong at Cy, but he showed no peculiar reaction to his father's proximity—besides being awash with joy. She'd need to discuss this with him later.

"Come along," said Mr. Augustus. "Let's get us to the house for a proper sit-down."

THE TWO MEN WELCOMED THEM INSIDE THE HOME AS IF IT WERE a manor house replete with a parlor. In truth, it was a modest place probably indistinguishable from other farmhouses around. The kitchen contained a sink, stove, and stacked orange crates for cabinets, with a board atop them as a counter. Reddy hurried to pull out a chair for Ingrid at a square table battered by use. Not five feet away, a thin wooden wall separated them from the rest of the house. The doorway to the bedroom was cordoned off by a curtain of stitched flour bags.

"I'm sorry to say we have no tea," said Reddy. "However, if you close your eyes, you might pretend the well water is tea. It's the right color."

"I suppose you don't have pie either?" Cy shook his head in mock indignation. "What a travesty of hospitality!" He sat, his father close by. Ingrid cast Reddy a look, which he answered with a small smile and a shake of his head. There was no chair for him, but even if there had been, a man of his station wouldn't have sat with guests present. It just wasn't done.

Ingrid wished she could have stood with him in solidarity, but to her chagrin, her legs needed a rest after that walk.

The sylphs had needed a rest, too. They had retreated into one of the big walnut trees just outside.

"We're happy to offer whatever we have, little as it is." Ingrid noted how Mr. Augustus shifted in his chair, and recognized her own recent behavior. He was in pain, but trying to hide it before his son.

"How did you end up here? What happened in the city?" asked Cy, leaning forward on his thighs.

"How is Mr. Roosevelt involved?" Ingrid asked.

"Where to begin?" Mr. Augustus glanced toward heaven. "We remained in the Bay Area for some weeks after the disaster. By some miracle, Mr. Roosevelt visited the refugee camp we were in. He saw me, had his men pull me aside. He well understood my request and established us here near Bakersfield. Folks here mind their own business and most don't hold repugnant views on folks of color." He nodded toward Reddy.

"There's even a thriving farm community of black folk a ways north, founded by freed slaves," Reddy added softly.

Ingrid was warmed by Mr. Augustus's consideration of Reddy; it fit with his kind reception of her as well. "And what was your request, sir?"

"To be dead." He looked at Cy, expression sober. "I know you didn't intend to fake your death. You simply deserted. When we talked at Quist's, I envied you, even as you were in the thick of danger. You were *free*. I've been chained to a desk for a long time."

"And the bottle," Cy added. Mr. Augustus recoiled at that, cheeks flushing. He did not meet Ingrid's eye.

"He hasn't had a drink in a month now. Since the earthquake." Reddy sounded matter-of-fact.

"Good." Cy nodded to his father, then looked at Reddy, brows drawn inward in concern. "I understand Father's reasoning, with the rest of his kin gone, but what of your daughter and her family?"

He flinched. "An autocar accident some five years ago took her and the little ones to Jesus."

"My God. I'm so sorry, Reddy. Ophelia was a good friend. We practically grew up together," Cy said to Ingrid. "She was seven years older than us twins. Probably saved our lives a time or two when our scientific mischief could've come to explosive results."

Emotion glimmered in Reddy's eyes. "I am proud of the woman she became. I hold no worries about her soul."

Respectful silence lingered for a minute. "I worried for

my soul," whispered Mr. Augustus. "I still do. That's why I wanted a chance to start over after I was reborn from the rubble. I hold no illusions that I can atone for what my machines have done, but I want a chance to set myself right with the Lord. I'll accept His judgment."

"You were still in downtown during the earthquake." Cy's voice trembled.

Mr. Augustus nodded and stood. He paced around the table, his gaze distant. That cold feeling crept over Ingrid again, and she fought the urge get away from him. Instead of prickles of heat, she sensed an utter void—the opposite of being near a fantastic. What did this mean? She studied him in the slant of light through the window.

Both times she had encountered this terrible coldness, she'd been in his shadow.

She was almost certain his shadow had passed over her at least once when they were together at Quist's in San Francisco, and she had felt nothing then.

"You met Captain Sutcliff, sir?" she prompted.

"I did." He rubbed his beard, the same gesture Cy often made these days. "You two fled from the restaurant. I went to the front door to distract the soldiers. Minutes later, I heard some of them mutter that they'd found the woman. I took that to mean you, Miss Carmichael." He grimaced. "I daresay, I wielded my clout. I demanded to speak to their commander. I waited a time, and heard whispers that an ambassador was taking over the operation. I feared for you. The restaurant shut but I lingered with some soldiers. Finally, Captain Sutcliff arrived."

Ingrid could imagine that scene well, and wondered how

Sutcliff had recovered from having his authority usurped by Ambassador Blum's arrival. He was such a pompous man, blond with a perfectly manicured mustache, his navy-blue uniform crisp and perfect even in the thick of disaster. She hated him. He had assumed Mr. Sakaguchi guilty of conspiring with the Chinese to destroy the auxiliary, of thieving the large kermanite. Even so, when Sutcliff had interrogated Ingrid after nabbing her at Quist's, she managed to break through his stiff facade. She had gotten him to consider the fact that the Thuggees were the real threat, that they were engineering an attack on the city that very night. And then Blum had arrived.

"I remembered, in our conversation earlier that night, you had mentioned the captain being in pursuit of the kermanite. I began our discussion with that subject, with nihonshu to soften the way."

Cy didn't disguise his grimace.

His father continued: "Sutcliff had suffered something of a crisis of faith regarding his role in the Unified Pacific. I reckon I was like a father figure. He wouldn't have spoken to me so openly otherwise, a man like him. That Ambassador—"

"Don't say her name," interrupted Ingrid. "There's power in names. She can wield it. Don't say my full name either."

Mr. Augustus's eyes widened. "I see."

"The ambassador's a kitsune, Father, at least four centuries in age," said Cy. "Her powers are many."

The shock of that news sent his father staggering back a step. Reddy balanced him with a hand on his back. "You'd best sit, sir," he murmured. Mr. Augustus did so; Cy took in his father's new feebleness with compressed lips.

"That old. That powerful. I had no idea." He shook his head. "When I first heard a woman ambassador had been ordained, I rejoiced. I've been a proponent of universal suffrage for years, and I selfishly thought this news would bolster our cause. Then I met her a time or two, and heard some of the scuttlebutt that swirled around her like a cyclone. I realized she was much *more* . . . but I had no idea about *this* . . ."

"Captain Sutcliff was terrified of her," Ingrid said.

"Yes, I could see that. That night, he grieved that he had abandoned his men to her whims. Soldiers under her direction are often subject to outrageous commands and abuses. Many die. Just before meeting me, he had penned a report and taken the terrible risk of addressing it to Ambassador Roosevelt."

"Bypassing his own commanders?" Cy shook his head with a low whistle. "Career suicide."

"Yes. And his career was everything to him."

"You're speaking of Captain Sutcliff in the past tense," Ingrid said.

Mr. Augustus nodded, staring away. "You had made quite the impression on him, miss. He was afraid he had committed an injustice by fixating on you and your mentor—by falling into the Imperial Japanese habit of guilt until proven innocent, rather than our American system of innocent until proven guilty. He worried that following the commands of the ambassador were to the detriment of America." He sighed. "Fact was, he was a man beset by demons. We sat talking until dawn."

"When the earthquake happened," Ingrid said softly.

Mr. Augustus said nothing. His fingers drummed on the table. Reddy positioned himself in his line of sight. "There's no need to drink for courage, sir. Tell the tale."

"Actually, I wish most of all that we had some tea and sugar." The words were flippant and rang false.

"Father, what happened?"

"Hell became real. But you know that. Theodore said you survived the worst of it." His hands stilled on the table. "The restaurant began to crumble around us. I'm an old man. I can't move fast. Captain Sutcliff all but carried me out. We just made it outside when the building's facade slipped down. The captain looked up and shoved me aside. He took a ton of bricks that Death had surely intended for me. The barrage still buried me to the waist. I dug through the bricks and I found him. Much of his body had been crushed, but Captain Sutcliff looked at me, his eyes defiant even as he died."

Mr. Augustus lost his ability to speak. Cy sat, elbows braced on the table, hand over his face. Ingrid blinked back tears. She had wished ill for Captain Sutcliff, but she never imagined that he was yet another death in Papa's terrible tally.

"I'd been upstairs asleep when this happened." Reddy's voice was soft. "I ended up in a room that tilted toward the street as the first few floors had compressed together. I climbed down the rubble, where I unburied George the rest of the way." The use of his employer's given name was awkward on his tongue, a new habit in their new lives. "We wandered for a while. It felt like forty days and nights in a wasteland, and then we found a park, and doctors. George's leg was crushed. For a few days, we worried it would need to be amputated."

Mr. Augustus waved a hand. "Reddy and the doctors worried. I was incomprehensible. I remember little of that next week."

"I do," said Reddy. "I remember every minute."

No one spoke for a while. "I want to find out more from you," Cy said, speaking slowly. "But we had best go check in with Fenris. He's surely anxious in wait for us."

"Fenris Braun? Your old roommate from the academy?" Mr. Augustus asked, brow wrinkled and perplexed.

"Yes, sir," he replied. "We were in business together in San Francisco." She noted that he omitted that he had been with Fenris during his full dozen years of exile.

Ingrid stood and waved back the gentlemen's attempts to come to her aid. "We can come back after a visit to the dock. You all need to talk more."

"Your company's welcome as morning sunshine," said Mr. Augustus. "We're doing soup tonight, weren't we, Reddy?"

"Yessir, George. I should start that soon."

They transitioned to the front porch and stood together in an awkward cluster. Cy and his father mirrored each other in their hesitant poses, neither able to say farewell.

Ingrid looked across the fields to see if she could sight the *Bug*. "Cy. There's a car coming."

He jerked to attention. "You get many autocars out here, Father?"

"Almost none. Most folks here rely on feet or hooves." As he spoke, Reddy retreated a few steps to where his shovel leaned against the porch rail.

A plume of dust illuminated the vehicle's approach. Cy shot Ingrid a look, and she wasted no time arguing. She stepped just inside the house, out of direct line of sight or gunfire.

"Is that a salesman's truck?" she asked, leaning forward to watch. "I can't make out the advertisement on the side."

"Looks to me like a Washman's truck," said Reddy. "One of those door-to-door sales folks vending soaps and household goods." The truck slowed to take the turn into their driveway. The men remained in place. There was no point in hiding now.

"Do you want me to greet them, sir? George?"

The porch creaked ominously as Mr. Augustus started down the steps. "No, Reddy. If someone's after us and our guests, perhaps they'll be more reluctant to shoot me."

True as the observation was, it made Ingrid cringe—she and Reddy would certainly be regarded as more disposable.

Ingrid couldn't see the truck as it rattled and bounced its way down the drive. She checked on the sylphs. They read her mood and immediately retreated deeper into their walnut tree.

The truck's engine whined as it shut down. The scent of dust drifted forward and Ingrid pressed fingers to her nose as she resisted the urge to sneeze.

"Howdy there!" Mr. Augustus called into the sudden silence. "Can I help you folks?"

Folks? How many men could he see in the truck? Ingrid leaned forward a tad. Reddy had blocked the doorway with his body, but around him she could see Mr. Augustus standing vulnerable on the scrubby grass, the truck dead ahead. She slipped her hand into the pocket with filled kermanite. She teased a stone between her fingertips, aching to be ready, but terrified of luring in another of Blum's hunters.

"Hello there!" a deep baritone boomed out. "We're here with a delivery."

That voice. Ingrid knew that voice. She stepped forward, a hand to Reddy's arm to motion him aside. "That's Siegfried!" she whispered to Cy.

Roosevelt's man hopped from the truck's cab. He wore a light blue cotton uniform, the fabric threadbare but tidy, the very thing one would expect to be worn by a salesman of home goods. Another man sat in the cab. She recalled him from their flight in Roosevelt's fancy airship. A heavy clang of metal indicated the back hatch of the truck dropping down. Fenris rounded the side of the canvas-back truck. Behind him strolled a stout, strong figure recognized the world over.

"Dee-lighted to see the reunion has gone according to schedule!" said Theodore Roosevelt, his white teeth flashing in one of his signature grins. "George, your leg looks to be healing well. Reddy, I doubt you'll need that shovel at the moment. No one needs burying today. Young Mr. Augustus." That greeting was as curt as could be expected. "Miss Carmichael. Good to see you upright again. I trust you had a lovely visit to the old Sandwich Islands?"

CHAPTER 15

George, Reddy, and Cy froze in place, stunned by the ambassador's arrival. Ingrid resisted the strong urge to swear.

"Greetings, Mr. Roosevelt. Yes, I had a productive visit," she said, her voice level, as if his arrival had been expected. Inside, she felt sick with worry. Did he know what she'd done to Warden Hatsumi? Did he even care? Why on earth was Fenris here?

She glanced up, but saw no iridescent glimmers. Maybe, just maybe, her name alone wouldn't draw in that thing again.

"T.R. never shows up unless he wants something," Cy muttered from beside her. She nodded. "And Fenris looks about ready to explode."

Indeed he did. As Roosevelt paused to chat amiably with Mr. Augustus in the yard, Fenris hopped up the steps to join them, his expression one of unrestrained fury.

"They made me leave the *Bug*," he spat.

Cy inclined his head to indicate that Fenris should lower his voice. "Did they board?"

"Of course they boarded. When that truck drove up, I pulled up the hatch. All the good that did. I couldn't disengage on my own. His brutes came up the mast, and gave me an ever-so-polite request to open the hatch or they'd bring crowbars."

"Did they take anything?" Ingrid panicked at the thought of the *guandao*. It was up in its usual place in the sylphs' bunk, but there were no sylphs to play guard right now. Then there was Mr. Sakaguchi's box of personal correspondence; Roosevelt would be aware of many of the secrets contained therein, but not all.

Fenris blew a raspberry. "As though I was allowed to oversee proceedings! They escorted me to the ground for a personal meeting with Ambassador Roosevelt."

"Damn." Cy looked tempted to say stronger words than that.

"How did that meeting go?" Ingrid asked.

The concern of the sylphs lashed against her. *are you safe?* She flashed back at them a sense of heightened alert, but that there was no immediate threat.

"Better than expected," Fenris said. "He complimented the *Bug* on its speed, said he was impressed at the time we made from Portland to Seattle, even with inept pilots in command. He noted that the airship thieves remained in lockup in Seattle, too."

"I never told him the details of what happened on the *Bug*

during its theft. He wants us to know he knows through other means," Cy muttered. "Did he leave anyone at the dock?"

"Yes. Three men with another truck. They are pretending to work freight."

"We'll need to search the *Bug* carefully when we return." Cy rubbed his face. "I hate to say it, but their strategy is smart. A second airship out here would garner too much curiosity, and they can't risk Roosevelt being recognized on a mast. Trucks offer cover and blend in."

Fenris snorted. "Blend in, to a certain degree. On the drive, a farmer stopped us to buy some stain removal powder."

Ingrid sensed Roosevelt's approach. The potent enchantments in his ring exuded heat and an onerous *presence,* though the man alone packed a wallop. There surely could be no one else in the world quite like Theodore Roosevelt. He was the sort of man who read a book a day and could recite much of the contents verbatim even years later, and could work a room in the same way—remembering names and details, and treating friends, enemies, and people of all walks of life with genuine courtesy. Even now, he greeted Reddy first, clasping his hand and asking after his welfare.

Roosevelt faced Ingrid with a bright grin, his eyes intense behind pince-nez lenses. He was not a good-looking man. He had a large head accentuated by his shortly cropped brown hair, his teeth appearing too large for his mouth. His small frame was packed with muscle, his neck thick like that of a walrus. But his unattractiveness was inconsequential when he grinned and looked a person in the eye. He embodied the charisma and might of a fantastic without a drop of magic in his blood.

"Shall we go inside and palaver?" Roosevelt asked, gesturing Ingrid in first.

"I'm sorry we don't have more chairs," said Mr. Augustus once they had again gathered near the table. With seven people in the room—Siegfried accompanying Mr. Roosevelt—the house felt even tinier than before.

"Nonsense. You have no need to apologize," said Mr. Roosevelt. "I set you up with the house. If anyone is to blame, it is me. Please, Miss Carmichael—"

"Sir, I know this sounds peculiar, but you must avoid using my name. Just 'miss' is fine. And I'd rather stand for now, thank you. Mr. Augustus, please."

The elder Mr. Augustus sat, and after a moment of everyone staring at the remaining empty chair, Fenris claimed it. He crossed his thin legs and folded his arms over his chest as if he had just stolen a throne.

Roosevelt studied Ingrid, taking in her walking stick and everything else. She stared back. Knowing him, he had already noted the elastic rig on her right boot. He knew her diagnosis had stated that it would be difficult for her to walk again. He didn't look surprised to see her up and about, but then, his confidence in her abilities was perturbing at times.

"Well then." Roosevelt gripped his suit jacket by the lapels. "I confess, my presence here is selfish. I wanted to see father and son reunited after the travails of the past month."

"I am forever grateful for all you've done, my friend." Mr. Augustus rose long enough to clasp Roosevelt's hand. The cold shadow drifted over Ingrid once again. "It does my heart good to see my only living child again. Seeing him, my suffering means nothing."

Ingrid looked at Cy at once, taking in his horrified expression.

George Augustus didn't know that Maggie was alive.

Mr. Roosevelt glared at them, his threat as evident as the reveal of a gun. *Don't mention Maggie.* Had he come here, not to bask in his role in this reunion, but to make sure they focused on the positive—and avoided the subject of Cy's twin?

Ingrid did not respond to threats well. But she also wondered how Mr. Augustus would take the news of his daughter's betrayal.

Roosevelt opened his mouth, but she spoke first. "We've been following news about *Excalibur*, sir. The culmination of the Gaia Project is as astonishing and dreadful as you said it would be."

"Wait." Mr. Augustus extended a hand. "I have seen mere drip-drops of news since coming here, but I wondered about this citadel. *That* is the Gaia Project? I recognized parts of it in a photograph—parts made by Augustinian, rush orders. But the sheer size of the thing would have required work by hundreds of companies across Atlanta and beyond. That must have been akin to herding cats as far as deadlines go."

"Indeed. An unparalleled effort in organization. I have had limited involvement myself, as this has been a special endeavor by my colleague Ambassador—"

"Don't say her name either, sir," broke in Ingrid quickly.

"She can utilize the power of names within her magic. We don't know if saying her name will act as a kind of invocation as well."

His expression flicked from annoyance to wide-eyed alarm. "That's why you don't want your name spoken aloud? What might she gain from hearing her own name from afar?"

"Our fear is that she might deduce who is speaking and maybe where we are. This is pure speculation on our parts, but we deem it a necessary precaution, in light of her interest in . . ." Cy motioned to Ingrid in lieu of saying her name. "We gave the matter long thought on our flight to the Vassal States."

"This brings about disturbing possibilities." Roosevelt's expression was dark.

"This woman ambassador—the fox—seems to have her claws in every pot," said Reddy.

"This project is her biggest pot of all, her means to secure Japan's dominance over China and to stop incursions by Britannia and Russia." Roosevelt's eyes smoldered, and she could tell he was readying himself for a tirade. "Here in America, even the Copperhead rags are praising *Excalibur* as the innovation of the twentieth century, the paragon of American technological might. Each and all ignore the fact that once it's in Asia, it will be used to secure Japanese possessions. It will only return to America's shores to be used here, upon our people."

Ingrid swallowed a comment on how Americans were already utilizing weapons against American people—Chinese citizens like Lee, who were born here, and others like Uncle Moon who had come here to live out their dream, not unlike immigrants from Ireland, Mexico, Italy, or elsewhere in the world.

"You reckon that to be her end game, then," said Mr. Augustus.

"Yes. Without question. Maybe not for another twenty years. Maybe not for fifty. But her eventual hope is for Japan to realize its divine place as ruler of our world. The Unified Pacific is a means to an end. There is no room for allies at the table she sets."

"I recall discussions you and Mr. Sakaguchi had on this subject. The 'sly invasion,'" said Ingrid.

Roosevelt nodded. "Yes. The integration of Japanese people and culture within American society. Which, in moderation, is not a terrible thing. America has incorporated elements of cultures from all around the world. One of our great strengths is our ability to absorb, to adapt. Yet when schools teach Japanese alone, when Japanese people are automatically regarded with privilege without regard to their achievements . . ." He shook his head, his cheeks ruddy.

"How are you working to counter *Excalibur*?" Ingrid asked, choosing her words and tone with care. Fenris had wondered before if T.R. might help them gain access to the citadel and Maggie.

"I wield a powerful weapon of war—bureaucracy." His grin returned. "I delayed its departure a month ago after a terrible fire at the assembly site. The incident did not harm any necessary equipment, but—"

"Or harm any people?" Cy broke in, clearly worried for his sister's welfare.

"Not to my knowledge. The citadel will make a long stop in Southern California to load soldiers and goods. I have already arranged for some vital shipments to go astray. I will seize other opportunities as they come."

No. He wouldn't be so bold as to help them board. Damn it. "Sir, where *is* the fox right now?"

His lips quirked, causing his mustache to twitch. "I don't know her current location, but *Excalibur* is the sun that she orbits right now."

"Father, how are you doing?" Cy asked, crouching beside him. Mr. Augustus seemed shaken by all the news.

"Oh, don't fuss over me." Mr. Augustus was rubbing his leg. "I'm old and I tire easily. I'm just so glad to see you, Barty."

Cy's eyes met Ingrid's, his expression troubled. She could see the question in his eyes—dare they tell him about Maggie?

Ingrid turned to the person who would best know that answer. "Could I bother you for a glass of water?" she asked Reddy. "I'm parched."

Reddy ducked his chin, somewhat embarrassed. "I should have asked everyone. Water . . . ?" The men shook their heads. "Come with me, miss. The best drinking water is from the pump outside."

Oh, blessed Reddy. He'd worked in high society circles for a long time. He understood that Ingrid wished to speak with him alone.

They walked out the front door and rounded the corner. Reddy stopped dead in his tracks. "Oh my."

Where only dirt had been before, garden plants thrived knee-high with scarcely a patch of mud visible. Even the scrub grass lawn looked greener. She could swear that the walnut trees were larger now, too.

Her mind raced as she wondered how large a group sylphs typically formed in the wild. If they were anything like the pixies often found in city gardens, their family clusters usually consisted of only five or so members. Her group of a thousand or more sylphs—bound together through their shared time in captivity—seemed far too potent for its own good.

Reddy raised an eyebrow at Ingrid. "Does this have something to do with your arrival, miss? I don't recall Mr. Roosevelt's visits ever being so . . . inspirational . . . for flora in the past."

"Would it be adequate for me to say yes, and plead for you not to ask how?"

His grin almost seemed to glow. "I'll accept that from *you,* as you have taken such good care of my boy."

"It's my pleasure," she said, and blushed at her poor choice of words. He only chuckled in response. "I wanted to talk to you, Reddy, about a serious matter regarding Cy's family."

Reddy sobered. "Please, tell me."

Ingrid took a deep breath. "Maggie is alive. She faked her death to get away from Augustinian. Roosevelt knows that, but he has kept the secret at her request. Maggie is the genius engineer behind *Excalibur.*"

Reddy took the news the way a well-rooted tree takes a blast of wind. He swayed, barely, his expression stoic. "I see."

Cy trusted Reddy. Ingrid needed to trust him, too. "We want to stop *Excalibur*. Not simply delay it with paperwork and mislaid deliveries, but prevent it from being used overseas. Cy grieves for his sister. He doesn't want the extermination of a people on her soul."

"I love her like my own, but . . ." Tears filled Reddy's eyes. "God forgive me for saying this, but when I heard that she had died, I was relieved that she would not guide Augustinian forward. She didn't care a whit about making money. She simply wanted to create, and be the best at what she created. For her to be the head of a weapons manufacturing business . . ."

"Mr. Augustus couldn't see this himself?"

"He saw her dark potential, yes. That's why he groomed her to be an administrator instead. She didn't take to that well. Neither did the rest of the board. They didn't like the presence of a woman in *their* space." His smile was thin. "George knew she didn't *want* to be there, but he thought he knew best."

That way of thinking reminded Ingrid all too much of Mr. Sakaguchi's governance of her own life.

An idea formed in her mind. "Mr. Augustus used to be a machinist himself, didn't he?"

"He can't handle tools like he used to, but give him a blueprint and he'll tell you what is what. He's a lot like Barty, really."

"Are you both supposed to stay here on this farm?"

"We're not prisoners, but going out brings the risk that George might be recognized. Are you plotting, miss?"

"I am." George Augustus could help them figure out the best means to infiltrate *Excalibur* and perhaps recruit Maggie to their cause. He might be able to help with the development of Ingrid's braces, too. "Everything depends on if Mr. Augustus is strong enough to take the news about Maggie. What do you think?"

"You really want this to come out in our present company?" He pondered that. "You said Mr. Roosevelt has known the truth all along. George is going to be angry, and Roosevelt makes an ideal target. If you told him later, my fear is he'd fixate that rage on himself, on Maggie's deceit and how he should have seen it coming, at how her death broke his wife's heart. Eva was near catatonic for months until she died."

"Oh no. No, no, no. Don't say that." Tears filled her eyes.

Reddy reached out an arm to steady her. "Miss?"

"Cy. He'll be devastated. He only just found out recently that his mother is dead." She wiped tears from her cheeks. "He'll blame himself for all the heartache he caused her, I know he will."

Reddy slowly nodded, sadness heavy in his eyes. "He would, that boy. I'll talk to George about this again. They need to work through this together."

"Without any liquor at hand."

At that, Reddy's nod was firm. "Amen to that, miss."

Ingrid steeled her resolve. Roosevelt was going to be very unhappy with her, but that was a risk she had to take. "Well then. Shall we go inside and light the fuse?"

"After you get your water, miss. Let's keep up the pretense for our errand."

They returned to find Mr. Roosevelt speaking of the situation in Seattle and how effectively the crises had been contained. Ingrid smiled in relief to hear that more geomancers had been brought in to stabilize the flow in the region. She waited for a pause in Roosevelt's tale and looked across the table to Cy.

"While we're all together, it's only right that we tell your father about the engineer behind *Excalibur*," she said firmly, before he could continue.

"Miss . . . !" Roosevelt flushed.

"What is it you're supposed to tell me?" Mr. Augustus asked, perplexed.

Cy assessed the situation, looking to Ingrid and Reddy, then crouched before his father again. "Father. I know this is going to be hard for you to hear . . ." He took a deep breath. "Maggie didn't die in a laboratory accident. She's alive."

"Alive?" George Augustus gripped Cy by the shoulders. "What do you mean? She's been alive all this time? How—"

Cy didn't give him time to finish another question. "She is the one who created *Excalibur*, the capstone of the Gaia Project. They didn't need your help anymore because they had her." He glared over his shoulder. Roosevelt glowered at him, red-faced. "Mr. Roosevelt has known all the while, but kept the secret on her behalf."

"I—Maggie—Theodore?" Mr. Augustus's jaw fell slack. No more sounds emerged as he slumped forward in a dead faint.

"That," growled Ambassador Roosevelt, "was poorly done. You had no need to deal the man such news—"

"You had no need to playact as his good friend while hiding from him the information that his daughter was still alive." Ingrid flushed with rage. If she had held any power, she likely could have shattered anything in hand.

They stood together on the front porch of the domicile. Siegfried lurked mere steps away, his back to the wall and eyes closed as if he dozed; she knew better. Roosevelt's other men sat on the ground and used a stump as their card table.

Cy and Reddy were tending to Mr. Augustus in the bedroom. His fainting episode had lasted mere seconds. Cy had caught him as he slumped toward the ground.

"This life of mine involves a constant struggle between loyalties. Moral lines are not as clear as they once were." Roosevelt didn't look at her, instead gazing over the rail to the sprawling farmland and distant derricks. She didn't think she had ever seen him appear so weary.

"The truth was going to come out soon," Ingrid said. "*Excalibur* is garnering incredible attention. Someone will let it slip—in a derisive way, I'm sure—that a woman is the lead engineer. Mr. Augustus needed to know while all of us were here to support him. What if he had found out from a paper?"

"You are not wrong." His tone was quiet. "In a way, I am relieved. Since George and I found each other in San Francisco, I have debated the time and place for the telling. I had thought today would work, but on the way here, I decided against it."

"Hence your not-so-subtle glare toward us when you arrived."

He acknowledged that with a tilt of his head.

Ingrid reached out with her senses to check on the sylphs. They were still resting in a walnut tree. Fenris lurked beneath those branches as well. He had sworn that he needed air, but she figured he simply could not bear being around so many people in tight confines.

"Have you heard from Lee Fong and Mr. Sakaguchi?" Roosevelt asked.

"I don't know where they are. I don't even know if they're alive." Not lies.

"You should know that the missing kermanite was intercepted by soldiers in Texas. As of yesterday, it's aboard *Excalibur*. The crystal will return to California, where its future usage will be a subject of great debate, and hopefully, innovation."

The innovation of another dreadful war machine. Her lip curled in disgust.

"The kermanite had been in the possession of British nationals, two with known associations with the Thuggee movement in India. I will be flying to Texas next to interrogate them myself, though their testimony already clears Mr. Sakaguchi of complicity in the stone's theft."

"I'm glad." She wanted to say more, but couldn't manage words.

"I had best leave. I don't want my presence to further trouble George." Sincerity softened his tone. "Will you be staying in Los Angeles for a while longer?"

"For the next week, at least. With *her* after us, we're afraid to stay anyplace for long."

"That's wise." He motioned to Siegfried, who stepped

forward. "Here are the funds that you requested, and more. I understand that George will be reluctant to ask for anything from me right now, but perhaps he'll accept aid from his son."

Siegfried pulled a sealed packet from his back pocket, and then a billfold. He slipped out several bills and passed them to her with the envelope.

Ingrid glanced at the billfold to find several hundred-dollar bills; the thick envelope remained sealed in her grip. She thought of the metal they'd taken from the Chinese storehouse and felt almost sick. They *could* have bought some orichalcum, had they only waited.

Mr. Roosevelt was right. Moral lines were foggy indeed.

"I hope this will suffice for a while. If not, you know where to reach my contacts both here and abroad." T.R. adjusted his bowler hat, and gesturing for her hand, planted a quick kiss on her knuckles. The steps groaned in the wake of his quick footsteps. The card game on the stump immediately concluded, and a minute later, the sales truck rumbled back up the drive.

The door clanged a minute later as Cy joined her on the porch. For a moment, they simply stood together, watching the truck vanish from sight, a dust cloud in its wake.

"He gave us money. A lot of money." She passed the wad of cash to him. "He wants us to help your father as well."

He flipped through the bills. A low whistle escaped his lips. "Of course we'll help him—and Father wants to help us, too. He asked to return to Los Angeles with us. He wants to assist us in regard to Maggie, and lend a hand with your braces."

"What did you tell him about *why* I need leg braces?"

Cy cleared his throat. "He came right out and asked me if you were a geomancer. He heard kermanite clinking in your pocket, and recalled that we spoke before about deviant geomancy. He connected that with the intensity of the UP's interest in you and . . . well . . ."

"I suppose it's just as well that he knows. We're all family now, aren't we?"

Cy's smile was both tired and happy. "We are. I'm going to get that autocar in the barn functional right fast. Reddy's going to drive us to the *Bug*. He's staying here to run the farm. You don't figure that . . . thing will return to this area, do you?" He studied the sky.

"I can't say for certain, but if it did, it'd only be looking for me. Your father's probably more at risk being in my proximity."

Cy offered a grim nod. "Where's Fenris?"

"Here he comes. He must have heard us talking." She pointed toward Fenris, who approached with his head down and hands tucked in his trouser pockets. That wasn't his usual demeanor at all. "Fenris?"

He glanced up. His pale brown skin was flushed, his eyes glassy. "I'm not feeling particularly well. It may be best for me to take a nap."

CHAPTER 16

"Fenris doesn't get sick." Cy's already pale face appeared ghastly in the dim light of the cabin. Beyond the glass, the hills were cast in gray as twilight descended.

"Everyone gets sick a few times a year. It's normal." She tried to keep her tone light because she knew Cy needed it, but she was worried, too. Fenris didn't nap. He defied slumber, period.

"Even when he was injured so badly back in Chinatown, he only slept extra due to pain and drugs. Back in our academy days, if he slept three or four hours a night, that was an extraordinary event."

"I must ask as a precaution: Do you have his wig and clothes aboard?" She kept her voice especially low. George Augustus didn't know all their secrets, nor should he.

"Yes, they're packed with his things, always."

She nodded, relieved to know that. "Fenris barely ventures

out in public, but he has in recent days. He must have contracted influenza somewhere."

"I hope Father doesn't catch it. He's much more frail than he used to be." His brow was troubled. Mr. Augustus had also lain down for a nap soon after they took off. "But, Ingrid, what if this isn't influenza? What if it's a side effect of the injection?"

Ingrid had wondered that, too. "Then you would also be coming down with symptoms, wouldn't you?" She paused, head tilted in thought. "I'll be right back."

She patted his shoulder as she stood. She had removed the alpha brace upon their return. Unsurprisingly, the skin of her left foot and calf had broken out in a rash, with large welts marking her where the creased cloth and brace plates had continually rubbed. She'd need to buy some soothing balm in Los Angeles, and hope that her skin healed before she tested the next iteration.

She returned to the cockpit with a handful of newspapers. Cy focused on piloting but she caught his curious glances her way. After a few minutes she had culled several sheets from the past week.

"The influenza outbreak started in Atlanta. Papers only began to mention it after *Excalibur* left. As of yesterday, Atlanta is in quarantine because the death toll has mounted so quickly. Maybe we've been thinking about this all wrong." She sidled up to the other copilot's seat to better talk to Cy as he flew. "We know the Chinese have some weapons, and training in their use, illegal though that is—but they certainly don't have the means to adequately defend themselves. They need a different tack to fight the UP. To fight America."

"My God." Cy breathed out the words. "The laboratories. They created influenza as a weapon."

"If it *is* influenza. Don't a number of digestive illnesses display similar symptoms? The papers have latched on to that label, but I'm not sure if it should be trusted."

"That's a valid point."

"I'd bet you a dragon's hoard that Lee immunized me back in San Francisco, and since he befriended the two of you, he wanted you to stay safe amid this attack, too. That's why he sent us to that basement."

"It's brilliant. These laboratories were probably in sizable Chinatowns across the country." His expression was pained. "This was planned for a long time."

"As an awful necessity." She blinked back tears. "Lee must have known for months. No wonder he grieved over how the war would develop here."

Both of them remained lost in thought for several minutes. "We dare not tell T.R. I don't trust how he'd use this information," said Cy.

Ingrid sucked in a breath. "Cy. The focus of the attack must be *Excalibur*. But the papers haven't mentioned any sickness there."

"If the influenza truly is on board, the UP would try to keep it secret as long as possible. That's helped by the fact that *Excalibur* is under way. It's essentially a vessel under quarantine, except for some supply drops. But they wouldn't be able to keep it hidden forever. Their flight path would have to change. They surely couldn't stop in Los Angeles and expose soldiers and civilians there."

Out of nowhere, the soft chime of a bell rang in Ingrid's ears, followed by the divine scent of apple pie—the fruity freshness of the apples, the magical melding of butter and flour in the crust. For a moment, she expected to hear the heavy clatter of the oven door in Mr. Sakaguchi's kitchen, for Mama to hum as she pulled forth her glorious creation, like an angel on high heralding a miracle.

"I smell horses and leather," Cy whispered, longing in his words.

Ingrid pivoted quickly in her seat and found herself face-to-face with the *qilin*.

The celestial being stood in the doorway not a half foot away, its head as high as Ingrid's knee. Its body was covered by shimmering gold scales licked by flames that caused no damage to the mat beneath its delicate cloven hooves. The dragonlike head with its two small antlers angled to consider her.

"Ingrid Carmichael."

The invocation resonated through her body as if she stood near taiko drummers. She felt a brief spike of panic at the sound of her full name spoken aloud for the first time in weeks, but she reminded herself that not everyone could hear this being's words. *"Qilin."* Gripping the seat, she awkwardly slid to the floor.

"Great *qilin*, I beg your pardon," said Cy. "If you'll grant me a few minutes I can get us in a place to safely stay at a hover—"

"Bartholomew Cypress Augustus. Please continue to pilot. I know you intend no disrespect, and your mission is indeed one of urgency."

Ingrid bit her lip to contain a gasp. Cy could hear the *qilin* this time?

"I'm honored, Great One," he said in a reverent tone.

"I'm honored, too," Ingrid said, lowering her face to the tatami. "I've been trying to communicate with you—"

"You have always communicated with me. I reply as I will."

Humbled, Ingrid pressed her face lower, nose almost on the floor. Her legs pulsed with agony in this position, but she dared not move. She had begged and pleaded for the *qilin* to come, and it had. She had to be thankful and grit her teeth.

"How may I serve you?" Ingrid asked. A sentence she'd willingly say to very few beings in this world.

"Lee Fong." The name emerged with infinite tenderness. Ingrid imagined Lee somewhere, hundreds of miles away, shivering and looking around with a puzzled frown. "His life will remain in immense peril for as long as he breathes, but we come again to a juncture. A point when you can channel the water's flow of his existence and ensure that it does not evaporate."

She recalled the metaphor the *qilin* used during its last visit, about fate as a flash flood, difficult to direct. "I love Lee. I'll do anything I can to help him."

"You must walk in the coming days, and then you must confront the orichalcum island where it stops. Lee and his companions will be there, hiding in the most obvious and clever place."

Ingrid waited, wondering if a living map would come to life in her mind as it had when the *qilin* directed her before.

After long seconds of nothing, she spoke. "Those are . . . minimal directions. Can you be more specific? Great *qilin*?" Her nose bumped the matting.

A sense of amusement flowed through her, along with a whiff of blooming jasmine. "You possess the power of the earth itself in your frail form, but you are so very human. I have told you enough. The variables, the possibilities, are myriad. A mother with a young child cannot govern how her offspring places each foot, nor can I direct your steps. Nor do you truly wish for me to do so."

Ingrid couldn't deny that.

"We're honored you're helping us as much as you are," said Cy, his voice a low rumble. "Thank you."

"Ingrid Carmichael." The *qilin*'s voice was a breathy whisper. Ingrid took that as a cue to raise her head. Its wide amber eyes were inches away, its curved lashes as long as her fingers. "You are entrusted with the *guandao* blessed by green dragon's blood. You must know when the moment is right to hand it to Lee Fong."

With that, the celestial being bowed, one foreleg extended. Ingrid froze. The two antlers grazed her cheeks, gentle as the brush of sun-warmed grass. As the *qilin* righted itself, it offered her a slight nod, and then blinked out of existence. Gone, as if it'd never been there at all.

A full sense of reality returned. She pushed herself to sit and groaned as she used her hands to adjust her legs. "I guess you heard the whole conversation that time?"

"I did. I am . . . in awe. I wish I could've done more to show respect."

"Keeping us from crashing was adequate, I think."

"I'm all the more glad we have Father with us now. We'll get you walking in the next few days." His grim tone left no room for failure.

Ingrid bit back a whimper as she edged back into her seat, still rubbing her left calf. Beyond Cy, the glass revealed that stars had begun to emerge, their sparkles hesitant and shy.

"As if there wasn't pressure on us already. How long did that conversation last, all of two minutes? There's so much else I wanted to ask about. Lee's health. If Mr. Sakaguchi is still with him. About the sickness spreading around the country. How badly off Fenris is right now."

Cy glanced back. "Ingrid, would any of its answers truly satisfy you?"

"No, damn it." She blinked back tears. If her ojisan and Lee were separated, they'd be so much harder to find. "But a few enigmatic hints might have been better than nothing."

"The *qilin* is ultimately a being of peace. Everything it says and does is to assist the survival of the Chinese people." Cy was quiet for a long moment. "I wish I'd thought to ask how many of the Chinese were inoculated, to get even a hint of that truth. That might make all the difference right now."

"Oh?" She was only half listening, distracted as she massaged her leg.

"If this sickness is as virulent as the papers make it sound, the Chinese may actually win the war after all," Cy said softly. "They'll be the ones who remain healthy and alive."

INGRID LIMPED TO HER COT AND LISTENED TO THE SOUNDS OF sleep from the racks above and across from her. Fenris rustled and whimpered in his sleep. Ingrid hoped he didn't experience fever dreams, but she had a hunch that he already frequently battled nightmares. He often bolted from his cot as if he were being chased.

How was Lee sleeping these days as he recovered from his brush with death? She wanted to hug him and ruffle his hair, pretend things were as they always were. What a mirage that would be.

She reached to the back corner of her bed and found the plaque gifted to her by Fenris. He'd removed the *qilin* carving from the wall and mounted it on a polished piece of wood. She stroked the divots carved by Lee's hand. Tears came to her eyes.

"I'm coming to help you, Lee. I'll do all I can, but . . . God. The *qilin* said your life will always be in danger." She shook her head. "I suppose that's true for any of us, but for you . . . what does it mean? I save you now, but you'll be dodging armies and assassins for the rest of your days? What kind of life is that?"

A life he had chosen. He'd been a child when he had faced that dilemma, true, but his eyes were wide open, even then. He'd seen what the Chinese endured in California. He heard the mutters all around. He knew he needed to do his part. If he hadn't been the emperor's son, if he hadn't been graced by the *qilin*'s visits, he still would have fought as a soldier. His life was set to be one of hardship, no matter his path.

"And thank you, *qilin*. I don't think I adequately expressed my appreciation for your help. I am, as you note, very human. I suppose I can only apologize for that so much."

She set the plaque aside and rubbed both legs in turn, flinching at the contact with her sensitive skin. Looking for any kind of distraction, she focused on the sylphs in their cot above, and her heart raced in sudden alarm. She lurched to stand, tottering against the opposite bunk to keep her balance.

The sylphs' presence felt *diminished,* their buzz at half its normal volume.

Had she accidentally left sylphs behind in Bakersfield? Her return to the *Bug* had been such an anxious blur, with Fenris sick, Mr. Augustus adjusting aboard, and the need to check over the ship to make sure nothing was gone or left behind to spy on them.

She listened with her ears for a moment, ensuring that Mr. Augustus was still sound asleep, and hobbled to the pantry. The sylphs read her intent and followed without coaxing.

Ingrid sucked in a breath. Their number *was* halved. She held out a jamu-pan on her flattened palm, the way one would feed a horse. The sylphs swarmed, pecking away at the pastry. In a matter of seconds, it was gone.

"Where are the other sylphs?" she murmured.

They flashed a profound sense of satisfaction at her. *gone!* Their emotions didn't convey any sort of alarm or regret. If they'd felt anything of that sort on the return to the *Bug,* she *would* have noticed it. Instead, they were as happy as ever.

"Did they go . . . home?" she whispered, sparing some of her energy to portray snowcapped mountains for them. She had to imagine the Cascades, as she had only seen the Sierras close up in pictures.

yes! they said with buoyant enthusiasm.

She couldn't help but feel sad. If only they'd told her of their intent! She would have expressed her deep gratitude, and fortified them with more baked goods for their journey.

Ingrid sat on her cot and watched the remaining sylphs flutter back toward their bunk. She bit into a jamu-pan of her own. These rolls weren't as good; the baker hadn't even punched a divot in the top, so they didn't even look right to her way of thinking. But at least the strawberry jam inside was delicious.

"Fed the sylphs?" Cy softly called.

"Yes." She debated returning to the cabin to talk to Cy, but he'd continue to mull over the *qilin*'s words, and she didn't want to do that right now. She wanted . . . she didn't even know what she wanted. Peace for her, for Lee, for Cy, for all of them, but that was impossible. Not even heavenly beings could make such things happen.

"Goddamn it!" she spat. She punched the mattress, causing it to emit a squeak of protest.

Nearby privacy curtains rattled as they were pulled aside. "Is something wrong?"

Ingrid flushed as she faced Cy's father. "Everything's fine, sir. I'm sorry if I woke you by accident."

He arched an eyebrow. "Ma'am, I was married over thirty years. Declaring everything to be 'fine' is like trying to sell me a lame horse."

"Well then, sir, let me say that I'm incredibly frustrated, but I don't feel comfortable discussing the matter."

"That's fair," said Mr. Augustus. "I can't expect you to confess to me as if I'm some priest."

"Honestly, a frock would make a confession even less likely, sir."

He guffawed at that, then quieted as she motioned above and pressed a finger to her lips. "I daresay, I agree with you on that." He sat up and straightened his clothing, then stood to grab his jacket from the hook. "Can't bear to be too un-dressed in your presence. It's just not right."

She thought of her men's cotton drawers with yearning; she certainly couldn't wear those with Mr. Augustus aboard. "You should be comfortable, sir. Of course, I say that with my feet and ankles scandalously bared before you."

His soft snort reminded her of Cy. "Pardon my saying this, but I never understood why feet are judged so differently for men and women. As children, we all gamboled about as barefoot as hares."

As he shrugged on his jacket, his shadow glanced over her, dousing her senses like a bucket of melting ice. She couldn't continue to ignore this strangeness, not when it could be a threat to them.

"Mr. Augustus, sir—"

"If we're doing away with formalities, please, call me George." He sat again on the jutted edge of the lower bunk.

"I'd like for you to call me by my first name, but I'm afraid to say my own name aloud right now." She gave him a rueful shrug. "George, have you noticed a kind of . . . coldness around you?" She winced at her awkward choice of words.

He arched both eyebrows. "Have *you* noted such a coldness around me?"

"I have, sir. Sorry—George. Cy said you figured out that I'm a deviant geomancer. I am . . . particularly deviant, I suppose. I can also sense the magic of nearby fantastics. They feel warm to me. This coldness . . . I have never felt the like before."

His expression was thoughtful. "I *have* felt an odd chill around me since the quake, but I ascribed it to my injury and my recovery. I still would rather attribute the sensation to that, until I find evidence otherwise."

"You're a man of science."

"I am, and when you say you find something odd about my shadow, well . . . it strains belief. I say that with respect for you, however. I do believe that you're sensitive to a range of energy that I can't perceive. But this . . . this is like asking me to believe I'm being haunted."

Ingrid sat straighter. "You were surrounded by a lot of death during the earthquake."

"So were you," he retorted gently. "Why would a ghost attach itself to me?"

"Because you were there when he died. Because he is a man with a mission to complete." She stared at the shadow at George's feet. Was Captain Sutcliff *here*? Blum had said ghosts required a resilient personality. Sutcliff certainly had that.

"Oh no. No. The captain couldn't have— No. Ghosts don't exist."

"You know souls can exist separately from bodies. Think about tales of kitsune. They can steal a body once every century as a new tail completes its growth. The soul is left errant. Death can leave a soul errant, too. Why is it hard to believe such a spirit might attach itself to a person or place?" She made an effort to keep her voice low. Fenris tossed about in the rack above her.

"I do believe in souls, as I try to redeem my own. And now Maggie's." His face briefly sagged with grief. "I believe in magic, too, as a finite energy source. Fantastics *are* fantastic because they have the capacity to carry magic." He mulled his own words for a moment. "I suppose I believe in ghosts, then. As supernatural energy left adrift."

"Sometimes, reality defies tidy classifications." She leaned toward the shadow at George's feet, fingers grazing the tatami, and imagined the strings of life that she had seen tugged on by Reiki and *lingqi* doctors. She could not see colors as they did, but by God, she found coldness. She seized it, willing it corporeal.

Her fingers went numb as a harsh chill traveled up her arm and caused her to shiver. Her leg muscles clenched slightly in response. The coldness gained weight like that of a feather pillow, almost nothing yet still *substantial*. She rose to her feet as she dragged the chilliness up and out of George's

shadow. The entity had slackness and heft, and she kept pulling upward. A strange sensation rose with it—the feeling of
presence. The way you know someone stands behind you, even
though they haven't made a sound. There was no malevolence
to it, nor did the sylphs react with any kind of alarm.

Ingrid's hand rose over her own head. Only then did she
feel that the full volume of the shadow had been revealed.

Captain Sutcliff stood in the corridor.

CHAPTER 17

Captain Sutcliff was transparent, his colors muted in a way that reminded her of old photographs colored by hand. He wore his Army & Airship Corps Unified Pacific uniform with its double row of buttons down the chest and neat pinstripes down the legs. Everything about him smacked of military precision, just as in his living days. He showed none of the injuries that caused his death, thank God.

He stared at her, then glanced around as he took a step back, taking in his environs. Finally, he plucked off his slouch hat to grant her an abbreviated bow. "Miss, whose last name I dare not state for reasons of safety." His words drifted over her face like a puff of arctic wind.

"Oh, good heavens." She hastily stepped back.

"Ingrid?" George stood. "What—"

"You don't hear him? You don't see him?" She tried not to sound hysterical. She had met so many powerful and strange entities of late, but none of them had been a dead man—the particular dead man who had made her life a living hell in those hours and days after the Cordilleran Auxiliary had exploded.

"He cannot. I've tried to converse with him for weeks," said Captain Sutcliff with an apologetic tilt of his head. "I hoped he might come across you again, but I didn't think we would be able to speak. I had no idea that you were so . . . attuned to the magical and spiritual. All I knew was that you would continue to pursue justice for Mr. Sakaguchi in regard to the kermanite. Our goal is the same."

Ingrid tried to take in all of that as she looked at George. "Captain Sutcliff's ghost is standing beside you right now."

George glanced every which way. "I see nothing different than before."

"Is it all right if we . . . attempt to touch your spectral form?" she asked Sutcliff. Once upon a time, she would have rolled her eyes if she'd read such a line in a dime novel.

"I can feel nothing as I once did. I will take no offense."

Ingrid held out her hand. Her fingertips passed through his arm as if she probed the interior of an icebox.

George followed her example, frowning. "The coldness could be from the ventilation system aboard." He gestured to a vent above.

"Miss, if you would, please tell Mr. Augustus that I regret that I won't get to enjoy a bottle of Red Hollow Kentucky bourbon with him again."

She repeated what Sutcliff said. George's face drained of all color, leaving him almost like a ghost himself.

"Oh, dear Lord," he whispered. "I told him I'd have a bottle sent his way. I didn't—I didn't mention bourbon before."

"No. You only mentioned nihonshu. Sit, George. Please." She hoped Fenris was using beeswax to plug his ears. It was a wonder he hadn't pulled open the curtain to grouse at them.

George shakily sat. "Why is he here? Why with me?"

"What can you tell us, Captain? Have you heard us all this while . . . ?" she asked. She realized that speaking with him was like any conversation, and didn't draw away any of her energy.

"I hear everything said around George, and an inhuman range beyond." He considered Ingrid. His manners seemed radically different than before. Softer. More thoughtful. Death apparently changed a man; but perhaps many of those changes had begun during his final night of life.

Captain Sutcliff cast his gaze downward as if ashamed. "As I died, I sensed that . . . a good place did not await me. I knew many regrets in those moments. I despaired for you, miss. I desperately wished I could have investigated the Thuggees. I raged that the kitsune had stolen that opportunity from me, that the city was being destroyed because I hadn't heeded your warning. I dreaded that the ambassador would recover the kermanite and use it as she wished. And so, I willed my spirit to stay on this realm."

She noted that he had adopted her avoidance of speaking Blum's name aloud. That was telling. "I'm sorry that you were in anguish at the end." All too recently, she had hated this man, hated the events he set in motion. Now, she realized, her hatred had been replaced by a deep sense of sadness. Sutcliff had been yet another of Blum's game pieces, and he'd lost everything as a result. Everything except this second chance as a ghost.

"Please apologize to Mr. Augustus for me. I have haunted him out of necessity. If I wander far from the familiar, I find that I begin to lose my sense of self. I become very confused."

Ingrid relayed the message. "I'm not aggrieved," George said. "He can linger with me as long as he needs to. He gave me my life. The least I can do is help him achieve his mission."

"What *is* your mission?" she asked Sutcliff. "If you can hear beyond a normal range, you know what Ambassador Roosevelt said to me."

"Yes. The recovery of the kermanite does not grant me the peace it would have when I was alive. I know more now." He dipped his head. "The kitsune cannot possess it. I cannot bear for it to be used to energize a machine of war that could later be used against *us*."

"You sound like Roosevelt," she said.

He smiled, and she realized it might have been the first time she had seen him do so. "I take that as high praise. My goal as an officer was to perhaps work beneath his direction one day. I welcome the chance to do so even after death." His expression sobered. "If the kermanite cannot be used for the sole benefit of the United States, it should be destroyed."

Destroyed. The very suggestion felt blasphemous, and yet . . . "That wouldn't be difficult to do, with how kermanite naturally fragments . . . but the shards would be incredibly dangerous." She paused. "I could destroy it in a more internal, controlled manner, though my close contact with such immense energy would bring a different kind of peril."

George arched an eyebrow. "I do believe I'm gathering enough of the gist of this conversation to state, emphatically, that such destruction is not a good idea if it places you in that much danger. I'm quite sure Barty would agree."

"Shattering kermanite and creating a wide radius of shrapnel is a poor idea as well," she said. "I knew an apprentice who once lost an eye after he dropped an average piece of kermanite." She held up her fist for size comparison. "But this dilemma is too inconceivable to dwell on right now. We don't know how we can even access *Excalibur* at this point."

Sutcliff cast his gaze downward. "Much of what has happened still feels inconceivable to me, even the reality of my own death." He took in a rattling, pointless breath. "I must use this opportunity to apologize to you for the aggressiveness of my investigation against you and Mr. Sakaguchi. I made crude insinuations about your relationship and assumed the worst of your motivations. There's a great deal that I didn't understand, and likely never will, but I know I was a cad and a fool. I am sorry." He offered her a bow, his hat over his heart.

"I . . . I don't hate you like I did back in San Francisco," she said, conscious of how that sounded in front of George. "But I can't say I fully forgive you either. I don't want to lie to you, not about something that important."

"I respect that, and you." He repeated his bow.

George stared toward the ghost. "I wish I could see him for myself. Or hear him, at least, so that we could palaver again."

"I wish you could, too," Ingrid said, voice thick. "The past month has been one surprise after another. I used to be a sim-ple secretary for the Cordilleran Auxiliary, you know."

George offered a sympathetic smile. "I can't even imagine all you've endured, but I doubt you were ever a 'simple secretary.'"

She shook her head ruefully at that, conceding the point.

"Ingrid?" Cy called down the corridor. "We're coming into Los Angeles."

"I'll retreat for now. I don't want my presence to be both-ersome to you." Captain Sutcliff shrank, his figure dwindling and thinning like smoke until it vanished completely. Ingrid shivered, even though she didn't feel any of his chill.

"The captain has returned to your shadow for now," she said, motioning to George, who remained in place.

"I'll follow momentarily," he said, his expression thoughtful.

Using the walls for balance, she walked to the control cabin, where Cy greeted her with a tired yet warm smile.

"Thought I heard you talking with my father."

"Yes. And another unexpected passenger on board," she said.

"Did the *qilin* return?" He sounded puzzled.

"I sensed something strange about your father's shadow. He's being haunted by Captain Sutcliff—"

"What?" That single word contained an ocean of panic. He began working a series of toggles on the dash. Ingrid reached to grip his elbow.

"It's not as bad as it sounds. You don't need to rush back there."

"But Sutcliff—"

"I *know*. Trust me, I know. And you might also remember that Sutcliff saved your father's life in San Francisco, and died because of it," she said, and Cy's tension abated some. "Sutcliff has been clinging to him ever since. I'm apparently the only person who can speak to him or see him."

"My father is being haunted by a ghost." His brow furrowed, and he began to adjust the toggles again.

"This isn't like something out of a gothic novel. Sutcliff is on a quest for redemption. He needs to stop the stolen kermanite from being used by Japan."

"Do you believe that's truly his aim?"

She considered that for a moment. "Even when he was alive, he never came across as a liar. What he believed, he believed with absolute conviction, no matter the folly. Now he thinks divine intervention has brought him here so he can help me and right the wrongs he did. He's lost everything but his soul, and if he errs now, he's very aware he'll lose that as well. So yes, I believe him."

"Those are mighty high stakes indeed." He glanced back, expression thoughtful. "How's my father taking this news about Sutcliff?"

"With proper southern aplomb, my boy." George braced himself on the doorway to the cabin. "Though do be aware that ghosts apparently have good hearing. There are no secrets in his presence."

"An important consideration," Cy said with a grimace. "Fenris still sleeping?"

"Yes, by some miracle. And he is alive. I could hear him tossing and turning up there." Ingrid claimed her usual seat, and felt a pang as George claimed the seat once frequented by Lee.

The cloudless night allowed the stars to shine in all their glory, with additional ornamentation in the form of diversely colored envelopes and galleys of various airships.

The settlements of Southern California sparkled in a similar way down below, each town like an island of illuminated cross-hatching. Los Angeles stood out with its tall buildings, though they looked diminutive from on high.

The *Bug* gradually dropped in elevation. The bright railway line provided them a guide straight south to Dominguez Field. The empty land that flanked the track resembled a black sea at night, the tracks like a long bridge.

"The sheer number of airships about is peculiar," said George.

"It is," Cy said. "They look to be small private and commercial vessels, too, not military."

They approached their port on the mesa. "The mast for vessels going to and from the hangars is still free," Cy muttered. "I count only four others vacant besides."

"The other nearby docks looked just as bad as we flew over," mused George.

"This traffic reminds me of how Seattle looked with the Baranov rush," Ingrid added.

"Something's drawn people here, and I don't like it one bit." Cy eased them toward the mast. Boys awaited them to assist in the docking. Ingrid and George remained quiet and tense as the engine noise wound down. Cy rose and opened up the hatch.

"Hey! You booked a hangar already?" called a faint voice. "Otherwise, you gotta—"

"We do, we're in seven. What's going on? We just flew out earlier today—"

"We didn't expect this either. It's all because of that *Excalibur*. People from all over are flying west to see it on the approach. Fares are going up, part and parcel of the demand."

"I see. I'll go to the depot to check on our account . . ." Cy's voice faded as his feet clattered down the steps.

"All of this hubbub because of *Excalibur*," she murmured. "The citadel is entertainment for them. A novelty."

"For some of them, I'm sure," said George, "but I imagine some newcomers are families coming to say farewell to soldiers set to deploy."

"*Excalibur* isn't even close to California yet. Why's everyone arriving now?" Frowning, she reached for the newspapers she had left pinned between her chair and the wall, looking at older issues first. "Oh. The citadel was originally due to arrive in Los Angeles two days from now. These people flew here cross-country based on the original estimates."

"Where is the vessel currently?" asked George. "I'm behind on the news."

"It just left Texas, headed into New Mexico Territory." Whenever it stopped moving, they had to be ready to intercept it.

George drummed his fingers on the back of the chair. "Curious, how *Excalibur* has slowed down so much. I wonder if this delay is Theodore's doing."

"Perhaps in part," she said, and desperately hoped that maybe, just maybe, the influenza would only make people on board really sick and wouldn't kill them outright.

What if Maggie fell ill? What if she died? How would that effect Cy—and *Excalibur*?

"We docked? We're in Los Angeles?" Fenris's voice was hoarse. Ingrid stood to better see him. He leaned against the pantry on the other side of the hatch.

"We are. How are you feeling? Did you sleep well?" she asked.

He shrugged in an apparent answer to the last question. "I feel better, actually. Still tired and achy, as if a titan used me as a footstool, but I can work."

"I don't think that's a—" started Ingrid.

Metal banged on the mast deck below, followed by heavy footsteps on the stairs. Cy's upper body emerged through the hatch. He looked both ways and gasped in relief when he saw Ingrid. "Come inside to the berthing. Away from the windows." He bounded the rest of the way inside and fastened down the hatch. "Fenris! You're looking better."

"I decided not to go keel-up today after all. Now, what the hell are you going on about?"

"This." Cy pulled a sloppily folded sheet from his pocket. Ingrid hobbled toward him to see. "Saw this posted in the office just now."

REWARD

FOR INFORMATION LEADING TO THE CAPTURE OF

INGRID CARMICHAEL

SUSPECTED OF COMPLICITY

WITH SAN FRANCISCO CHINAMEN

Ingrid's jaw dropped. She yanked the paper from his hands and skimmed the contents. "How nice of them to ask that I not be harmed. My goodness, with a five-thousand-dollar reward in the offering, I hope I'm being delivered encased in velvet."

Five thousand dollars. That was more money than most folks would see in a *lifetime*. She felt light-headed and groped her way along the wall to her usual sitting spot on her bunk. She read the sheet again, dry-mouthed. She looked up as the others joined her.

"You're named on here, too, Cy. You need to be careful."

"I'm also an average-looking white man and therefore a dime for three dozen."

The last thing Ingrid would call him was average-looking, but now was not the time to argue over the matter.

"We need to walk the docks and major rail stations throughout the area," said George. "See how widely distributed this is. It may be posted in the major papers as well, as deserter notices are."

She skimmed the paper again and again, her fingers trembling. Tears burned in her eyes. She just wanted peace. For the world, for herself. She wanted Blum stopped once and for all.

"Should we leave in the morning?" asked Fenris.

Cy pursed his lips. "She only went out in daylight a few times, and wore her hood for part of that."

"I don't think we can risk that again, not with this everywhere," she murmured, shaking the paper.

"We can't head out to the boonies," Cy continued. "Our orichalcum needs to be processed and we need access to other supplies, too."

"How soon until we're in the hangar?" she asked, her throat tight.

"Another hour, they estimate. The crews are shuffling other airships around."

"Very well." She looked at the men gathered around her. "I'll stay in berthing for now, away from the windows, and I won't go beyond the hangar while we're here."

Cy looked stupefied by how readily she had accepted such confinement. "Are you sure . . . ?"

The presence of George prevented her from snapping her reply. "I'm not sure about much of anything these days, Cy, but we need my braces done and we need to stay here to do that. My question is, can you truly get something made in the next few days?"

Cy rubbed his beard. "We're under a mighty deadline to work a miracle, and we'll work it."

"Good thing she has a crew of geniuses at the ready," said Fenris with a yawn.

That made both Cy and George smile. "Father, you get to relive your machinery-by-lamplight days," Cy said wryly.

"Sounds a mite better than the paperwork-by-lamplight I've known in recent years. Show me the schematics you have and this alpha brace of yours. Let's get going."

Cy clapped his father on the arm and guided him to where the project was stored.

Fenris plopped down on the bunk across from Ingrid. "We ended up with a ghost on board after all, eh?"

She shakily laughed. "You did overhear us. I'm sorry."

"Beeswax can only block so much." He shrugged. "Don't waste your time feeling guilty over it. The ship is small. Not like there are a multitude of places where you can sit and talk."

"I can't believe I'm hearing you speak critically of the *Bug*. You *are* sick." She still wondered again if his illness was due to the injection.

Fenris gave the wall an affectionate pat. "That wasn't criticism, just a gently stated fact." He stood. "Keep the gun with you, just in case, but Cy might notice it soon."

"I'll talk to him about it," she said. "Fenris? Since you'll likely be out on errands soon, can you do me a favor?"

"Maybe?"

"Can you please get me some books to help me pass the time these next few days? Some adventures, perhaps—ones that don't feature swooning women on the cover."

"That may limit the available selection, but yes, I can get some books for you. I can get tamales, too. You should try some other than pork—they're all good. I can't let you starve in captivity."

"Thank you. I think you make a far better prison warden than the fox."

"That's the nicest thing anyone's said to me all day," said Fenris. He reached up to his bunk and slid out the slender copper length of his Tesla rod. He twiddled with it, frowning, manipulating some setting she couldn't comprehend. "There. If anyone comes after you, one strike with this and it'll cause an instantaneous heart attack."

She believed him. He'd already used that technique, or something similar, in Honolulu. "That's about the nicest thing anyone's said to *me* all day, too."

Fenris's intense gaze lingered on her for a moment, and then he moved to join the other men in their lively discussion of her brace modifications. Ingrid remained in place, the crumpled paper on her lap.

Amid all her fear, she knew a strange sense of peace that was not provoked by the manipulations of the *qilin*.

She was loved.

CHAPTER 18

WEDNESDAY, MAY 23, 1906

The chilly presence of the ghost contrasted with the heat of the noon sunlight that sliced through the curved window of the control cabin. Captain Sutcliff stood at the back of the chamber, behind the copilot's chair. Since he had tethered his spirit to the *Palmetto Bug* rather than George the previous day, the temperature throughout the ship had dropped several degrees.

Ingrid leaned forward in her seat as if she could make the *Bug* fly faster. They had exited Los Angeles in the middle of the night so that they could arrive in Phoenix at midday.

Having seen the forested hills of Cascadia and the unreal greenery of Hawaii, she had been eager to view the desert southwest. However, after enduring the scenery for several hours, she was less enthused. The color green didn't exist here. Endless wasteland sprawled to the far curve of the horizon, the hills and rocks in varied shades of brown. She had seen no active rivers since they crossed the Colorado at the territorial border, only dry fissures choked with trees and shrubs that tenaciously clung to life. Even the blue sky seemed bleached of its normal vivacity.

This, not the lava lake of Kilauea, was Ingrid's idea of hell.

Cy's socks whispered on the tatami as he returned to the cabin and sat across from her. He'd been a bit withdrawn today, understandably sad after having said good-bye to his father the previous evening. George had returned to Bakersfield. He'd volunteered to continue on with them, but his health had already suffered due to long hours of work in the hangar bay.

Excalibur had reached Phoenix two days before. It had idled there ever since. According to Cy, the rumors as to *why* had been downright imaginative, and the Unified Pacific had done little to placate the public with its bland statements that all was well. No one believed that now.

Ingrid could only hope that they could still find Lee in town, and that Mr. Sakaguchi was with him.

"I'm spying some reflected light far in the distance," said Fenris. "We may finally be nearing that citadel."

Ingrid bolted upright to look out the window, her braces granting her new pep. "Oh. It just looks like clouds to me."

"That's the point. The papers called it the White Cloud Fleet, remember?" Fenris's voice was still a touch raspier than usual. They could only conclude that he alone had experienced a mild reaction to the vaccine, as he had slept more in recent days and run a low fever. It was clear he hadn't contracted the sickness that had now caused quarantines in Atlanta, Little Rock, and Amarillo—all places along *Excalibur*'s route—and had continued to spread from there. Reports had related gruesome details of boarding-houses with two thirds of the occupants deceased, of babies found screaming with parents rendered too ill to move, or dead.

If this epidemic was indeed the Chinese attack, then it might prove more effective and efficient than the triggered earthquakes and the technological might of the Unified Pacific.

"That is the fleet," said Captain Sutcliff. "Seven Pegasus gunships in formation around the citadel. I am in awe that this project was carried out with such secrecy. The Gaia Project was a mere rumor a month ago."

"The captain says there are seven gunships around *Excalibur*." Ingrid repeated the words for the benefit of Cy and Fenris.

"Damn. Ghost has good eyesight. Can he see *through* that floating chunk of orichalcum?" asked Fenris.

Captain Sutcliff considered this. "I don't see as I once did. I believe I am . . . sensing the ambient heat of the kermanite on each vessel. I can tell where the largest piece is on the far side, and that a chain of other strangely large pieces is being utilized to power the craft."

Ingrid didn't contain her surprise. "That's right. T.R. described how the kermanite was rigged aboard, back before you joined us. You could guide us straight to the engine room on board! Why didn't you mention this during all of our plotting over the past few days?"

Sutcliff's expression became rather dreamy. "I didn't

know. The closeness of my goal seems to have increased my sensitivity to kermanite all around."

She repeated the relevant information to the others.

"That will prove useful, if we can get on board. If our spectral soldier can find a way to do *that*, then I hope he shares right away," said Fenris.

The current plan was to find Lee and Mr. Sakaguchi while conducting reconnaissance on *Excalibur*, and, if possible, seize an opportunity to infiltrate the citadel and retrieve Maggie while the crew was largely incapacitated. If she would help them sabotage *Excalibur* while they were there, then all the better. Ingrid wasn't betting money on that outcome, though. It sounded like Maggie would need an awful lot of convincing.

"A way will open for us," Sutcliff intoned. "I have come this far. I am blessed in this mission."

Ingrid arched an eyebrow. "Blessed, other than the fact you were crushed to death by a falling building?"

"Life is finite. I'm looking toward immortality." His tone was gentle in a way that unsettled her. Sometimes she almost preferred the brash, arrogant, easy-to-despise Sutcliff to this newly enlightened one.

Cy slipped into his copilot's chair with a sharp intake of breath. "Look at that thing."

Past a rocky mesa curved like a saddle, *Excalibur* hovered several thousand feet above the ground. It truly did resemble a castle keep constructed of rounded towers and turrets, its matte-white paint allowing scant reflection from the intense sunlight. Even at a distance, Ingrid could see mooring masts that crested it at various levels, and the broad doors that allowed access to the holds.

Closer still, white-painted airships maintained their positions to guard *Excalibur*. The nearest gunship flew toward them. Lights flashed along the hull.

"What does it mean?" she asked. The sequence repeated again. She needed to acquire a book to learn this language, even if she never became a full pilot herself.

"A clear message of 'Stay away, or we'll shoot,'" said Fenris. "I would like to offer a message as well—"

"I'll handle the reply without your contribution, thank you kindly," said Cy, already working at buttons along the panel. Fenris aimed the *Bug* in a southeasterly direction, skirting far around the designated perimeter.

"Are the Pegasus gunships there to prevent civilian ships from attempting to dock, or to stop anyone from fleeing the citadel?" asked Ingrid.

"Both, I imagine," said Cy. "I hate to think of the hell that has occurred on board, with so many sick and dying. Some men would try to flee. Some always do. But others would maintain the presence of mind to know that escapees might spread the illness to their parents and wives and children—some of whom are probably waiting to see them in Los Angeles, not that far away."

Ingrid glanced at Sutcliff, surprised he had no comment. He looked lost in thought, one hand pressed to his mouth as if he might be ill himself.

She returned her focus to the window as the *Bug* began to descend.

"That's Phoenix?" she asked, skeptical.

"Yes, and quite the bustling center of civilization it is, too," said Fenris.

Phoenix proper looked like scarcely more than a village, its streets bare dirt and buildings no more than two floors in height. An especially large canal cut to the north, to high mountains in the distance. A few sizable mountains squatted right near town, the vivid red of their rocks bold against the sun-weary dirt. Patches of agriculture were a surprise against the brownness of the desert, the way a hiccup might interrupt a sentence. A scrub-covered mountain range clustered to the north.

"The town doesn't look like much, only about five thousand folks, but it *is* civilization for this valley. Maybe, without the war and so many men lost this past decade, the west would've been settled more. There are a lot of places like this out here, places of promise that've withered on the vine," said Cy. "Fenris, look for a tin roof with 'Cortez' painted on it. That'll be our dock." He'd had the foresight to call from Los Angeles to find a dock willing to reserve a mast for the *Bug*—and he promised a rather exorbitant payment for the privilege.

Fenris grunted. "Another Pegasus is flashing lights at us as a reminder. Huh."

"What?" asked Ingrid.

"Its guns are out, and I do believe I see smoke."

"The gunship shot down another airship," said Captain Sutcliff. "You cannot see the wreckage from here. The citadel blocks the view. Five people died."

Ingrid looked at him, aghast. "How do you know *that*?"

Cy jerked his gaze to where he knew the ghost stood.

"I . . . I don't know." Sutcliff's spectral visage looked fright-ened. He sank into a crouch, hands pressed to his head. "Dear God, why am I aware of these things? This is too much."

"Captain Sutcliff?" She moved closer to him, feeling the need to provide some kind of comfort.

The ghost softly sobbed into his hands. "This is too much. My eyes are *seeing too much*."

Ingrid quietly repeated this to the others as Captain Sutcliff remained inconsolable. They all remained silent after that, no one sure what to say.

With the airship dock in sight, Sutcliff stood again. He straightened his transparent clothes and regained much of his bearing.

"Deaths seem to create puncture wounds in the living world, punctures that seep hints of the next life beyond. On *Excalibur* . . ." His voice quavered. "There are many such wounds on *Excalibur*. More than I can even estimate."

INGRID THOUGHT CY MIGHT ARGUE AGAINST HER SUGGESTION TO walk about town together, but to her surprise, he readily agreed.

"Sounds good to me. Let's scout out the place." He had returned from his talk with the stationmaster, his pockets lighter. He didn't wear his jacket. It was strange to see him openly carry a gun holstered at one hip and the Tesla rod on the other. Arizona Territory didn't discourage such things.

"No wanted posters?" Fenris called from the engine room.

Cy shook his head. "Not a one, but plenty of others for local wanted men. This is a speck of nothing, far as the UP's concerned. I doubt that even the fox would expect us out here, almost in the shadow of *Excalibur*. Smart folks would steer clear of a place with such a strong military presence overhead."

"Smart folks? *Us?*" Fenris guffawed. "She clearly isn't considering everything we've done in the past month."

"We're still alive," Cy said.

"Likely proof of divine intervention rather than intelligence on our parts." He ducked back into the room and began to clang on metal.

Ingrid cringed at the noise. "How many soldiers are out there?"

"None. The local garrison was withdrawn in advance of *Excalibur*'s arrival, and right as curious folks invaded to take a gander at the citadel above. Those people are starting to leave now. That downed airship today isn't the first."

She frowned. "The garrison actually *left*? It sounds like the A-and-A is saving their own in case the sickness spreads here. Why not warn the public?"

"Because they'd riot, for one. For another . . . this is a geographically isolated area. If they need to impose a full quarantine, they'll strafe the docks to destroy the airships and blockade the roads." He said this matter-of-factly.

Ingrid paled. "That extreme hardly seems necessary when the sickness has already spread elsewhere."

"That's the very reason why they *would* go to that extreme.

Whatever this is, it's highly contagious with a high mortality rate. They're trying to contain it however they can." The worry in his eyes revealed he was thinking of Maggie and how she fared aboard. "Have you sensed any other magical threats?"

"No, nothing since we set off." She hadn't held any power since their close call in Bakersfield, though she had faintly heard one of Blum's *things* fly over Dominguez twice during her seclusion.

Cy glanced behind him. "The sylphs are sure being loud."

The fae cloud advanced down the hallway. Ingrid had seen them abuzz when they had landed before, but never like this. They emitted an undulating trill as they wavered in place. She reached out to them, but found herself denied. The sylphs were fully engaged in whatever it was they were doing.

"Are they trying to leave?" Cy asked.

"No. It's like they're in a deep conversation right now, or some such." Was this part of a mating ritual? Maybe she didn't want to know.

A few minutes later, she clambered down the stairs behind Cy.

The combined brilliance of George, Cy, and Fenris had been almost frightening to behold. By the end of the weekend, they had worked through four more tin prototypes, and by Monday had placed an expedited order for the ori to be processed.

The finished braces fit inside her boots, with strategically placed orichalcum reinforcing her from the arches of her feet to her upper calves. The sliver-thin plates added no extra weight to her step. Her stride felt stronger, though a bit strange. With practice, Ingrid hoped to soon walk down stairs without feeling as though she could fall flat on her face at any moment. Glory be!

Four days of confinement in their airship hangar had left her restless yet ambivalent about venturing into public. Therefore, she had thought ahead to attire herself in a way quite unlike the staid auxiliary faculty photograph used in her wanted poster.

Cy had acquired a broad-brimmed hat for her. The finely woven straw curved to one side, rather like an ocean wave, and was crested with a cascade of ostrich feathers. With it, she wore one of the smocks Lee had packed for her, an understated gray gown in Orientalist cut with kimono-styled sleeves and an obi to cinch her waist.

"Perhaps my body has adjusted a bit too much to the new coolness aboard the *Bug*," she said. "It feels awfully hot here."

Cy chuckled. "This is spring in Phoenix. You should see August, when the temperature doesn't drop below ninety degrees at night and violent monsoons roll in during the afternoon."

"Don't you ever bring me here in August, then."

The early afternoon breeze reminded her of peering into a searing oven. Sudden homesickness welled in her. She was a San Francisco girl. She wanted coolness and fog and *greenery*. From their vantage point, she knew none of those elements were available here. There was dust, so very much dust. The ground below the dock was paved over with bricks, but even those were yellow with dirt that swirled and choked the air as an airship at a neighboring mast lifted off.

Downtown had only some five streets running east and west, the buildings of wood and brick with no evidence of Japanese influence. They looked like relics preserved from the days of early photography, before the War Between the States.

"You lived here for a while, did you?" she asked, then sneezed.

"Bless you. Yes, we were here for almost a year. One of the things I liked best was that folks here prize independence, don't ask too many personal questions."

"Let's hope that's still true. Have you given thought to where we should look here? We were advised they'd be in a place that was *obvious and clever*."

He glanced at her sidelong. "I reckon we're thinking the same sort of locale."

"A laundry," she said softly, though acknowledging the stereotype made her wince. Laundering clothes had been the most common, socially acceptable job for Chinese residents across the western states and territories. She once heard some geomancers—white, wealthy men—state that Chinese were mentally suitable for no other line of work. She'd been about to open her mouth to retort when Lee kicked her shin. He'd been beside her, eyes downcast as appropriate, acting as if he hadn't heard a thing.

Later, when they spoke about it, Lee had let his true emotions show. "Let them underestimate us," he'd said, his eyes smoldering with fury. "They'll learn our hands can do a lot more than wash clothes." She'd been too ignorant—too damned oblivious—at the time to realize he was hinting at the life-and-death fight ahead.

"A laundry," Cy repeated. "A place so obvious for the Chinese to be, no one would think to look there now—not if they took proper care to hide their whereabouts."

"Do you know where to find the laundries in town?"

He nodded. "I know of two."

Only five masts occupied this dock, so it was a quick walk to the gate. A group of men conversed there in the sparse shade cast by a booth.

"Howdy there, folks," Cy said, flashing one of his winning smiles. Ingrid stood back, head angled down, arms demurely crossed at her waist.

One of the suited men shook Cy's hand. "How are you? Just landed? Come to see our war machine?"

"War machine, at war against whom?" grumbled one of the others. "Us?"

"That crashed airship tried to get too close to the perimeter. They got what was coming." The suited man shook his head. "Folks who can't follow the language of lights shouldn't be pilots."

Ingrid was confused for a moment, then realized they must be talking about the airship that was shot down by a Pegasus gunship.

"Reporters should also know when to mind their own affairs," added another man with a husky grunt. He wore dusty dungarees and a plaid shirt. "Tried to fly close to take photographs, he did."

"I heard it's cursed," added another man. He jerked his head toward the hovering white citadel barely visible above buildings on the far side of the dock.

"Cursed!" scoffed the suited man. "Do you realize how much concentrated effort it takes to curse something? If the chankoro could have cursed us, they'd have done it a decade ago, when they still had *numbers*!"

"Well, something's seriously wrong, innit?" The man breathed out cigarette smoke. "That contraption didn't fly like they said it would, and now it's stopped here. They're not pulling up supplies like they should either. Just one ship went up yesterday, and it hasn't come back down. Any way you squint at the situation, it looks peculiar."

"Maybe you just need glasses," said one of the other men, spurring a round of laughter.

"I heard there's sickness aboard. That influenza that's spreading bad back east." The man's eyes were troubled. "That's why I come down here to the dock. Buying the wife and children tickets down to Las Cruces to her kinfolk. I'm getting them away from that thing."

"I'm keeping my wife here. She could use some influenza, might help her lose some weight." The men laughed again. Ingrid clutched her hands together, utilizing the calm she had so often practiced in the auxiliary. The men likely wouldn't have engaged in such crude banter with a lady present, but then, to them Ingrid's skin tone meant that she was no lady.

"Thank you for the welcome, gentlemen." Cy said the last word as if he meant it, but she recognized the annoyed undercurrent in his voice. He tipped his hat, and the others did the same in turn, continuing their talk. Cy and Ingrid moved on.

"And people say women gossip," Ingrid muttered.

"Gossip makes for good currency for us. Few newspapers would have the gumption to publish anything less than patriotic about *Excalibur.* Angry men have looser lips."

"I wonder at his mention of one supply ship going up yesterday. We'd considered hitching a ride like that ourselves," she whispered as they traversed a walkway into the modest business district. "If the Chinese used that method to infiltrate *Excalibur,* what can they do on board?"

Cy remained alert yet nonchalant. "Depends on their numbers. I imagine *Excalibur* can stay aloft on its own with a couple crew, but to actually pilot it, you'd need dozens. Maybe a hundred. Maintaining balance on a craft like that must be tricky."

"It'd be far easier to crash it, then. Or try to blow it up," she muttered.

"Those would be easily achievable with a handful of men, especially if Sutcliff's right about the number of dead crew up there." He was silent, studying signs as they passed by. "God Almighty, I hope Maggie is all right." He had voiced that thought many times since they had returned from Bakersfield.

Ingrid grazed her elbow against his to offer brief, supportive contact. "If we make it up there, you're going to experience a rather awkward family reunion."

"Yes." He sighed. "But I think I can talk sense into her. Get her to walk away. Go with us. She likes a challenge, and helping the Chinese would be a fine mental exercise for her. Maybe she can eventually join Father. Start over, with no fuss about profits and board meetings and annual expectations."

"They could start a business making braces. There's demand these days. Maybe we could all join in." She had to lighten the mood; she didn't want Cy falling into despair.

"That's a wonderful idea. Might be a good new angle for our trade." He smiled, then nodded to motion past her. "There's a German bakery across the way. We need to stop in as we return to the dock. Hopefully the critters won't mind a new nationality of pastry."

"I'll eat what they don't. Strawberry strudel is manna from heaven, far as I'm concerned."

"Let's hope strawberry is available, then. Perhaps we can find some tamales around, too."

Such light chatter, as if they were on a casual stroll together with no worries about Ingrid being recognized, even as other men appraised her the same way they regarded passing horses. Few women were about, and none of them made eye contact. She and Cy weren't the only ones who were tense here. *Excalibur*'s literal shadow didn't darken the town, but its looming presence cast a deep pall indeed.

The roar of kermanite-powered machines warned them of a laundry just ahead. Ingrid and Cy shared a look.

"Would any Chinese be working in the middle of the day?" she murmured.

"I reckon not. Sentiments are too high right now. But let's amble by and see."

A glance inside showed a white woman at the counter,

while darker-skinned women worked around the machines. Perhaps more notable were the two signs in the window: HIREING NOW and NO CHANKORO HERE.

"Figures; they can't spell the word 'hiring' but they get the epithet right," Ingrid growled, trying to hide her scowl.

"Indeed. Let's go on. I recall another laundry near the park."

They reached the end of the business district along Adams and walked south through a park with a small fountain in the center. Dozens of small trees featured strange green bark and green leaves, the colors washed out, the shade cover minimal.

"This is the better prospect, I think. It was Chinese-run back before," Cy muttered. "Let's not get too close just in case there are folks inside who might recognize us from Seattle."

They paused beneath one of the green-yet-not-green trees. Cy angled himself to view the building and the street, and pulled out his pocket watch as if they were waiting for someone. Ingrid positioned herself behind him, knowing all too well that she was the more recognizable one. She fidgeted in place. Sutcliff's chilliness had felt pleasant on her skin but caused her calves to cramp more often. This awful warmth did help her leg muscles flex.

The laundry building was a single-story adobe brick structure with a more modern addition in red brick that looked as though it about doubled the floor plan. Paper trash and nuggets of horse manure mounded on the front stoop. Boards crisscrossed the entry door in a completely chaotic manner, as if to secure some dread demon inside. The windows were likewise blocked.

Yes. This had to be the place.

"We need to come back tonight. We have to hope they're in there." The thought of Lee and Mr. Sakaguchi perhaps being only thirty feet away made Ingrid's heart pound with longing and eagerness.

"I can't help but think of Seattle and how it all went so god-awful wrong when you went in to save Lee." Cy's voice was low and hoarse.

She couldn't help but think of that, too. Of her slowness to create her energy shield. Of Lee, shot in the stomach, dying in Cy's arms, continuing to die even as Uncle Moon poured more and more life into him, siphoned from his surrounding men.

"I say that," he continued, "but I also know you're the most qualified of us to infiltrate this building. You've been careful in how you're been handling your energy. That . . . that is a comfort to me. Even so, in a crisis . . ."

"That's why we need to discuss our strategy now and be ready for emergencies." She walked back toward Adams, Cy at her side. "First of all, this is a region with low geomantic output. Certainly no active volcanoes. I've never heard of earth-magic Hidden Ones in this vicinity. I'll be sure to bring both filled and empty kermanite. The sylphs will be happy to help." She felt a spike of worry and hoped that their strange trilling ritual would be done soon. "I have you, and Fenris. And I have something more, an advantage that I didn't have in Seattle."

"More sense?" he said with a teasing smile.

"God help us all, I hope I have more sense." She wanted to reach up and kiss him, but too many people were around. Still, her intention must've been clear on her face, because his gaze turned even warmer. She cleared her throat. "But we have something else, something that will make a mighty difference. We have a ghost."

CHAPTER 19

The night offered a mild reprieve from the heat of the day, and Captain Sutcliff's presence granted Ingrid even more mercy. Binding himself to her for this journey meant she constantly felt the icy tendrils of his proximity.

"I committed a series of grave injustices against Warden Sakaguchi that resulted in his current captivity," Captain Sutcliff had said. "I'd be honored to assist in retrieving both him and Lee Fong, and to ensure your safety as well."

The sylphs' motivations were simpler yet still profound. Ingrid discovered they were inordinately fond of deep-fried jelly-filled doughnuts from the German bakery, and so they were well fortified for the night's espionage. She still wondered about the odd ritual they'd finished up earlier in the day, but her polite inquiries had garnered no comprehensible reply.

The fae moths hovered mere feet over Ingrid. She had

asked them to avoid encouraging plant life here, a request they found odd but had agreed to nevertheless.

Ingrid felt better with that assurance. She didn't want to worry that the sylphs were creating a new Eden in their wake.

Cy, she knew, trailed a bit farther behind her. He'd keep an eye on the building as she went in. Fenris stayed with the *Bug* in case they needed to make a quick exit.

"Amazing, how much kermanite is all around us. I see it like sparkling constellations in every building," murmured the captain. He suddenly waved her forward. "Hide over here. Men are coming along the sidewalk across the street."

She stepped into the shadows behind a rain barrel. All was silent; the sylphs emitted no buzz. After a delay, she heard laughter and loud voices from the approaching group. She gave Sutcliff a nod of gratitude.

When all was quiet, she continued along the street. She recognized the outline of the laundry building ahead and ducked into the nearest alley, beside a dilapidated mercantile. A cat yowled and scrambled from a garbage bin. She pressed a fist to her chest and willed her frantic heart to calm down.

In the past, holding energy had left her feeling empowered in many ways. Now she felt terrified, wondering what the energy might do to her body, and what it might lure down from the heavens. She couldn't help but study the sky every so often, in dread of Blum's trackers.

"What can you sense from the laundry?" she murmured.

Captain Sutcliff walked to the head of the alley and tilted

his head, as if listening. His transparent form had a wispy gray outline against the bleak night. Not even gaslights illuminated this street. "Minimal kermanite inside. No recent deaths have torn the veil within."

"What can you tell me about the living people inside?"

"I can't say for certain there *are* people inside. My new senses can do only so much. My apologies."

"There's no need to apologize. Let's do more reconnaissance."

"Yes, ma'am." He practically puffed up in eagerness.

Back on the *Bug,* they had engaged in brief tests after he had tethered himself to her. As Sutcliff had observed, his hold on reality frayed if he tried to wander far from a familiar person or place. That boundary seemed to be at about twelve feet. At that point, the appearance of his spectral form faded, like a hot cup of tea cooling to emit only a trace of steam. Sutcliff had become addled, too, unable to answer where they were—though he could repeat his rank and deployment history. Knowing him, that hadn't surprised her.

The laundry building was shallow. That was to their advantage. Also an advantage: Sutcliff's incorporeality.

Ingrid clung to the shadows as she approached the building. As she reached the corner of the newer brick addition, Sutcliff paused for a moment, as if to take a deep breath, and entered the wall. Even though she expected his disappearance, it chilled her to see him pass through solid matter.

She also felt a surge of sympathy for Captain Sutcliff. He often acted like his brash self, but he couldn't hide how it perturbed him at times to face the fact that he was dead.

She took slow, measured steps along the wall going toward the adobe side of the building. Sutcliff's bond to her was like holding a dog on a leash. She knew where his cold essence was on the other side, how his steps kept pace with hers. Nearing a boarded window, she stopped. Sutcliff drew closer.

"I'm going to lean through the wall to speak with you directly," he said, voice muffled. Only his chest, head, and arm emerged from the bricks. Ingrid stifled a small gasp. His warning could never have fully prepared her for such an unnerving sight.

He acknowledged her reaction with a sad, brief smile. "Don't speak. Only listen. I found your Mr. Sakaguchi. He's sleeping on the other side of this wall. I see no outward signs of abuse."

Ingrid nodded and blinked back tears. Ojisan was here. He was alive. This time, God help her, she would leave with him.

"There are two young Chinamen playing a game in the room ahead. Another is sleeping." No Uncle Moon, then. Good. He had demonstrated a strong awareness of the life forces of those around him; she would not have been surprised if he could see ghosts as well. "Lee Fong is not here," he said in an oddly gentle way. "I studied his photograph in San Francisco. All of the men here are older, closer to your age. Tread carefully as you go forward."

She swallowed, forcing away her disappointment. No time to dwell on Lee's absence now. Mr. Sakaguchi was here. Maybe he knew if Lee had indeed smuggled himself aboard the craft to *Excalibur*.

She edged forward, dodging sticks, broken bricks, and

more manure. As she stepped around the latter, she was keenly aware of her tether to Sutcliff and how thin it stretched. To her surprise, the thick adobe walls seemed to lessen some of Sutcliff's chill.

Sutcliff stopped moving forward. She felt him waver in place, as if suddenly confused.

Oh, damn it. He *was* suddenly confused.

Ingrid pressed herself against the wall. Sutcliff still wasn't moving. She carried only a smidgen of power, enough to better communicate with the sylphs. She called on that heat as she grabbed the cold chains that bound her to the ghost, and *yanked.*

Captain Sutcliff staggered through the wall and stumbled to the ground before her. He panted heavily, as if he still had need to breathe. "Thank you." He rose with grace. "I apologize for worrying you. I leaned through another wall to check the far side. Apparently, adobe walls insulate against more than the weather."

"What did you find?" she murmured.

"I confirmed that only four men are in the building. This door here"—he pointed ahead—"is the easiest entrance. Let's go closer and I can examine it in more detail." He withdrew inside the building without hesitation this time. He seemed to be acclimating to his spectral nature.

Ingrid stood in a shadowed nook. Outwardly, the door looked as battered and abused as the door facing the public garden. Only when she was up close could she see the precision cuts through the boards that allowed the door to open.

Captain Sutcliff walked through it to rejoin her.

"There is a single hallway along this back portion of the building. Most of the rooms are empty, the laundry machinery gone. There are no traps in place on the door or elsewhere in the structure. I have always had an eye for such things," he said, not bothering with modesty. "Therefore, I perceive your greatest obstacle to be the door itself. You said that your fairies can cover your noise, to some extent?" She nodded. "That will prove useful. I believe I can work the latches on my side."

"You can?" she dared to whisper.

"Ghosts *are* known to fling about objects when they're riled. I believe that with some focus, I can indeed manipulate the latches. The door is not within ready line of sight for the Chinamen—a strategic error on their part. Can your sylphs cover the door itself when it's in movement? We then wouldn't need to worry about any sounds that it makes."

Ingrid blinked. That was brilliant. She was beginning to see why Sutcliff had achieved the rank of captain while so young. And yet . . . "What metal is in the door and hinges?"

"Brass hinges, I believe. Call forth the fairies so that they may inspect it for themselves."

She did so. The sylphs flowed along the door, like a fog seeking a way inside. They swirled around to rejoin Ingrid. A few hovered in front of her long enough for her to see their smiles.

"The door has no iron," she confirmed to Sutcliff.

With a thought, Ingrid called on her held *mana* to shield her skin against the pain of fae magic. A blurred, gray veil fell over her.

"This tether between us," she whispered, showing them

the bond with Sutcliff. "It must stay intact." The sylphs hummed in the affirmative. They seemed to know *something* was there, but since Sutcliff was not perceived as a threat, they ignored him.

Sutcliff stepped through the wall again.

Ingrid imagined the door for the sylphs, showing them how it would open and that they must make sure that no sound escaped. To her surprise, the veil around her thinned as sylphs siphoned away, finding crevices to penetrate the interior of the building. A series of soft clicks followed. She scarcely breathed.

"Open it, slowly," said Sutcliff. "I cannot see the door at all."

She did, with hope and dread twined together. The door groaned, the sound loud and agonized, like a banshee's lament. She froze.

"Incredible. I can't hear a thing. Keep going," hissed Sutcliff, his voice low from habit, not necessity.

He truly couldn't see or hear anything? The sylphs' geas worked on ghosts? Incredible indeed. She hurried forward and shut the door behind her. Within seconds, the full retinue of sylphs resumed their circuits around her.

"I see the door again. Good. I will leave it unlatched to allow you a quick egress, and hope that the guards persist in their ineptitude. Don't tarry."

She nodded, though he couldn't see, and walked forward.

Ugly gouges marked where laundry machinery and massive tubs once stood. What couldn't be moved looked as though it had been assaulted with sledgehammers. That included the walls themselves, which were host to what looked to be holes from cannon blasts.

She moved down the hallway. The two men chattered softly in Chinese. An oil drum between them was covered in two-toned brick shards; she guessed they were playing the ancient game Go. She passed an empty room; the door had been ripped from the hinges, the wooden frame left jagged like a broken bone. Blankets and cases of items lined a wall, tidy and in wait of people to return.

Another room with no door awaited her at the end of the hallway.

Mr. Sakaguchi lay curled on the floor, his arm as his pillow. Sutcliff stood beside him, his ethereal illumination granting her a modicum of light.

Sutcliff was right; Mr. Sakaguchi showed no outward signs of injury, but he looked so *old*. The past weeks had aged him by years. He seemed to be attired in the same cotton work clothes he'd had on in Seattle a month before, now stained and frayed by sweat and wear. She couldn't see any shackles on him. The room had no window, nor had the one next door. A chamber pot on the far side of the room buzzed with flies and exuded a foul stench.

She willed the sylphs to rest and let the shielding over her skin dissipate. The hive withdrew to the floor near her feet; despite their exertions, they weren't hungry yet, which was good. Pastry time needed to wait awhile longer.

"Marvelous creatures," murmured Sutcliff. "A travesty that they are best known as a culinary delicacy."

"Watch the guards for me," she whispered, low as she

could. Sutcliff acquiesced with a crisp nod, stepping toward the doorway a few feet away.

Ingrid reached into her pocket and pulverized a sliver of kermanite between her fingertips. She took in the ebb of energy with a shiver. Gripping Mr. Sakaguchi's shoulder, she shook him gently as she constructed an energy bubble around them.

"Ojisan. Ojisan!"

He awoke with a gasp, lurching backward. He would have bumped into the wall but met the glass sheen of the bubble instead. Ingrid focused to make it absorb all sound.

"Ojisan, it's me. I'm really here."

"Ingrid?" Mr. Sakaguchi blinked rapidly, looking stunned. "But how?" Mr. Sakaguchi's hair had grown out, tangled and shaggy. A black-and-silver beard obscured his jaw and neck.

"I'm using a bubble to absorb our sounds, but I can't keep it up for long. I need to be careful about how much energy I expend. Has Uncle Moon healed you recently? And do you know where Lee is?"

"I haven't been healed in two weeks. His ability to track me will have decreased by now. He's not here, anyway. He went with Lee to board *Excalibur*." He blinked, regaining his bearings. "Yesterday, I believe."

She thought of the *qilin* and *guandao* and Lee's future, and shoved those thoughts away. She had other things to worry about now. "Let's stand. Next, I'll evaporate our protective bubble. I have Sierran sylphs with me. They are going to fly around us to render us invisible and mask our noise. Their magic might hurt you. If it does, clench my arm hard and I'll create a shield over your skin."

"Which will drain you more," he murmured.

"You may not even feel pain. *I'm* the deviant." Her smile was wry. "We're also in the company of the ghost of Captain Sutcliff." At that, Mr. Sakaguchi's eyes widened. "I will speak with him at times. I'll mediate a conversation between both of you later. He has a fervent need to apologize for how he treated you before."

"My goodness," Mr. Sakaguchi murmured.

Ingrid dropped the bubble and took in a deep breath of fetid air.

Captain Sutcliff looked their way. "The 'guards' remain distracted. Will you use the sylphs for the door again? Or your own shield? You might even make yourself invisible, if necessary."

She shook her head. She knew she could make her bubbles do many things, but she also knew how much that effort took out of her. A motion toward the sylphs indicated her answer. They flew over, radiant with the happy scent of lavender. Mr. Sakaguchi barely contained a gasp. Ingrid allowed herself a small smile, even as she was sick with fear.

She had reached this stage when she rescued Lee. She thought she had him, that she'd keep him safe. Then her attention had lapsed.

She couldn't let that happen with Mr. Sakaguchi. She wouldn't.

Ingrid twined her left arm around his, their hands clasped. They stepped forward as the sylphs encircled them. She glanced at Mr. Sakaguchi as she shielded her skin. He cast her a nod and smile; good, he felt no pain. More energy for her to preserve.

The walk was, perhaps, fifteen feet, but it felt like a mile. She recognized the long and even nature of Mr. Sakaguchi's breaths; he relied on his meditative practice. She relied on barely contained panic.

The Chinese men didn't so much as look up, but Ingrid took little comfort in that as she walked past. If the guards were alerted now, she and Mr. Sakaguchi could easily be stabbed or shot in the back. Energy writhed in her veins, ready. If the guards moved, she would bring up her shield.

They reached the door. Sutcliff waited behind them where he could monitor the Go players. "Wait one moment while I check outside." He took a few steps through the wall, and returned seconds later. "The street is empty."

She coaxed the sylphs to swirl around the door again, then opened it. Her hold on Mr. Sakaguchi was slick with shared sweat. They walked forward. Outside. To a dirt street and a sky of diamond-sparkling stars. She turned and shut the door, her fingers trembling. The sylphs resumed their full circuits around her and Mr. Sakaguchi. Soft clicks on the far side indicated Sutcliff fastening the locks again.

The ghost joined them, silent, and waved them along. She pushed her legs to walk faster. Tears streamed down Ingrid's cheeks. Had they made it? Had they? Her gaze raked over the sky, her ears wary for any whispers. She couldn't assume they'd made it free and clear, she couldn't.

The sylphs, however, could not cloak them for the entire walk back to the dock, not with their current numbers. Their circuits had begun to slow. Oddly enough, they seemed distracted, too. More and more of them hovered, looking ahead while emitting a low, resonant susurrus.

Ingrid guided Mr. Sakaguchi to the niche where she had hidden behind a rain barrel. Cy was almost invisible there in dark attire, his gaze focused on the laundry building.

Sutcliff walked closely past him; their agreed-upon signal. Cy stood straighter at the sudden chill. Ingrid and Mr. Sakaguchi filed behind him as she willed the sylphs to disperse.

"All well?" Cy asked. Sadness flickered over his face as he recognized Lee's absence.

"Yes." Her voice was a dry croak. She let go of Mr. Sakaguchi's hand to wipe tears from her cheeks. Her relief at making it this far was tempered by the reality that they still had a ways to go.

"I'm delighted to make your acquaintance again, Mr. Jennings," murmured Mr. Sakaguchi with an abrupt bow.

Cy offered a bow in turn. "Same to you, sir. We have maybe a quarter mile to the airship dock." He stroked Ingrid's cheek. The gesture held its usual affection, but she knew he was also assessing her body temperature.

"I'm being careful," she said. He granted her a tiny nod, the tension around his eyes softening. Mr. Sakaguchi took in the intimate exchange and said nothing.

The sylphs hovered at her head level. *go go go go home home home everyone home!* Their tiredness seemed of little consequence now, nor was there the slightest hint of hunger.

Ingrid blinked at them, alarmed at their sudden change in behavior. "Captain Sutcliff?" she whispered. "How does the way ahead look?"

"Quiet, far as I can see and hear. If an officer of the law stops you, rely on Mr. Sakaguchi's appearance. Make it clear that he's Japanese. Play on him being a drunk and that you're getting him back aboard his airship."

Ingrid murmured this advice; the men nodded. Mr. Saka-guchi took position between her and Cy in case he needed to develop a stagger.

Captain Sutcliff walked ahead, his posture alert. His hand angled to his waist as if to draw the firearm that was hol-stered there in ethereal form.

They walked fast, but not fast in a way that might draw unnecessary attention. The sylphs flew above Sutcliff, their eagerness adding an elated tingle to the air. They reminded Ingrid of a horse fighting the bit in an urge to gallop. More male voices carried from a block away. Dogs barked. Doors slammed. The dock lay dead ahead. Past it, the wide sky yawned over the desert. *Excalibur* hovered like a falling star frozen during its drop to the earth.

At the dock's gate, the man on duty granted them a curt nod and continued to carve a block of wood by lamplight. The sylphs couldn't contain themselves anymore. They surged ahead. The *Bug* was a hundred feet away, fifty. They passed the neighboring mast and their airship was fully in sight.

Immense magical pressure walloped Ingrid across the head like a plank.

Weakened as she was by exertion and fear, not even the braces could hold her up anymore. She dropped to the pave-ment on a knee and hand, gasping for breath, mind reeling. She forced her gaze up to the *Bug* again.

"Oh my."

Sylphs. So many sylphs. Thousands upon thousands. Maybe a hundred thousand. She couldn't actually see them, though—they knew the dangers of human cities and thus were invisible, but through their ambient magic, she could tell their cloud was almost the size of the *Bug*'s envelope. The comparison was easy to make, as the sylphs had clustered on and around the airship, causing it to sag slightly on its moorings.

"Is it the fox?" asked Cy. He hadn't looked at the *Bug* yet.

"Has the ship sprung a leak?" asked Captain Sutcliff.

"No, but I imagine Fenris has, as he stares at the dials and panics," she whispered, pushing herself to stand again, the men on either side of her this time. "It's not the fox, it's—"

A sinuous line of sylphs flew down to greet her. *we returned! we returned! friends came! an-pan! jamu-pan! need to try jelly doughnut!* They cheered with a low, subtle buzz.

She turned to Cy. "Did T.R. give us enough money to buy a bakery?"

CHAPTER 20

Cy was a naturally pale-skinned fellow, but upon hearing the nature of their problem, he blanched as if he were about to faint. "Can you get the fairies off the envelope? Lord, they might be inside, too. The hatch is open. Fenris must be apoplectic about the weight on the ship." He paused, a hand pressed to his head. "How many sylphs are there, to weigh that much?"

"Where should they go? Where can they be safe?" Ingrid asked.

"We don't need them to completely vamoose. Tell them to land on the top deck for now. It can support heavy freight, so it can stand up to them. I hope. How long can they stay invisible?"

She thought of what she'd learned of sylph biology in recent weeks. "Their invisibility provides natural camouflage for their survival in the wild. It drains them quickly when they cover us, but I think they can hide themselves for hours and days, so long as they have food."

"Food may prove to be problematic with such a large number of sylphs," added Sutcliff.

"Perhaps it may be necessary to rent an empty barn in the morning?" murmured Mr. Sakaguchi, taking this new development with characteristic calmness.

"I doubt I can find an available barn. The farmers around are likely using theirs. We'll figure out something." They started up the mast.

"I promise you, Cy, I had no idea that the sylphs that left had decided to recruit all of their friends from the Sierras to come to the *Bug*." Ingrid leaned on the rail, her legs weary but able to maintain a good upward rhythm.

"I know. These are fantastics. They think on a different level than us."

"One with an apparent fondness for pastry." Mr. Sakaguchi softly chuckled. "Oh, if your mother were here, Ing-chan, I can well imagine how she would have busied herself with baking for them!"

"I can, too," she whispered, and almost burst out in tears all over again. Mr. Sakaguchi was here. Boarding the *Bug*. She could talk with someone who knew Mama. Who knew *home*, as it once was.

Dizziness overwhelmed Ingrid on the final flight of stairs. Cy moored her with a hand to her waist. Sylph magic warmed and thickened the air and felt as if it contained a physical weight. It wasn't painful, though, like when they directly utilized their magic on her. It simply was *too much*.

She would have laughed, had she the breath. Truly ancient beings like the two-headed snake and Pele had carried immense, deep power, but the sylphs' high numbers radiated something more akin to sweetness. Ingrid could readily believe that eating them embodied a delicious, magical wallop.

"Bring your friends down to the deck," she said to the familiar sylphs who hovered nearby. "But slowly." She wanted to make sure the metal structure could indeed support them.

As they walked across the deck, invisible sylphs descended in a slow torrent but left a clear path for the humans to access the *Bug*. She felt as if the way were flanked by fire.

"Fenris!" Cy called into the *Bug*.

"Cy! Cy! Something is terribly wrong, the dials! It's not a leak, but the pressure and elevator readings . . . !" Fenris's voice echoed from the cockpit.

Cy, Ingrid, Mr. Sakaguchi, and Captain Sutcliff climbed into the airship.

Cy drew up the hatch and locked it. Ingrid stood there, Mr. Sakaguchi beside her. The moment felt utterly unreal. She was afraid to move, to breathe, to do anything that might shatter this wonderful dream. Mr. Sakaguchi was a mere foot away, but that distance still seemed so far, so fragile. If she awoke from this moment, to find out it was all in her imagination, she wouldn't be able to bear it.

Mr. Sakaguchi must have felt the same way. He gazed at her with love and longing, his feet pressed to the tatami mat, his arms slightly outstretched as if ready to catch her.

After a minute or forever, Ingrid moved forward and they fell into each other's arms. Sobs shuddered through him, his tears soaking her shoulder. Mr. Sakaguchi was crying. Him, the stoic warden from a culture averse to any public shows of weak emotion. Ingrid bawled. She squeezed him in a hug. He felt too skinny, he stank, but she didn't care. He was here, he was alive, this was real, real, real.

"Fenris, we've been invaded by what may be tens of thousands of sylphs." Cy's voice was low in respect for the moment. "Ingrid's sending them all to the deck below. How are the *Bug*'s numbers reading now?"

"Better, but the gas readings are not where they should be at this elevation, the pressure's been—"

"Then we'll take care of that at sunup, along with buying every available pastry in town. Deep breaths."

Ingrid pulled back from Mr. Sakaguchi. "When did the problem start, Fenris?"

"About thirty minutes ago." He stood in the doorway, face flushed, his thin frame still heaving from anxiety. "Oh. Hey. You made it."

"Nice of you to notice," she said, laughing as she swiped at her tears. "Mr. Sakaguchi, I'd like to introduce you to my dear friend Mr. Fenris Braun. He was Mr. Jennings's business partner in San Francisco. With the help of him and his airship, the *Palmetto Bug,* we've stayed alive this past month."

Fenris's face was strangely sober as he moved forward to shake Mr. Sakaguchi's hand. "An honor to meet you, warden, sir. Ingrid has said a lot about you."

Mr. Sakaguchi returned the handshake and then bowed. "The honor is mine. Thank you for taking care of my Ing-chan. I know she can be something of a handful."

At that, Fenris gave a customary snort. "That's an understatement."

"I rarely had the chance to speak to Lee in recent weeks as he recovered. We were kept apart or under watch most of the time," Mr. Sakaguchi said, turning to her. "How did you escape from Seattle? Has Ambassador Bl—"

Ingrid motioned for silence. "Don't say her name. It carries too much power. We've been referring to her as 'the fox.' I . . . I will explain more about that later. It's best to avoid saying my full name, too, though I think 'Ing-chan' is fine." There was so much to tell him. "Thank you, Cy." She accepted a canteen and took a long drink of water before passing it to Mr. Sakaguchi. Captain Sutcliff stood to one side, reverent and patient. Her feet took in the warmth of the sylphs like the heat of a fireplace through exterior chimney bricks.

She continued, "We evaded her by traveling to the Vassal States. I met with Mrs. K." That evoked both happiness and sorrow in his smile. "And we met with my grandmother, Madam Pele."

"She truly is your grandmother . . . ?" Mr. Sakaguchi murmured, with a wary glance at Fenris and Cy.

"You can speak freely in front of both of them, Ojisan. They know everything." Fenris snorted again. "Madam Pele is . . . beyond description. She has a way of putting things in a proper perspective." She glanced down. "I went to her for help. In Seattle, I inlaid magic into a ward to prevent the fox from tracking me. That effort pulled significant energy directly from my body. According to doctors, I damaged the nerves that connect my extremities and my brain."

"For a few days there, we were afraid she might not ever walk again," Cy added quietly.

"I recovered, to a point, but I journeyed to Madam Pele with the hope she could tell me more about my power and that my legs could heal further." Ingrid shrugged. "The damage is permanent. Most of the time I still manage to get around, though. Cy and Fenris have helped a great deal in that regard."

"I noticed a difference in your stride," Mr. Sakaguchi said. "New stiffness."

"Orichalcum support braces within her boots," said Cy, with a small measure of pride.

"Incredible." Mr. Sakaguchi shook his head and took another drink of water.

Cy waved him to the control cabin. "Please sit—make yourself comfortable."

As Fenris fiddled with dials and jotted notes in his records book, Mr. Sakaguchi and Ingrid faced each other in the wooden seats by the door. Sutcliff lingered nearby, a cold shadow.

"Ojisan, we need to know about Lee. What's their plan?"

"I was kept insulated from most of my captors' conversations, but I did hear them speak of the flying citadel, *Excalibur*."

"The culmination of the Gaia Project," Ingrid murmured.

"I feared as much." His eyes fluttered closed for a moment. "To my knowledge, Lee is there now. Yesterday a number of *tong* members departed to smuggle themselves aboard the citadel along with a shipment of pharmaceuticals. *Excalibur*'s crew is incapacitated—I do not fully understand how. The

Chinese men's goal is to commandeer the craft, and if they can't figure out how to fly it, they will employ explosives to bring it down here."

"How many in this infiltration team, sir?" Cy asked sharply.

"About ten."

"That number's not enough to pilot *Excalibur,* just keep it afloat."

"I imagine they will realize that soon, then, and do what they can to destroy the vessel."

Cy released a hiss of breath. "My sister's likely aboard. She's the brilliant fool who created that thing."

Mr. Sakaguchi's expression was sorrowful. "They won't show any mercy to a woman."

"No. And I'm not certain she deserves any. Pardon me." Cy pushed himself from the doorway and stalked down the corridor. Ingrid considered following him to offer comfort, but she wanted him to have space to control his emotions, too.

"The crew is incapacitated by some sort of influenza that is now running rampant in Atlanta and other cities," Ingrid said. "The mortality rate is high. I . . . I believe I have been inoculated by Lee, as have Cy and Fenris. I don't suppose you were jabbed with a needle in recent weeks?"

"No." Mr. Sakaguchi's eyes were wide. "Are you saying this illness was engineered by the Chinese? That Lee knew what was planned?"

Even as he spoke, it was evident that he knew what the answers would be. Even so, he still had to ask.

Ingrid's throat clenched with emotion. She nodded. Grief

swept over Mr. Sakaguchi's face. He wavered in his seat.
Ingrid reached out to steady him and realized anew how
frail he was.

"I'm fine," he murmured.

"You're still trembling. Do you need anything?" Ingrid
asked. She hadn't let go of him.

"No. I need to know these things. I need to accept them."
He took in a deep breath, his eyes half shutting. This was
how he had so often appeared when entering meditation—
and yet he looked unlike himself, too, emaciated and shaggy.
It tore at her heart.

He gave her a tiny nod. She let her hand return to her lap.

"Meanwhile, the UP is biding its time as sickness runs
rampant through *Excalibur*," said Fenris, his voice low.

"If the Army & Airship Corps suspects the Chinese are
aboard, the gunships will open fire," added Ingrid. "The UP
would never stand for their prize to be in Chinese hands."

"I bet the Chinese could shoot down the gunships first.
The weaponry on board would be easy to figure out compared
to the engineering and piloting systems," said Fenris.

"If we could get aboard—" Ingrid started to say, then
gasped. "We *can* get aboard. Fenris, can you open the hatch
for me?"

The full magical radiance of the sylphs filled Ingrid's
senses as she carefully climbed down to the deck. Captain
Sutcliff remained at her side, his expression one of blatant
curiosity. Though still invisible, the sylphs' sheer density dis-
torted the air like a faint heat mirage. She'd need to find out
if the others could see it, too. If so, the sylphs would need

to split into smaller groups before sunrise when dock traffic picked up.

She drew on her well of power. "Greetings."

The response was a happy cacophony, rather like announcing to the young geomancers-in-training that they were about to have a surprise cake and lemonade party, but magnified by a thousand. Their power buffeted her. She hadn't realized she had staggered backward until she bumped into Cy's tall, solid form, his hands brushing her arms to steady her. She had been so distracted, she hadn't noticed that the men had joined her.

Ingrid glanced back at him. "I'm going to have a conversation with the sylphs. If you feel my skin start to cool, give me a pinch. That *shouldn't* be necessary, since talking with fantastics drains little energy compared to other tasks, but still . . ."

He squeezed her oh so gently. "I'm here for you. Do what needs doing."

His faith buoyed her spirits. She gave herself a nod and closed her eyes, letting her consciousness dip into her reservoir of energy. Her awareness flowed out, seeking the original sylphs she had rescued in Seattle, including the ones that departed in Bakersfield. They had congregated in a group right before her.

"The first-come sylphs." She sent an image to the cloud of the cage in Seattle, the salt-crusted iron bars, the sylphs limp as molted feathers. At the dread memory, the entire cloud quivered in abject horror, which changed to ecstasy as she changed the vision to that of freedom, companionship, and pastries. "There are so many of you now. My first-sylphs, will you speak for all of your number and relay what I say as well?"

yes! No hesitation.

"Why have so many sylphs come here?" she asked.

mountains hot too early. little snow to melt. many people. Visions flickered through her mind. Spring flowers blooming and withering all too soon. Blank, blue skies. Dead grass, and subsequent fires. Men plowing hillsides. Wandering with guns. Some bearing nets and laying traps laced with honey to lure in desperate sylphs. The sylphs knew these traps were bad, but they were starving, and the honey smelled so sweet . . .

Damn it. How could she ask the newcomers to leave soon when that meant their death? But they couldn't stay with the *Bug* for an extended time either, or they'd still starve—and deplete their human allies of money and resources as well.

She couldn't think that far ahead. Right now she had to concentrate on how they could all survive the next day.

"The *Palmetto Bug* here—" she started to say.

home! Their happy vibrations made the air quiver.

"Yes, home." She laughed. "You first-sylphs have made me and my friends invisible before. Can you hide the entire *Palmetto Bug*?"

She felt Cy's gasp. He murmured something to Mr. Saka-guchi and Fenris, but she kept her focus on the sylphs.

They considered her proposal as a group, buzzing among themselves for a minute. *it is home. we keep small nests invisible when threatened. many sylphs here now. if bellies are full, we can hide our home's sight and most sound for . . .* They showed her an image of the sun moving a quarter of the way across the sky.

She nodded. "I want to initiate a new business transaction with all of the sylphs present." She pictured the breaking of sweet bread, an equal exchange in return for their assistance. "I have an existing agreement with the first-sylphs. That remains. With the new sylphs, our transaction may only last a few days." She showed them the passage of the sun and the dark blink of nightfall.

Ingrid waited in suspense for her message to be relayed. The sylphs were silent for several long seconds, then a positive surge struck her. *second-sylphs agree. airship will be a night-by-night nest. will work once they have bread. will continue to work for more bread in days to come.*

"Very well." Local bakeries had better not let them down. "Everyone you see here with me"—she motioned behind her—"is a friend. Every other person is a potential threat. Hide from them. Stay here on the deck for now." She gestured around her.

yes, said the first-sylphs. *we will continue to hide here.*

With that, Ingrid opened her eyes. She touched Cy's hand on her neck. She hadn't even fully registered his contact there until now.

"Your skin feels about as cool as before," he said, answering her before she could ask. "We could feel the sylphs' happy buzzing. I take it they want to deal?"

"The newcomers know this won't be permanent, but they'll work for bread over the next few days." She turned to face him. The lights beneath the *Bug* were set to dim, but she could easily read the chagrin on his face. "I know. I'm sorry. I can't even guess at how many pastries we'll need."

"We'll buy out the town and hope it's enough." He shook his head. "Using sylphs to cloak a full ship. I don't think anyone's tried that before."

"Sounds like a good plan to me," said Fenris. "As suicidal as anything else we've done."

"I believe there was an attempt some years ago to create an invisible airship envelope, but the inventors utilized the wings of dead sylphs, and they underestimated the sheer number of wings required," said Mr. Sakaguchi.

Ingrid shook her head. "No one would think to *ask* the sylphs."

"Most folks wouldn't have that option," Cy chided.

"Well, true."

"Rendering the ship invisible is useful, but what good will that do if a UP sailor recognizes the distinct roar of an airship from the otherwise empty sky?" asked Mr. Sakaguchi with a skeptical eyebrow.

"I'll ask the sylphs to muffle our sounds, not hide them completely. That way they won't exhaust themselves too quickly."

"I rather like the idea of baffling some poor sailor with an unexplainable roar of sky," mused Fenris. "But the sylphs' health must come first."

"The gunships won't shoot us once we're docked and visible," said Cy.

"Not unless they regard the entire Gaia Project to be expendable at that point," added Captain Sutcliff. Ingrid didn't feel the need to repeat that for the others. "There's something more you must consider. The fox has invested great time and effort in *Excalibur,* and it's now in peril. She is almost certain to arrive soon. Her ring would enable her to board without risk of sickness."

Ingrid frowned at him. "I can sense her within a few hundred feet. At least, I could soon after she had forcibly healed me."

"Would your ward impair that ability?" Cy asked, joining in on the one-sided conversation.

"No. When I constructed the enchantment, my full intent was to block her from tracking me and to establish myself as superior. I couldn't undo the effects of her healing magic. Nor did I want to at that point." She shivered at the memory.

"I feel," murmured Mr. Sakaguchi, "that I am painfully ignorant of your tribulations in recent weeks, Ing-chan."

"I'm sorry, Ojisan. I want to catch up with you, but we should probably get sleep soon. Tomorrow looks to be a busy day."

Fenris waved a hand. "Before you people decide to sleep, I should point out that one important detail has been omitted. *How* are we going to moor with that thing? I doubt that any of the sick airmen will be so kindly inclined as to tether us."

"We'll figure that out tomorrow," she said.

"You say that, and your solutions usually place you in imminent peril." Cy scowled at her.

"I suppose that has become a pattern of late," she said, her arm lightly wrapped around Mr. Sakaguchi. He felt so frail. "Come along, Ojisan. We have food aboard. No tea, unfortunately. *They* rely on coffee," she said, making a face of disgust.

He paused, one foot on the hatch steps, and smiled at her. "I think, with all I've endured of late, I will find within me the fortitude to drink some coffee in the morning."

Ingrid smiled back as they helped each other up the steps.

CHAPTER 21

THURSDAY, MAY 24, 1906

Ingrid sat on the tatami by the open hatch. Paper bags of pastries surrounded her on all sides. The first-sylphs supervised as the new arrivals flew aboard in small groups for their introduction to the glories of bread. Ingrid thanked the Almighty that she no longer had to eat half of each piece as a show of balanced trade; if that'd been the case, she would have keeled over dead by now. Which would have been a sad way to go, considering all she had survived of late.

The sylphs operated with assembly-line precision. As soon as one cluster finished—which probably took all of twenty seconds—the next one entered. The sylphs became visible upon entering the security of the *Bug*. Their emaciated condition broke Ingrid's heart, and made her wonder how many hadn't attempted the journey or had died along the way.

Cy had bought all of the available stock from the two

bakeries in town. His haul included doughnuts, amashoku, an-pan, croissants, and cinnamon rolls, and he had promised to return later for more. Better to have too much than not enough.

She set a jelly doughnut on the tin plate. Sylphs descended with a waft of lavender, their buzzing escalating like a cat's purr. Footsteps whispered on the tatami mat behind her. She turned.

"Mind if I join you?" Mr. Sakaguchi asked. At her smile, he lowered himself to the mat. "Where's your young man?"

New sylphs entered the cabin. "He's getting the latest scuttlebutt. He was a bit worried that his massive purchases of pastries might create alarm that he's intending to feed a garrison of troops or some such."

"You are feeding a kind of army, one unlike any other. My, what incredible creatures." He leaned forward to study the sylphs as they decimated a croissant. His voice sounded hoarse. He hadn't been allowed to speak much during his captivity, and then he and Ingrid could not stop talking the previous night. Hours had passed. Many words were shared; many others were restrained.

She couldn't confront him about her forced sterility. She couldn't ruin their blessed time together by giving voice to her anger and frustration. There would be a time for that talk, later. If she survived.

"My flight will leave in a while." He tapped his chest out of habit, as if he carried a pocket watch, and chuckled at himself for the error. He wore a cheap yet functional Western-style suit that they had optimistically bought for him in Los Angeles. Ingrid had provided Mr. Sakaguchi's old measurements out of habit; the clothes hung from his frame.

He had also cleaned up using Cy's grooming kit. The shaggy beard was gone, but he kept his hair long, tucked into a samurai-style knot. She remembered photographs from his youth when he had styled his hair in a similar fashion.

"You're scheduled to leave in about an hour." She pointed to the clock over the doorway to the control cabin. "We'll head out soon after."

Mr. Sakaguchi nodded as he observed the voracious stream of fae. "We each have our own roles in this opera. I'm glad that I can do my part as you undertake such a dangerous mission."

"Roosevelt needs to know about the immunizations. I hate for all of the hidden treasures in that warehouse to be exposed as well, but . . ."

"I will do what I can to have the belongings cataloged and stored, with the borrowed orichalcum included as well. The only exception, perhaps, will be that poor gorgon's head. It should somehow be granted peace. I'll research that." Of course he would. "That said, our highest priority must be for the government to know about this vaccination so that it can be replicated for public benefit." Grief shadowed his face. "For Lee to be party to such an act of subtle, devastating violence . . . for him to have known about this plot in San Francisco, to have had the foresight to inoculate you . . ."

"This is war, Ojisan," she said softly. "Even more, Lee is not in command. He didn't unleash this sickness."

"I know. It's illogical for me to grieve over his choice, and selfish for me to debate if I erred in my teaching of him. Dr. Moon certainly thinks so." He gave a rueful smile.

"You know Lee. You know the nature of his conscience. Guilt and grief will stay with him."

"I hate for him to be haunted by such darkness."

"All each of us can hope is that we have a chance, at the end, for redemption." Captain Sutcliff's voice was a whisper from where he stood on the far side of the hatch. She acknowledged him with a nod. She had mediated a conversation between him and Mr. Sakaguchi during the night; Sutcliff had been lost in introspection ever since. He acted like a man in constant prayer. She had tried to ignore him, granting him whatever privacy he required.

"Guilt serves a purpose," she said, both to the ghost and her ojisan.

"Yes," they said, almost simultaneously, their voices alike in softness and regret.

She set another melon-pan on the plate and was surprised to recognize the distinct presence of her first-sylphs.

we are last! They promptly inhaled the pastry.

Ingrid extended her senses to verify an incredible sense of delight and satisfaction radiating from the deck below. The strength of the sylphs' magic had increased, too. Amazing, what some baked goods could do.

She looked around, pleased to see many bags remained. Fenris would need those once they moored at *Excalibur*. She almost giddily laughed aloud at the thought. They were going to *Excalibur*, to finally search for Lee and for Maggie. All these weeks of wondering how and when they could make their move, and the moment had arrived.

Faint footsteps clanged on the mooring mast below. Ingrid scooted forward and eased herself down the short stairs to the deck. She hadn't put on her braces yet. Wearing them for so long the previous day had irritated her legs and caused her to bust out in a mild heat rash, too; she wanted her skin to air out as long as possible.

"Good, I'm glad you're coming to greet me." She could see Cy looking up at her through the steel cross-hatching. He was still several flights down. "Vexes me to walk on the deck right now. I'm afraid I might step on something." His tone was mild, as he was at a point where his voice might carry below.

"Don't worry about that." Already, the invisible fairies shifted to form a path in advance of his arrival.

Cy reached the top. Sweat sheened his face and created dark crescents at the armpits of his blue-checkered shirt. "My worry is legitimate. I'd never want to disrupt peace accords because I flattened a sylph like a flapjack. G'morning, Mr. Sakaguchi. Thank the Almighty you're already up. Your flight out's leaving early."

Mr. Sakaguchi came down the steps behind Ingrid. "Why? What's the matter?"

"The A-and-A is coming in." Cy looked grim. "They've ordered local docks to clear out as many airships as possible."

"Damn them all," said Ingrid.

"I wondered when this would happen," Captain Sutcliff murmured from beside her.

"Is Fenris up yet?" Cy asked.

A dull thud echoed from just above. "I'm up. I heard you. What's the deadline?"

"Ten o'clock, but most folks aim to go sooner, if they can. The rumor mill's churning something fierce—that there really is a quarantine aboard *Excalibur,* or a mutiny, and if it's the latter, that there may be a battle."

"I can be ready to go within minutes," said Mr. Sakaguchi, his hand sweeping over his hair. "It's a good thing I'm traveling light." With a faint smile, he hurried aboard, his socked feet soft on the steps.

Ingrid turned to Cy. "Did they say who leads the fleet?"

"No."

"It has to be her." Ingrid swayed in place. She breathed in deeply, as if she could already detect Blum's awful musk above the stink of dust and the fragrance of happy sylphs. Cy steadied her with a light grip on her shoulder.

"We'll deal with her, best as we can," he said.

"That means nothing. She's nigh invincible with that ring. An artifact that powerful can likely only be counteracted with another artifact, likewise powerful. Like the *guandao.*" Her eyes widened. "We *know* Lee is aboard *Excalibur*. This is the time to return the Crescent Blade to him."

Bags of pastries still flanked her sitting spot by the hatch. The voices of Fenris and Mr. Sakaguchi carried from the control cabin, but she hurried—as quickly as she could hurry, anyway—the opposite way, to the racks. She stared up at the nest where the *guandao* lay hidden.

"You're not considering a climb up that ladder, are you,

Ing-chan?" Mr. Sakaguchi came up behind her, his tone chiding.

"Actually, no. I figured if I waited, someone would fetch the blade for me." The confession of weakness didn't bother her as it might have even a few days ago. *My body will never be as it once was, but that doesn't mean it's not strong.* Nor was she stupid enough to injure herself now, out of sheer pride.

Mr. Sakaguchi's eyes widened. "Do you think—would I be allowed to touch it? To bring it down?"

"If the *guandao* doesn't want you to handle it, it'll let you know."

"An important consideration as I will be standing on a ladder at a precarious height." He slowly climbed up.

Ingrid glanced back at her cot, where the *qilin* plaque rested. "Please lend some of your good fortune right now," she murmured. "He is a good man. Don't let him be judged by the sins of his government. Please." She knew what it would mean to Mr. Sakaguchi to handle such a weapon of legend.

"I have hold of the parcel," he said, and took careful steps down.

"Do you feel anything from it?" she asked, even as she sensed the blade's inherent holy aura.

"Is giddiness expected?" A bright grin lit his haggard face.

"Here, we can unwrap it—"

"No." He stayed her with a hand on her arm. "I am not worthy to behold its full glory. It's enough to hold it like this." Tears filled his eyes as he gazed on the leather bag with awe. "Perhaps it is irreverent, but I'm filled with pride that you'll carry the Green Dragon Crescent Blade to Lee. I think the *guandao* chose well." He bowed, as much as the space allowed, and passed the parcel to her hands. She immediately set it on her bed.

"I hope I can find Lee and deliver it to him at the right moment. I hope . . . I hope for so many things."

"The *qilin* trusted you to carry the weapon, Ing-chan. Trust that you will find Lee when the moment is right. And keep your hope burning, even if only a spark. You must always keep hope alive." His words trembled with grief and love.

"You're going to your flight now," she whispered.

"I must." Tears swam in his eyes. She and Mr. Sakaguchi embraced. The cloth of his baggy jacket rustled against her.

"I'll stay in Southern California as I wait for news. I trust in Mr. Roosevelt's people to set me up somewhere. I shouldn't be too difficult to find through his channels."

They pulled back, gazing at each other.

"Sir?" Cy's voice was soft from where he stood at the hatch.

"I'm going." Mr. Sakaguchi pulled away from Ingrid. From his rack, he grabbed a battered hat that Cy had acquired for him. He set it on his head, slightly askew, and walked down the hallway. He and Cy clasped hands. "I'd tell you to take good care of her, Mr. Jennings, but—"

"We'll take care of each other, best as we can," Cy said.

"Yes, you will." He faced Ingrid. "Farewell, my beloved daughter."

"Good-bye, Ojisan," she whispered.

Like that, he was gone.

She looked away, blinking fast. Cy's footsteps came up behind her.

"There's that song about Federal soldiers in the opera *Lincoln*," she said, without turning around. "'I will gird myself for battle. Squire, kindly fetch my greaves. Today we fight, we fight.'"

"'And tonight, tonight, we likely grieve.'" Cy completed the punned verse as his arms wrapped around her tightly, completing her.

THE *BUG* FLEW SOUTH, DIRECT SUNLIGHT GLARING THROUGH THE wide window of the control cabin. They had flown far enough north to transcend the sight and concern of the Pegasus gunships stationed around *Excalibur*. Now they looped back around. The steep hills below contained full forests of saguaro cacti, an army of spiny green soldiers standing at attention.

"How close dare we get without the sylphs?" asked Ingrid.

"We'll need 'em soon," said Cy from his copilot's seat. His gaze was intent on the view ahead. At this distance, *Excalibur* resembled a strange, squat cloud. Many other airships filled the sky, too, as the docks throughout the valley emptied out.

Cy had observed that Phoenix had no masts to accommodate Behemoth- and Tiamat-class vessels; the newcomers would be small crafts and traveling in formation. Distinct, in other words. No such sight marred the skies yet.

"Thin bank of cumulus up ahead," said Cy. "Might provide some scant cover."

"Thank you for helpfully stating the obvious, Cy." Fenris's arms were tense, his grip on the wheel white-knuckled. They flew toward the clouds. "How close is our fairy mob?"

Ingrid reached out her awareness. Magic warmed her skin, and she had more filled stones to draw on as necessary. She also carried empty rocks, in case one of Blum's magical scouts flew near.

"They're maintaining our speed just above the envelope."

"You made sure they're aware of the stub wings, right? This trip'll be over nice and fast if—"

"Yes. You were right there. I told them, and passed along the graphic imagery you shared about the currents around the stub wings and what would happen if they were sucked in. They understand." The sylphs had been rendered silent in horror. A spooky thing, to hear them go from happy buzzing to dead quiet. Immediately following that, however, they had mobbed Fenris in a happy, grateful cloud. The safety warning had almost pleased them as much as fresh pastry. Almost.

"I just want to make *sure*," muttered Fenris. Worry creased his brows.

On the subject of spooky things, Captain Sutcliff had claimed the empty seat across the doorway from Ingrid. He maintained adequate corporeality to sit there, legs crossed, his pleats perfect and shoes shined. Like Ingrid, he had geared himself for battle. His regular belt was gone, re- placed by a thick utility version that hosted several laden holsters and a knife of wicked size. A shoulder belt carried a canteen and a thick pouch that she could only assume car- ried food. All of the equipment was useless. Sutcliff knew that, too. Even so, there was something powerful about being physically ready for battle, even if one was a ghost.

"Kindly tell the sylphs to encompass the airship once we're in the clouds," said Cy.

"Very well." Ingrid closed her eyes, and extending her magic, beckoned to the hive. They surged forward as the airship itself slowed, the engine noise changing to a soft purr.

The heat of the sylphs draped over the airship. Ingrid sucked in a sharp breath, anticipating pain from their magic. To her surprise, she felt nothing. Maybe the orichalcum-plated hull provided a buffer, or maybe it was due to the distance they had to fly in their circuits. Whatever the reason, Ingrid was relieved she could preserve more energy.

She opened her eyes. "The sylphs are at work. Let's go." She gripped the length of the Green Dragon Crescent Blade across her lap. In its leather bag, it was about as long as her forearm. The weapon's holy aura warmed her lap, not unlike a sprawled cat.

Fenris glanced back, his face skewed in worry. "Are you *sure* the sylphs are active? I don't see anything."

"They are blending in with the cloud. You'll see a kind of gray veil once we're out."

"Just go, Fenris," said Cy.

"Yeah, yeah, forgive me for some hesitance so that I might make certain we're *not flying straight into hot cannon fire*." The *Bug*'s engine slowly revved and the ship flew forward. Clouds dissipated but the sky was not pure blue. "Well, damn. I see what you mean. Time to sidle up to some gunships, then."

"I hope you're joshing," said Cy.

"Being within a few hundred feet *is* sidling up. Under most circumstances, that coziness would be incompatible with staying alive," said Fenris. He pointed ahead. "Hey, Captain. Is this the best place to park?"

Excalibur loomed closer and closer, the gunships surrounding it like points of a star. No matter how many times Ingrid looked at the flying alabaster castle, it never seemed quite real, more like some fanciful creation out of an N. C. Wyeth painting in a fairy-tale book, only missing a dragon perched on a parapet. Mooring masts crested the citadel at several levels. Only one airship remained docked at a mast— the last supply vessel.

"Yes, the kermanite is closest to this side," said Captain Sutcliff. Ingrid relayed this news.

"Good. Those should be the main holding-bay doors. Makes sense for the kermanite, large as it is, to be stored near the tanks and other equipment of size. That matches our map, too."

During their last days in Los Angeles, the men had made several trips to view more newsreels of *Excalibur,* and then engaged in vigorous discussions to plot out the interior layout and points of vulnerability.

A minute of tense silence passed by as they crept closer. Ingrid could count the windows along the gunship's hull.

No one in the other ship could have heard a sound from inside the *Bug*'s cabin, but even so, Cy, Ingrid, and Fenris said nary a word as they glided by. Ingrid knew the sylphs were concealing much of the *Bug*'s engine sounds, but there was still the risk that an alert crewman might detect a distortion in the air, hear some nebulous soft roar from the empty sky. She waited in dread for a klaxon, for gunfire, for a hailing light sequence.

The gunship passed from view. Ingrid released a rattling breath, a hand to her chest as if to prevent her heart from galloping away. The castle keep loomed large, too large. The *Palmetto Bug* was like krill drifting close to a whale's maw.

"No one say a positive word right now." Fenris's voice was tight. "Don't jinx this."

"I never thought of you as the superstitious type," Ingrid whispered with a glance at the image of the "saint" tucked among the dials.

"Well, yes, but I also decided years ago that there was no such thing as God—or gods. Being in your company has reintroduced the idea of faith to me in very real and complicated ways."

"I'd like to ask a question of Captain Sutcliff, if I may," Cy interrupted. She nodded for him to continue. "Captain, you're able to manipulate physical matter to a degree. Do you think you could moor an airship?"

Sutcliff bowed his head. "The issue there is not with me handling the winch and cables, but of the distance it would take me from our lady geomancer here. I would lose hold of my sense of self." Ingrid considered his words as she repeated them aloud.

"I can form a bubble and fling myself to the deck," she suggested.

"When you flung yourself the distance of three stories,

that action pulled a lot of power from you. Here, you have to account for wind as well as gravity." Cy shook his head. "And once there, you don't know how to moor us."

"You can tell me—"

"It takes experience," said Fenris, not unkindly. "And a strong arm on the winch."

She looked to Captain Sutcliff. "Once I landed on the deck, *you* could tell me what to do next."

His blond brows pressed together. "I cannot disagree with the other gentlemen in this. The risks of overextending your body, and perhaps overexerting your magical force, are high and add peril to the mission."

Ingrid's throat clenched in frustration. Sutcliff was probably more worried that she might die and he'd never find his peace. She recognized the pettiness of the accusation and couldn't give voice to it. Even if it were true, his fear was legitimate with his immortality at risk.

Excalibur filled the window, a slight copperlike sheen beneath its white paint. The recently moored supply ship twisted slightly at its mast. Two other masts stood nearby. The deck curved out beneath the masts as if to form a bay. The points at either end were guarded by deck-mounted guns, unmanned. No people were visible at all.

"So much death," Sutcliff murmured. "I cannot help but think of a lamp screen I made for my mother when I was a child. With the help of my uncle, I used an ice pick to puncture a sheet of metal. The intent was for the light to shine through the holes, the effect like stars. I punctured the metal too much, set the holes too close. The screen allowed through too much light." His whisper dropped to an almost incomprehensible level. "There's so much light leaking through."

Cold chills crept along Ingrid's spine, and not from Sutcliff's proximity.

"Cy, take my chair." Fenris stood, stretching his arms and legs as much as he could within the tight space between the seats. "I've gotten it nice and warm for you."

"Where are you going?" Cy asked as he switched chairs.

"I'm going to jump out of my perfectly good airship. It's troublesome, really, how everyone else has done that but me." He thudded around in the storage cabinet along the hall. "I've always been slow to follow trends. Ah, here we are. Cap, goggles, jacket."

"What?" snapped Ingrid. Wind caused the ship to quiver.

"Fenris! You can't jump out!" said Cy. He set the *Bug* in a hover and angled himself to glare down the corridor.

"Why not? The only other option is for *you* to leap out, and you're pretty important here. I've never met Maggie in person, and I'm not about to introduce myself as your old academy chum and then apologize for the fact you just jumped to your death from a few thousand feet in elevation."

"I don't like this," growled Cy.

"Surprise! I don't like it either." Fenris stepped to just inside the control cabin. He wore a slim-fitted leather jacket that emphasized his narrow hips. A leather cap covered his cropped black hair, and he had a pair of goggles propped up on his forehead. "Do I look adequately equipped for an act of derring-do?"

Ingrid didn't know what to say. She didn't want Cy to jump

either, and they had effectively argued against her taking action herself. She checked on the heat lingering in her veins. She had lifted Cy over a chasm in Olema, but this, as they had pointed out to her, was considerably more complicated.

"You hated when we had to practice 'derrings-do' at academy." Cy guided the *Bug* to a gap between the masts. The curved wall of *Excalibur* looked to be only some fifteen feet away—not far at all. Wind shoved at the ship, relentless as a play-yard bully.

"'Derring-do' was the noble name our school gave to weekly athletic competitions," said Fenris, casual as could be. "Wretched things. Climbing steep walls with ropes, running sprints, sumo bouts, that sort of thing. I was terrible at most of the drills, but! . . . I was agile. I could tumble and roll and land on my feet. I earned a medal once. I melted it down to make something. I forget what."

"If you've been practicing your gymnastic exercises in the last decade, you've been sneaky about it," said Cy.

"Bah, *practice*. I remember what to do." Fenris stepped farther into the cockpit to study the gauges. "This wind adds a new level of difficulty, though. Ah, well. That's life for you. Or death." His hand glanced Cy's shoulder, and he turned away. "Angle the ship around."

Cy's broad hands were tense on the controls as he pivoted the *Bug* in place. Their view changed from the sleek hull of the citadel to a span of blue sky gauzed in moving sylphs. Two gunships hovered at a distance.

Now Ingrid couldn't judge how far away *Excalibur* was at all—or where the masts were on either side of them. She could move to view the exterior mirrors, but somehow she doubted that what she saw would provide any comfort.

Nor would she be able to see if Fenris actually landed.

"Ingrid, come here," Fenris said. She immediately joined him at the hatch. The *guandao* in its leather bag bobbed against her thigh. She self-consciously checked the ties that secured it to her belt. "Here are some security straps. I'm belting you so you stay put. It'll be awfully windy once I drop out. You have to haul up the hatch door again as soon as you can. It can't be flapping around as Cy approaches the mast."

He handed her a simple harness. Nervous as she was, her shaky fingers managed the broad buckles. Meanwhile, Fenris fastened another strap to the hatch door and tethered that to the wall.

"See this?" He tugged on the rope. "Lean into this rope with your body weight to bring up the door. Even if you only get a latch or two, that'll help with the pressure in here until Cy can finish securing it. Got it?"

She nodded. "Don't die."

"I will, but hopefully not today. Give the sylphs some extra pastries for me." He worked the latches.

The sylphs. Ingrid couldn't see what was happening, but the sylphs could.

The door swung free. Wind roared inside the cabin. The heat of the sylphs' magic flecked the icy wind that gusted into her face and prickled like nettles.

Fenris gripped the lip of the opening and lowered himself. His arms swung back and forth, back and forth.

And then he let go.

CHAPTER 22

Fenris dropped away, and Ingrid threw her awareness outward to the sylphs, ready to scream at them, only to find they
were already alert. They had sensed the pressure change as
the hatch door swung open. They had recognized the familiar, wonderful presence of Fenris, a person the first-sylphs
strongly associated with the joys of pastry, a person whose
scent was evident through every inch of their beloved home.

fenris fenris fenris! chanted the sylphs. *you cannot fall
from the nest. you have no wings!* Their tone was playful,
chiding as a small group ceased their rotations around the
Bug, and, as a sinuous ribbon, dived after Fenris.

"Ingrid! Pull up the door! I need to turn us!" Cy shouted.

Without opening her eyes, she lurched belly-first onto
the now-taut rope that anchored to the hatch door. Her mass
dragged it down. She lay almost level on the floor. The door
clattered, unwilling to completely shut, but the wind had
been greatly reduced.

She wondered if she should seal the door, but the metallic banging reminded her of a metal jaw, ready to chomp down on a hand. She could shield her skin as a precaution—and likely damage the hatch if it did snare her. Better to just stay put. She heaved for breath, her lungs aching at the sudden shift of temperature and pressure. Her ears popped.

The sylphs' happy hum told her everything she needed to know.

They had him. Dear God, they had him.

Ingrid folded over and sobbed in relief. "The sylphs! They got him!" she choked out.

"What? Did he miss the deck?"

She flashed that question to the sylphs as the airship began to turn. Images immediately entered her mind: Fenris falling, the cruel wind taking his trajectory just short of his goal. The lead sylphs caught him as he would have dropped past, the rest joining in to scoop him up and over a matter of feet to safety.

"I see him!" yelled Cy, a hitch in his voice. "He's on the deck!"

All of the sylphs sang in a mighty chorus. They were not yet hungry, but they knew they had done well and would later feast for their efforts.

The *Bug* stilled. Rapid footsteps approached her. "I'll seal up the hatch. One thing Fenris didn't take time to mention is that the flapping door could easily slice off a hand or fingers if you don't grab it right."

"He was in something of a hurry." Her voice rasped. The wind was gone, but she still felt especially cold. That's when she noticed Captain Sutcliff was right beside her, his eyes squinted shut.

He was focusing to grant himself as much mass as possible to help her with the rope.

Cy jerked the door up the rest of the way and latched it to stay put. His hand brushed her cheek. "Oh God, Ingrid, you're like ice, did you—"

"No, I didn't use my power to grab him. The sylphs did that on their own. It turns out that they take good loving care of people who feed them. I'm merely cold from exposure, and the company of the captain. Does the ship still need to be invisible now?"

"No. The sylphs have earned their rest."

She extended her gratitude to the fairies and bade them heed Fenris; when they'd planned this out, he'd promised to find a safe place for the sylphs to recover while the *Bug* was docked. The magical presence faded from around the ship.

As Ingrid's limbs remained rubbery from terror, Cy helped her to stagger to the cockpit and to the copilot's seat.

Fenris was climbing the mooring mast. A few sylphs—the first-sylphs, she realized—shadowed him all the way, as if to make sure he didn't fall again. The other sylphs had retreated into the shadows of the wall behind the mast.

Cy pointed to the barely visible sylphs and nodded in approval. "Even the best spyglass from a gunship won't be able to see the sylphs in such deep shadows."

"He has made the effort to train them, though I think they've trained *him* in turn."

Cy eased the *Bug* forward. "If we survive this, I'm praying the bakeries in town have replenished their stock. Those sylphs deserve all the baked goods they desire."

"If we survive this . . ." she echoed. "Cy. If we do survive, and the fox isn't sniffing after us, where should we go? Where can I find 'my mountain,' as Tacoma put it?"

The tip of the mooring mast grew larger as the ship glided forward. Cy snorted softly and shook his head.

"What?"

"You said that, and I had one specific place come to mind, though I don't know if it'd do. It might be too geologically active. Down along the central California coast, there's a little town called Morro Bay. It features this massive four-hundred-foot rock right in the bay. A veritable mountain, quite the landmark when you're flying over."

"I think I've seen pictures of it." The central coast. It'd be wilder and more remote than San Francisco, sure, but also forested and green and foggy.

That thought spurred a deep yearning that brought tears to her eyes. "We'll need to investigate the place. After."

"Yes. After." The *Bug* powered down. Cy sat slack in his chair. Ingrid stood and wrapped her arms around him and the headrest, her hands against his chest. The rapidness of his heartbeat reminded her of when she once cupped a baby bird in her hand. The wild thrum of its heartbeat made her feel as though she held a heart entire, not simply a small bird.

Cy tilted his head against hers, and they remained like that for a moment, taking in each other's strength, only to be interrupted by banging at the hatch door.

"I suppose we should let him on board again." Cy shifted,

as if waking up. Ingrid remained behind the chair as he sidled past to the corridor.

"I can see why you survived the earthquake and your travails since." Sutcliff's voice caused her to turn in surprise. "You and your friends are audacious and brave. You've been blessed."

His words caused her to hesitate as she walked past him. "I have been. Truly."

"I'm fine. Don't act like a mother hen." Fenris's voice sounded muffled as he clambered back on board, his sleeve pressed to his face. He gave Ingrid a nod and lowered his arm. His face was a grisly mask of blood, with fresh red still dripping from his nose. "Ingrid, for future reference, try not to have the sylphs catch you face first. I imagine it's rather like crashing into a brick wall. You'd think they'd be softer, but then, we were all traveling quite fast." He accepted some rags from Cy. "I'm not complaining, mind you. No. I take that back. Yes, I will complain, but I'm still grateful."

"Oh no. Is your nose broken?"

"I don't think so. Maybe I'll be lucky and end up with a permanent bump on the arch of my nose. It'll make me look tougher." His grin revealed gory teeth.

"We cannot dawdle," murmured Captain Sutcliff. "To both A-and-A soldiers and Chinese guerrillas, this is an enemy craft."

"Cy, Sutcliff says we need to move."

"Fenris, will you be all right here?" he asked.

"As well as can be expected. I'll feed the sylphs and see if I can adjust the angle of that gun to face the nearest doors." He looked perky at the thought, even as he continued to mop his face. "I have the gun you bought for me in Phoenix, too." He motioned to Ingrid as a reminder that she was armed as well.

"We'll check on that airship moored beside us before we enter the hold. I'd like to know how the Chinese went about their plot," said Cy. "Ingrid, can Sutcliff please take a gander inside the bay doors as we go that way?" He checked his pistol and holstered it again.

She listened to the ghost as she moved to the hatch. "He can, though he thinks orichalcum will be hard for him to move through. He theorizes that's why he's able to stay on airships without difficulty. Fenris." She met his eye and gave him a nod. "See you soon."

"Yes, well, take care of Cy. He's likely to get into trouble."

"I'll do everything in my power to keep him well."

Fenris offered her a brittle smile. "I know you will. Go. Shoo. Sooner you go, sooner we all go. Right?"

Right. Ingrid followed Cy down the mast. She tried to be wary of the placement of her feet as well as any threats that might emerge along the citadel's deck below or from the sky beyond. Cy had prepared a pack for her with water, food, basic medical supplies, and more kermanite; the gun was in an outer pocket, within easy reach. All were essentials, but the extra weight added more strain to her body.

They reached the deck and headed across the open space toward the bay door. Cy angled himself to protect Ingrid, alert for any sound at their level and from above. They stopped to one side of the door. Sutcliff walked through; the chill of his presence dimmed, but she could feel where he was just on the other side. He returned seconds later.

"There's a dead soldier within. It appears he died of influenza, but he's been stripped of his weapons. I saw no sign of any living guards in the vicinity."

Ingrid related this to Cy as they continued to the mooring mast. She looked up the stairs with dread, readying herself for the slog. Cy hesitated.

"Take cover behind the barrels here. Watch the doors. I'll go up."

"But if I go up with you, the captain can scout ahead—"

"He can keep an eye out for you here, too."

Ingrid took out her pistol and sat on a low box behind the barrels. With her gaze on the doors, she used her free hand to rub her left calf as best she could through the boot shaft.

"You hide your discomfort well, most of the time," Sutcliff murmured.

"I was protected from my own pain for much of my life, but I did learn how to hide the symptoms of energy fevers. This isn't so different, really."

Sutcliff was quiet for a moment. "There is a great deal I wish I could have comprehended while I was still alive." He took a few steps away. "Pardon. I would like a closer look at the gunnery over here."

Ingrid obliged, moving around the barrels so that Sutcliff could study the large gun mounted to the deck.

"It's a prop," he murmured.

"A prop? It doesn't work?"

"It can't even hold bullets. Beautiful work as a dummy piece, though."

Her jaw dropped. "There are guns like this all over these outer decks. Are they all fake? Why?" She paused, then answered herself. "They posed soldiers by these in the cinema footage."

"*Excalibur* was assembled in a hurry, but it's necessary for it to look like a ready battle station."

"Do those gunships nearby know the truth?" The *Palmetto Bug* on its moorage now looked all the more vulnerable.

"That is the question, isn't it?" he muttered, stroking his blond mustache. "I doubt they know about the faux armaments, but at this stage they almost certainly know about the illness on *Excalibur* and why no other ships can come near. They are guarding a contaminated graveyard."

"It's a wonder they allowed the supply ship to come up at all," she said.

"An act of desperation." He shook his head with deep weariness.

Footsteps tapped along the stairs above. She glanced upward to confirm Cy's approach, and moved to the base of the tower to intercept him. Moments later, he joined her, panting heavily.

"No one alive up there. Ugly fight." He offered no more details, for which she was thankful. "A large crate was left open. It's clearly how the Chinese smuggled themselves aboard.

"They are surely roving the citadel even now, killing anyone who has survived the sickness."

Picturing Lee as a soldier, as a murderer, made her feel sick. She felt *revulsion*. This was war, but . . . damn it.

"Our position here might be more precarious, too." She moved to show the deck gun to Cy. He immediately recognized it as a fake as well.

"Damn it all. I hoped we could use this gun to our advantage. I need to let Fenris know."

Ingrid waited beneath the *Bug* as Cy dashed up the mast again. Questions raced through her mind, questions she knew they could not answer: What would they do if a gunship moved in? Was there any possible way to defend the *Palmetto Bug*?

The low buzz of the sylphs caused her to face where they rested in the shadows.

The sylphs could attack; they had acted in her defense before. But she could not ask for them to commit suicide by throwing themselves into battle. Ingrid thought of the warning she'd already given them about the stub-wing engines and how they had reacted, and she shuddered. No. She had already asked too much of the sylphs.

They sensed her attention and flashed a query her way.

"If another ship comes and threatens the Bug, listen to Fenris," she thought at them. They replied in the affirmative.

Depending on the situation, he could verbally request their aid. Or he could yell at them to leave.

Cy returned, and they walked together to the holding bay doors. "Captain Sutcliff, can you please scout ahead for us again?"

"He's going in," she murmured as Sutcliff stepped through the wall.

"Ingrid, remember, if we're separated, plan to meet at the engine room. Some crew *must* be alive there, keeping this hulk afloat." She could see in his eyes his fervent belief that Maggie must be among them. "That'll be among the most defensible areas on the craft, if people had the foresight to bring down the fire doors."

Even if Lee and the others couldn't understand the engineering controls, they would know that destroying the chained kermanite that powered the citadel would be an easy way to crash it. Since that hadn't happened, maybe they hadn't been able to access that area at all. This was Cy's repeated logic over the past day, anyway.

Ingrid released a heavy breath. They were on *Excalibur*. They were going to find Maggie. Maybe Lee, too. Would they have to fight him and his companions? How could she pass along the *guandao* if they stood on opposite sides of a battlefield?

"Hey." Cy's fingers stroked her cheek, startling her. "You're worrying about Lee, aren't you?"

"Yes."

"For the sake of your own life and mine, you must stop. You need to be focused." Cy's gaze on her was hard. "You hear me?"

"I hear you." She took in a deep breath. "I love you, Cy."

"And I love you, Miss Ingrid," he said, drawling out her name as he had done in the first days of their acquaintance. "Take care of yourself in there."

"You be careful, too. Engage in chivalrous acts, only in moderation."

They stared at each other and leaned together for a tender, bittersweet kiss. She pulled back as she sensed Sutcliff's return.

"Still no signs of life nearby," he said. "The hold is spacious. Multiple levels are visible in the central portion of the citadel. Those decks offer vantage points into the hold."

Cy looked grim as Ingrid repeated this information. "Wonderful spots for snipers, then. If the Chinese didn't have guns and ammo when they boarded, they surely have aplenty now. Does this door offer decent cover?"

"As good as any of these smaller doors, Sutcliff says. He agrees—the best course of action is to get out of the hold as quickly as possible, but we do need to get him to the kermanite. It's off to the left."

"I don't suppose he'll dally a bit longer, to help us survive this?"

Ingrid listened and relayed Sutcliff's words. "He says he has no desire to abandon us, but he also *needs* to get there before we leave. After all, if we're required to make a quick escape . . ."

Cy nodded, expression sorrowful. "Far be it from me to keep a man from his peace. Please lead the way, Captain."

They slipped inside the hold.

She could not see a ceiling above, only darkness, but had a strong sense of a great open space that was scarcely filled. Sporadic kermanite light cast faint blue illumination along the curved exterior wall and from support pillars throughout the broad cavern.

Cy scrambled forward, and she traveled in his wake. Her crouched posture caused her calves to clench, and she relied on momentum and fear to propel her forward. She had to keep up close to Cy in case she needed to create a shield around them. The pistol felt heavy and uncomfortable in her grip. The longer she held it, the more she realized she'd prefer to rely on magic alone.

At her back, the door shut again. The click would have been a mild sound in a regular building, but here it seemed to echo loud as a gunshot.

They reached the first stack of crates about twenty feet into the hold and hunkered there. Sutcliff began to take shelter as well, then gave a chagrined shake of his head as he stood tall.

"No one in sight," he said. Ingrid conveyed this to Cy in an "okay" hand sign. He nodded and led her onward—not straight forward into the central portion of the citadel, but on a zigzag route among the spaced-out islands of supplies. Sutcliff studied Cy with blatant approval.

Ingrid almost tripped over a man lying in a fetal position in the shadows behind a pillar. The smell of him—good God. She gagged and fought the compulsion to vomit as Cy hurried them along. Her backpack thudded against her spine.

"Wait." Sutcliff had stopped behind her. He gestured to a side path, his head at a curious tilt. She beckoned Cy to follow. Sutcliff walked about fifteen feet into the blackness of a chasm between boxes and studied the floor.

"There is a massive pile of papers strewn about here, circular burn marks on each and every one," he said.

"Do they look like confidential papers?" she whispered. Evidence might prove useful later. She tucked the pistol into the side pouch of her pack and wiped her sweaty hands on her hips.

"No, that's what is odd. There is no writing on them at all.

They are absolutely blank. If enchanted ink were being used, protocol states that the entire sheet must be destroyed, not simply one spot." Sutcliff motioned her forward to look.

His eyesight was far better than hers, as she couldn't see the sheets at all until they were underfoot. She stopped at the very edge of a pile roughly ten feet in length and wider than the path; papers filled the passage ahead and protruded from the boxes above, as though they'd been dropped from the ceiling. Just as Sutcliff had described, each sheet bore a circular burn mark about the size of a wax seal. What he hadn't mentioned was that every sheet was folded, and not in a haphazard way. The folds were unique to each sheet, angling this way and that. Many sheets fit together, creating a strange puzzle.

She took in the wormlike length of the pile, and bit her knuckles to smother a loud gasp. She couldn't help but take a hasty step back.

"What is it?" whispered Cy.

"One of the fox's constructs. Those things she had on patrol for me. The sigils that powered it have been burned away." Her voice shook.

"We know these things were all over California. The search must have extended far beyond," muttered Cy, his brow furrowed.

"The person who enchants an object has the easiest time disenchanting it. That means she was likely *here*." Ingrid motioned to the ground at their feet. Inert as the creature was, she wanted to get away from it, away from a place where Blum had perhaps stood.

Cy gripped her trembling hand. "We already know she was on board when *Excalibur* was in Atlanta. This may have been here all the while. The soldiers aboard could have been ordered to leave it undisturbed." Sutcliff nodded in agreement. He stood in the open, vigilant as they spoke. "Or someone else made this one, and unmade it."

"Or perhaps this construct wasn't used to track you. It may have served some other purpose for her or someone else," added Sutcliff.

"I don't dare think optimistically, not when it comes to *her*." Nor did she want to think pessimistically either—that this might be one of the trackers from California, and that it flew here to intercept its maker. That Blum was already on the citadel or in Phoenix or somewhere else far too close for comfort. By their expressions, Cy and Sutcliff were thinking the same thing, but no one dared to give voice to the fear.

"Let's get away from this thing," she whispered with an uneasy look around. No one naysaid her. She briefly embraced Cy, her head against his shoulder as if to borrow more of his strength, and then they continued their trek.

Cy guided them deeper into the hold. Ingrid concentrated on the soft tread of her feet, the sound of her breaths. The citadel's hull was no longer visible. The world was rendered to boxes, barrels, and other odd parcels, all lit by scant light. The darkness high above resembled a night sky, minus the glory of stars.

They crept into an open area between rows.

Sutcliff shouted, "Above!" Reflexively, Ingrid formed a

shield, her focus on Cy. Bullets zinged past and impacted nearby with sharp pings.

Cy kept on running, hunched low. They reached the cover of a Durendal tank, one in a row of about ten. The central cannons hadn't been mounted yet, creating black cyclops eyes in the low turrets of each shiny new tank.

In her rush, Ingrid had formed the shield too close to them. She let it drop so they could take in ragged gasps of fresh air.

"There is one man a deck up along the railing. He's taking shelter behind a pillar." Captain Sutcliff stood in the open about five feet distant. "About thirty feet away, someone's throwing—"

Cy must have seen something, too, as he jumped up and scrambled away before she could repeat a word. Ingrid tried to follow. She couldn't. Her left calf muscle locked with a lightning bolt of agony. Cy slipped around the corner of the tank and vanished.

Metal pinged close by. An impact with her right calf sent her rolling onto her back.

"Shield!" barked Sutcliff.

She flared out a bubble to encase herself again. Something crackled against the floor nearby. Smoke unfurled around her in a billowing cloud. A smoke bomb, perhaps with a toxin inside.

Was she shot? She groped at her good leg—*ha!*—and found a chunk of her boot sheered away. The smooth orichalcum plate beneath had been dented. The pain beneath that point was already starting to fade.

"It looks like you caught a ricochet, and sent it ricocheting again." Sutcliff's disembodied voice carried from the fog.

She rolled onto her side and forced both feet flat underneath her body. Even though she was trapped with a clean air supply, Ingrid's mouth was parched with acute terror. She could see nothing in front of her but the expanding cloud, and nothing behind her but the mighty chassis of the Durendal.

"Jennings slipped away in time. Crawl away—under the fake tank, the same direction he went. Use the fog to cover you from the sniper."

There was no way Ingrid could crawl beneath the tank. Instead, she crouched and blindly scurried after Cy. Her left leg dragged, but the braces enabled her to keep moving.

"Straight," snapped Sutcliff. "Left, left, left. Keep going!" As if directions made any sense! Move forward, forward, that's all she knew. The fog seemed to expand and follow her. Her ragged breaths echoed inside her enclosure; sweat wept down her back.

The cloud finally dissipated. She staggered another twenty feet and barely managed to sit rather than collapse face first. "A minute," she croaked, with a weak wave to Sutcliff. She leaned on a high stack of boxes.

"I hear footsteps and voices close by. We cannot stay here long."

She hesitated, then let the shield fall as she inhaled with a soft gasp of sheer relief. Her skin still carried a slight fever. She rubbed at her bruised leg, wincing.

Sutcliff spun around, alert as a cat in an aviary. "Our attackers are near. You should move."

She nodded. Using her hands, she slid on her backside around the corner of the crate. Energy tingling through her extremities, she edged along the side of the box and peered around the next corner.

To find herself staring into a pair of dark eyes wide with alarm. A black bandanna covered the lower half of the person's face.

Ingrid recoiled in a panic, her hand rising to shove out energy. That's when the realization struck her. She knew that face, that shaggy black hair, those eyes.

"Lee?" she whispered, almost unable to get the word out.

"Ing?" He poked his head around the corner and tugged down the bandanna. He wore a sooty gray cotton work uniform. Relief flooded across his familiar features. "It's really you? You're here?"

With a choked sob, she launched herself forward, both arms around him. He was real and warm and alive. Too skinny, yes, but he was *alive*. They rocked in place, both in tears, both trying to stay as quiet as possible.

"How are you feeling?" She pulled back to study his face. His skin looked sallow, deep bags under his eyes—but it was a hell of a lot better than he had looked the last time she'd seen him, blood-soaked and a mere breath from death.

"I probably haven't been getting as much sleep as I should, and I know I haven't been eating enough vegetables, but . . . well." He studied her, reaching up to roughly scrub his tears away. "How did you get here? Where are Fenris and Cy? Jesus Christ, I almost shot you just now."

"Someone else is nearby." Sutcliff's voice startled her. In

the joy of the moment, she'd forgotten he was there. "By the soft tread, I don't believe it's Jennings."

"Should I use a bubble?" she murmured over her shoulder.

"Ing?" Lee's voice was barely audible.

"The footsteps are fading again," said Sutcliff. "Be judicious if you use a bubble to hide both of you. That magic expenditure will drain you quickly."

She nodded then whispered to Lee, "Someone else was close by, but they crept away. I have the ghost of Captain Sutcliff with me. He's acting as my lookout." Lee's expression was outright aghast, but she couldn't really tell him the whole story right now. "Cy is with me—or was. We were separated by a smoke bomb. Fenris is with the *Bug,* docked outside."

Horror flashed over his face. "I threw the smoke bomb, Ing. That was me. We thought soldiers had landed. I didn't know—"

"There was no way you could." She hugged him again, her face pressed to his shoulder.

"Why are you here?" His whisper was insistent.

"Cy's twin, Maggie. She's not really dead. She's the engineer behind this." Ingrid waved around them. "We're hoping she survived the sickness and we can get her help to sabotage this thing."

"You know about the sickness? Then—"

Ingrid's left leg pulsed with pain. She hissed and drew it closer, changing her sitting position to take pressure off that hip. Lee glanced down. Ingrid's skirt flared up to the knee, showing the shiny orichalcum of the brace that protruded above her boot.

"What's that?" he whispered. "Are you hurt?"

"Constantly." The painful tingles eased off again. "In Seattle, my body was permanently damaged by my power. I can barely walk on my own. We went to the Vassal States, where I met my grandmother, Madam Pele—"

"Your grandmother? *Her?*"

"She told me the damage was permanent. Cy and Fenris've helped me find ways to adapt."

"They would. I'm glad you found more family, Ing. Mr. Kealoha would have been thrilled—"

"I met his wife. She helped us. She was just as sweet as we always expected she'd be."

Raw joy lit Lee's face. Mr. Kealoha had been the only other warden who treated Lee with kindness and respect—as a human being. "I'm so glad, I—"

"Someone is coming!" barked Captain Sutcliff. Ingrid gripped Lee's arm, her other fingers pressed to his mouth. "We cannot stay out here. More people are converging."

Ingrid pushed an energy bubble around them and forced it to hide their sound. She let her hands fall to the ground as she pushed herself up. "We have to move. I can make us invisible, but—"

"No. You can't risk damaging yourself more." He stood, flinging his arms around her waist. "Which way was Cy going?"

"Engine room. That's where we hope to find Maggie."

"We haven't been able to break in there. Someone is alive in there—or was. Go that way, to the big corridor." He jerked his head to the left. "I'll try to guide my people the other way.

You get his sister and get out. I can only do so much. Some of the men here . . ."

"I understand." They'd spoken before about factions within the refugees, and she could imagine her efforts to help save Lee in Seattle had made him look all the more untrustworthy.

Sutcliff positioned himself behind Lee and urgently waved her forward. The shield dissipated. She gave Lee a final squeeze then she let go, their hands meeting for a brief moment as they moved in opposite directions. Ingrid determinedly forced her tears back. It physically hurt to be separated from him so quickly.

"To this side," Sutcliff said. "Stay still. Perhaps you won't need to use more energy to hide."

She nodded, too close to sobs to dare speak. She stood with a crate at her back. Around the corner, she heard Lee speak softly in Chinese. Another man answered, then another. Ingrid ached to peer around the corner, to have one last glance of Lee, but Sutcliff's hard gaze pinned her in place. A minute passed. Two.

Sutcliff's posture softened. "How are your legs now?"

"Better now that I'm standing."

His nod was crisp. "Good. Move out."

She followed him at a jog, backpack rustling, the Green Dragon Crescent Blade bouncing against her thighs.

Oh, dear God. The *guandao*.

"I didn't give him the Crescent Blade!" She spun around in a panic.

"Ingrid. You can't go back. He's with the others—"

"But I must hand it over! Everything depends on it!" Despair caused her to waver in place. The *qilin* had trusted her. Mr. Sakaguchi had trusted her. "I have it right here. Damn it, the blade was right between us as we hugged."

Captain Sutcliff stood before her, spectral hands on her shoulders. She convulsed in a vicious shiver. "The moment is gone. Follow me." His voice contained both military authority and compassion. With a final glance back, she followed him, her jaw taut with self-directed rage.

Had her carelessness doomed not only the mission, but Lee's very purpose in life?

"Don't blame yourself alone. I, too, should have remembered the *guandao*." Sutcliff spoke without meeting her eyes. "Do not regret the reunion you just experienced. Life is too fragile, too precious. The love you two share . . ." Grief rattled his voice. "Don't waste time on regret. You may see him again before we leave."

"I hope so." She prayed so, with all her being.

They wound their way around more freight, eventually reaching the corridor. Unlike the hold, it was fully lit. "This is too exposed," Sutcliff muttered. He motioned her through an open doorway to her left.

Ingrid paused in the doorway, stunned by the size of the room. She breathed in the intense greenery of *Excalibur*'s garden as she moved forward among the rows and towers of plants. Her wonder at the place pushed some of the despair from her mind.

She recalled seeing the gardens briefly in the reel footage, but those few seconds of film had done the scope of it no justice. The greenhouse had to be a quarter mile in length. She couldn't see exactly where it ended. Towers of greenery seemed to stretch on forever. She had never seen plants growing up in this manner—not in a contained environment—with pillars hosting cups of plants in tiers stretching up to the ceiling. It put her in mind of the thick growths of vines on Hawaii Island.

Rail tracks lined the floor and ceiling along each row. Some devices were parked along these tracks. By the long copper spouts and attached tanks, she could only imagine them to be part of an automated watering system. She moved deeper into the rows, still traveling parallel to the corridor she left behind.

"At the cinema, the footage said the soldiers aboard could survive for months in the self-contained environment aboard." She stroked a growing yellow squash as she moved past.

"Survive, perhaps, but not happily," said Sutcliff. "American men require *meat*."

"I bet they have chickens elsewhere on board, and the ability to process compost." She reached a kind of booth set up in the middle of a partitioned section—perhaps an office for the overseer. The room featured two windows, a desk and chair, and a simple lavatory. The wall over the desk had exactly what she needed, though—a map. She pulled it from its nail and sat on the floor to study. Her calf muscles spasmed, but she didn't dare take off her boots and braces.

"This door will take you toward the engine room," Sutcliff said, pointing.

She took in the multiple levels of the station, the massive berthing areas, the presence of several kitchens across different floors, the placement of munitions at loading areas on every level. The sheer scope of the flying fortress boggled her mind. How had the construction of its segments been completed in such secrecy over the past year? How had it been assembled with nary a peep reaching the public?

Had all of those menial workers been killed to keep the word mum?

Magnolia Augustus was brilliant to conceive such a citadel and to make it fly. Brilliant, yet a figure of terror. For Cy's sake, she hoped Maggie was alive and sealed away in the engine room. For all of humanity's sake, Ingrid hoped that Maggie could be reasoned with to sabotage or otherwise work against *Excalibur,* and to redirect her imagination to other endeavors.

"I need to intercept Cy in the engine room or the corridor there." She gnawed on her chapped lip. "I hope that Fenris has a gun ready. Lee will try to keep the men inside, but . . ."

"Mr. Braun is resourceful, and the sylphs are devoted to him, even without you present to moderate."

Ingrid nodded, recalling words Cy had uttered to her amid the bedlam of Seattle. *Control what you can.* "We need to find Cy and Maggie before that fleet arrives."

Sutcliff offered a crisp nod of support. "You must maintain hope."

That brought to mind another piece of advice from Seattle: *Hope is a kind of gangrene.* Ingrid grimaced as she stood.

She encountered more dead men and evidence of illness as she worked toward the corridor again. On the map, she had seen where the hospital was on board, and fervently hoped she had no cause to go there. It must be a morgue by now.

Captain Sutcliff hurried ahead of her, a hand on the useless gun at his waist. He motioned her to lurk behind a pillar of plants as he advanced to the central hallway about ten feet away.

"I hear multiple footsteps," he said, motioning her lower.

That's when Ingrid smelled it. That musk. That goddamned, horrible musk, the stench of her nightmares. Ambassador Blum.

This wasn't a trace whiff, like that of Blum's insidious scouts.

Blum was here. *She was already here in the citadel.*

The breath seized in Ingrid's lungs as she dropped flat to the ground, a hand to her thigh and the burned ward. She stopped herself from trying to will more magic into the mark. She couldn't. Her exertion in creating that enchantment had already irreparably damaged her body. The ward was working; Grandmother had said so. It would surely work at close proximity, too.

Faith. Ingrid must have faith.

Captain Sutcliff. He remained in the open. She seized the cold tendrils that stretched between them and reeled him toward her. He dug in, looking back at her with indignant shock.

"What—"

"Shh!" she said, loud as she dared. "Hide!"

He didn't fight her further. Seconds later, he was beside her, an ethereal form on hands and knees amid dangling strawberry vines with crisp white buds. "What is it?" he whispered.

The *guandao*'s leather bag lay uncomfortably between

her body and the floor, but she didn't try to raise her body. The heat of the ancient weapon offered a strange kind of comfort.

"*Her*. She's here. I smell her. She can see and hear ghosts. She's interrogated them before."

Ingrid wouldn't have thought it was possible for the ghost to grow more pale, but he did. "God help us," he whispered. His arms quivered as he bowed his head to face the floor.

Sutcliff's terror did not ease her fears, but his presence did prevent her from falling into the deep pit of her nightmarish memories again. She had to be strong for him—to protect him. Protect the ghost of the man who was once her sworn enemy. She would have erupted in hysterical laughter, if she could.

"You're bound to me. I will fight for you," Ingrid murmured.

He lifted his head, and in a blink, the ghost in A&A battle attire was gone. Ingrid had to clamp her hand over her lips to choke back a cry of shock at the sudden change. Instead of the Sutcliff she knew, a child with tousled blond hair and wide, blue eyes stared at her. "You'll keep the monster away?"

Unable to speak, she nodded. Then, just as quickly, the adult Sutcliff returned, though his eyes remained much the same, blue and terrified. Translucent tears shone against translucent pupils.

What was it he knew or sensed about Blum that evoked such primal terror? His worries about Blum seemed to go far beyond concern for the men in his command. Sutcliff had seen *monsters*.

Ingrid thrust her hand into her pocket. Kermanite crunched in her grip like dried bread.

Taking a steadying breath, she focused on custom-building a shield around both of them. This shield would amplify their hearing but obscure their noise; she knew all too well that Blum had the sensitive ears of a fox, even in her human forms.

"We're shielded. Whisper. The effort to conceal noises will drain me."

"Are we invisible as well?" he asked.

She shook her head. "That would deplete me too quickly."

Sutcliff nodded, tilting his head. "Do you hear that?"

She did. Her amplification had worked. The sound of two pairs of footsteps rang out clearly, along with a murmured male voice. Cy's voice.

He drew closer . . . and Ambassador Blum was following him.

CHAPTER 23

Ingrid's first instinct was to scream at Cy to run. Instead, she rocked in place and mouthed *no, no, no* to an anxious rhythm, her heartbeat at a gallop. If she screamed, she'd give away her location as well as Cy's. And if Blum was already stalking him, his effort to run away would mean nothing. She was preternaturally fast. Shooting at her meant nothing either, not with the protection of the ambassadorial ring.

Ingrid's hand went to the leather bag tied to her belt. She had to find Lee again.

Blum's foulness clogged Ingrid's senses like the stench of rotting bodies, but as much as she wanted to block it out, it was the only way she could track Blum's location.

"I keep wanting to look at you, Maggie. It's a miracle you're alive." Cy spoke at a whisper from what had to be fifty or seventy feet away and through a wall. Through the amplification of Ingrid's magic, he sounded as if he were there next to them. It took a moment for his words to register, and then Ingrid realized—he was talking to Maggie! She was alive!

But why were they walking toward the hold? That place was a trap.

"A miracle? I suppose it is—"

"You *suppose!*" Cy teased. Ingrid could imagine the joy and relief on his face, despite the lingering dangers. She muffled a moan against her hand. He had no idea Blum was so close to them.

"My sole focus has been keeping this thing afloat, but it's been hard. It's been lonesome. Everyone dying around me . . ." The words came across as soft and stilted.

"You don't have to talk about it if you don't want to." Concern rang through his voice.

Captain Sutcliff motioned for Ingrid's attention. "We can follow this row of plants running parallel to the hallway and continue to listen. Can you ascertain where the fox is?" He moved forward, stooped over.

Ingrid followed. "Only that she's out there, somewhere near them. Obviously, Cy hasn't seen her, wary as he is." She had to figure out some way to save him.

"She will track him to find you," Sutcliff said.

"Yes," Ingrid whispered. "And after that, he's disposable."

"We can talk about it more later," Maggie murmured. "Right now I just hope we find your lady friend soon. Maybe she'll be along this corridor. Save us a search of the hold."

"Lord, I hope so. I wish we weren't out here at all, Maggs. The engine room would be the best place to wait—"

"I'm not staying locked in there anymore." Maggie's voice was shrill, dangerously high-pitched.

"Shh, Maggie. Stop. I thought I heard something."

Ingrid and Captain Sutcliff stopped, too, though no sound had escaped from them. Her calf ached, reminding her that it was developing a hell of a bruise. Long seconds passed. Finally, Cy resumed his walk. The presence of Blum loomed, close as his shadow.

"I haven't had anyone to speak to for days, other than those Chinese banging at the door—as if I'd let them in! I—"

Ingrid couldn't understand why Maggie was talking so much, even at a whisper. Didn't she comprehend the danger? She might not have firsthand experience in situations like this, but Cy had said many a time that she was brilliant.

"Maggie, we'll talk later." He sounded exasperated by her behavior, too. "Hold's coming up."

Strategy. Ingrid needed a strategy.

She had more kermanite in her pack, and she might need every nugget if she was going to try to protect three people and a ghost all the way across the hold. Her shield could block Blum, too, but leading the fox straight to the *Bug* seemed like a poor idea.

Maybe they could shove Blum off the deck. Surely her ring couldn't save her from falling thousands of feet.

If only Ingrid had more kermanite! And then she realized, she *did* have more kermanite at hand. The biggest known piece in the world.

"Captain, how far are we from the stolen kermanite?"

He glanced back, surprise evident on his face. Blum's

presence had horrified him to such an extent that he'd forgotten about his own mission. "The rock is located deep inside the hold. Going that route would require us to abandon
Mr. Jennings and his sister."

"I can find them again, with my hearing enhanced like
this." It took everything in her to resolve to abandon Cy in
this moment, but Ingrid needed more power if she was to
save him. Somehow.

Sutcliff considered her. "I want you to be careful." His
voice was strangely soft. "I don't want this action to place you
under additional duress."

"Look where we are, Captain. I'm under exceptional duress already."

"You know very well what I mean. I can't cross to the
hereafter if I believe that your contact with the kermanite
will kill you."

Ingrid bowed her head. "I don't want to die either. I
want . . ." A life with Cy, and Fenris, and Lee, and Mr. Sakaguchi, and voracious little sylphs, and strange contraptions
all around, and days gloriously gray and misty.

He seemed to sense what she was feeling, and it was
enough to reassure him. "Follow me." Captain Sutcliff cut
away from their parallel track, taking them farther into the
greenhouse. Ingrid released the shield around them. Her
skin was almost normal temperature. They wound through
the rows, past two bodies, and to a door to another hallway.
The echo of the door's closure was slight, but they froze in the
shadows for a moment to see if anyone stirred nearby.

At this far side of the garden, they could no longer hear Cy and Maggie. Guilt gnawed at Ingrid. She kept glancing back that way, wondering.

Sutcliff glanced back, too. "This is a strategic retreat. You're not abandoning him."

"I know." Her whisper was hoarse. "Or so I am telling myself." The only comfort came in leaving Blum behind. Ingrid breathed deeply, trying to cleanse her lungs and her spirit.

They entered the hold again from a far different angle, and to an area packed with far more crates and barrels. By the burned designations on the freight, most of the parcels included weaponry: guns, ammunition, pouches, parts.

They approached another row of Durendals, again minus their main guns. Ingrid did a double take.

"Before, when we were fired upon, you mentioned the tank was fake. These are fakes, too."

Like the guns outside, they were masterful frauds. The tanks had full treads, turrets, and outer rails for additional troop transport. But a look inside the gaping hole of the gun showed it to be an empty shell.

"Yes. I have yet to see a genuine Durendal aboard."

"Are these intended for display somewhere?" She approached one of the boxes labeled as RIFLES. A peep between the wooden slats revealed the box to be empty. She checked more and more around her. Empty, empty, empty.

"I think much of the freight in the hold merely set a stage for visiting cinematographers," murmured Sutcliff, shaking his head. "I anticipated most of the *Excalibur*'s supplies to come aboard in California, but I didn't expect *this*. I hope that the hospital stores weren't treated with such disregard as well."

"I agree." She did not want to think of the suffering aboard being even worse than she had previously imagined.

Sutcliff guided her onward. Hidden among the empty freight parcels, they found a massive box with very real and dangerous content.

The crate was almost the size of an autocar, the wooden slats battered, scraped, and splintered away in chunks. "It's been in the same box all the while." Captain Sutcliff pressed a palm to the wood, and recoiled in surprise as his hand sank through.

Ingrid touched the wood. Coarse splinters pricked the tender skin of her palm, but she didn't pull away. Instead, she pushed out power. Just a touch. The battered wood blackened and all but disintegrated beneath her hand, the reaction spreading like smokeless fire outward to form a hole some three feet in diameter.

She pulled her hand back and stared at it. Not even a smudge marred her skin. She had wanted to create a hole without making a sound, and as a result, the wood had been consumed as if by lava.

Sutcliff peered inside the hole. "The rock is still well padded. Good." Then he laughed at himself. "How foolish of me. I'm here to see the thing destroyed. I'm such a being of habit.

"I once would have cushioned this rock in the feathers of pegasi and angels, had I the budget." His gaze grew distant. "I saw in this kermanite my chance for promotion, for medals, for the notice of Roosevelt. And when it was stolen, I mused that perhaps that would be for my benefit, too. I

could be the hero, retrieving it from the scheming Chinese."
He laughed again, this time the sound laced with bitterness
and regret.

Ingrid pried down layers of quilts, dozens of them, several
feet worth, until she finally saw the kermanite at her eye level.
She paused to fumble inside her pack for a flashlight. She
propped it on the smashed-down quilts to illuminate the dark
recesses of the box. The deep blue of the crystal held a smoky
whirl of contained energy.

Its facets were coated with blood. Long, thick dribbles
like crusted wax from a tapered candle, some of it smeared by
the swipe of a hand.

After a month, the color of the dried blood was more
black than red, and created an odd contrast with the surreal
Hawaiian-ocean-blue hue of the kermanite itself. The azure
March batch of kermanite at the auxiliary must have been
mined in the same vicinity as this massive piece. She had
been handling tiny parts of this rock for weeks, and hadn't
even known.

"Your father's blood?" Sutcliff asked.

"Yes." She was glad he had picked up enough context in
his afterlife that she didn't have to explain the how or why.
She put away the flashlight.

"It's appropriate, in a way, that the kermanite was never
cleaned," he said. "Much blood has been shed because of this
rock, and more would be shed yet."

He pressed a fist to his chest, and she noticed a gleaming
thin strand leading from his neck to his hand. He clutched a
cross pendant. She had never seen it before. Had the jewelry

always been obscured beneath his clothes, or had he manifested it now, when he needed it most?

"I'm ready," he said.

"I'm . . . sorry you died and have had to endure time as a ghost, but I'm grateful for this time to know you, Captain Sutcliff." She meant every word.

"And I, you," he said, head still bowed. "Thank you for your kindness. I did not deserve it. But please. Beware of the temptation offered by that rock. You can't fight the fox spirit if you're paralyzed or dead. I want . . . I want you to have a happy ending after all of this, like in those pulp novels you read."

Tears slipped down her cheeks. "You *did* find my stash when you nosed around in my bedroom. I hope you enjoyed them."

He gave a small shrug. "I always preferred nonfiction histories, but sometimes other diversions are necessary." He smiled. "Godspeed."

"Godspeed, Captain. I wish you peace." Ingrid touched the kermanite. The plane was smooth and cool beneath her palm. She focused, probing outward with her mind and magic.

She found heat. Swirling, boiling. Pele's lake of fire, bound in a priceless hunk of rock. But she was not immersed in it. She hung back, taking in the potential, the power. Papa had been bound to this crystal and tortured to cause the San Francisco earthquake, and the geomantic energy from that horrific disaster had been imprisoned here. So very much energy. Even if Mr. Thornton had supplemented the flow, it was horrific to think of that much magic flowing through Papa . . .

and how the earthquake would have been so much worse if he hadn't channeled what he had.

This rock was his dying legacy. And now she needed to destroy it without destroying herself.

When she had previously drawn energy from charged kermanite the size of a football, the effort had almost killed her within seconds; this kermanite was the size of a horse's body.

She assessed the power she held inside. It wasn't much. She tried to picture it like the last dregs of tea in a pot; she needed to pour the contents into a near-full cup without causing it to splash or overflow. That imagery in mind, she pulled *mana* through her body to well in her fingertips. They buzzed with heat. It'd be all too easy to blast out power like she had before when she shattered walls, but this time she needed finesse. She needed that perfectly filled teacup.

She took a few deep breaths then tipped energy from her hand in a smooth, measured trickle.

The large kermanite needed almost no encouragement to break as nature intended, though in a controlled manner that caused an implosion rather than an explosion. A thousand fracture points spread from her fingertips, the pieces creaking and chiming together as cracks spread and new portions fell and broke again, again, again, in a cascade. A whiff of dust blew over her face, the taste of kermanite on her tongue. A small rumble carried through her feet. Boards along the base of the crate bulged and groaned as the falling shards tried to spread from their nest of quilts.

Captain Sutcliff was gone. She missed the now-cozy coldness of his presence.

"I'm alive," she whispered, just for the joy of hearing her own voice.

Mindful of splinters, Ingrid used a shred of quilt to pick up numerous walnut-sized pieces that were average for fragmentation. She set them in her bag, with some more quilt scraps for padding, then sifted out small pieces to mound in her pocket.

Now she needed extra power to carry within herself. With the crystal fragmented, this was much safer than before. She focused as she plucked up three more pieces, rendering them to dust as heat tingled along her limbs and swirled and stewed near her heart. Sweat beaded on her skin.

"Still alive," she whispered again, and immediately retreated into the maze of freight. Sound carried too well in this cavernous space. Someone was sure to investigate the noise of the kermanite as it shattered.

She held her power close to her skin, ready to form a bubble, but sent a tendril of energy to her ears to enable her to listen again. She immediately detected footsteps on the level behind her as well as overhead.

"Oh, how stupid of me," she hissed beneath her breath. She should have cracked open the kermanite crate from the other side. A person on the viewing decks above could probably see the gaping hole, but not the kermanite inside—not unless the bulging weight broke the crate the rest of the way. Yet another reason to get away, fast.

Ingrid relied on the cover of boxes to hide her as she scurried along, her teeth clenched together. The longer she hunkered over, the worse her lower back and legs ached. The laden pack didn't help.

She suddenly realized her intense thirst and hunger, exacerbated by her use of energy and her current fever. Cy's now-familiar chiding rang through her mind: *Take care of yourself.* This time she would spare a minute and take his advice.

She found a shadowed crevice between barrels and slipped inside, taking several gulps of water from her canteen and eating a handful of smashed dates with pecans. Thus fortified, she continued on her way as she listened with preternatural ability.

Cy. She had to find Cy. She had to get him away from Blum. They had to get Maggie off of the citadel.

A gunshot echoed from the far side of the bay, followed by another.

She swerved in that direction as she pushed more power to her skin, armoring herself as if with orichalcum. Someone yelled in Chinese, and another voice called out from above. Neither sounded like Lee. She missed Sutcliff's vigilant presence.

She pushed out her awareness, as she had when searching for the sylphs, but this time she reached for Cy. Blum would have been easier to find, but Ingrid had no desire to tickle the fox's whiskers. She *knew* Cy. She knew the contours of his body, the softness of his beard pressed against the top of her head, the way his eyes crinkled when he smiled.

Cy was a bright spark in the darkness. He drew her in, a moth to the flame.

Blum remained near him. Ingrid dryly swallowed, fighting a renewed swell of terror. Nausea twisted in her gut. She used magic to soften the fast tread of her feet, the rattle of kermanite in her pockets and pack, the thump of the *guandao* against her thigh. She slowed down.

"I should never have taken you out of the engine room. Let's get you back there, Maggs." Cy's voice again carried at a distance.

"No," Maggie hissed. "We need to keep looking."

Several people walked among the crates about a hundred feet away. They didn't seem to know quite where Cy and Maggie were. Ingrid did. She edged that way, staying low, dashing across gaps between the rows.

Finally, she glimpsed Cy through the stacks. He appeared to be well. He looked this way and that, wary. He knew he was being hunted.

Blum was close. So very close, the magic of her looming and crackling like a thunderstorm ready to boom and break. Was she more powerful than before? Was that possible? Ingrid closed her eyes for a moment as it occurred to her . . . Yes, it was possible according to the old stories—if Blum had completed growth of another tail.

Ingrid angled herself to see Cy's twin. Maggie wasn't quite as tall as Cy, but she easily topped six feet in height. A simple navy-blue jacket fit her form and flared out at the waist. A knit snood contained a heavy burden of dark auburn hair. Maggie gestured to Cy, and Ingrid could see she wore gloves.

Ingrid could feel the weighty enchantments embodied in her ambassadorial ring.

Cy didn't stand next to his sister. He stood next to Ambassador Blum, adorned in Maggie's skin. She had stolen Maggie's form. Maggie was dead.

INGRID SANK TO THE FLOOR, BONELESS IN HORROR. SHE HAD TO save him. Save herself. Save the present Chinese men, even. Blum would kill them all, luxuriate in it, all while wearing Maggie's face.

Cy was going to be completely heartbroken.

"We need a more defensible position than out here among the freight," Cy murmured.

"Maybe we should go to your airship?" Blum asked.

"No. She'd try to find me on *Excalibur*."

Ingrid pushed herself to stand. Other footsteps circled around her at a distance; she couldn't dally here, she had to figure out how best to get Cy away. She *could* grab and lift him with her power—she'd done it before—but with so many obstacles around, she'd likely injure him, too. Damn it! She peered through the gaps but he had moved. She had to get closer.

"I've missed you, Maggie. I mourned your death." Cy whispered as Ingrid hurried toward him.

She stood just on the other side of the crates from the twins, with a view of them both. Cy faced away, fists balled at his sides, shoulders bowed. She knew that posture.

He was readying himself to attack.

He turned, Tesla rod extended and tip sparking. Blum dodged with a hiss, but Cy followed up with a leg swipe. Blum toppled backward. For an instant, it looked like Cy might have a clear blow with the rod, but Blum bounded onto both feet, faster than any human should move, especially in a uniform skirt and boots. She landed a fist to his gut, doubling him over, then punched his inner arm. The Tesla rod flew out of sight and landed with a clatter. In a deft move, Blum unsheathed the bowie knife at his belt as she slipped behind him. She clubbed his hat off and gripped him by his topknot. His head craned back, his long neck exposed to the blade.

"I suppose my acting skills are a bit rusty," said Blum. "I'm not accustomed to playing roles like this, not anymore."

"Maggie was quiet as a dryad compared to you, Ambassador Blum." Her name wheezed from his throat.

"I always admired your cleverness, Cy."

"My sister. You killed her." He faced to the right, Blum pressed against his back.

"Actually, I didn't. A terrible explosion occurred in *Excalibur*'s engine room as final preparations were being made. Maggie suffered severe burns to most of her lower body. After dealing with that Seattle Chinatown fiasco, I hurried to attend to her myself, but it was clear that she wouldn't survive. She would be the first death in the on-board hospital.

"I hadn't planned on making her my newest acquisition, but I couldn't pass up the opportunity, even if it means constant pain while in her form. A woman's lot in life, really." She shrugged. "It's worth it to play with the incredible potential of your sister's brain, Cy. My oh my. To her, everything is a machine. Mere parts, for utilitarian applications. I had no idea we had so much in common."

"You couldn't contract the sickness," he said, speaking

louder as if to telegraph his position. Was he trying to make his position known to Ingrid, or the Chinese? Did he care at this point? Better to be dead than used by Blum.

"No, I could not. I kept the citadel running, and until earlier today, I had a small crew of able-bodied people assisting me and trying to nurse others back to health. I was secured in the engine room when the Chinese infiltrated. I'm not certain how everyone else has fared, though I imagine the answer is 'not well.'" She jerked on his hair. "Call out to Ingrid, Cy. Warn her that I'm here. You know that will bring her running all the faster. You two are so nauseating in your need to save each other." Blum's tongue lapped Cy's ear. He jolted, his face in an appalled grimace. A line of crimson slid down his neck.

"Don't do that," he gasped.

Blum giggled. "If you're not careful, you might slit your own throat. Call out to Ingrid or I'll have another taste."

"Calling out'll bring in the Chinese, too."

"Good. It's been boring here, with everyone *vomiting* and *dying*. This should be more fun." She pulled his head back further, her mouth dangerously close to his ear.

"Ingrid?" Cy croaked.

"Louder!" Blum hissed, nudging him.

"Ingrid!"

Distracted as Ingrid was, she didn't hear the footsteps until they were practically upon her. She jerked back as Uncle Moon emerged from between the crates, a finger to his lips. He didn't wear the distinctly Chinese outfits as he had before, but shabby cotton work clothes like those Lee had been clad in. His hair, though, fully announced his status as a rebel. The top of his head was shaved, the rest pulled back into a tight, tapering braid that draped to his waist.

"Lend me your silence," he whispered.

Ingrid eyed him with blatant distrust. She respected Uncle Moon and his magic, but she also knew that her life was of no consequence to him. He would use her skills with vicious enthusiasm, not unlike Blum.

But she needed help. She needed an ally.

She expanded her bubble around them both, as she had with Sutcliff. "I cannot keep this up for long," she said.

"I will not ask you to." He tilted his head toward Blum. "You know what *that* is."

"Yes. Where's Lee?"

"Alive, elsewhere in here." Uncle Moon glanced at her waist, frowning. "What are you carrying?"

She pressed a hand to the *guandao,* not surprised that Moon could sense its intense power. "Something for Lee, courtesy of the *qilin.*"

His eyes narrowed. "*You* haven't seen the *qilin.*"

"Yes, I have. We've shared full conversations twice."

He continued to glare at her, mouth twisted in disgust, but he didn't make a move to grab the bag. He must have understood that few people would be permitted to act as its courier.

"Ingrid!" Cy yelled, louder.

"I have to make my presence known," she said.

"As do I." Uncle Moon took a step back. She accepted that as her cue and let the shield fall from around them. An energy fever still lingered in her skin.

Ingrid rounded the corner of the crate. "Moshi moshi!" she shouted, evoking the customary Japanese telephone greeting—a phrase intended to test if the person on the other end of the line was a kitsune.

"Moshi moshi!" Blum returned the greeting with a delighted squeal as she whirled around, Cy still clutched close. "Ingrid! My dear! You have joined us at last. I daresay, I'm *very* surprised to see you up and so spry. Last I heard, you had some difficulties with walking, though your ability to *kill* has improved. I heartily approve! A woman ought to be capable of her own defense, and your methods are certainly worthy of more study." Of course, Blum knew of what had happened to Warden Hatsumi.

Cy's gaze met hers, his expression one of impotent rage.

"I would love to know how you've evaded me, Ingrid," Blum continued. "I haven't had anyone do the like in *centuries*."

"And I would love to see you permanently die in an excruciatingly painful manner befitting your crimes," said Ingrid. "Let Cy go. Don't hurt him. I'm here."

"As am I." She lurched in surprise as Uncle Moon stepped alongside her.

Blum's countenance changed in an instant. *"You,"* she breathed. "Oh my."

Uncle Moon said something in Chinese, to which Blum responded in turn before belting out a laugh. Then she looked at Ingrid again. "Hurt Cy? No, I won't *hurt* him."

Blum's foul magic intensified as she shoved Cy away— but she merely released her physical hold. Ingrid couldn't see the strings of life, but she could sense the manipulation of magic. She felt the tension as one of Cy's life cords stretched taut in Blum's grip and snapped. He impacted on the concrete floor with a soft thud that nevertheless shook Ingrid to her core. She rushed forward and grabbed his shoulders. He flopped backward in her grip, limp as an overcooked noodle.

"What did she do to me?" he whispered. His face looked drawn and pale.

"Stole some of your life force. I don't think it's permanent," Ingrid said, but she didn't truly know. She boosted her strength to drag Cy away, her legs and lower back screaming agony with every step.

Uncle Moon stalked toward Blum, an eerie grace to his movements.

"Don't go far, Ingrid," called Blum. "This shouldn't take long. I would like for us to have tea together later. Perhaps we could discuss the books I possess from the library in Alexandria. Remember, I mentioned them in Seattle? There's one about fantastics in the ancient world that I think you'd find to be of particular interest."

With that, Blum began to shift.

Her malodor deepened, leaving Ingrid gasping for breath amid severe nausea. The stench was the substance of regurgitated nightmares. Muskiness. Feces. Rot. Death.

Maggie's body blurred as her head craned back, her hands curved at her sides like claws. Moon didn't hesitate. He dashed forward as he pulled a long knife from his belt, but in the span of time it took him to travel ten feet, Blum's transformation was complete. She wore the face of a woman slightly older than Maggie. Pockmarks pitted her cheeks and her somewhat flattened, crooked nose. Her eyes were wide, pupils like midnight. Glossy black hair now filled the mesh snood.

She parried Moon's blow with a cry, then spun in place. Her kick sent the old man staggering backward. With him away, she pulled the collar of Maggie's A&A jacket forward and brought her knife down along the line of buttons and cloth. She shrugged off the constrictive burden as Moon attacked again.

Whoever this woman had been, it was evident why Blum had claimed her body. She was an athlete, a poem in muscle. She kicked, she sliced, she propelled herself off the sides of crates. She *danced*. Blum's face glowed with exertion and delight.

Though Moon was old and not as fast and flexible as his younger-bodied opponent, he moved with surreal grace. He bounced back from her attacks, he dodged her arcs, he forced her to retreat, then conceded ground again. Back and forth, back and forth. Not even a minute had passed.

"Cy, can you walk?" Ingrid murmured, her eyes on the fight and the crates around them.

"I feel like I've had influenza for a week. I'm a deadweight." Fear shimmered in his eyes.

"Don't you dare use the word 'dead,' not even in that context," she snapped.

A Chinese man stood in a gap among the freight. Blum bounded his way and extended an arm as if to stroke his face. The man staggered back a step. Uncle Moon shouted in

Chinese; the warning came too late. Blum tugged her arm back toward her body. The man crumpled to the ground.

Blum's increased vitality was evident as she rejoined the battle with Moon. She had the relentless energy of a young child who had feasted on a meal of ice cream and cake, and she clearly rejoiced in her increased power, giggling as she parried Moon's thrusts. She said something in Chinese, her tone taunting. Moon remained stoic. Sweat sheened his face, his movements slowing.

Blum could have easily killed him already; instead, she toyed with him, like a cat with a cricket beneath its paw. Even though he surely knew that truth, Uncle Moon wanted this fight. That was evident in his intensity, his deliberation. And for the time being, Blum was happy to oblige him.

More of Moon's highbinders emerged from among the stacks. Blum sprinted toward the nearest newcomer, her gap-toothed grin exuberant. Moon shouted, but his words would come too late yet again.

"Ambassador Blum, *no*." Ingrid didn't merely lace magic into the invocation. She bludgeoned with the words.

Blum staggered, momentarily stunned. Her target scampered backward and out of sight.

Moon took advantage of the distraction. His blade caught Blum along her back, painting a diagonal slice from shoulder to hip. Ingrid gaped—Blum had been hurt! She bled! However, it was immediately apparent that the wound was superficial. Blum pivoted on a foot to counter Moon's next swipe. Her attacks redoubled. She swiped and slashed at Moon, forcing him backward one step, two steps, three. Her teeth remained bared in a vulpine snarl.

She brought down her arm, the swipe sure to hack his neck. With a small *tink* as if it met glass, the blade bounced off an invisible layer inches above his skin. Moon stayed in place, heaving and gasping for breath. Blum turned, the curved-tip knife blade lowering as she faced Ingrid.

"I said *no*, Ambassador Blum." Ingrid added an anvil's weight to the denial again. She held out both arms to help her focus on the shield. "*No* to stealing vitality from people. *No* to the war. *No* to your very existence."

"How wonderful that you've learned how to tap your geomantic powers to wield some sorcery!" Blum had barely broken a sweat.

"I've been educated by our encounters."

Ingrid had already found out the hard way that the Green Dragon Crescent Blade was useless in her hands. But maybe her magic alone could strike at the kitsune's hoshi no tama: the onion-shaped pendant bulged beneath Blum's shirt collar.

"No wonder you were able to avoid my efforts to find you." Blum sniffled as if upset, then turned, chopping at Moon. He raised his blade to block, but Ingrid hadn't let down her guard. Blum's knife clattered off the bubble yet again.

Ingrid felt Cy's hand brush against the back of her boot. She knew without looking that he was attempting to touch her skin and gauge how much energy she held. She wished she could reassure him in that regard, but shielding Uncle Moon at a distance was draining her fast.

Blum had to be aware of that as well.

Ingrid advanced, both arms still held outward. Uncle Moon retreated several feet. Blum stood where she could monitor them at either side, grinning, clearly relishing this new complication.

"Ingrid Carmichael, Ingrid Carmichael, Ingrid Carmichael." The singsong invocation annoyed Ingrid more than it provoked her. "I would like to hear more about your trip to the Vassal States. Such a bold move! I never expected you to go there. For any other geomancer, that would have been suicidal. Or an indicator of insatiable greed. You're certainly not the latter, not like old Hatsumi."

"I needed a vacation." She let the bubble drop from around Uncle Moon.

"Really. A vacation? That's the tack you're going to take?" Blum tsked. "I think the trip meant something more. Your father was captured there, too, you know."

"Yes. I know."

Blum lunged at Moon, the cut along her back like a thin crimson bandolier. It had scarcely bled. Moon repelled her attack with new energy; his brief respite while shielded had done him well.

With Blum turned away, Ingrid flung out a ball of writhing blue fire. Her mind flicked to Hatsumi, what she had done to him, but she forced the image away. If anyone deserved such a fate, it was Blum.

The missile arced toward Blum's neck, but she spun around with preternatural quickness and bowed backward. The fireball soared harmlessly overhead.

Ingrid knew she could bring the concentrated energy around for another pass, but she also knew her reserves were almost depleted. She let the fireball dissipate into nothingness.

Blum's gaze flitted to Cy on the floor, telegraphing her threat with a bright grin.

"So curious, your family's interest in that volcanic island." Blum jumped toward Ingrid, but Ingrid was ready, pushing out a pressure wave with the hoshi no tama her target again. Blum angled her body so her shoulder took the blow instead. The force slid her into a crate ten feet away. Wood cracked and splintered at the impact, revealing the box to be empty. She bounded to her feet again an instant later. The protective ring had nullified Ingrid's attack.

To destroy the hoshi no tama, she'd need to *only* hit the small jewelry that housed the fox's true soul. Not Blum's body.

The horrid stench of Blum's magic snapped outward like a whip. Ingrid brought up both arms to flare a shield around herself and Cy just in time. The impact jarred her to her bones, but the shield held.

She didn't dare lower her hands. Instead, with a thought, she jerked on her pocketed kermanite. A handful's worth surged into the air. She swiped at the floating rocks as she let her shield fade again. New magic surged through her body, delicious as a cold drink of water after a long trek.

Sweat trickled down her neck. She'd been so close to drawing on her own *mana*. So very, very close.

"Your powers are wonderfully *godlike*." Blum straightened her baggy attire as best she could. "Perhaps you and your father were there to visit a powerful relation. One with renowned geomantic powers of her own."

There was no point in attempting a denial. "I would like

to see you match wits against Madam Pele. You pretend to be a god. She actually *is* one."

"Match wits?" Blum giggled. "Why would I waste time with a debate? I know her measure. Like so many old gods, she wants to be left alone, though she still cares a great deal about the people on those islands, doesn't she? It'd be a terrible shame if we had to use aggressive force to quell the strikes out there."

Rage seared against Ingrid's skin.

Blum sighed. "I understand the anger and vulnerability you're feeling right now. I bear a similar weakness myself. Japan is *my* home. I love its people, its language, its food, its everything. I work for Japan's benefit in all I do."

Uncle Moon dove at Blum and the two scuffled again and bounded apart. She had scarcely looked his way.

"You say you love Japan, but how many have died because of your ambitions?" Ingrid asked.

"Oh, millions." Blum dismissed the number with a wave of her free hand. "But such sacrifice is necessary. Plants must be pruned back each winter so that they grow and bloom in spring. Japan's population is surging now. We'll fill up Manchukuo and China soon enough, and after that?" Her prim smile said it all. "But I digress. I want you to come with me, Ingrid. It's clear to me now that the best way to ensure your cooperation is to target your vulnerabilities. I can't threaten San Francisco. It's already been obliterated, and besides, its rebirth is important for Pacific commerce.

"I suppose I could threaten some random group of children or cute animals, but that's so *cliché*.

"But the *kanakas*? Their numbers have already been dismally reduced in the past century, and those that are left never cease their grousing. Sometimes there's only one way to shut someone up. We can bring in plenty of other people to settle the islands."

"No."

The emphasis on the word didn't make Blum flinch this time. "Oh, Ingrid. You should realize by now that as long as you're free, you will never be *free*. I won't simply pursue those you love, like Cy. Every person you meet, every single place you visit, will be in danger because of you. If you think San Francisco's destruction was bad . . . well, piffle. You haven't seen a full hellfire bombardment. You haven't *smelled* it."

Ingrid's mind reeled in horror at Blum's declaration, but she remained alert enough to shove Blum back when she attempted another approach.

"I have smelled the bombardments." Cy's whisper trembled. "You would not and could not ever cause such a thing, Ingrid. It's all on Blum. These are her games, her manipulations."

"Yes, it is," she murmured, well aware that Blum heard their every word. She placed a hand on the leather pouch at her hip. The time for games was done.

She had used her magic to search for Cy; she could find Lee the same way. They'd known each other for over five years. He was her brother in every way but blood. They had scrubbed floors together. Competed in watermelon-seed spitting contests in the backyard. Acted as partners in crime to steal fresh, forbidden cookies from the kitchen. Together, they had mourned the death of Ingrid's mother.

She pulled on the power of those memories and her love, and melded them with the magic that surged through her body.

"Lee Fong!" she whispered. *"LEE FONG!"*

The invocation reverberated through the hold like a radio wave—and found him. He was coming. Walking, at first, drawn toward the sound of a distant scuffle, but then he *heard* her. The magic hooked him, but he didn't fight back. He ran.

"Ingrid!" he yelled, her name booming out in an echo. "I'm coming!"

"What are you doing, Ingrid Carmichael?" Blum asked as Uncle Moon advanced on her again. She scored a gash on his forearm and forced him back.

"I'm doing what needs to be done," said Ingrid.

For all of Blum's scheming and spies and centuries-long plans, she didn't know about Emperor Qixiang's living son.

Ingrid slashed energy to cut the strings of the leather bag. She pulled forth the cloth-wrapped weapon's head. With another swipe of her hand, she sliced the weapon free of its swaddling cloth.

"Lee Fong!" she screamed.

Lee ran at her from between the crates. Heaving for breath, his cheeks flushed, his black hair as unruly as ever. Emotions flashed over his face as he took in everything—Cy on the floor, unbloodied and helpless—Uncle Moon battling a woman who could only be Ambassador Blum—and Ingrid. He looked on her with adoration and relief.

She held forth the strangely curved weapon's head as if

passing a baton in a relay race. His eyes widened with abject terror as momentum carried him forward, but he didn't hesitate. He reached for the blade stained with a green dragon's blood.

Trust that you will find Lee when the moment is right, Mr. Sakaguchi had said.

This was the moment.

CHAPTER 24

Raw energy exploded within Ingrid's grasp, not a physical detonation, but the stuff of heaven and creation, of making and unmaking at a level beyond human comprehension. She smelled ozone and jasmine and mud and sweat-soaked leather, everything and nothing. The blade writhed as a pole grew out from its base to perfectly fit Lee's waiting hands. He didn't stop moving. Ingrid let go of the weapon's head and Lee hoisted the pole arm upward. The weapon now stood taller than him, the mysterious metals of the blade subtly aglow in the scant light, like blackened coals that still carried a hint of heat deep within.

He entered the battleground, the pole gripped against his forearm. Uncle Moon flowed to one side. Ambassador Blum leered at Lee.

"Oh, now a Chinese boy wishes to fight me with some magical weapon?" She sounded amused.

"Do you see that many magical weapons?" asked Ingrid, surprised that Blum didn't more seriously regard the holy aura of the *guandao*. Perhaps she couldn't sense it all.

"You'd be surprised," said Blum with a shrug.

"You may be surprised, too," said Lee. His voice reflected his absolute conviction.

"I doubt it. So you're Lee Fong, Sakaguchi's houseboy? I thought you were dead in San Francisco."

"I did die, but not there."

Ingrid scooped more kermanite into her hand. The powder sifted between her fingers as new energy whirled through her. She momentarily wavered, dizzied by the influx.

"Ah, yes, I see how this is going. You have returned from the dead to kill me, achieve vengeance for your people, et cetera. Are you an orphan as well? Perhaps a farm boy? If you have an ambition to be a hero, don't be such a tired cliché."

He swiped at her. Blum danced to one side.

"My ambitions are much simpler, actually. To stay alive. You've made that difficult for me and many of my people." Lee spun the *guandao* again, the blade flashing this way and that. Blum's eyes widened as she leaned to one side, then rolled away to land again on both feet. Lee kept the pole aligned with his arm part of the time as he thrust, bowed, swiped. Blum leaped and took shelter behind the corner of a box. The Crescent Blade sliced through the crate with a violent snap. Wood shards exploded across the battleground.

Ingrid watched him, stunned. Had the weapon endowed him with some skill—or had he trained for this moment? Or both?

Blum's grin was vulpine. "My oh my. You actually know what you're doing to some degree. And yet, look at me, armed with a mere bowie knife, while yours has such reach." She tumbled, skirts flaring, to dodge a blow. "Have you no honor, Lee Fong?" The taunting invocation rang with magic.

Uncle Moon called out something in Chinese. Blum spat a reply.

Lee pivoted on one foot, bringing the *guandao* around at waist level. The blade caught Blum at the hip, the impact flinging her against a stack of crates. The top box teetered. Several Chinese men cried out and scrambled away as the box smashed five feet to the ground. Lee remained posed, one knee uplifted, Green Dragon Crescent Blade against his extended forearm.

Blum snarled and jumped upright again. The skirt dangled, exposing white cloth beneath. No blood.

Lee didn't hesitate. He knew the stories about kitsune, and where best to strike. He spun in place in a vicious ballet move, and lunged again. This time the blade directly impacted with Blum's chest. Ingrid stepped forward, her body a-thrum with energy and terror. Had he damaged Blum's pendant?

Blum smacked into the floor and slid backward, still very much unharmed. She slashed an arm outward just as she skidded to a stop. Lee was not prepared for that sort of assault—nor was Ingrid. Lee raised the pole in time to partially block the blow, the attack sending him staggering back with a cry. Blood sprayed over his shoulder. Blum slashed energy again as she bounced to her feet, but this time Ingrid shielded Lee from afar—a massive bubble, by necessity. She felt the decline in her own body temperature and ceased her hold as soon as Blum's blast dissipated.

The Green Dragon Crescent Blade was too long for her to effectively shield Lee for any length of time. She could cover six people or more within the span of that pole.

Blum laughed, a merry, delighted sound. "Now, this is a fight!" She clapped her hands and bounced in delight. "I daresay, I haven't been up against a halberd-type weapon in *ages*. This body trained in their use, centuries ago. It wasn't trendy then—not for a woman, certainly—but perhaps now the time has come. I should start a new fashion."

Lee glanced at Ingrid. Sweat soaked his face. "Damn it, I thought I had it!" His left shoulder was bloodied, the shirt in tatters with the sleeve tenuously attached.

Blum sprang forward, aiming low. Lee scrambled, his movements slower now. He swiped low to deflect the knife. Blum was a blur as she spun up, flinging an energy blast at Lee, then at Cy. Lee batted away the first attack, sending it ricocheting into the remains of the shattered crate, while Ingrid shielded Cy.

Uncle Moon dove in, striking at Blum, only to be pounded backward by a series of impossibly fast stabs. He only avoided being gutted by the arrival of Lee, who sliced through Blum's skirt again as she pirouetted to one side.

Blum wasn't slowing down. She wasn't drained. She held an abundance of stolen life energy, in addition to her own considerable power. She was playing with them. This combat was a diversion to amuse her, nothing more. She had already worn down Uncle Moon, and Lee could only last so long. Cy was out of the fight. Ingrid had limited kermanite, and was already weak.

No. Not weak. Her body wasn't what it once was, but she was still strong. Most importantly, she was *smart*.

This was not a battle to be won through honorable combat.

Ingrid looked at the high ceiling, the freight around them, the orichalcum panels underfoot. Her body felt incandescent with captive magic. If this worked, her reserves would be depleted quickly. She needed to be fast, fast and effective.

And at the end, God help her, she needed to remain alive and mobile.

She shoved her fist into the floor along a riveted seam. The ground bucked as she focused the energy forward. In the span of two seconds, the floor seam split to Lee's right and rippled and expanded beneath Blum's feet. The kitsune sneered as she jumped—directly into the shield that Ingrid had formed above. She smacked her head and crumpled downward. A full leg slipped into the gap, just as it had in Seattle.

But unlike in Seattle, Ingrid wasn't working with familiar, conductive earth. Orichalcum had been strong enough to keep Sutcliff's ghost afloat in midair, after all; it resisted magic and bullets alike. But Ingrid didn't need to break the ori, only bend it, sculpt it, and not with any finesse. She brought her twined fingers together, the metal floor closing inward like teeth—but not attempting to pierce Blum's flesh.

The drop in Ingrid's fever flashed over her as if she'd opened an icebox. She'd need to grab more kermanite from her backpack very soon, though the fifteen seconds that might take could give Blum a chance to counterattack.

Objects chimed and rolled across the floor around Ingrid's feet. Kermanite chunks. She spared a glance behind her. Cy had opened his stash, and weak though he was, flung rocks her way. Good God, she loved that man. She exerted more power to summon dozens of kermanite shards to her hand; they melted against her skin like hot snowflakes.

"Ingrid Carmichael, haven't we played out this trapped-leg-in-ground scenario before?" Blum's voice was at a strangely higher pitch. "Will you have the Chinese throw bricks again as well? I should tell you how the soldiers—"

"No more!" screamed Ingrid. Her voice boomed. She sounded like her grandmother, ancient and bold, even as she wanted to sob and run away in terror. She advanced on Blum, and with each stride, she armored herself. She forged geomantic magic as strong as orichalcum.

Then she was at Blum, breathing in her putrid musk. Blum swiped at her. The bowie knife shattered against the shielding. An instant later, Ingrid gripped Blum's arms at her back, the way Blum had restrained her before.

This time Blum was the one who writhed and fought. The iron-rich scent of blood filled the air as Blum's leg scraped against its imprisonment. Perhaps the ring's power was limited when the injury was self-inflicted.

There was much that Ingrid could never understand about the rings of the Twelve, but everything depended on one technicality: the rings guarded the ambassadors' bodies, not their souls.

Dark magic flailed against Ingrid, in search of any chink in her armor. Blum didn't speak. She snarled. She was a crazed fox, still bound in human form.

She had never before shown fear.

Ingrid knew offensive tactics wouldn't make Blum stay still. Instead, the situation required defense. She thought of how she shielded the pipe in the *Bug*'s engine room. She shoved energy along Blum's arms, forming a hardened layer like *pahoehoe* lava over her enemy's skin. Blum stopped struggling as if she had looked the gorgon in the eye. Her neck froze, head tilted to one side.

Ingrid diverted a sliver of energy to tear open the layers of cloth at Blum's collar, baring the star ball pendant to the world.

There was no honor in pinning down Blum in such a way, but there was honor aplenty in Blum's death. That was enough.

Lee didn't hesitate. He spun the Green Dragon Crescent Blade against his arm then lunged forward with just enough momentum to plunge the blade's point into the hoshi no tama.

The sound of shattering glass filled the hold—not the sound of a single cup falling, but of a row of chandeliers striking the ground in a cascade. Unleashed magic buffeted against Ingrid, but she maintained her shield and increased the protection over her ears. Even so, the ethereal crackling resounded in her skull.

Lee withdrew the *guandao*. The hoshi no tama came with it, the pendant speared like an alligator pear's seed removed by a knife chop. The broken necklace chain dangled. Dark fumes, the stench as rank as burning rubber, escaped the cracked ball. Grimacing, he tapped the object on the floor to force it free. It lay there, bleeding out Blum's original soul.

Lee stomped on it.

The sound stopped.

Then Blum herself began to shatter.

Her clothes exploded from her form. Ingrid bowled backward as if smacked by a gale, then scooted back farther on her hands. Different female bodies of Blum flickered past too fast to register who was who, only that they were different women, all bare as the day they were born.

The final human shape shriveled down to that of a large fox standing upright with one leg sunk into the floor. Blum-as-a-fox remained still for a moment, her array of tails flared, then collapsed, her body partly in the crevice.

The musk and might of her power dissipated with a thunderclap. Light fixtures flickered throughout the hold, some failing with an electrical sizzle.

No one moved for a long moment. Lee stayed in a fighting stance, even as the tip of the blade lowered over the fox.

"She's dead." Ingrid pushed herself to her feet as she let her shield dissipate. "She's dead."

"Ingrid? How're you?" Cy grunted and began to rise in painful slow motion like an old man.

She glanced down to inspect herself. "Alive." She walked to meet Cy, her strides shaky.

"I think some of what she stole came back to me. I'm not so weak now." Even so, he looked like hell. He reached for her, and they fell into a hug. The comfort of his body so close to hers felt like a touch of heaven's own grace.

"We did it. We killed Blum." Lee's voice was low. "Well, you did most of the work—"

"No." She listened for a moment to confirm that the other Chinese men were drawing close again. "You carry the weapon. You fought her. You struck the final blow. That must be the story you tell."

Lee scowled. "But that's not all—"

"The story is more important than the facts, Lee." Cy shook his head, expression aggrieved. "Much as I'd like to see Ingrid made a hero, the truth here won't do her favors. You need the story. You need the glory."

"A necessary deceit." Uncle Moon regarded Ingrid with new respect, then looked to Blum. "The fox's body must be burned hot enough to destroy the bones. Nothing of her must remain."

"She still wears the ring." Ingrid pointed to the band, which had grown to resemble a bracelet on the fox's paw. "It still holds power but it's . . . different than before. Dimmer."

"I can destroy the ring as well," said Lee, moving the blade that way.

"Stay your hand," snapped Uncle Moon, surprising Ingrid. "These rings are older than even Guan Yu. They cannot be destroyed, and to touch it now would impose a terrible cost."

Ingrid and Cy shared a look. Modern mythology around the rings made them out to be a creation of recent decades, proof of the magical might and divine favor conferred on the Unified Pacific.

She wondered at Uncle Moon's use of "cannot," too. Did he mean that the Crescent Blade would fail to destroy the ring—or that the ancient rings should be allowed to exist?

"Lee, use the blade to move her tails so we can count them," she murmured. He did, with delicate care, as if Blum slept and he didn't want to wake her.

"Lord in heaven," muttered Cy. "Seven tails. *Seven.*"

The tails were beautiful, truly. Red plumes with tapered white tips. Their sizes varied slightly. The oldest was evident by the flecks of white hair among the red. The newest tail was obvious, too, its red sheen especially bright. Who had Blum intended to nab before Maggie met her fate?

"Seven," Ingrid repeated. A nine-tailed kitsune was akin to a god. If Blum's long game had played out, she would have become a deity and overseen her homeland as the ruler of the world.

"Maggie died because of one of those tails. What did Blum truly do to her, to take her skin? Her voice? Oh Lord, I can't bear to know." Cy's eyes squeezed shut as grief rocked through him.

"Blum stole Maggie's body?" Lee stared at the kitsune with new horror. "I'm sorry, Cy. I'm so sorry."

"I wish I could have known her," Ingrid said, voice thick.

"I wish you could've, too." Cy's smile was bittersweet. "You'd have liked each other." Ingrid twined her arm with his and they leaned on each other.

Other Chinese men emerged from among the freight. Two of them checked on their slumped comrade and shook their heads.

"You should know a UP fleet is going to arrive anytime," Cy murmured to Lee. "What's your plan from here?"

Lee looked to Uncle Moon, who began to speak in Chinese as he gestured to the blade. Whatever he said made the other Chinese men speak among themselves in rapid tones. Lee set the pole upright. The strangely curved blade reminded Ingrid of a torch, one that cast a dark light.

"Apparently, I am now in charge," he murmured.

Even as he said it, Uncle Moon and the other men bowed to him.

Lee stood tall, but Ingrid was close enough to see the flicker of fear in his eyes. He was only fifteen, and now . . . what was he? Commander? Emperor over the refugees? Ingrid ached to gather him in a hug and rumple his hair and rejoice in the fact that he was alive, that they were both alive, but she didn't dare touch him again. Based on her experience with Uncle Moon, she could well imagine how the other men regarded her.

She could not jeopardize Lee's tenuous new position.

Captain Sutcliff was right. Those few minutes she had to hug and speak with Lee before were moments she would treasure to the end of her days.

Lee looked at Cy. "We were setting charges to explode this thing. That was our last resort. We had hoped to figure out how to fly it, but we could never get access to the engine room, and none of us could make sense of the other controls."

"You barely have enough men here to resume the most basic operations aboard, and that's assuming these men have experience in piloting and engineering." He glanced around, and the men shook their heads. Of course. The Chinese wouldn't have been trusted to hold such positions for years now.

"We have more crew awaiting us at a rendezvous point, if we can make it there," said Lee. "But if a fleet's incoming, it's even more important that we destroy *Excalibur*. We can't let it get to China."

"Is there no one else alive?" asked Ingrid, trying to keep an accusatory tone out of her voice.

"There are locked rooms around the ship. Only a few people were in the open to put up a fight." Lee did not meet Ingrid's eye. "Was Blum here all along, in the engine room?"

"Yes," said Ingrid as Cy gripped her hand harder. "Cy, how long would it take you and Fenris to assess the scope of operations aboard and to teach people what to do?"

His mouth opened and closed without a sound as his brows drew together in thought. "Hard to say. Depends on the skill of the people we are training, too."

"Ingrid, what are you suggesting?" Lee's voice was very low. She felt Uncle Moon's unreadable gaze on her.

"This is a floating city designed to be self-sustaining for months on end. It can hold up to ten thousand people. You have a hospital. A greenhouse. *A greenhouse.*" She paused, laughing to herself, then faced Cy. "Those new sylphs need a home."

Understanding dawned on his face. "Well, I'll be. The folks aboard might end up living in a jungle, though."

"I can confer with the sylphs to arrange a transaction,"

she said. "Perhaps some Chinese bakers can be found, though flour may not be able to be produced aboard. If the sylphs have a thriving home, though, that may be enough to satisfy them."

"Something tells me I missed out on a lot." Lee looked wistful for a moment, then remembering his new position, settled into stoicism again. "We *could* use this place as a new, temporary homeland. We could take on the refugees. We could cross to China, too." He turned to Uncle Moon and began a flurried conversation. The other men chimed in at times, too.

"I'm not sure how they can even make it off America's shores, truth be told," Cy murmured. "Those gunships are hovering just outside, and more ships are on the way, and the military reception in California would be ugly indeed."

"It looks like the only weapons aboard are personal firearms," she added. "The Durendals are props. Every crate that's labeled as armaments appears to be empty. The captain thought that most of the real equipment was coming aboard in California."

"The captain. He's . . . ?"

"At peace. Yes."

Cy absorbed that news thoughtfully. "Well, if by some miracle this craft does make it across the Pacific, China might make some new allies. Blum's gambit in Baranov will have the Russians antsy to make some kind of strike against America. I can well imagine Russia's willingness to form an alliance with the Chinese if their cause doesn't look hopeless."

Ingrid felt her hopes spiral downward. Had all their efforts

merely changed the players in this war? Could anyone survive this?

Lee turned toward her, aglow with excitement. "Ingrid, think of the good you could do with us. And Fenris
and Cy, too, of course." His eyes shone. "With what you can
do—if we can get more kermanite—we could not only go to
China and free the people there. *We could go to Japan.*" He
grinned. "We could—"

"Lee. No. *No.*"

He took in the horror on her face and realized what he
was saying. "Oh my God," he whispered. "I sound like Blum,
don't I. Like Roosevelt, like everyone else. Using you. Making
you into a weapon. I'm sorry, Ingrid, I'm so sorry."

In that instant, he was a vulnerable teenage boy again.
Ingrid knew she couldn't play the part of his big sister for
much longer; she had to use her influence while she had it.

"Lee." She spoke low enough that the men beyond their
circle couldn't hear. "I accept your apology, but you cannot show weakness now. You carry Guan Yu's weapon, but
that doesn't guarantee your place. I don't expect you to treat
me . . . derisively, but neither can we act as we always have.
Our relationship . . . our places . . . are different now." She
kept her voice steady, even as her heart broke.

"You are right, of course," murmured Lee, his face twisting in pain. "You usually are. I must tell you, too, that Mr.
Sakaguchi is being held in an abandoned laundry building
in Phoenix." Now, *this* was the poised side of Lee, his skills
honed by their mentor.

"Mr. Sakaguchi is well and away from Phoenix," said Cy

with a purposeful glance at Uncle Moon. "The men who were guarding him were unharmed."

Curiosity bloomed in Uncle Moon's face. "How did you find—"

"Good," Lee cut him off. "Now about the operations—"

A door banged open with a terrible echo. The Chinese men hefted their guns. Ingrid and Cy shared a look of dread.

"Miss Carmichael!" boomed a familiar voice. "If you can hear me, speak out. We have your man Mr. Braun here."

Ambassador Roosevelt had arrived.

CHAPTER 25

※

Lee whirled to stare at Ingrid, his face tense and flushed. "Did you— No, you didn't know he was coming."

"We reckoned an ambassador was coming with the fleet, but we figured it'd be *her*." Cy gestured his thumb toward the dead fox.

Uncle Moon muttered something to Lee, and they engaged in a rapid-fire exchange, their tones curt.

"I need to be seen. They have Fenris," said Ingrid as Roosevelt belted out her name again. The invocation carried no magical weight, but made her flinch nevertheless. He didn't know Blum was dead, and he knew the perils of using her name, and was choosing to do so anyway.

With her now-normal hearing, she detected the sound of several heavy bootsteps. Not a full squadron. She'd bet T.R. was accompanied by Siegfried and his other guards—maybe they were immunized, enchanted, or simply ready to endure quarantine.

"I could kill Roosevelt." Lee's voice was low. "Uncle wants me to." He considered the weapon in his hand then looked back at her, his gaze older than his years. "I told him no. Uncle sent me to learn from Mr. Sakaguchi so that I could become a leader. He regrets that choice now. He would have us slaughter all Americans." Lee considered the man he referred to as his uncle. "He forgets that I'm an American, too."

Uncle Moon spat out a retort, his sentiments clear without a word in English.

Lee cocked his head to one side, not deigning to reply. "I know Roosevelt. I know he's bullheaded and obstinate, but I also know he's smart. He can be reasoned with."

Ingrid left her pack on the floor and clambered onto a small box, and then another, moving upward. Her legs ached but remained steady.

"Pardon my saying so, Lee, but you don't exactly have an advantage in your negotiations," said Cy.

"No denying that." Lee's grin was cold enough to make Ingrid shiver as if she'd brushed a ghost. At this distance, he looked like the Lee she had known for ages, and yet a stranger. "But I know what Roosevelt really wants, and I can make it happen."

Ingrid climbed as high as she could. The view was incredible, a vast topography of hills and valleys, all formed of freight. "Ambassador Roosevelt!" she called.

"I see her!" his voice boomed out.

She found him working his way through the maze. Alongside him was the tall form of Siegfried, with more of his devoted men following closely behind. As they passed through

394

an open space, she saw Fenris as well. He looked irate, undoubtedly fuming at Roosevelt for forcing him away from the *Bug* a second time. Ingrid remained on her perch until the men were close before scooting down to rejoin Cy.

Only Lee and Uncle Moon remained by the fox's corpse. The other Chinese men had retreated into the freight maze. God help them all. This could get ugly fast.

"Miss Carmichael." Mr. Roosevelt's grin was not as exuberant as usual. "I did not expect to find your wayfaring airship docked here."

"Mr. Roosevelt." She offered him a slight curtsy. "I didn't expect to meet you here either. I assumed Ambassador Blum would accompany the incoming fleet. Instead, she was already here." At that, Ingrid made a showman's gesture and stepped aside, affording them a view of the dead fox with multiple tails.

"It can't be," muttered Siegfried.

"Oh, it can," said Roosevelt, expression more thoughtful than surprised. "The rings don't offer immortality, after all. All it takes is the right tool, be it a failing heart or an ancient weapon." He took in the sight of Lee and the strange pole arm without any fear. "Mr. Fong. It has been a while."

"It has." Lee's voice was soft yet strong. "Ambassador Roosevelt, I'm here to negotiate on behalf of the Chinese people."

"Negotiate? Negotiate for what? Possession of *Excalibur*?"

"Yes. That and more."

Roosevelt snorted. "I'm afraid you're delusional, Mr. Fong."

"Hope is a kind of delusion." Lee shrugged.

"Even if you could crew this technological marvel and monstrosity, the war with China is at an end. Killing *her* can't undo that." Roosevelt motioned to the dead fox.

"You're right. We can't change the past. The Chinese, as a people, have lost this war. We have lost our homeland, our identities, our clothing, our culture. But you, sir, aren't simply focused on this war, but the next. The one against Japan." Roosevelt studied Lee with narrowed eyes as he continued, "You know that conflict will come. The invasion is already under way. I've heard you discuss that with Mr. Sakaguchi, time and again. There will come a time when America will either be absorbed as another imperial dominion, or will be forced to fight once more for its independence. We can help you win that fight."

"How?" The word was blunt.

"By *existing*. We can be the splinter that Japan can't dig free from its flesh. We can be proof of their failure."

Roosevelt considered this. "You truly wish for me to let *Excalibur* stay in your possession? Preposterous. You would use it against us."

"Define 'us,'" retorted Lee. "I was born in San Francisco. I've never been outside of America. I *don't want* to fight America unless I'm forced to do so in defense. What I want is for China to be free—and for America to be free, too."

Ingrid could scarcely breathe. This was what Roosevelt wanted most—to break the Unified Pacific from within, to allow America to achieve its manifest destiny on its own terms.

"You propose an alliance, even as your people face an-nihilation."

"I have heard you say yourself that we're all children of God."

"I'm well aware of what I say," snapped Roosevelt. "And what I believe."

Ingrid looked between the men, and to the surrounding crates. The other Chinese men would attack at the slightest signal. They surely knew it'd be suicide, but they would never submit to captivity. Lee mentioned they had been setting up explosives, too.

"How much kermanite do you have handy?" she mur-mured to Cy.

"A pocketful."

Good. She could get to that faster than the contents of her pack.

"The death of the fox—Ambassador Blum—changes the balance of power among the Twelve." Roosevelt walked to-ward the body. No one else moved. Tension crackled in the air like electricity. He stooped to pull the band from the fox's leg. As he held up the piece of jewelry, it reverted to being a ring again, its power still subdued. He tucked the ring in his jacket pocket.

Ingrid looked sidelong at Uncle Moon and wondered what terrible cost T.R. had paid for donning his own ring.

As Roosevelt stood, he picked up Cy's hat as well. He walked back toward them and passed along the hat to Cy, who accepted it with murmured thanks. "You would use this citadel as your refuge."

Lee's gaze was wary. "Yes. I request that any Chinese who are willing to leave America be allowed to do so without harassment."

"And those who cannot be accommodated aboard? Or who don't wish to leave?" Roosevelt asked.

"We'll need to engage in an ongoing dialogue regarding other Chinese people in America. Continuing to imprison them for 'their own safety' isn't acceptable."

"I agree, but there are still many problematic elements to your plan. Like how I could possibly explain how and why I let you simply fly away." He fluttered his hands like butterfly wings. "Especially when the scourge that is killing thousands of people at this very moment is likely Chinese in origin. Hmm?" Roosevelt's gaze was as sharp as a knife. Lee and Uncle Moon shared a look. "You have some nerve, Mr. Fong, some nerve indeed to propose that I give you this war machine, that we ally ourselves." His face flushed.

The men stared each other down.

"Mr. Roosevelt, sir," interrupted Ingrid. "We have discovered new information ourselves in recent days. In Los Angeles, there's a hidden Chinese laboratory that contains an immunization against this contagion. We freed Mr. Sakaguchi from captivity yesterday, and he's flying to California as we speak. He's going to connect with your contacts there and lead them to the lab."

"Ah, so the Chinese immunized themselves, did they? Bully for them!" T.R. looked even angrier than before.

"Mr. Roosevelt, you should know we—" Lee began, only to be interrupted by Uncle Moon. They argued until Lee seemed to snap, smacking the butt of the *guandao* against the floor. An ethereal thunderclap resounded through the broad chamber and made Ingrid's ears pop. Lee himself looked shaken for a mere second, but he regained his bearings to face down Roosevelt.

"Sir, you should know that this virus was engineered by Japanese scientists in Manchukuo. It was utilized against the Chinese people when they were at their most vulnerable, in the aftermath of the Peking earthquakes. We assumed the sickness was natural until late February, when one of the Japanese laboratories was discovered."

Roosevelt went utterly still. "This was a *Japanese* innovation?"

"Yes, sir. It's our understanding that, at minimum, elite Japanese soldiers and the nobility have been immunized, but programs are ongoing to treat the larger Japanese populace as well, especially in newly colonized areas."

"Few Chinese people have traveled abroad of late," said Cy. "If this started in Atlanta, right as *Excalibur* was setting off, the culprit was likely Japanese."

"Yes, yes," Roosevelt murmured. "Many Japanese officials and soldiers flew into Atlanta for the unveiling. With that many people gathered together, no wonder the virus has spread as it has! But you are still culpable for holding this immunization secret and—"

Ingrid burst out laughing. Roosevelt stared at her, almost bug-eyed in rage. "Listen to yourself, sir. What did you expect them to do? Sentiments against the Chinese have been outright violent for months, and far worse since the San Francisco earthquake. They couldn't simply walk up to a soldier and say, 'Pardon me, here's an immunization for an illness that has ravaged people in China and it might spread here, too.' They'd be blamed as the source. Good God, *I* blamed them for it based on the evidence I'd seen."

Lee nodded. "We figured it was only a matter of time until the sickness spread here. All we could try to do is protect our own."

"We can supply names, addresses of Japanese scientists in Manchukuo," said Uncle Moon, his grudging voice like wheels on gravel. "Also the locations of mass graves. American scientists can identify that the viral strain is the same."

"Thank you, Dr. Moon," said Roosevelt. Ingrid wasn't surprised he recognized the *tong* leader. The ambassador's gaze rested on the dead fox. "This sounds like one of *her* projects. Did she truly think she could hide a weapon this . . . virulent?"

"Yes," snapped Fenris. He had cleaned up his face, but his nose had swollen, distorting his voice. "And she apparently did quite a good job of it since the Peking quakes happened in January and it's now late May."

Roosevelt was quiet for a moment as he took in everything. "The newspapers keep boasting about the power embodied in *Excalibur,* but I think they forget that *they* are the ones embodying it with its greatest might, that of a symbol. Not simply of America's brilliance and glory, but of its future. A future based on trade, compromise, and *independence.* For all of our people."

No one moved. Everyone seemed afraid to even breathe.

"We have many details to discuss," Mr. Roosevelt continued, tone brisk. "The dead on board must be attended to. Any living A-and-A soldiers must be found and provided with medical treatment in preparation for quarantine. That fox must be destroyed. The issue looming over everything, of course, is the story to explain the whole affair. We can credit Japan with manufacturing the illness that devastated *Excalibur*'s crew, but losing custody of the vessel over American soil reflects poorly on us."

"If you're creating the narrative, control it in every way," said Ingrid. "Publicize the illness that occurred aboard. Say you're bringing another crew here, when in truth you're smuggling out as many Chinese as possible. The citadel can bypass Los Angeles and fly onward over the Pacific. Find some excuse why. The gunships could even continue to supply an escort, up to a point, to keep the curious away."

"We would need to coordinate the departure of the gunships and the timing of the revelation about Japan's role behind the contagion," Roosevelt mused. "Then there is the matter of the war and how it will resume. Mr. Fong, I won't believe any assertions that this will remain a Utopian floating island for refugees."

"I have no intention of lying to you. We're going to fight to regain China. However, it's my hope that we won't be battling the *Unified* Pacific as we work toward that goal."

"Mr. Roosevelt, sir, how many American civilians are estimated dead by this virus at this time?" Cy asked. "I hesitate to believe the hyperbole in the papers."

"In this case, believe. Reports state fatalities range as

high as seventy percent among those infected, and it's striking down many young adults of otherwise high vitality, not simply the very old and very young." Roosevelt's face reflected grief. "I've prayed for America to stand alone as an independent power, but I never would have wished for the schism with Japan to come about in such a way."

That many dead. Ingrid could not even imagine the numbers involved.

"Then we have come to a tenuous agreement?" Lee asked, extending a hand. Roosevelt hesitated only a moment, as if surprised to see such an American gesture. Their hands met with a small clap.

"Will you now call your other men out from where they have obscured themselves among the freight?" asked Roosevelt. It figured that he knew he had walked into a potential ambush.

"Yes," said Lee. "They'll set down their arms for now."

"I imagine you will not be relinquishing *that,* however." Roosevelt eyed the *guandao* with blatant curiosity.

"Sir." Siegfried coughed.

"Ah, yes, my men are unsettled by your weapon. That's part of their job." He waved a hand in dismissal of their concern. "I think it's rather refreshing to be near a weapon that can kill me. Comforting, I would even say." His voice softened.

"The thought of immortality frightens me more than mortality," said Lee, his tone similar. The two men—men, not man and boy—regarded each other, an understanding met without words.

The soft tintinnabulation of bells rang throughout the hold. Ingrid suddenly smelled Cy's leather jacket as if her face pressed against him in a hug, though he didn't wear the heavy garment now.

She smiled at him, and caught him smiling right back.

"I smell that fine stew you were toting about that first day we met," he murmured. "And I can't help but think of when we stood together by the bookshelf in your home, and how delighted I was to converse about Twain with such a beautiful woman."

"A woman who'd almost shot you a short while before," she murmured. He waved that off as a minor detail. Together, they turned to look at the source of the chimes.

The *qilin* stood on the crate top where Ingrid had called out to Roosevelt. She heard soft cries behind her as the Chinese men reacted to the presence. She didn't turn around. They required privacy. To her, the *qilin* was a fascinating celestial entity; to them, the *qilin* was that, and so much more.

She lowered herself to her knees and bowed; Cy did the same beside her.

"Thank you," she murmured, voice thick.

"My thanks to you, Ingrid Carmichael." The *qilin*'s voice carried the smoothness of strummed harp strings. "I wish for you to find peace upon a mountain of your own."

The profound emotional weight of the statement brought tears to her eyes. She wanted to say more, but her tongue was too clumsy to manage speech. She mouthed the words "thank you" again and rose with the help of her hands.

The *qilin*'s thickly lidded eyes focused on Lee and Roosevelt, who were likewise prostrated before the golden entity haloed in unburning flames. By their soft murmurs, she knew a private conversation was under way.

"I'll be damned. It actually talked to me this time," said Fenris from a few feet away. "I thanked it for not incinerating my airship. The *qilin* laughed."

At that, Ingrid gawked at Fenris. "I didn't know it *could* laugh."

He shrugged. "It's a heavenly entity that promotes peace and prosperity, right? I'd expect it to laugh and smile much of the day."

Ingrid looked back at the *qilin*. Its head tilted, just a touch, to meet her gaze directly. A new sense of solace flowed over her like a waft of fresh-from-the-oven sourdough bread, and then the *qilin* was gone.

The vacuum left by its departure resonated as if they had all abruptly awakened from a beautiful, soul-deep dream. The other men, even Roosevelt's lackeys, were left stammering and stumbling with tears in their eyes.

Fenris stepped closer. "It's good to see you two survived. You do look . . . tired, Cy."

"Blum yanked away part of his life force. He's doing better than he was." Even so, she twined her arm with his. The extra power she held could still come in handy.

"This is no time to rest. We need to find the survivors, help with the dead. They can't bring on other soldiers to do it." Cy looked weary to the marrow.

"Suddenly, being immune doesn't sound so pleasant," muttered Fenris. He absently touched his nose, then flinched.

Ingrid felt sick at the thought of what they must do aboard, but she nodded. This needed doing. She had to get to the citadel hospital, in any case. That was where Maggie had died. If she was anywhere near as tenacious as Cy, perhaps her ghost could be found there. The twins might still have their reunion, and just maybe, peace.

That's what they all needed. Peace.

"I promised you world peace, back on that day we first met," she murmured to Cy. "I never thought it would come to this, for China to have its chance at survival, but for America and Japan to be drawn into conflict instead."

Cy leaned into her, a gesture not entirely inspired by affection. He needed help to stand. "That conflict would have happened no matter what we did. Blum made sure of that. Only now, the war won't happen on her schedule."

Ingrid nodded, her eyes drawn to the fox's body again. "From here, she looks so normal. You can't even see her tails. You can't see the horrors she created." Ingrid looked to her hand, her fingers twined with Cy's. She didn't look noteworthy either. Most of society would dismiss her with a quick glance at her skin, classify her as a servant, a maid, a nobody, yet she had also contributed to her own share of horrors.

She had strived to do good works, too. To be kind, to be merciful, to *forgive*. She wasn't defined by Papa's sins. She wasn't Mama either, even if she could replicate her near-divine dried apple pie. Ingrid was her own person, to be damned or redeemed by her own decisions.

After all, if Captain Sutcliff could redeem himself. . . well, surely there was plenty of grace to go around.

"Penny for your thoughts?" asked Cy, giving her hand a gentle squeeze.

"I'm thinking I still need to make you a dried apple pie at some point," she said. "Because I love you, and nothing says love as eloquently as pie. But for now, I think we should get this grim work over and done, and help the Chinese on their way. I miss the feel of the earth beneath my feet."

EPILOGUE

MONTHS LATER . . .

Cy had constructed a covered deck for Ingrid right above the rock-laden beach so that, on mornings like this, she could tread down the stone steps and sit for a while where the brisk wind could bring her the spray of the ocean. The morning was cold and gray, as Central California summers liked to be, but for Ingrid, gray was forever the color of coziness and home.

She knew better than to try to walk across the sand just below her. Even with her braces on, her leg muscles could not negotiate the uneven, shifting grains beneath her feet—and what manner of person wanted to walk across a beach wearing *shoes*? The deck allowed her to get as close as she needed to be. Cy had even constructed her a bench of orichalcum—they had a surprising excess these days, with business booming—so that in the event of an earthquake, she had an effective buffer between herself and the ground.

The risk of geomantic activity in this part of the central coast was negligible. A short drive south, the volcanic plug Morro Rock sat in its bay, part of a chain of similar gigantic rocks dubbed the Nine Sisters. Ingrid didn't want to live in a place devoid of earthquakes—she still wanted to help ensure public safety by drawing in energy on occasion—but she knew she didn't dare live somewhere with catastrophic potential.

She also needed deep mists and the salty freshness of the Pacific Ocean, and greenery. The village of Cambria offered her what she needed.

From here, she could stare west, and she often did, as if she could see beyond the horizon to where *Excalibur* hovered somewhere near the Hawaiian Vassal States— obedient vassals no more. Full rebellion had erupted after film emerged of a Bayard obliterating unarmed women in a picket line. The Chinese aboard *Excalibur* had formed an alliance with the native Hawaiians as well as subjugated Korean and Filipino plantation laborers. Ingrid knew nothing beyond what the papers said, but she knew Lee was sending a message her way. That he remembered her—and the Kealohas. That he wouldn't forget others who had suffered under Unified Pacific rule.

Ingrid had also read that a sudden lava flow from Mauna Loa had obliterated vast stores of UP armaments. This had given the rebels a major military advantage on Hawaii Island, but perhaps more importantly, buoyed belief that Madam Pele had blessed their side of the fight. Ingrid had no doubt that was true.

The Chinese possession of *Excalibur* had changed the dynamics of the world. Uprisings had been sparked throughout Asia, even as Roosevelt stymied the Unified Pacific's demands for more American support. Sometimes, sitting here, it felt unreal that she had played an integral role in everything—that even now, thousands of people lived and died because of her actions.

She was no longer directly involved in the world's power struggles, but she still intended to fight, in her own way.

Even with her braces on, she took the stairs with slow care, her gaze on her feet to make sure her foot placement was solid. Cold and moisture seemed to cause her muscles to misfire more often.

She paused at the ground floor of the house to rest for a moment and take in the ocean's shush and roar, the wind rattling through the Monterey pines, and the near-constant grinds and clicks from the workshop nearby. Fenris had worked the night through, as usual; he delighted in his new smithy and its capability to work orichalcum. More orders for custom braces came in every week, forwarded by a Los Angeles doctor associated with Mr. Roosevelt. George Augustus did similar labor at his place over near Bakersfield. The Augustus men had decided it was best for them to stay separated by distance as George continued his new life. George remained a highly recognizable figure from the social pages of newspapers, and if he were to be outed, he didn't want Cy identified along with him.

She continued upward. The kitchen and main living areas were on the second story, allowing Ingrid the freedom to rove barefoot through her favorite rooms, if she chose. The deck just off the kitchen granted her a full view of the rocky beach and the dark sprawl of the Pacific. This was where she had most often engaged in her writing these days.

She had just settled into her chair to skim a source book when Cy's footsteps padded up behind her. "Isn't that the book you described a few days ago as 'best used as a weapon against burglars, because it will soak in blood so well'?"

Ingrid placed her bookmark and closed the tome. The leather-bound geomancy textbook was a solid eight hundred pages in length. If she held it on her lap too long, it restricted nerve signals through her legs.

"I'd like to amend that with a comment, if I could. The text is so dry, the moisture from the blood *might* make for better reading, too."

Cy laughed. "That awful?"

"All of them are." She gestured over her shoulder to the bookshelf inside, host to a full array of geomancy texts sent along by Mr. Sakaguchi. "These books offer some instruction on geomancy, but they are far more effective as soporifics."

A soft clunk indicated a cup being set on the table beside her. She looked over in surprise.

"I saw you coming up the stairs, and put the kettle on."

"Bless you." She touched the porcelain with the backs of her knuckles. Too hot to drink. "Green tea. Perfect."

"I hoped so." He set a steaming coffee mug down and claimed the seat across the table. "Mind some company for a time?"

"I do welcome any excuse to procrastinate."

"I need to go down in a few and finesse an ankle brace we

made yesterday." He took a sip. "I never get tired of this view." He wasn't looking at the ocean, but at her.

"You're not allowed to say something like that without being close enough to kiss me."

"I beg your pardon." He set down his cup, and a moment later his lips were on hers. He tasted like coffee, which she found more than tolerable under the circumstances. She cradled his face with both hands, his jaw clean-shaven and soft under her fingers. He deepened the kiss, his tongue stroking hers. A soft moan escaped her throat. His fingertips—warm from carrying the cups—wandered down her neck to tug at her collar. Her chilled skin broke out in goose bumps.

"If you wish to procrastinate, I'd be happy to oblige you." His eyes sparkled with promise as his fingers teased along the scooped neck of her dress.

"Is that so?" She sounded breathless. "Any particular activities in mind?"

His hand found her right breast and enjoyed the full curve. Her layers of clothing suddenly felt quite cumbersome. "A few." He pulled back to gaze upon her with stark appraisal.

"I wouldn't mind having my braces off. Do you think a leg massage could be worked into your agenda?"

"Always, Ingrid. Whatever you'd like." The tone of his voice made her squirm in her seat.

"Goddamn it!" Fenris's voice echoed from down below, accompanied by a thud.

Ingrid sighed and pulled back. "Sounds like he might be coming upstairs." Fenris had made a habit of not-so-subtly granting them a few minutes' warning before he made a visit. A precaution much appreciated by the newlyweds.

"He might. May be best to wait and see." His tone turned wistful. He kissed her again, his lips hungry. He kept his eyes open wide, his gaze intent behind his lenses. "I'd rather us not be interrupted while we're busy procrastinating."

His hands trailed over her curves again as he withdrew into his chair.

She stared at him in dismay. "That's it? You're going to stop, just like that?"

"Ingrid, it's taking every bit of my self-control to resist whisking you away to the bedroom, at which point, I'd be particularly cross if Fenris were to come a-knocking." His words were even and measured. "I am trying to be patient for a few minutes more, with the hopes that we can then carry forth our plans."

She laughed. "In other words, we're procrastinating in our plans to procrastinate?" She shook her head as more swearing boomed from below. "I suppose I do love to sit here and be serenaded by the birds, the sea, and the distinctive arias of Fenris."

"I suppose it's a good thing we own the land around, or the neighbors'd surely hate us." He took another sip, an ear tilted toward the stairs in wait of stomping footsteps. An interruption was sure to be imminent with this amount of warning. "I was thinking that maybe next week we could take the *Bug* up to San Francisco so you could visit Mr. Sakaguchi for a few days. I need to settle on some new suppliers now that the city's growing back. We could take in the sights. You could borrow more books for your project."

Ingrid stared into the grayness. She had once entertained

the notion of being a respected geomancer, in a position to teach young geomancers. She now knew that could never be. For now, she had to continue to hide her abilities. Blum was gone, but there could be others like her out there, those who wanted to utilize her as a weapon.

But she'd be damned if she idled away without using her insight into geomancy for *something*. Therefore, she was quite literally rewriting the texts on the field. Mr. Sakaguchi was setting up everything on her behalf.

Ingrid, the housekeeper's daughter, the secretary, the woman often assumed to be an exotic and illiterate plaything, was writing the books that would train geomancers for generations to come. Her name would be on the cover: *I. Carmichael.* Her identity would be neither a secret nor promoted.

Even though half of the previous textbook authors hadn't had a lick of magical talent, she expected her authorship to create some fuss among the curmudgeons of the ol' boys club auxiliaries. She welcomed it.

Ingrid might be a woman, and one of color, but she would not be silent. All her life, what she had craved most of all was respect. She wanted to be looked in the eye and to have her intelligence recognized. She would no longer ask for that kind of acknowledgment. She *demanded* it.

"I'd like to take a trip up to the bay," she said, smiling at Cy. "He's been sending me updates on the construction of the new auxiliary, but I'd love to see it in person."

"It's been some two weeks since your last letter, right?"

She nodded as she sipped her green tea. "Yes. He's being

kept busy as the sole senior warden. He'll have more help once the auxiliary is set to open, but for now, he's trying to do everything himself. Of course."

"Mmm. He'll have to slow down if you're there for a visit."

"Yes," she said softly. But he wouldn't slow down for long; he had too much to do. Nor would she stay for more than a few days. The presence of other geomancers kept her pain from aggravating the two-headed snake in the fault line, but she didn't dare test their capabilities as a buffer for long. She did enjoy seeing some of the changes in the city, though, even as many more perturbed her. The buildings were all *wrong*. The maps in her brain could not adjust.

She didn't want to adjust her way of thinking either. She didn't want to walk the streets, her gaze studiously avoiding that of the men all around. She didn't want to wear a servant's clothes. She didn't want to pretend she was Cy's lesser, not his wife and equal. Not that they were married under the law, of course. Such a thing wasn't allowed in California. But she and Cy had held a small ceremony anyway, laws be damned. Mr. Sakaguchi, George Augustus, and Fenris Braun had witnessed their vows. Lee hadn't been able to attend, of course, and she had missed him with a sorrow too deep to put into words. Even so, it'd been a happy day. The sylphs had responded to Ingrid's joy with an enthusiastic tizzy that caused her flower bouquet to grow roots.

Ingrid remained happy, too. Life was quiet here. Neighbors minded their own business, but if an autocar became mired in mud, everyone pitched in to get it free. Cy and Fenris worked with their metal and gadgetry, and for minimal profit. Ingrid read textbooks and wrote notes and cursed about what some fool man wrote in 1883 and read and griped some more. The original sylphs from Seattle had stayed with them. They roamed the hillside and kept Ingrid supplied in strawberries every day of the week.

She stood and dropped the textbook into the chair, which creaked beneath its onerous burden. Far below, she heard footsteps on the stairs. She and Cy shared a smile. Sure enough, they were right to procrastinate—for the time being.

"Cy," she said as she walked through the open door to the kitchen. As always, her eyes found the carved plaque of a *qilin* upon the wall, which she acknowledged with a dip of her head and a smile. "When we fly the *Bug,* let me take a full hour in the chair this time."

"A full hour?" He followed her, empty cup in hand. "That's a long time. I'm certain you can handle it, but I'm not sure if Fenris can."

"If Fenris can what?" Fenris clopped across the deck and trailed them inside.

"Handle a long stint of me learning how to pilot," Ingrid said. "You wheezed and moaned during my last lesson."

"That was meditational breathing, thank you very much. I need pastries. The sylphs are hungry." He threw open the pantry door to pull out jamu-pan she'd made the day before.

"I just fed the sylphs at bedtime! They shouldn't be starving already."

"Yes, well." He spoke with a mouthful of yeast roll. "There are more sylphs now."

Cy froze. "Beg your pardon?"

Fenris flapped a hand dismissively. "Oh, nothing like that cloud we left on *Excalibur.* These are itty-bitty sylphs. Maybe

415

they hid a bunch of chrysalises somewhere along the slope, and these just hatched? I don't know. In any case, we have more sylphs, and we need more bread." He grabbed an extra roll as he swiped the door shut with his elbow. Seconds later, his feet thundered back down the staircase.

"Oh goodness." Ingrid pressed a hand to her forehead. "I've been worried about how our passel of sylphs is impacting the ecology here, and now we'll need to contend with *more*?"

Cy slid an arm around her waist, drawing her close slowly so that she had time to adjust her footing. Their lips met, demanding and full of promise of more activities to come. His nose nuzzled hers as he pulled back. "We've had to contend with far worse conundrums. We'll manage. Besides, this means more strawberries, right?"

"Says the man who always happens to be in the thick of some engineering dilemma in the workshop when I'm making jam."

"Cy? Ingrid?" Fenris called from below, a tremulous note to his voice. "You'd better, ah, come see. I think a few more, um, hatched. Spawned. Whatever."

Cy and Ingrid shared a look. She worked her hand into the pocket where she always kept filled and empty kermanite, just in case.

"We'll be right there!" she yelled down to the ground, a hand on the orichalcum railing and Cy a step behind.

Yes, they'd handle this new crisis as they handled each catastrophe before—together, and with the proper application of both magic and pastries.

Writing an alternate history requires carefully twining reality and fiction. Some of my changes have been on purpose; others are the result of my ignorance. I beg forgiveness for any inconsistencies and errors.

Japan's ambitions for possession of the Asian mainland began long before World War II. The Japanese tussled with Russia in the 1890s and 1900s, and won—and President Theodore Roosevelt was awarded a Nobel Peace Prize for his integral role in their treaty negotiations.

Chinese immigrants to America were subject to persecution, abuse, and outright murder. The Geary Act and its "Dog Tag Law" in the 1890s truly did force Chinese residents to carry photo identification cards at all times as evidence that they were legal residents of the United States.

An early scene in *Roar of Sky* describes downtown Honolulu festooned with Japanese flags and banners celebrating the emperor and the Imperial military. This wasn't a fanciful scene created from my imagination alone, but one based on a real celebration in Honolulu immediately following the first Sino-Japanese War in 1895.

At the start of the twentieth century, six out of ten people in Hawaii had been born elsewhere. The native population had been devastated by foreign diseases; therefore, sugar and fruit plantation workers were imported from China, Japan, Portugal, Korea, the Philippines, and Puerto Rico. In my world, these demographics have shifted, with Japanese residents granted more privileges and Chinese workers shuffled elsewhere. Honolulu's Chinatown really was largely destroyed in 1900 when an effort to burn down buildings that hosted victims of bubonic plague ended up scorching much of the neighborhood.

The description of the journey into Kilauea is heavily based on travelogues from the late nineteenth and early twentieth century, and my own January 2017 visit to the island. I journeyed down the Halema'uma'u Trail, the one used a century ago to bring guests from Volcano House to the lava lake. During my visit, the trail ended at the crater floor, as volcanic fumes had rendered it unsafe to venture beyond that point. Even if I had been able to trek farther in, I would not have had the liberties that visitors once experienced. All of the behaviors I describe—from cooking sausages over the lava to singeing postcards—are accurate to the period.

Sightings of Pele as a white dog are a phenomenon of the twentieth century. My bibliography for *Call of Fire* already featured resources I relied on to write about Pele, and I want to repeat some of the most useful ones here: *Pele: Goddess of Hawai'i's Volcanoes* by Herb Kawainui Kane, journal articles by H. Arlo Nimmo, and *The Burning Island: Myth and History in Volcano Country, Hawai'i* by Pamela Frierson. Yes, Mark Twain really did write a travelogue about his visit to the lava lake.

I chose Dominguez Field as my characters' Southern California base of operations as a hat tip to very real events: the Los Angeles International Air Meets held on Dominguez Hill in 1910 and 1911. Over 250,000 people attended, and for many of them it was the first time they had ever seen airplanes and other innovative aircraft, including various dirigibles.

Los Angeles was a young city in 1906—proud of its Main Street Station, the largest building in the west—and not yet a film capital. I advanced cinema technology a wee bit to suit my needs. In Japan, silent films did host benshi to provide narration and character voices throughout the experience. Tamale (also spelled "tomale" in some books) carts were indeed a feature of downtown Los Angeles, a fascinating regional novelty described in several travel guides of the period; I combined them with Japanese yatai food carts, which were also common throughout the Meiji period. Tamale carts also sold pie and other weird new food creations called "hamburgers" and "wienerwursts."

When creating a new version of Phoenix, I had to consider the effects of ten years of war and how that would impact the settlement of the western frontier. Historically, Phoenix was a small town in that time period—it really didn't experience tremendous growth until World War II and widespread use of air conditioning. I decided it would need to be smaller yet in my alternate history, and therefore I kept the territorial capital in its original location of Prescott.

The Blood of Earth trilogy is fiction and intended for entertainment, but I sincerely hope that readers are surprised, enlightened, and even angered by the bits of real history they encounter in these books, and that they might read more about this often-ignored period of history.

The full research bibliography for the series consists of some seventy works. The sources for *Breath of Earth* and *Call of Fire*, as well as the ones that follow this section, are also listed at BethCato.com with links to where they may be purchased online or are available for free legal download. I want to emphasize the latter. Many of the old travel guides I read for Hawaii and Los Angeles are available for free, in a wide variety of e-book formats, courtesy of the New York Public Library. They have over 144,000 books on Archive.org. Go there and fall down a wonderful rabbit hole.

Hawaii

The Japanese in Hawai'i: Okage Sama De by Dorothy Ochiai Hazama and Jane Okamoto Komeiji

The Islands at the End of the World (A Novel) by Austin Aslan

Hawaii: A History, from Polynesian Kingdom to American Statehood by Ralph S. Kuykendall and A. Grove Day

Vacation Days in Hawaii and Japan by Charles M. Taylor Jr.

Seven Weeks in Hawaii by an American Girl by M. Leola Crawford

*The Hawaiian Archipelago: Six Months Amongst the Palm
    Groves, Coral Reefs, and Volcanoes of the Sandwich
    Islands* by Isabella Lucy Bird

The Real Hawaii: Its History and Present Condition by
    Lucien Young, USN

*Hawaiian Legends of Volcanoes: Collected and Translated
    from the Hawaiian* by W. D. Westervelt

"The History of Mana: How an Austronesian Concept
    Became a Video Game Mechanic" by Alex Golub, *The
    Appendix: Bodies* 2:2 (April 2014)

EARLY TWENTIETH-CENTURY AMERICA (GENERAL)

Inventing the Dream: California Through the Progressive Era
    by Kevin Starr

California Revisited 1858–1897 by T. S. Kenderdine

Victorian Los Angeles from Pio Pico to Angels Flight by
    Charles Epting

Southern California by Charles A. Keeler

A Tenderfoot in Southern California by Mina Deane Halsey

Phoenix: Valley of the Sun by G. Wesley Johnson Jr.

California Wings: A History of Aviation in the Golden State
    by William A. Schoneberger

"On the Wings of To-day: An Account of the First Interna-
    tional Aviation Meet in America, at Los Angeles, Califor-
    nia" by Charles K. Field, *Sunset Magazine* 34:3 (March
    1910)

The Giant Airships (The Epic of Flight) by Douglas Botting

ACKNOWLEDGMENTS

The research involved in the Blood of Earth trilogy has been daunting, and, at times, downright overwhelming. I'm grateful to everyone who has provided guidance along the way. In particular, I want to call out Codex Writers for helping me with numerous queries over the four years I have spent on these books.

My work on *Roar of Sky* included a trip to Hawaii to walk where my characters would have walked and to get a genuine sense of the place. Thanks to Wilma and Zarli Win for the wonderful day tour around Oahu; I will never look at feral chickens the same way again. At Hawaii's Plantation Village, ninety-year-old Charlie (with the help of his little dog, Tomo) "talked story" for two hours about growing up on a local sugarcane plantation. On the Big Island, we had a wonderful stay at the Kona Bayview Inn Bed & Breakfast, where Sharon and Thomas embodied the aloha spirit. The access to fresh-off-the-tree macadamia nuts and softball-sized avocados (alligator pears, in my book's parlance) has spoiled me forevermore. If you're planning a visit to Kona, do look them up. At the Jagger Museum in Volcanoes National Park, it was a delight to hear the rangers talk with such enthusiasm about the Big Island. I fell in love with the place, too. Nothing in my life can compare to watching the distant lava lake churn at sunrise, or hiking miles across the dried lava bed of the Kilauea Iki crater with full knowledge of the catastrophic potential of the ground beneath my feet.

Many people helped me to try to do justice to Ingrid's spasticity and the daily challenges that she would face. I want to thank Pat Esden, Erin M. Hartshorn, Tina Smith, Jolenna and Bill Cullum, Dr. Geoffrey Habershaw, DPM, and others unnamed. Rebecca Roland read the full rough-draft manuscript and provided pointed advice on making Ingrid's assistive devices as accurate as possible. Any errors and inconsistencies that remain, of course, are my fault alone.

Rachel Thompson critiqued this book, as she did the previous two. At some point, my immense gratitude will be expressed via cheese.

My agent is Rebecca Strauss at DeFiore and Company. She's worthy of an entire thesaurus entry of synonyms for "awesome." Here's to more books to come!

Many thanks to the sloth-loving crew at Harper Voyager, including David Pomerico, Caroline Perny, Angela Craft, and my editor, Priyanka Krishnan. I'm so happy to work with you all.

ACKNOWLEDGMENTS

Last but not least, I need to thank my family: Mom and Dad; Scott; my husband, Jason; and my son, Nicholas. Jason deserves particular praise, as much of his vacation time the past few years has been used so that he can stay home and kid-watch while I go to conferences and frolic with plush sloths and flaccid foam breadsticks. He's the best hubby ever.

Nebula Award–nominated author **Beth Cato** hails from Hanford, California, but currently writes and bakes cookies in a lair west of Phoenix, Arizona. She's the author of the Clockwork Dagger duology and the Blood of Earth trilogy from Harper Voyager, plus scores of other short stories and poems across a multitude of publications. She shares her household with a hockey-loving husband, a numbers-obsessed son, and three feline overlords.

www.bethcato.com
Twitter: @bethcato
facebook.com/beth.cato